also by Fae

Cloudy with a Chance of Bad Decisions

FAE QUIN

Cover Art and Interior Artwork by Fae Loves Art

WWW.FAELOVESART.COM

Typography and Interior Formatting by We Got You Covered Book Design

WWW.WEGOTYOUCOVEREDBOOKDESIGN.COM

Edited by Angela O'Connell

A full list of content warnings and tropes

is available on my website:

WWW.FAELOVESART.COM

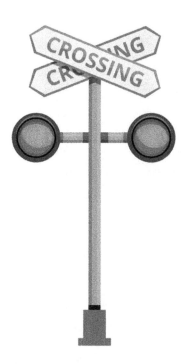

Dedicated to my husband,
for loving me as fiercely as I love him.

For anyone who's ever been afraid
To fall in love—and did it anyway.

The Reluctant **LEAD**

GEORGE

ALEX

the **HEARTTHROB**

the **BRIDE**

JUNE

JOE

BEEFY
Snow White

One

George

JUDGING BY THE DILDO in my backpack, letting Missy—my roommate turned cat-sitter—help me pack last night had clearly been a bad decision. One that was worse than wearing the loafers I'd chosen that morning which soaked up the New York rain like dry sponges. Hell, it was even worse than waiting until I'd left the office before telling Brendon, my immediate supervisor and ex-boyfriend (another bad decision), that I had scheduled time off. Which, of course, subsequently left me having a panic attack on the subway home.

I hadn't *actually* forgotten.

It was on my calendar.

Which was sacred.

I'd consulted both our boss and HR to get approval for the dates I'd be gone. All my bases were covered, so to speak.

Brendon had, predictably, blown up my phone the entire ride, but I'd ignored

1

every buzz in my pocket. Despite his fury, a sick wave of relief had flooded through me at the realization that I wouldn't have to see him for eight blissful days.

Truthfully, I'd known that if I gave Brendon notice, he'd find a way to keep me in New York. And even though going back to small-town Ohio for my other ex, Roderick's, wedding was not exactly the homecoming I was dying for, I couldn't stomach the thought of causing my mother to make *that* face.

Her disappointed face.

The same face she'd made for the last eight years every time I'd cancelled a trip home.

She always loved it when her "big city son" came to visit. She'd gossip with her friends, ask me thousands of questions, and parade me around town with her head held high and a smile on her round face.

But those visits had grown sparser and sparser as the years had dragged on.

Which had created a rift between us, leaving me both apprehensive and eager to heal the damage.

Life wasn't fair.

At thirty-three, with soggy rain-soaked socks, I knew that better than anyone. Which was why there was a dildo in my backpack. Or, more accurately, there *had* been a dildo in my backpack—before I'd accidentally knocked it out.

I immediately knew who the culprit was.

"*Missy*," I gasped in horror as the veiny silicone soared through the air, right over the edge of the conveyor belt, and down to the floor.

A sane person would not bring a sex toy to their ex-boyfriend's wedding. A fact that everyone—and I mean *everyone*—in the entire world knew except Drunk-Missy-From-Last-Night, apparently.

There was no telling if she'd done this to fuck with me on purpose, or if she'd thought she was "helping". *This*, as in, packing my fucking *dildo*— nicknamed Nine-Inch-Neil for his length and girth—in my back-up backpack. The same backpack I took with me every time I traveled, full of a variety of clothing options on the off-chance fate fucked me in the ass and lost my checked bag.

It was a just-in-case bag.

A *precaution*.

Which was *why* I hadn't thought anything of it when Missy had offered to shove the clothing I'd laundered earlier that day inside it. I should've known she'd been up to no good.

Missy had been a wild card the entire decade we'd been friends.

At fifteen years my senior, with gray hair, a wardrobe full of pastels, and an unrepentant taste for *chaos*—she, for some odd reason, thought she knew better than I did. Maybe because, even though she tended to opt for the most wildly unhinged choice available in any given situation, things always seemed to work out for her.

Some of us—and by that, I mean *me*—were not that lucky.

Once, Missy had stolen a shopping cart straight out of a drugstore. Walked out the front door with it and down the street with no interjection from the staff or police at all. She'd spent the weekend weaving ribbon through the metal till it resembled a satin basket on wheels. And then she'd returned it the following Monday—directly to the store manager, might I add—with a note that read "Merry Christmas."

In July.

He'd offered her a job.

Knowing her, she'd probably thought the dildo would be a good omen.

But it wasn't.

How could it be?

As it rolled across the floor and my stomach dropped along with it.

The Kindle I'd been digging for inside my backpack fell into the plastic bin with a clatter. On the move already, the tray scooted down the conveyor belt toward the X-ray machine.

I hardly noticed.

Because my soul was too busy evacuating my body.

I bent over fast enough my spine cracked. When I lunged forward, my fingers whistled through open air, missing Neil by a scant few inches. The dildo continued to roll. And because life wasn't fair, the damn thing rolled straight into the very expensive-looking Italian leather loafer of the man standing in line behind me—before I could catch it.

He made a sound. Half laugh, half cough. His foot moved, blocking the dildo from view of the row of people at the conveyor belt to our right.

And I wanted. To. Die.

Slowly, I looked up, cheeks burning, and what I saw only made everything worse. Way way worse. Because the expensive shoes were connected to muscular calves and thick thighs.

Oh *Jesus*.

And the man himself? Yes. Fuck my life.

He was objectively hot as hell.

Broad shoulders. A square jaw. Full lips. An air about him that screamed mischief—and an almost overwhelming confidence—even with a dildo currently pressed to his foot—as though this were his world and the rest of us were borrowing space within it.

Like mine, his hair had been affected by the rain. Lightly curled, a single ebony-colored lock fell across his forehead, escaping what I was sure had previously been an artful style. Everything about him looked like carefully manufactured effortlessness. Dressed in a charcoal gray Armani suit, but with the collar undone, like he was too cool to make proper use of the buttons provided.

His pale blue eyes were ringed by lashes so dark they smudged like eyeliner. They flickered with wicked understanding, making it obvious that he knew *exactly* whose dildo had tapped his toe. He'd probably observed the whole goddamn thing, spine-snapping and all. His almost domineering vibe was softened only by the smirk on his lips and the dimples that framed said smirk, twin companions to his chaos.

Deliberately, he met my gaze as he squatted, thick thighs flexing, tanned fingers reaching for—

Oh Jesus.

No, no, no, no.

Why was he touching it?!

When he stood, I stood too, heart pounding, hands clenched into fists at my sides.

"You dropped this." His voice was slightly higher than my own and buttery warm. His obvious mirth at my expense made my hair stand on end.

What sort of asshole witnesses the apocalypse and smirks?

Did he think this was *funny?*

This was the antithesis of funny.

I was so offended by his blasé attitude, it took me a second to realize that my *Neil*—my nine-inch Neil—was still in his hand. Snatching the dildo right out of Armani-man's grip, I wasted no time shoving it into my backpack, germs and all. It wasn't until the sex toy was zipped back up and out of sight that I could breathe.

I triple-checked the zipper was shut. Shakily, I shoved the plastic tray that the backpack sat inside onto the conveyor belt. My Kindle had already rattled down to the end, passing through the airport security's X-ray machine with zero problem.

Relax, George.

It's over.

Just get through security.

You never have to see this man again.

You're fine.

For the first time since Mom had sent me my plane ticket home, I was *ecstatic* to go. I couldn't wait to get as far, far away from this whole *situation* as I possibly could.

I hadn't said a single word to Mr. Armani, and I didn't intend to.

No.

He'd seen too much.

For a brief, unhinged moment, I debated whether or not I needed to kill him. But…that felt extreme.

Even given the circumstances.

Besides, the only pointy item I had on me was a ballpoint pen—which would be an ineffective murder weapon, even in a pinch.

It was better for everyone if I pretended he didn't exist.

Unfortunately, he was making that very difficult. The weight of his gaze made the hair on my nape stand on end. An electric fizzle of something— fear, maybe?—tempted me to acknowledge him, but I didn't.

Through sheer force of will, I maintained what I hoped was an air of unbotheredness as I waited for my turn at the body scanner. There was a bit of rustling, no doubt him taking his shoes off.

"Hey," he tried. I pretended I didn't hear. If he'd been anything other than an asshole he would've let me slowly implode in peace. On a good day, I abhorred the idea of being seen as less than perfect. Today was *not* a good day.

Therefore, I refused to acknowledge what had happened.

There was a balding man in front of me wearing a Hawaiian shirt and khakis. I studied the shiny spot on the back of his head to distract myself, relieved when he finished his turn inside the body scanner, and I was next. Immediately after he'd passed through to the other side, the TSA attendant waved me over.

Which was excellent.

Wonderful, even.

I'd officially survived a whole thirty seconds without having to speak to the man behind me.

If I were lucky, I might get through security before Armani-guy managed another word. When I stepped forward, so did he—far closer to my back than he needed to be.

"There's no need to be embarrassed," his voice dropped low, quiet enough only I could hear. There was no denying the mirth that danced in his tone, though. The asshole really did think this was funny.

No need to be embarrassed? Ha!

Don't respond.

Ignore him, George.

The weight of his gaze remained as I strode away from him and into the machine. The whole time it whirred, my hands held high above my head, my back vulnerable, I willed a hole to open up in the floor and swallow me. But it didn't. Anxious to escape, I stepped free when directed. It took a lot of effort to waddle-walk in damp-socked feet while attempting an air of nonchalance.

Like I wasn't running.

When I so clearly was.

Bald-guy was taking forever. As I waited for him to finish putting his shoes on, I glanced over my shoulder. Fuck. Armani-man was nearly through the body scanner.

Fuck. Fuck. Fuck.

Nervous sweat beaded at my temple. Just then, the balding man finally stopped blocking my access. He moved out of the way, and as quickly as I could, I jerked my shoes and backpack on.

Move, George. If you speed-walk, he won't be able to catch up.

Speed-walking was my specialty. I often ran half-marathons to catch the subway, or to avoid Brendon when he tried to terrorize me at work.

I had the legs for it.

A fact I was more than a little grateful for at present, as I hurried away. Paranoia got the better of me right before I turned the corner at the end of the hall. When I glanced back toward security, I was relieved and totally *not* disappointed to see the sexy stranger was still slipping his watch around his wrist.

He wasn't paying attention to me anymore.

Instead, he was chatting with an employee in a spiffy blue uniform. His smirk remained, like being smarmy was simply a part of who he was.

Good.

That was good.

He'd already forgotten about me. At least one of us had moved on from the dildo incident.

Maybe my luck was turning around?

Maybe…despite the hell that'd been this morning, the universe had decided I'd suffered enough. I could only pray that I would never see those dimples again. Unluckily for me, fate—like Missy—had a strange sense of humor.

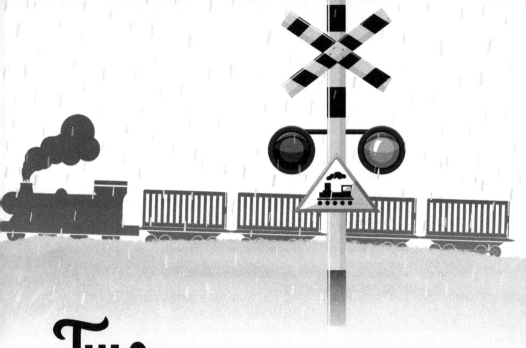

Two
George

IT TOOK THE ENTIRE walk to my gate to calm my racing heart. Rain drizzled down the glass windows overlooking the tarmac below, planes en route to their next destinations parked like dominoes. Their white exteriors stuck out like sore thumbs against the rather dreary backdrop, but I was too lost in my own head to really pay attention.

My shoes squelched with every step, a reminder of today's poor, poor luck.

I didn't know *why* I was so worked up over this.

It wasn't like he had been about to hunt me down and demand answers. I wouldn't be subjected to an interrogation. Nor would he openly laugh at me—though that felt far more plausible.

And yet…I couldn't get that damn smirk out of my mind.

So cocky.

Self-assured.

Playful and infuriatingly unflappable.

My complete fucking opposite.

Maybe it was his lack of reaction that bothered me, actually. The fact that this horrible-awful-mortifying experience meant absolutely nothing to him. Not that I wanted it to. Of course I didn't. But still. I both envied and loathed that casual nonchalance.

Still on edge, I scanned the rows of chairs at my gate for an empty seat. *There. Perfect.* With a rustle, I slid into place against the back wall. I preferred being seated as far from other people as possible. Especially as I was debating digging in my bag for a pair of dry socks, even though the idea of having my naked feet out in an airport, of all places, made my skin crawl.

I felt bare as it was.

My phone buzzed in my pocket, and without thinking, I pulled it free. With a groan, I turned it off again. But Brendon's texts had been short enough I'd caught the gist.

Brendon

Why am I only now hearing you'll be out of town?

I am your supervisor.

Did you go over my head?

How childish can you be?

To distract myself, I shakily unzipped my backpack to double-check that I'd gotten everything safely inside it. The whole thing had been a blur. I still felt off-center, and Brendon's texts hadn't helped. He was my supervisor, yes. But he wasn't actually my boss. Charles, the man above him, was a lot easier to talk to—all things considered.

I'd known going to him to schedule my accrued PTO was a recipe for disaster. But it felt like the lesser disaster of the two options.

I refused to disappoint my mom again. Even though choosing this path had meant opening myself up to Brendon's negative attention. A sick feeling of dread curled cold and tight in my chest. Heavy enough it was hard to breathe.

I almost wished the embarrassment would come back—finding the flush and horror preferable to this.

To this…icy guilt.

Biting at my chest and fingertips.

Frostbite of the heart.

We'd been over for a year now, and yet, it still felt as though he loomed above me, casting his shadow over everything I did.

"At least you're loyal," I muttered to Neil without heat as I hunted past the back-up t-shirt I'd packed for a pair of socks. Nothing was in its correct place, unsurprisingly—again, because Missy had been the one to pack. Neil's fat crown poked out of the fabric innocently, as if in agreement. "Even if you are an exhibitionist." I was half-tempted to sneakily toss Neil in the trash so that I wouldn't face potential future humiliation.

But…*that* felt disloyal.

And I couldn't bring myself to do it.

So instead, I quickly and efficiently switched out my socks, relieved when the soggy bundle was shoved into a separate pocket and my feet were more comfortable. I was straightening the hem on my pants when I heard it.

The click of expensive shoes.

Like any sane introvert in a crowded space, I ignored their approach. It was only natural to hope the newcomer would find somewhere else to sit. Unfortunately for me, the footsteps didn't stray or change course.

They steadily became louder as they headed straight for my gate.

With a sigh, I lifted my head, only to balk when I spotted a familiar stranger striding purposefully down the hallway. *Oh dear god. Hell no.* Once again, it seemed that life had decided to demonstrate how unfair it could be.

His sturdy thighs flexed as he walked, challenging the seams of his suit pants. He was so much more muscular than I'd realized during our brief encounter only twenty minutes prior. I figured that was probably a result of the fact that at the time I'd quite literally been dying of embarrassment. There had not been a lot of time to ogle his quads.

I shrank in my seat, quickly turning my attention to the water-speckled glass to hide that I'd been staring. A few incoming planes wheeled toward our section of the terminal.

There was no denying it was him.

The guy from security.

And he was headed my way.

Fuck. My. Life.

Tall, dark, and handsome paused at the end of my row.

The footsteps drew closer and closer.

Don't sit by me.

Don't-sit-by-me!

Don't—

Fuck.

He sat by me.

A beat passed in silence.

When I was nervous, I had a bad habit of fixing my hair, even when I didn't need to. That was no different now as my anxious fingers fidgeted with my half-ruined gelled-back waves, desperate for some semblance of control.

I swear to god my shirt collar was growing tighter by the second.

I suddenly regretted my decision to wear one of my casual powersuits to visit home. I'd hoped it would make me feel more confident. That it might make my mom smile—maybe influence more bragging to her friends. But… as I sat there in silence, yanking on my bangs, I didn't feel more confident.

Didn't feel put-together.

Didn't feel in control.

Every breath was arduous. Especially as the silence stretched. I wasn't sure if I should be more ashamed about Neil, or about running when he'd tried to speak to me. Either way, I was not eager to be called out for my childish behavior.

Why had he approached me?

This was just…mean.

Wasn't it?

He had to know I was embarrassed. Was he here to make fun of me? Sure, he'd been…somewhat kind earlier, but that didn't negate the fact that his presence was ambiguous at best. If I had been in his shoes—and what a pair of shoes they were, damn—I would absolutely not be terrorizing the poor dildo-yeeting man. I genuinely could not understand his motivation.

Up close, Mr. Armani's smell was tantalizing. Like sandalwood and crushed up money. It was the type of scent that belonged between the pages of a smutty romance novel—not here, in my very real life. Underneath the layer of cologne was an underlying musk of sexy-man sweat—which made sense, seeing as he'd crossed the terminal, same as I had.

It was infuriating.

Peeking through my lashes at his legs manspreading beside mine, I was forced to come to the conclusion that he *must* be an asshole. No one smelled that good and sat like that if they weren't.

He was enjoying watching me squirm.

Mr. Armani shifted until the heat of one of his supple, *glorious* thighs pressed snug against mine. It was nearly a rub, and the simple brush made the hair on my arms stand on end. I snapped my knees together, practically pinching my balls to get away.

Was he doing this macho-posturing thing to intimidate me?

Why?

He leaned over, his bulk even more distracting the closer he became.

"Hi again, Georgie." His breath tickled the shell of my ear, and I had the oddest urge to reach up and slap him away like he was a petulant fly. The stranger's tone was chipper now and just as devastatingly attractive as it'd been earlier.

Time screeched to a halt.

There was only his voice, my name, and the weight of his body leaning into mine.

And theeeeen, the panic set in.

It took me less than two seconds to leap from my seat without a word. I tripped over my backpack, and decided to abandon it in retaliation. There was no time to right its topple as I fled across the hall and into the men's restroom.

The entire walk of shame, I could feel those same infuriating eyes on me.

Why the fuck did I run away?

How childish can you be, George?

Christ.

I splashed my face a few times, hoping to clear my head. It was only when my flush had faded beneath chilly droplets of water, and I'd stopped gawking at my own panicked expression that it finally struck me what had really been odd about that whole interaction.

He'd known my name.

How the hell had he *known my name*?

A man finished peeing in the urinal behind me. He flushed, and with an oddly demure sniff, walked over to me only to completely bypass the sink and exit the doors without washing his hands. Disgust nearly overwhelmed my confusion.

No, no.

Focus on the problem at hand, George.

Nails biting into the surface of the counter, I glared at my reflection, then pointed an accusatory finger at my own splotchy face.

"Just because he knows your name and how big you like your dicks doesn't mean the man can intimidate you. You've won employee-of-the-month six months in a row. You successfully tamed Mr. Pickles into somewhat of a pet. You survived *Brendon*. You're made of tougher stuff than this. Stop freaking out."

I didn't respond to myself because I was already feeling out of my mind, and good god, *what the fuck was I doing?* Talking to myself in the mirror. Giving myself a goddamn pep talk.

I was ridiculous.

Today had been disaster after disaster after disaster—and I hadn't even boarded the plane yet.

I was exhausted by it all, to be frank.

It didn't help that I'd been up all night, fretting about the wedding and working overtime from home to finish a design for a client that needed approval while I was away.

But no more.

I would not allow myself to be intimidated any longer, dammit, karma be damned.

I'd figure out what the hell this man wanted—how he knew my name—and then pop my headphones in so that I could zone out until it was time to board my flight. If I cut him down with an efficient interrogation, he'd leave me alone.

We'd all be happier.

Me, especially.

Splashing more icy water onto my face and fueled by righteous indignation, I practically stomped out of the bathroom, across the hall, and back to the seat (and backpack) I'd abandoned a few minutes prior.

Unsurprisingly, the asshole had not left the chair beside mine.

In fact, he'd settled in. His legs were still spread, his own carry-on parked on the seat to his right. He hadn't pulled his phone out—like a normal person would. He'd obviously been waiting for me, because as soon as I paused in front of him, his trademark smirk graced his lips.

If he wasn't an asshole it would've been a nice smile.

But he was.

So it wasn't.

In fact, I kind of wanted to punch it.

He had ridiculously pretty eyes. Far lighter than my solid, basic blue. Framed by thick dark lashes that drooped rather than curled, they gave him a striking appearance when paired with his other features. There was a slight crook to his nose, almost like he'd broken it and it'd set slightly wrong—but aside from that, he was infuriatingly perfect.

Eyes sparkling with amusement, the stranger nudged my abandoned backpack with the toe of his shoe. It was the same shoe that had touched Neil, a fact that had not escaped my attention. "Don't worry, I kept your bag—and its contents—safe." He waggled his brows. "There's no need to thank me. Just doing my civic duty."

He looked far too pleased with himself. Like he truly thought that he'd done me a favor by not allowing me to be robbed.

What a dick.

"How did you know my name?" I demanded without acknowledging his words, still flushed, and...*dripping*. I slashed my blond bangs out of my face, irritated when they only fell forward again. What was the point of gel if it didn't fucking work?! "Are you a *stalker*? Is that what this is? Dear god, am I about to be *murdered*?"

A voice in the back of my head whispered, *if you die, you won't have to go to Roderick's wedding.*

Ugh.

Roderick.

My first boyfriend. We'd remained friends even after the breakup. Another bad decision. I should've known that keeping that door open would lead to being strong-armed into attending his pending nuptials.

We'd broken up before I moved to New York over a decade ago so I wasn't necessarily *surprised* he was tying the knot. I was happy for him, honestly. Even though he'd never been the best match for me, I'd always hoped one day he'd end up happy. He and his fiancé, Juniper, had looked...peaceful, honestly, on their wedding invitation.

I could admit, I'd looked at it for an unhealthy amount of time the day it arrived in the mail.

Not because I felt jealous of Juniper's place on Roderick's arm. Of course not. But because…it hurt to see two people living the dream I'd held onto for so long. I'd wanted that with Brendon. Begged for it, really. Had our life planned out like it was a spreadsheet on Excel.

And look where I was now.

Boyfriend-less.

Stuck in a job I'd worked my ass off for that wasn't what I wanted anymore. Stuck trying to keep my mom proud even though I'd kept her at arm's length for years. Stuck working every goddamn day with my cheating ex-boyfriend. Stuck half a country away from my family—and for what?

Because I didn't want Mom to stop smiling and introducing me to her friends as her "big city son".

"So you *can* speak," Mr. Armani said, as though he was pleased and not annoyed by my interrogation. Oddly enough, his interruption was welcome. As effective as the swipe of Mr. Pickle's claws had been when I'd opened Roderick's invitation.

"Of course I can speak," I snapped, waspish.

"My bad. I assumed, given the fact you ran off without so much as a thank you, that you couldn't."

"Well, I can."

"Ah. So you were *choosing* to be rude, then?"

"Rude?" I scoffed. "Says the *stalker*."

He laughed.

It was a nice laugh.

A fact that made me even angrier than his smirk had.

"To answer your many dramatic questions—" *Dramatic? I was not being dramatic.* All my questions had been perfectly valid. My eyes narrowed, but he remained unintimidated. "No, I'm not stalking you. Just observant. Your name is embroidered on your backpack."

Shit.

He was right.

I deflated.

The embroidery on my backpack—embroidery I'd genuinely forgotten was there—mocked me as I plopped into my seat with an embarrassed sigh. It said George, not "Georgie". But…hell.

Mr. Armani cocked his head to the side with a wicked grin. He twisted to face me better, his thigh bumping mine. "Besides, if I *was* a stalker, I'd be an awful one, don't you think? Considering I approached you openly."

My cheeks felt hot all over again.

"And to answer your third question: no, I am not about to murder you in the middle of the airport in broad daylight. That would be poor planning."

He winked.

Winked!

And I…*wilted*.

Now I was the one acting like an ass.

"Oh," I said dumbly. "I…suppose all of that makes sense."

"Now that *that's* out of the way…" he trailed off with a thoughtful hum. "I'm curious. You don't look like the kind of man who travels with a…" I watched his lips begin to form the word dildo, and I panicked, waving my hands to shut him up. His lips softened into a naughty smirk, dimples flickering.

Of course that was the first thing he'd ask me. A totally invasive question about something that was *private*.

"What *do* I look like?" I asked, even though I probably shouldn't have humored him.

Part of me was intrigued.

There were a lot of answers I expected.

Boring, for one. Average? Another. Brendon had said I was too fussy, too needy, too colorful. I'd spent years trying to fit into the mold he'd made for me.

And it had worked.

Maybe too well.

Because Mr. Armani's next words hit harder than he'd meant them to—

based on the still-playful expression on his face. "You look like the kind of guy who spends more time with a stick up his ass than a dildo." He looked expectant, like he anticipated a laugh or something equally optimistic.

But I didn't laugh.

Instead, I glared at him.

My fury came back full force.

"That may be true," I admitted, and then added in a darker tone, surprising myself. "Do I also look like the kind of guy who wouldn't hesitate to stab you? Because I assure you, I'm that too."

Instead of being frightened, as he should've been, Mr. Armani chuckled. Like he did not believe me. Which was fair—and frustrating. I kind of couldn't believe that had come out of my mouth either. Fighting was not normally something I did.

And yet.

I knew my threat had not been empty.

Which was…odd in and of itself.

And only made his blasé attitude piss me off even more.

"Hey, man. *You* were the one that asked! It's not my fault you didn't like my answer." The stranger shook his head. "I'm Alex, by the way." His playful smile was *horribly* attractive and *irritatingly* gorgeous. Alex held a hand out to me, massive tanned palm hovering expectantly in the air.

Ass.

I took his hand, surprised by how much bigger it was than mine. Though I was only a few inches shorter than him, he was maybe double my mass. Thick where I was thin, as broad as I was willowy. Alex's skin was hot and dry. He had calluses—not something I'd expected, given what he was wearing.

Most men in suits like his did not have rough hands.

Begrudgingly, I introduced myself, "George-Arthur Milton." Alex arched an eyebrow at me in question. "Two first names. Hyphenated."

"Do you prefer George or Arthur? Or both?" he asked, though I was having difficulty paying attention to what he was saying when his hand was still clasped possessively around my own.

Should I pull away?

No…no.

That would be weird, wouldn't it?

Like I was losing this unspoken battle of wills.

"I'd *prefer* you stay out of my business." And then, because I didn't want him getting any ideas, I actually answered. "But if you *must* address me, George is fine."

"Georgie it is."

I'd had my fair share of men try to intimidate me via the good ol' handshake. This was my first time responding to macho posturing this way, with goosebumps that prickled up my arms and a surge of lust so fierce it made me breathless. Electricity zapped down my spine when he squeezed.

What the hell?

Quickly, I withdrew my hand, accepting my loss. Something flickered in Alex's pale gaze that made the hair at the back of my neck stand up.

"You know, there's a bathroom further down the hall that no one ever goes to." He tilted his head, and I narrowed my eyes at him.

Was he…propositioning me?

"In case you wanted to wash your…" Alex waggled his eyebrows, "not-so-little friend."

"Neil is never leaving my backpack again, if I have anything to say about it," I found myself blurting on autopilot.

"Neil?" Alex blinked, then snorted. "You named your—"

"*Travel companion,*" I interjected before he could say the actual word out loud.

"You named your *travel companion?*" Alex looked far too entertained by all of this, tone dripping with disbelief. "*Really?* You don't seem the type."

"Why? Because you think I look like I have a stick up my butt?"

"Your ass," he corrected. "And sure." Alex shrugged. "Let's say that's the reason. Why Neil?"

I glared at him, unamused. "He looks like a Neil," I defended.

Alex's grin only grew. Like with every quip we shared, his evilness multiplied. He was chaos incarnate. "He looks…like a *Neil*," he echoed slowly. "*Fascinating.*" I did not like the glint in his eyes. At all. "Do you name all inanimate objects? Or just the ones you fuck yourself with?"

Demon.

He was an actual goddamn demon.

No one had ever looked at me like *that* before.

Like he wanted to crack me open and peer at my insides to see how they worked.

We were interrupted by the announcement that my flight had begun boarding. Relieved that this confusing and irritating conversation was over, I stood up. On autopilot again, I gathered my backpack, and belatedly figured I should probably say goodbye.

And also, maybe thank you.

Because as he'd unhelpfully pointed out, he had, in fact, saved me.

"Thanks for, you know…whatever *this* was," I said, stiff as a board. And then, because I couldn't help it, the sarcasm slipped free. "I'd say it's been a pleasure, but it definitely hasn't."

"You're welcome," Alex said, far too chipper all things considered. "And I beg to differ. It's *definitely* been a pleasure—for *me*, at least."

At least one of us was entertained.

I was still contemplating stabbing him.

"Goodbye." I almost saluted, but realized that was stupid and odd and not appropriate given the circumstances. So I didn't. I simply stalked off, head held high—you know, in case he watched me leave.

He'd seen my ugly sides enough for one day.

After waiting in line for an ungodly amount of time, I boarded my plane with one prayer—one solid, beautiful, wonderful prayer.

Dear God, please don't let Alex be on my flight.

Three
George

ONCE ON BOARD THE plane, all it took was one proprietary glance to realize my prayers had not been answered. Because Alex had flirted his way into the line directly behind me—cutting the rest of the people who'd patiently waited, and yet, no one complained. In fact, the woman he'd asked to step in front of simply giggled, like it was a goddamn honor to assist him in his plan to torment me.

Not that I looked at her—or him. Of course not. I stared resolutely ahead, guarding my sanity.

"Long time no see," Alex purred.

Asshole.

I ignored him, desperate to get to my seat and as far away from him as physically possible.

He occasionally bumped my back as we shuffled past the already full seats that lined the aisle, headed toward the empty rows at the rear of the plane. It was slow going as the passengers in front of us found their spots, and I did my best—but failed—not to inhale his cologne. In my defense, Alex was inappropriately crowded right against me. It was nearly impossible not to breathe him in.

"What's your name again?" a feminine voice cooed. More than likely the woman Alex had charmed to get in front of.

"Alex," he replied, warm and flirty.

"Oh!" She laughed, the sound grating on my nerves. Almost as grating as Alex's presence, but not quite. I could not wait for this whole ordeal to be over.

"Are you from New York?" she questioned, and I rolled my eyes heavenward, begging for patience. The pen in my pocket taunted me. It would be so satisfying to pull it free. To pop the cap off. To jab it into those fancy, fancy slacks and see if I could wipe that smug look right off Alex's face.

Not that I knew for sure he looked smug.

I was actively refusing to turn back.

I was less than zero percent interested in watching Alex flirt.

But that didn't mean I couldn't picture his face. The twinkle in his eyes. The smirk that made me want to do evil, wicked, not very nice things to him. Those dimples that begged me to act on impulses that were as foreign as they were…mildly liberating.

It'd been a long time since I felt so strongly about anyone new—even if my feelings were negative.

"I'm afraid not," Alex said in response to the woman's question. "I'm here for business in New York."

"Business?" she echoed, sounding delighted. I was sure she'd noticed how expensive his suit was too.

"Yes, ma'am."

She tittered, and I had to fight not to gag.

The closer we got to my assigned seat without separating, the more I despaired. There was no point wishing for a different outcome. Not when it was clear that fate had decided to fuck with me. Alex continued to flirt, and as my unease grew, I gave in to the urge to turn around and sneak a glance.

What I saw nearly made me stumble.

Because the woman Alex was currently chatting with was well into her eighties. And I was...shocked to say the least. She was beaming at him, her round face lit up with delight that this young, flirty thing was giving her attention.

I had no idea what to do with that—especially not when he blew her a kiss as she slid into her row beside two other older women who all seemed equally delighted by Alex. They whispered back and forth to each other as we moved on, voices quickly lost in the murmur of the rest of the crowd as the distance between us grew.

By the time we reached my assigned row, I had already come to terms with the fact that this journey was not going to be a pleasant one. Proving me right, rather than move the rest of the way down the aisle, Alex stopped when I did.

His body pressed into mine as he reached up to stuff his carry-on bag in the compartment above our seats. There was no use denying it now, was there? We, no doubt, were about to sit right next to each other.

Fuck my life.

"You 16B?" Alex inquired against my ear. I had to fight the urge not to smack him away. He did not sound surprised by this turn of events. Which... was odd, but not overly alarming. His breath tickled and sent a hot flicker low in my belly that I pointedly ignored.

Twisting around to glare at him, I opened my mouth to say something biting—but nothing came out. Judging by where Alex was looking, he'd clearly been peeking at the boarding pass that was still pulled up on my phone screen.

"*Why?*" I huffed, despair and irritation growing stronger with every second that passed.

"I'm 16A. Window seat." Alex's grin turned wolfish as he tilted his head to the side, arching a brow at me. "I'll need to get past you."

Right.

I'd anticipated this.

I should not be surprised.

And yet, hearing him say it out loud made the situation far too real. Sitting beside him at the gate had been bad enough. Being stuck with him for hours? Yeah. Not my idea of a good time. If I wasn't careful I really might stab him by the end of the flight.

Alex wasted no time swapping places with me. There was a lot more brushing and pushing than was necessary as he did so. I made sure to project my displeasure so he'd know I did not appreciate his lack of respect for my personal space. I suppose he couldn't help that he was large, though—so I cut him slack. Once finally settled into his spot by the window, Alex turned to me.

He patted the seat to his right invitingly.

My hands clenched into fists, and it took everything I had not to snap.

Maybe someone would sit in 16C—so we wouldn't have to be alone.

They could act as a buffer so I could listen to one of the audiobooks I had downloaded to whispersync with my Kindle for the flight. Perhaps another wrinkled woman for Alex to throw himself at?

I had no such luck.

The person who sat next to us was a woman in what I guessed to be her early twenties. She would not be my savior, that was for certain. Because she fell asleep immediately after giving me an affable nod, her headphones tucked around her ears, making it clear she was not open to conversation.

I could feel Alex staring at me. I sighed before turning, very slowly, to meet his gaze.

He was *still* smiling.

Little shit was obviously his default setting.

Leaning into me in a friendly but domineering way, Alex's stupidly massive shoulders pushed against mine.

"Why the suit, you have a meeting in Ohio?" Alex said, as if he expected me to want to talk to him. Goddamnit. The knowing glint in his eyes gave the illusion that he already knew what I was about to say.

"This is a *casual* suit," I gritted out, shuffling to get comfortable. I was hyper aware of the heat of his thigh where it snuggled tightly against mine. His legs were much wider than my own, and he flexed them so I could feel the muscle tense.

"A casual suit?" Alex echoed, and then he shifted his knee in a way that felt an awful lot like a rub. "Didn't know that was a thing."

I shuddered, then surreptitiously attempted to move away from him, because what the hell else was I supposed to do?

"Well, it is," I said. His knee shifted again. "You have big legs," I blurted with a grimace.

"Thank you," Alex's voice dropped lower, sweeter.

"Wasn't a compliment."

It had been. We both knew it had been.

"You ever heard of this thing called personal space? Truly revolutionary," I asked as I bent down to scrounge around inside my backpack for my headphones—very carefully not knocking Neil free or allowing the woman to my right to see the contents of my bag.

"I like your personal space," Alex flirted.

I didn't know how to respond to that.

Maybe if I put my headphones in, he'd get the message? No talky-talky, please and thank you.

I mean, objectively speaking…Alex was *hot*—like fire—but…the urge to stab him was growing with every passing minute. What had started as a preposterous idea was beginning to feel like a solid plan. I needed him to stop paying attention to me or I was going to implode.

I was not used to this kind of attention, and certainly not from a man who looked so out of my league he might as well have belonged to another planet entirely.

It made me feel like…

Like…

I don't know.

It was better for all involved if we parted ways now, no speaking, no bonding—and no more of Alex's personal brand of meaningless flirting.

I couldn't survive it.

I fumbled with the audiobook app on my phone, headphones sitting pinched between my thighs as I did so. Alex's eyes were laser-focused on my now slightly sweaty neck before his attention drifted to my screen.

Could it get any hotter in here?

"I love audiobooks," Alex said. My head thunked against the seat with a groan.

"Let me guess. You read a lot of self-help books," I rolled my eyes. "Get rich quick schemes?" Alex laughed, not offended whatsoever.

It really *was* a nice laugh.

"Try again."

"Memoirs from men who work in the stock market?"

"Colder."

I squinted at him as I tried to figure out what the hell someone like *him* would read. "I give up."

"Boo," Alex pouted. "I'm disappointed, Georgie. Where's your stamina?"

"Don't tell me you're into the hard stuff."

"Hard stuff?"

"Non-fiction?"

"Ehhh," Alex made a sound like a buzzer going off. "Nope. Think sexier."

I scrutinized him. There was no way…right? "Romance?"

"Erotica."

"You read *erotica*," I echoed, disbelieving.

"Religiously. I've dabbled in romance in general, but my sister and I buddy read, and we both lean toward smut more often than not. Right now we're on a BDSM kick."

Well, that was too close to home. I didn't dwell, already overwhelmed as it was.

Alex's eyes were twinkling, his lips twitching. He took my attention for the permission it was, leaning even further into my bubble.

"I didn't expect that," I admitted, cheeks hot. "You buddy read erotica with your sister?"

"Sure do."

"And that doesn't get weird?" I couldn't imagine listening to the same smut as my two sisters. I enjoyed it, yes. But the idea that one of my siblings could be turned on by the same thing? Absolutely not. No. Not interested.

"What about you?" Alex asked. "What do you read?"

There were only a few scant inches between our mouths. All I could think about was how good he smelled, musky-sweet, sultry enough to make my cock twitch where it lay trapped inside my silk panties.

I'd always liked panties.

I ordered custom ones to accommodate my cock, always careful the cut would sit low enough that when I bent over, my suit pants wouldn't show a thing. They were my secret. My power move. No one knew but me. Which was why I was wearing them today. I'd needed the extra boost of confidence both the panties and my suit would give me when visiting home.

Another bad decision.

Because the way Alex was studying me made me feel like he must have X-ray vision. Like he could see through the clutch of fabric at my hips to where my cock lay nestled safely in silk and lace.

Stop thinking about Alex looking at your panties, I reprimanded myself.

"What I like to read is none of your business."

"Why?" Alex's eyes crinkled in amusement as he crossed one of his ridiculously long legs over the other, his ankle bumping my thigh. It wasn't his fault he was massive—but fuck. I blamed him anyway.

I hadn't been lying when I told him he had big legs.

"I don't appreciate you getting off on bothering me," I muttered.

Alex's thick, dark brows shot up, and his grin turned wicked again. The urge to stab was back. Unconsciously, I pulled my pen from my pocket, fiddling with the cap nervously as Alex continued to tease.

"You seem to think you already have me figured out, don't you?" He asked, once again entertained rather than offended.

"You're not that hard to figure out." Another glance at our seat neighbor confirmed she was still asleep, and not listening to our verbal sparring. Good. Ink spread across the pad of my thumb as I rubbed it back and forth, self-soothing.

"Speaking of hard, you never did answer my earlier question."

I frowned, confused. "What question?"

"About whether or not you name all your sex toys?" His voice was quiet, intimate. There was no way anyone else could hear, but my cheeks still flamed. "I'm guessing you do."

"Jesus Christ." He was such an asshole.

"That's not a very sexy name." Alex pouted.

"I'm about five seconds from stabbing you with my pen."

"So you've threatened." Alex's whole body was quaking with mirth. "Believe me, I'm terrified." He did not *sound* terrified. He was as infuriatingly unbothered as always. Like he truly did not expect me to follow through on my threat.

Like I was a joke to him.

A giant fucking joke.

Someone to laugh at, to poke and prod and taunt.

Well.

Joke's on him. He wasn't leaving this flight unscathed. If he was going to push me past the breaking point, I was going to demonstrate why that was a bad idea. I couldn't quell the bubble of both excitement and irritation mounting inside me.

For the first time since we'd met, I knew exactly how to shut him up.

And no, it wasn't the perfect or "socially acceptable" thing to do. And it wasn't ignoring him, or verbally confronting him, because both of those things had thus far only egged him on.

No.

I was going to shut him up by doing exactly what I'd promised I would.

This wasn't the kind of thing I'd ever consider with anyone else.

But Alex brought out a side of me that I hadn't known was there.

Raw and unfiltered and honest.

So, even though it was an unhinged choice to make, and totally out of character, I still did it. Still flipped the pen around, squeezed it tight in my fist, and slammed it down on his leg. The tip of the ballpoint planted right into the meaty part of his thigh with enough force to leave a spot of black in the charcoal gray.

Alex's eyes nearly popped out of his head.

His jaw dropped open, pearly teeth flashing.

Surprising him—*actually* surprising him—was the single most satisfying experience I had ever had. Alex's leg jumped beneath the point of my pen, and ink spread in a streak that I hoped would remind him every time he looked at it not to be a dick.

"You *actually* stabbed me." Alex gasped, shocked. He was gaping at me like I'd grown a second head. For once, that infuriating smirk was absent. "Holy shit."

"I said I would," I replied immediately. To be honest, I was a bit surprised too. Not that he needed to know that.

"Yeah, but I didn't think you were serious—"

"Not thinking is probably a common problem for you," I interrupted, recapping and returning my pen back into my pocket. Finally, I had the upper hand.

My skin was buzzing.

Electrified.

I'd never fought back before.

This was…invigorating.

God. I'd never been this turned on in all my life. I was half-tempted to stab him again just to see what face he'd make. More surprised? Shocked? The first time had certainly been satisfying.

"I was only trying to be friendly," Alex grumbled. Though he didn't actually look upset, merely puzzled, like he'd thought he had me figured out, only to be proven wrong.

I shrugged, reaching for my headphones and popping them in with a grin of my own.

"So was I," I replied, tipping my head back, closing my eyes, and tapping play on my book.

Maybe my day wasn't ruined after all.

Alex's shoulder continued to brush against mine, warm and somewhat comforting. I didn't pull my Kindle from my bag, content to bask in superiority for as long as it lasted. I was sure, soon enough, Alex would do something to steal my attention again.

And even though he kept accidentally touching me, I didn't push him away.

Instead, as the plane took to the sky and the tarmac disappeared, I simply enjoyed my win.

I hadn't had one of those in a long, long time.

Four
Alex

GEORGE-ARTHUR MILTON WAS nothing like I'd expected. Sure, he was blond. That part was no surprise. Every single member of his family was. He had the Milton charm—serious to a fault. Just like his dad and his three siblings, he was tall with a pale complexion and a smattering of moles on his throat. But aside from that, he wasn't at all who I'd thought he'd be.

For one thing, rather than exhibit the stoic demeanor his siblings shared, George was positively fiery. He was an open book. His nose scrunched, his eyes squinted. Wrinkles and divots, and pursed lips to demonstrate his displeasure. His facial features were so incredibly responsive, I had the urge to collect each new expression like they were Pokémon.

He was also gorgeous.

A delicate, sharp sort of pretty. Constantly marred by each scrunch and scowl.

The most interesting thing about George, however, wasn't his expressiveness or his fire. It was the fact that, unlike the rest of his family, he didn't fall for my charm.

I spent the majority of our shared flight doing my best to crack his hard shell, only to be wildly unsuccessful. He didn't respond to my flirting the way most people did. Questions only seemed to make his hackles rise. And like a grouchy cat, he was unafraid to swipe me with his goddamn claws.

He showed no remorse about that either. In fact, his soft-looking lips and been pulled into what could only be described as a triumphant smile as he'd pocketed his pen and proceeded to ignore me immediately after he'd literally fucking stabbed me in the leg.

Unexpected—totally fucking unexpected.

He was a challenge.

It wasn't often that I encountered challenges.

Most of the time, all it took was a flash of my dimples to get what I desired.

George was honestly the first person I'd met in a very long time who didn't simply bend over and take my flirty bullshit. His dark blue eyes held a guardedness that I could relate to, even if I couldn't understand. When I pushed, he pushed back. Unyielding.

Which was, suffice to say, electric.

I couldn't wait to see him again.

Couldn't wait to surprise him the way he'd surprised me.

It was going to be amusing to watch those expressive brows twist. Maybe he'd scowl again? God, that scowl was adorable. He had this little dimple in his chin when he frowned that I found disarmingly captivating. It was the grumpiest dimple I'd ever seen.

A *grimple*, if you will.

So fucking cute.

Seriously.

When I'd finally annoyed him into abandoning his book, George had evaded as many of my questions as he could. The flight duration was nearly two hours, and I'd learned very fucking little about him, despite how doggedly

I'd worked for answers. When I'd asked him if he'd been raised in Ohio, he'd flicked an eyebrow and said, "Obviously."

It hadn't been obvious at all.

At least, not if you looked at how tightly wound his ass was in his dark suit and silver cufflinks. He had New York practically tattooed on his face. It was hard to believe he was from the same small rural town that Roddy was from. Raised surrounded by cornfields beneath the same wide blue sky I'd always called home.

There was nothing "small town" about George.

He was the opposite of friendly.

Not that I'd necessarily call the rest of the clan "friendly", per se, but George had *bite*.

A fact I begrudgingly respected at the same time I found fascinating. Maybe that was why he'd moved so far away? Why he'd become the black sheep of the family despite being Mrs. Milton's golden boy. Her pride and joy. The only Milton to break the mold.

He was as tightly wound as a yo-yo, and I couldn't wait to watch him spin. I felt no remorse. Why would I when I knew this would lead nowhere fast? This was a bit of flirty fun. Nothing more.

I mean…sure, I hadn't planned on flirting at all—I certainly hadn't with June's other matchmaking efforts. But…a little wouldn't hurt.

I didn't date.

I never would.

I knew better than anyone that I was unpalatable. Too much. There was no point pretending otherwise. And I wasn't going to. If I found George fascinating, that was private information.

It didn't mean anything.

Nothing at all.

Especially when he made it so goddamn clear how incredibly uninterested he was in me. I wasn't used to being disliked.

"Favorite thing to do in your spare time?" I tried, ignoring the heat that pooled between my legs when he glared at me.

"I'm not playing twenty questions with you."

"Harsh," I laughed, unrepentant. I maybe shouldn't have pushed, but I couldn't help myself. Not when he was so fucking cute—especially when he was annoyed. He didn't want to be vulnerable when it wasn't on his own terms. This wasn't about privacy—at least, I didn't think so. It was about control. I could respect that.

"Please?" I said, curious to see what he'd do next. There were limits to how far I'd go. I didn't want to actually make him uncomfortable, and though I continued to prod, I was careful not to cross the line.

George didn't reply.

I'd stumped him.

I could see the flicker of confusion in his eyes as he scrambled to figure out what to say.

George had the kind of eyes poetry was written about. There was a sadness in them I recognized far too intimately. My own neediness projected onto him—given how brutally and efficiently George shut me down.

A vivid, bottomless blue, as dark as mine were light. It was difficult to look away once caught inside their depths. Like the Mariana Trench, his irises were so blue they were nearly black. Layers on layers, rippled waves of emotion buried on top of one another so far down they muddied. And though the color was gorgeous, best of all was their shape. Angled upward at the ends, the wrinkles at the corners of George's eyes betrayed how often he scoffed or squinted. Years of emotion bundled in every permanent crevice. Framed by see-through blond lashes, he was a study in contrast.

Dark eyes to complement the honey blond of his hair.

A plush mouth with a sharp tongue.

Long, long legs. Lean shoulders. Sharp angles and soft hands.

I'd never been a poet, but looking at George made me want to try my hand at it—if only so that I could attempt to remember how frustratingly fascinating he was. Which was infuriating seeing as I'd promised myself I wouldn't be drawn in by him.

It would have been impossible not to be.

He was as stunning as he was prickly, and I couldn't recall the last time I'd flirted with someone and been shut down so goddamn efficiently.

"I'm not going to tell you my hobbies," George finally settled on, though it'd taken him a solid forty seconds—and counting—to get there.

"I play sports," I offered in reply, hoping that if I opened up, he would too. I'd yet to meet a single person who'd glimpsed beneath my walls and liked what they saw, so I didn't understand why my mouth kept fucking opening, bullshit spilling free.

"Good for you," George huffed, sinking lower into his seat. He had narrow shoulders, though his suit had done a pretty good job of concealing it. Narrow shoulders, narrow hips, long, limber legs. God, those fucking legs, kill me now.

Made me want to squeeze and knead and shove them wide apart.

"I'm not picky about which one. I've dabbled in most—" I continued, like he hadn't spoken. "Though hockey is probably my favorite—and the one I play often. Recreationally. I'm by no means a professional."

Jesus, Alex. Why are you telling him all of this?

George's mouth opened like he was about to ask a question, then it snapped shut the moment he thought better of it.

"What?" I asked, excited that I might have *finally* inspired something other than a biting remark. "You a hockey guy?"

"No," George scoffed. "I'm wondering if a puck to the head is the reason you don't know when to shut up."

"Oof," I slapped a hand over my heart. "You wound me."

"I sincerely doubt that," George sighed, gaze fixed resolutely on the seat in front of him. "I literally wounded you, and you're still bothering me." His cheeks were pink, though, which was adorable.

Christ. It was impossible to break through his walls.

This was not a script I had memorized.

Normally, by this point, I had people eating out of my hand. Sometimes literally. Other times, there were fingers on my biceps, and dark pupils peering up at me as whoever I was trying to woo inquired if *sports* were the reason my physique was as sculpted as it was.

To which the answer was no.

But I'd lie and say maybe.

They'd titter and laugh.

Five minutes later I'd have my dick snug inside whoever I had seduced.

Rinse and repeat.

It was the same thing over and over and over again.

But not with George.

No.

George was…

George was *George*.

A lost cause, honestly. He wasn't interested in me. Which was fine. Anything with him was bound to be messy, and I seemed to be the only person who realized that.

That didn't mean George wasn't super entertaining, though.

Or that I wasn't fascinated by him.

Fascinated enough that I couldn't seem to stop flirting, even if my usual MO when it came to June's set ups was to go icy cold.

When our flight landed—unfortunately too quickly for me to get anything real out of him—George was gone before I could blink. Those leggy legs had eaten up the distance as fast as they possibly could. He'd practically teleported off the plane.

I would've been offended if I truly cared.

Which I didn't. Except, apparently I did. At least…a little.

Again, he wasn't interested.

A thought that rankled more than it should have, considering I was bound and determined not to feed into the madness that was my sister and her matchmaking.

"What's up with your face?" The aforementioned twin sister, June, said in greeting.

"Nothing's up with my face." I yanked the passenger door to her truck open. We both knew I was lying. I hadn't schooled my expression quickly enough. And besides, she knew me better than anyone. My thoughts were full. Full of soft lips, chin dimples, and scowl lines.

"You look constipated."

"Thanks," I replied dryly, sliding into my seat.

June drove a hilariously massive pickup truck. Hilarious because of how fucking tiny she was. Climbing in and out made her look like a cartoon character straight out of a picture book. Which was exactly why she'd bought the car in the first place. She enjoyed the looks she received when she hopped out and people realized the monstrosity was being manned by a big-boobed hobbit. (Her name, not mine.)

If there was one thing June didn't lack, it was good humor.

Case in point.

That was one of the things I loved most about her.

That and her knack for calling me on my bullshit. As frustrating as it could be, she grounded me. Constantly proving that not everyone in the world was a superficial asswipe, even if it sometimes felt like it.

"So..." June said as I grabbed a couple empty Coke bottles at my feet. I tossed them into the back to make room. A wayward fast-food bag crunched beneath my heel, but I left it alone. Too much nitpicking and I'd incite her ire.

I didn't want to do that.

Not when I knew I was about to piss her off—a fact I hated, even if I couldn't really help it.

I knew what she was hinting at.

As infuriating as it was.

"So?"

"You met George." She grinned a shit-eating grin. The kind of grin that made me want to smother her with a pillow.

"Yes."

"*Aaaand?*" June waited eagerly, already slamming her cowboy boot on the gas and peeling out of the arrival zone at the airport. She drove like a woman possessed—and yet somehow, we always managed to be late for everything. Like being chronically behind schedule was simply a facet of who she was. She blamed the trains that ran through Columbus, even when it wasn't their fault.

Almost like I'd summoned one, we were cut off from the road by the gates lowering. With a groan, I leaned back, the *ding, ding* of the approaching train acting as background noise as I settled in for an interrogation.

"And he's…" *Sexy, cute, grumpy, not interested?* "Blond," I finally decided.

"*Blond,*" June echoed unenthusiastically.

"Okay, he was nice." He was not nice.

"Nice? *Wow.* That's boring."

"Shut up."

"Nice is what you call the weather, Alex. Not a cute guy who is exactly your type."

"I don't have a type."

"Sure you do. You know, anything with a pulse." June's grin grew wolfish. It was the same smile I wore half the time and I decided I really didn't like it being directed at me.

"Ha, *ha.* Fuck you."

"Fuck yourself." June flipped me off.

I flipped her off back.

The train finally departed, and we were on the move again.

Silence filled the cluttered truck as June gathered her thoughts.

Leaning my head against the headrest, I watched the city melt into the country. Endless fields, tall golden corn, trees that drifted along the sides of the road casting long shadows we drove right through. A sunny summer sky and puffy white clouds spread as far as the eye could see, no high-rises or mountains to break the never-ending blue. The dotted yellow line that curled like a serpent down the winding road led us deeper and deeper into the countryside. Away from Columbus and toward Chesterton, the small town Roderick—and George—had been raised in.

"For real, though," June spoke again, quieter this time. "Did you like him? We were hoping you'd like him."

"We" as in June and her gaggle of matchmaking accomplices—Roderick, her fiancé, among them. Most of June's matchmaking efforts had been made on her own. Not this one, though, nope. Because apparently, one person trying to hook me up for her wedding wasn't annoying enough. I needed a whole goddamn army.

Though I highly doubted Roderick had been outright involved in the ticket purchasing aspects of June's plan. He wasn't diabolical enough for that.

"I know you were." I knew why June had set this up in the first place. And because I knew, even though my first instinct was to blow her off, I couldn't do that. Not when she looked so cautiously hopeful. Not when her pale blue eyes were bright.

Not when she'd admitted to me in confidence before I'd left home for my business trip in New York that her greatest wish for her wedding was to make sure I wasn't alone, even if it was only temporary.

It was my own fault, really.

For stupidly trusting her with my secrets.

She knew better than anyone how badly I wanted what she had. When I'd informed her I wasn't bringing a plus-one, she'd made it her mission to find me one. Even though she also knew I'd written off love.

Love meant being known.

Being seen.

Being accepted for all your flaws.

And I knew, least of all, no one was going to look at my pile of dirty socks and think "wow, this one's a keeper."

I was a romantic.

A romantic who was terrified of romance.

What a joke.

"George is cute," I admitted, because it was true. I didn't often open up about real feelings. But I figured I owed her *something*. "Especially when he's grumpy."

"When he's…" June groaned. "*Christ*, please tell me you didn't *intentionally* piss him off?"

"I don't want to lie."

"*Why*, Alex?" June slammed on the brakes, the truck screeching to a halt at a stop sign she'd only now noticed. Fuck, she was the worst driver I'd ever had the displeasure of riding with. Because of our dad's recent accident, I was even more on edge. I could feel my pulse skittering as she hit the gas again, accelerating fast enough the wheels squealed. The engine roared, this angry, awful sound—that she ignored.

Of course she did.

She ignored lots of things—like my attempts to thwart her plans, and my protests.

An engine light popped up on June's dash, and before I could point it out, she slammed her fist on the glass until it turned off.

"Stupid thing."

"You should get that checked," I replied, attempting to change the subject. "Just because the light is off now doesn't mean you fixed the underlying issu—"

"You should get your *brain* checked," June interrupted. "*Why* did you piss him off, Alex?"

I blew out a breath. I should've left it at "he's cute" and let her think what she wanted.

"I only teased him a *little*," I defended, as if that made it any better.

"What, did ignoring him like you have with every other plus-one I've arranged not work? So you had to outright *antagonize* him?"

I didn't know what to say to that, called out as I was.

"You make it really fucking hard to set you up with somebody," June growled.

"Did it ever occur to you that I might be doing that on *purpose*?" I replied, more biting than I'd intended. "I don't want you to set me up with people. I have told you that, repeatedly."

Play nice, Alex.

Stop antagonizing the dragon.

"I don't know why you thought setting me up with a Milton would go any better," I muttered. "Way fucking worse, actually. Because I actually know his family."

"I *hoped*," June stressed, "that the fact we know his family might make you act like less of a dick."

"Yeah, well. Sorry to disappoint."

"I don't get you," June lamented. "You want a partner to spoil. You want a family. You want kids. And yet, you're allergic to monogamy. You do realize you can't have the picket-fence kinda life you want without dating someone first, right?"

"I know."

"Then why do you choose to be such an asshole? You're intentionally self-sabotaging. Not a cute look, dude. At all." June's words hurt more than she'd intended them to. She cared about me. More than anyone had ever cared about me. We'd literally shared a womb. And since the day she could walk, she'd made it her mission in life to look out for me.

She'd always given me everything I'd ever asked for.

All her toys. All her treats. All her attention.

She was the best sister in the world.

42

So why did I always feel the need to…to upset her like this?

Maybe something really was wrong with me.

"I'm sorry," I said sincerely. I genuinely felt like a dick. "I…I honestly don't know."

Maybe I did know, though.

Because any time I'd given someone a part of myself that was vulnerable, they'd crushed it. There was no point trying. Not when I needed too much. When my heart was an open, gaping black hole—and I was "too much" for anyone to handle. George had certainly thought so, if the way he'd bolted from me as soon as he could was any indicator.

"I know." June wilted, taking a hand off the wheel—oh god—to give my shoulder a squeeze. Her hand was so fucking tiny. Ridiculously so. Sometimes it was difficult to believe we'd been the same size at birth.

"I'm sorry for pushing you when you're not ready," June said, putting her hand back on the wheel. I missed it when it was gone. That simple contact had been more than welcome.

June had no ulterior motive.

None at all.

Not like the people I hooked up with. Not like the clients I worked with at Dad's company. Not like the socialites I schmoozed at the parties I had no choice but to attend, lest I make our father look bad.

She loved me.

Simple as that.

She wanted to see me as happy as she was.

She knew my aches, my hollows, my wants—how could I fault her for doing her best to help?

I couldn't.

"You didn't do anything wrong," I replied, because I hated the idea that she'd feel guilty about this. "You're trying to be helpful. And you were right. He *is* my type."

"You're not just saying that because it's what I want to hear?" She sounded dubious, not at all excited like she had earlier.

Self-loathing curled black and heavy in my gut.

"No." Honesty felt odd and unfamiliar.

Why couldn't I have just said I liked him in the first place?

Why had I pushed her?

Why was I always pushing?

What was wrong with me?

"I'm not his, though," I managed. I couldn't help but recall how very uninterested George had been on the plane. "So it's pointless."

June's smile was back, even brighter than before. Sunnier than the summer day. She arched a brow at me. "You're everyone's type."

I snorted. "That was suspiciously nice."

"Don't get used to it."

"Wouldn't dream of it," I said.

The fact that I'd caused that grin made me feel like I'd won an award, and yet, guilt still waged a war in my gut. Because the truth was, though George had walls—so did I. Fortresses, really. And as selfish as it was, I'd rather disappoint than be disappointed.

Which meant I was going to do what I always did. Treat George the way I'd treated the rest of June's "miss-matches". Stop flirting with him—when it was clear he didn't want it.

I wasn't sure if I was protecting her, or myself. Maybe both?

I'd prefer to get the awkwardness over with before the beginning of her "wedding summer camp". It would be better that way.

George-Arthur Milton wasn't my soulmate.

He was a grouchy size queen from New York.

There was no way he was the one person in the world who'd want all I had to offer. It was glaringly obvious that *I* was the real lost cause. And once again, June had given me no choice but to show everyone that.

Five
George

EVEN THOUGH I KNEW that responding would only fuel Alex's curiosity, I hadn't managed to ignore much during the flight home. When I'd bolted off the plane, Alex had stared after my retreating back with puppy-dog eyes. I'd done my best not to acknowledge him. I'd already given in enough earlier, due to my inability to tune him out.

I genuinely had no idea how to handle someone like him—and the attention he'd given me. I was used to being ignored or berated, not whatever *that* had been. I was still mostly convinced he'd been making fun of me. But…I figured that wasn't something I needed to worry about anymore.

Stop thinking about him.

You're never going to see him again, I reminded myself as I made my way toward baggage claim to retrieve my checked bag.

Maybe I should've said goodbye?

No, *no.* Absolutely not.

What if he'd assumed it was an invitation for more and asked for my number or something? The thought was enough to make me pause mid-walkway and laugh hysterically.

Yeah fucking right.

The family that had been shuffling beside me paused, the mother pulling her children behind her as she aimed a judgmental look my way. To which I only managed to laugh harder. Fuck. Then I slapped a hand over my mouth so I'd look less unhinged. It didn't work.

Something was clearly wrong with me.

Because discovering that my luggage had somehow ended up lost had only made me laugh again. Of course it had. Today was a day for fuckery. I tried not to think of the implications of that—grateful I always packed my backpack for this exact fucking reason.

I'd have to go into the city to buy a suit at some point. There was no way in hell I was wearing a *casual* suit to a wedding. Tacky as hell. Absolutely not. I had an image to maintain. The one thing in life I had going for me was my mom's pride.

My brother, Joe, was waiting for me in the designated pick up zone.

I sighed when I saw him, relieved to have someone to help me get my mind off of how completely awful today had been. I could taste summer in the air, the thick cloyingness of pollen and sunshine—though the bustle of the city almost drowned it out entirely.

For the first time in years, I was home.

Joe waved at me, all six-foot-five of him, dressed in awful pale-blue flannel and his usual Levi's and white undershirt. I waved back, making a beeline for him. His expression didn't change, forever as stoic and expressionless as Dad.

Joe was older than the last time I'd seen him—obviously—and he wore that age well. He was broader somehow. Had new creases at the corners of his mouth from frowning. At twenty-eight years old, Joe looked far more world-weary than he deserved, considering he was basically a giant puppy inside a grumpy, intimidating-looking body.

He was different.

But there was no denying *this* was my little brother. My *only* little brother. The same kid who'd followed me around for half our lives, desperate to prove himself.

In contrast with the blank expression he sported, Joe wasted no time demonstrating how enthusiastic he was about my return home. I only had a moment to mentally prepare before he yanked me into a tight embrace. His massive hand smacked my back a few times as he crushed me into him. The sweat-sunny musk of Joe's natural scent filled my lungs.

"Hi, buddy," I wheezed, face smashed into his chest.

I did my best not to die.

Which was genuinely a struggle.

Joe was too big and too dumb to realize how strong he was—and how easily breakable I'd become now that he was double my goddamn size.

"*George.*" Joe squeezed me tight enough my bones rattled. When he finally set me down, he wasted no time ambling around to the back of the minivan to open the trunk.

It was Lacey's minivan.

The car she used to transport my adorable niece, Mavis, who I hadn't had the pleasure to see in person since she was a tiny baby three Christmases ago. My family had flown back East to visit me, and I'd spent the holiday at war with myself. Ecstatic to see Mom, and apprehensive, because Brendon had been pissed off they'd "stolen me" from him.

Joe pulled the trunk open almost ceremoniously. He gestured at the empty space, obviously urging me to toss my backpack in.

"No luggage?" he confirmed, pale brow furrowed in confusion.

"No." Because my luck could seriously not be worse. Reminded of the uncomfortable encounter at baggage claim, I pinched the bridge of my nose. I'd been apologized to about a half-dozen times. And I would've been more pissed about the whole situation, considering how many important items had gone missing, but…

After Alex's flirting, I'd been far too frazzled.

The employee had looked miserable enough without me beating him up over something he couldn't control. I'd given him my number in case it turned up, but figured I'd need to cut my losses.

"Why?" Joe looked perplexed. Well, as perplexed as he could, considering his face was made of stone.

"It got lost." I shrugged a shoulder as his dark blue gaze grew stormy. I had no doubt if I asked, Joe would glare the unlucky employee into submission. But that wouldn't solve the missing bag issue—so there was no point. "Don't worry about it."

Joe nodded.

And that was that.

He waited for me to toss my backpack inside—obviously eager to help, even though it was only one bag. I didn't think we really *needed* to use the trunk, all things considered—but I didn't want to dampen Joe's mood by pointing that out.

So I didn't comment.

"Just cleaned the back," Joe grunted. "Figured you'd appreciate the lack of junk. I even vacuumed."

Last I'd heard, he'd been borrowing Lacey's van and acting as an official babysitter on the side while he saved up for a farm of his own. He'd even moved back home, every penny he earned going toward his dream.

I wasn't the only Milton interested in living back East.

Joe had his heart set on Vermont, a fact that made Mom apprehensive. At least, that's what she told me when we'd chatted on the phone about it. I didn't share that apprehension. It was easy to picture Joe on his own. He'd thrive there, especially if he found a farm close to wild life. Animals flocked to him like they saw him as one of their own. He was basically the gigantic, manly version of Snow White—only if she'd been interested in owning an apple orchard and dreamed of going bird watching on the weekends.

Joe's cleaning left much to be desired. The trunk looked like a cornfield had thrown up in it. There were muddy boot prints. A few broken crayons. A half dozen unicorn-themed toys—all Mavis's.

It was the thought that counted, right?

And Joe had obviously…tried.

Which was why Joe was my favorite.

The passenger seat was covered in Cheez-It crumbs and Kool-Aid stains. And yet, I melted into it gratefully, absorbing the scent of dirt and family. I was a bit anxious to see my other family members, worried Mom would take one look at me and know how miserable I was, and I'd be unable to play her golden boy the way I desired.

Which was why I let myself soak up Joe's presence and enjoyed the companionable silence we shared during the forty-minute drive home.

The cornfields were thriving, green, glorious blurs on either side of the windows. Eventually, Joe got me up to date on the family drama—nothing more than a few tiffs between siblings—and updated me about Mavis and her newest obsessions.

The way he spoke to me, all quiet, gruff honesty, made it seem like no time at all had passed since we'd last talked. Despite his efforts, I could feel the chasm that Brendon's presence in my life had left behind.

It was always bizarre returning to Ohio after living so many years away. Like visiting an alternate dimension of the place I'd grown up. Some things were the same, yes—more paint chipped than when I was a kid, maybe—but mostly unchanged. And others? Other things felt like transplants. Foreign buildings that didn't fit into the Chesterton of my memories. Too new. Too different. Out of place.

Family, though.

Family was the same, no matter how many years went by.

My phone buzzed in my pocket, and I pulled it free. Like a slap to the face, another text from Brendon broke the calm Joe had lulled me into.

Brendon

I know you read my earlier text, George.
Ignoring me is a new low, even for you.

"What?" Joe's voice was a welcome distraction. But even its familiar cadence couldn't chase away the shadows left behind from Brendon's words.

"Nothing. Just work," I replied, shoving my phone back in my pocket, hands shaking.

I shouldn't stress over this.

Over something as small as a text.

I wasn't obligated to reply. Not during my time off.

But it still…Christ. It still bothered me.

Was he going to go to our boss and tell him that I'd been ignoring him? I was past caring about Brendon's personal opinion of me. But I wasn't ready for him to ruin my reputation at work.

No one had even known we were dating.

They'd take his words at face value, wouldn't they?

There was no reason to believe he was vindictive.

And yet…I couldn't help but think that all of this was my fault.

Because I'd known our relationship wasn't healthy, yet I'd let him twist me up over and over just so I could feel gratitude on the days he decided to help me untangle the knots he'd tied.

I was never enough for him.

Never what he wanted.

Always begging for scraps of attention, perpetually left empty.

Unbidden, a more pleasant thought rose to the surface.

Namely, Alex James.

His laugh, his massive tanned hands, his gorgeous eyes and the way they'd crinkled at the corners. His dimples, so full of mischief. And the way he'd commanded my attention like it was his right to do so.

Alex hadn't left me feeling empty.

He'd paid attention to me.

Maybe too much attention.

And as we pulled into the driveway of the picturesque farmhouse that I'd grown up inside, I realized how desperately, horribly, *awfully* I'd needed that.

My childhood home was a frankly massive three-story country monstrosity. It had white siding, ivy climbing up the walls, and a window for each of the bedrooms. I could vividly remember summers here, chasing Joe and Lacey around the yard with the hose, water casting fragmented rainbows wherever it sprayed. Marcille would watch from the front porch swing, and Mom would ply us with sandwiches and reminders not to track mud in the house come lunch time.

"You sure you don't need help?" Joe confirmed.

"It's a backpack, Joe. Pretty sure I can handle it." I rolled my eyes.

"Sure." Joe grunted, and I smiled at him. "You dating anyone new?" he asked.

My smile fell immediately.

Well, that was random.

"No." Slinking out of the car, I catalogued each change.

The lawn was more manicured than I remembered—Joe's handiwork. Dad's shed, full of tools and the like, had been repainted a cheerful red. There were scribbles in chalk on the driveway, probably Mavis's doing. And a different set of curtains hung inside the window that'd been mine growing up, facing across the street to Roderick's house. I popped my back with a groan, shaking off the funk I was in as I headed toward the trunk to retrieve my backpack.

This felt surreal.

I wasn't sure if it was good or bad.

Already, I could feel my walls coming up, the need to perform rising to the surface.

"If you're looking—" Joe recited, almost like this conversation was scripted, and he'd been put up to it.

"I'm not."

"Roddy's fiancé has a brother."

Joe blocked access to my backpack, his large frame waiting expectantly. Held hostage by him and the script he seemed determined to follow, I groaned.

"Not interested."

"But—"

"Even if I *was* looking—which I'm not—the last thing I'm going to do while I'm home is entertain the idea of hooking up with the *bride's* brother."

"He's…cute." He winced, like he knew exactly how painful this was for both of us but was determined to follow through with it anyway.

"Cute isn't my type."

Joe's brow furrowed. "Huh," he said, rather eloquently.

He dropped the subject.

Thank God.

I was drained enough already—from the drama of this whole damn trip—and I did not need to add "man troubles" to the mix.

I could hear the party that was raging in our backyard before I saw it. Frowning, I turned to Joe. "Mom went all out with the barbecue," he said in explanation.

"Barbecue?"

"It's a welcome-home-George-congrats-Roddy-party. To kick off the celebration." He nudged me conspiratorially with one of his ginormous shoulders, nearly bowling me over.

I stumbled, trying not to fall flat on the pavement.

"Mom bought your favorite brand of pickles."

My heart fluttered, light chasing away the shadows Brendon's texts had left behind. "Oh." I bit back a smile. I *loved* pickles. And no, that wasn't a euphemism.

Apparently, Joe had forgotten that I'd told him I would handle my own backpack. Because before I could catch my balance, the blond giant stopped blocking the trunk and pulled it out.

He didn't give it to me.

Instead, he slung it over his shoulder, and I sighed, sulking after him as he headed toward the white wooden gate that separated the front from the backyard. Small butterflies flitted along the shrubbery. A tall, drooping maple tree cast a puddle of shade across the grass. Cricket song croaked somewhere in the bushes, the whistle of a summer breeze carrying it through the air.

Dodging a wayward grasshopper, I eyed my backpack distrustfully. I knew, realistically, Neil wasn't going to jump out all on his own, but I was still truly terrified he'd make a second appearance.

I had to fight back the urge to reach out and yank the damn thing off of Joe's back.

No one is going to open your bag without permission, I reassured myself. *It's fine.*

"I'm assuming Roderick is already here?" I grimaced, glancing behind to check the house across the street. Just looking at it made my heart hurt. I'd grown up there as much as I'd grown up inside my own childhood home. Roderick and I had been friends for far longer than we'd dated. It felt strange to look at his home through the lens of thirty-three-year-old George.

I didn't want Roderick. Not anymore.

That wasn't a pain I still carried.

"Yep." Joe said. "Is that weird?"

It was definitely weird.

"No," I replied as we finally reached the gate. "Why would it be weird?"

Joe leveled me with a look that made it clear he thought I was being an idiot.

I was not fooling anyone, least of all myself.

"Do you still love him?" Joe frowned.

"*No,*" I bit out. "Absolutely not."

"Good." Joe nodded seriously. He pushed open the gate, and I prepared to see Roderick in the flesh for the first time since we'd broken up a decade prior.

You're fine, George.

It doesn't matter what he thinks of you.

He's just a guy you used to date, nothing more.

I fixed my hair, anyway. Then I adjusted my suit and checked my shoes for dirt streaks or wayward airport gum. Nothing. As spiffy as when I'd shined them that morning. I was grateful they'd dried enough not to bother me anymore.

When I decided I was as physically ready as I'd ever be, I followed Joe through the gate. He was only a few feet ahead of me, and I hurried to catch up, eyes tracking the sway of my backpack as it sat tiny on Joe's broad back. As soon as I'd ensured the zipper was still firmly shut, I took in my surroundings.

As per usual—in typical Mom fashion—the yard had been invaded by a small army of white foldable picnic tables. There were a myriad of tablecloths thrown across each one. Splashes of Christmas, fall, summer, and spring decorations coated the yard in a rainbow-meshed tableau.

The party was a potluck, judging by the giant bowls full of food lining the table designated to house the plethora of options. Joe slapped me on the back in lieu of a goodbye. Then he headed off toward where my dad was grilling on the porch, bringing my backpack up the stairs with him.

Dad said he liked to be up high. It made him feel like the king of the world as he gazed down on the rest of us peasants wandering around his massive backyard like barbecue-fueled ants.

I loved my dad. Even though he was bad with words, allergic to affection, and made the worst burgers in the history of the universe.

Every one of my siblings was present today—aside from my oldest sister, Marcille, who Mom had told me hadn't been able to make the trip back home. It felt surreal to stand in my backyard like no time had passed.

Mom found me a second later.

She was dressed as she always was, curvy body drowning in a dress so colorful and garishly patterned she might as well be wearing a neon sign. Her giant blonde hairstyle was even rounder than usual, rising easily five inches above her head in the classic beehive she and the other women in town considered fashionable.

Mom was the local hair stylist. She took great satisfaction in making everyone in town look just like her.

"*Mom*," my voice broke.

Suddenly, I was a kid again, transported back in time.

"George." Mom enveloped me in her arms, holding me tight. She was so soft. So warm. She always managed to smell like the oddest combination of sunscreen, cookies, hairspray, and laundry detergent.

For a moment, I simply breathed her in, squeezing back as my face buried in the crisp round of her over-hairsprayed updo.

"You're too skinny," she said the second she pulled away, hands rubbing my arms. "You look tired. Have you not been sleeping?"

I laughed, chest aching. "I've been sleeping just fine."

Another lie.

Mom made a disapproving sound, then pulled me into another hug. Longer this time. "Welcome home, baby," she said.

And just like that, my fear dissipated.

Gone like it'd never been there at all.

After Mom had paraded me around to all her friends—making me recite what I did for a living and tell them about the many "big-name" companies I'd designed for, she finally left me alone. I missed her, but felt settled in a way I hadn't for a very long time.

It was good to be home.

I was grateful for the opportunity to feel like something other than a failure.

The last year had been horrible, to say the least. Between the breakup, getting over the breakup, and Brendon's refusal to leave me alone both in and outside of work, I was spread thin—two seconds from snapping at any given moment.

Mom's pride was the tether I'd desperately needed.

Dad gave me a nod from his perch on top of the porch.

For him, that was as good as declaring his undying love.

Lacey flipped me off as she stacked her plate high with snacks—again, a show of obvious affection. So, I was feeling pretty fucking good about myself—and my decision to come home by the time I turned back to the crowd of people that spread across the lawn.

I'd almost forgotten about Roderick.

But there he was, sitting unobtrusively at one of the picnic tables. He clearly saw me too, because he smiled at me and waved. My heart skipped a beat, anxiety sending a cold wash through me.

Yes, I'd flown all this way because he was getting married.

Yes, he'd invited me.

Yes, we'd stayed distant friends since our breakup when we were younger.

And no, I hadn't been lying when I told Joe I didn't love Roderick.

But that didn't stop my body from reacting like he was going to jump on top of the table, point at me, and start laughing.

Maybe it was the trauma of the dildo incident.

Or the lingering pessimism that accompanied my suitcase going missing.

Either way, I couldn't help but expect the worst, my good mood dissipating as I realized there was no getting out of this.

Roderick patted the empty place next to him in a way I figured he thought looked inviting, but wasn't. The last thing I wanted to do was crease my suit by sitting in a camping chair—but I did so anyway, consequences be damned. It creaked beneath my weight, sucking my butt inside it like a nylon black hole.

Roderick was older now. Obviously. Unfortunately for me, he'd aged well. His brown eyes twinkled as he peered at me from overtop the rim of his glasses.

"Hiya, George." Roderick's lips pulled into a smile that I couldn't help but return. It felt as natural as breathing was supposed to. He'd always had that effect on me.

"Good afternoon, Roderick." I opted for formal, figuring it was the best way to go. "Congratulations on your pending nuptials."

Congratulations on your pending nuptials?

What was I? An automated email?

"Thank you." Roderick cocked his head at me like he was trying to figure me out. "I'm glad you decided to come. June and I have a whole itinerary planned. She's excited to meet you."

Why in the hell would she be excited to meet me?

"A whole…itinerary?" I frowned, confused. "On top of the ceremony?"

"Of course!" He beamed at me. "You only get married once!" Roderick had a nice voice. Boring but soft. Like something you'd hear on an infomercial about blenders. "We're both outdoorsy so we're more excited about the lead up to the wedding than the wedding itself."

What the hell did that mean?

"How…modern of you," I replied, because it felt like a nice thing to say.

"That's what I said!" Roderick's smile softened. "You don't mind attending, do you?" He inquired, tone gentle. "I don't want to make you uncomfortable."

Jesus, why was everyone asking me this?

"I'm not in love with you," I blurted out, my cheeks growing hot. "So no. It's not weird."

"Good." Roderick's grin was back. "I wanted you here."

I debated asking him *why*, but figured that would be rude. Besides, I knew why. Before we'd dated, we'd been friends. And before we'd been friends, we'd been neighbors. We'd grown up practically living inside each other's pockets. It would've been odd not to attend Roderick's wedding—when I was the one in the Milton clan who had actually mattered.

"I wanted to be here." The words surprised me almost as much as the fact that they were true. "I admit…I thought it was a little…unorthodox to invite me, considering our history. But I understand. I'm happy for you, Roderick. Truly, I am."

"Thanks, George," Roderick said, laying a hand on mine and giving it a squeeze. "Means a lot coming from you. You were a big part of my life when I was younger. I don't think I'd be who I am today without you."

Oh.

Well.

That was just—

I blinked, misty-eyed. "I feel the same."

We sat for a beat in silence, but that silence was comfortable.

"Friends?" Roderick offered me his hand. "No weirdness attached?" I shook it, unfairly reminded of the other handshake I'd received that day. Alex's skin had been hotter, drier. And I could tell by the almost limp hold Roderick had on me that our lack of desire for one another was mutual.

"Friends," I agreed, releasing his hand without feeling any sort of drive to linger.

"So—"

"No more sincerity," I interrupted him. "Please. I've reached my quota for the day."

"Deal." Roderick laughed. "Good to see you haven't changed."

He was wrong.

I *had* changed.

And not for the better.

Roderick was still talking, but I zoned out. A numb sense of sadness came over me as I watched the crowd mingle and laugh. People were gorging themselves on potato salad and red Jell-O. An unnamed child I didn't recognize with jet black hair and an inflatable baseball bat was screaming at the top of his lungs.

"Anyway, we all thought you two might hit it off," Roderick continued, oblivious to the fact that I wasn't listening.

It took me a second to realize what he'd said.

"Not you too," I groaned.

It seemed even Roderick was trying to play matchmaker.

"June's brother is a really nice guy, George," Roderick promised. "He's all *professional* like you are. A career man. Big job. Briefcase. The whole shebang." There were plenty of "career men" out there. I sighed despondently. "— aaaaand he wants kids."

Oh.

Oh.

Well, that was interesting.

My full focus was now on Roderick. He smiled at me, pleased. "June says he wants a *lot* of kids."

It was no secret that I, too, desired a large family.

I'd always loved children. More so than anyone. In fact, when I'd gone to college, I'd originally been planning on becoming an elementary school teacher. That hadn't happened, but the sentiment remained.

I wanted to be a dad.

I knew I'd be good at it too. Firm where firm was needed. Kind and fair. I'd love all of my children the way they deserved to be loved—with my whole fucking heart. The problem was…I'd never been brave enough to attempt to adopt on my own.

And thus far, obviously, I'd had an incredibly difficult time finding a partner who was interested in the kind of brood I desired. Brendon had convinced me he wanted that too—that it was only a matter of time before we adopted our first.

Stupidly, I'd believed him.

Only to find out later that it—like most of his promises—was only a ruse.

"How many kids?" My eyes narrowed, and Roderick's smile grew even slicker. He was shorter than me by an inch or so, though he was thicker, especially as he'd filled out the last few years. Fuller around the middle than he'd been when we were younger, and he wore that width well. Juniper was a lucky woman, that was for sure.

"Last I heard, three to five," Roderick said.

"Five kids? Or five total people?" Inquiring about Juniper's brother didn't mean I was committing to actually dating him. I was curious. That's all.

"Kids."

Five kids?

Christ.

I'd never met another man interested in that many before.

Juniper's brother was getting more and more attractive by the minute—and I hadn't even seen him. Ready to interrogate Roderick further—about health plans and savings—I was interrupted when the crowd erupted in a riotous cheer.

What the fuck?

"Juniper! Juniper!" I turned my head, watching as everyone scattered toward the gate that Joe and I had come through in anticipation. It slid open, and a tiny woman in a frankly *giant* dress popped through. She wore an oddly recognizable shit-eating grin.

Had I met her before?

No, no. I would've remembered that. I'd seen her on the invitation, that was why she looked familiar. No other reason.

Juniper's blue eyes flashed, big skirt swirling as she waved both hands up at the sky and bellowed her hello. For a itty bitty thing, she had a surprisingly deep voice. Nearly as deep as mine, honestly.

Double-fisting two beers, Juniper twisted to face the gate, waiting for someone.

Her brother, probably.

Right.

Yes.

That made sense.

The man of *many* matchmakers.

Was there something wrong with him? Not to be mean, but it was a fair conclusion to come to, considering how desperate everyone seemed to set us up.

The shade from the maple tree mostly concealed him, so it was hard to catch details. I squinted, but that didn't help.

"There they are!" Roderick rose from his seat. "Over here, June!" It was impossible to look away. Roderick's waving was as awkward as it was adorable. These awful, clumsy jerks of both his arms that kicked up enough wind that I worried he'd muss my hair. The two lovebirds were only twenty feet apart, and yet, he was acting like he was beckoning a plane down a runway.

I didn't see why he needed to be so…exuberant.

But I suppose…it was cute. Especially when I glanced at Juniper and realized she was waving her arms just as excitedly back at him.

"That's June's brother," Roderick whispered to me through the corner of his mouth, arms still jerking. "The tall one behind her."

I wanted to act aloof—to prove how very uninterested in this little matchmaking endeavor I was…but nosiness got the better of me. So, instead of looking anywhere else, I found myself observing a tall, muscular man as he stepped out of the shade and into the sun.

His thighs tested the seams of his jeans, flexing in an oddly familiar and distracting way. For a moment, I let my imagination run wild. It was almost too easy to picture a kid attached to each leg, holding on for dear life as Juniper's brother played with our children.

Those were excellent fathering thighs.

Sturdy.

Capable.

His hands, too.

Even from a distance, I could tell they were nice and big, just the way I liked.

He shoved them in his pockets, and I sighed wistfully as my eyes traveled up his gorgeous forearms. Ropey muscle, covered in dark hair. One wrist sported a lovely watch, expensive no doubt, round face glinting in the sun. It looked worn. An heirloom perhaps?

Eager for more, after nothing but pleasant surprise after pleasant surprise, I dragged my gaze up the stranger's full pectorals to his throat—surely something had to be wrong with him? Thus far, I couldn't fathom why he'd need help getting dates at all.

At least…until I saw his face.

I don't know what I expected.

But—it certainly wasn't what I got.

Because familiar, taunting dimples haunted the edges of Alex's smirk. And those pale eyes burned bright, zeroing in on me like a hunter who'd spotted prey.

His eyes said, *there you are.*

And I was once again tempted to run.

That's right.

Juniper's brother was Alex from the goddamn plane.

Dildo-saving, suit-wearing, infuriatingly-sexy Alex.

Jesus Christ, I was so fucking fucked.

Six
George

SPOTTING ALEX IN MY childhood backyard was like a fever dream. Unreal. Panic twisted tight as a noose around my neck, and my shirt collar, like earlier, suddenly felt far too tight. Simply breathing became laborious— short, panicked bursts escaping as I processed the fact that my own personal demon had reappeared. Too soon, reality set in, and my initial shock and horror evolved into bewilderment.

Roddy turned back to me with a clueless expression. "You can ask him yourself!"

Ask who what?

Alex?

It took me a second to remember I'd been in the middle of interrogating Roderick about Juniper's mysterious family-loving brother. Seconds that had passed like lifetimes as the summer sun set, and the chaos I'd thought I'd abandoned at the airport followed me home.

I'd been intrigued before.

Roderick was expecting me to still be intrigued. And if the look on his face was any indicator, he assumed my ogling was caused by interest—not horror.

I couldn't blame him.

That would be the more logical conclusion.

"Don't worry, June told me you're his type," Roderick promised, attempting to soothe. "One sec—"

Don't do it.

Don't do this to me, Roderick—

Before I could open my mouth, Roderick whipped his hand in a circle, tossed it back, and threw an invisible lasso toward the two siblings—like a total dork.

What transpired next was the most heinous thing I'd ever witnessed.

Namely, Roderick making these awful hand-over-hand motions. He pulled the siblings across the yard like a cowboy—and in response, instead of becoming disgusted, Juniper giggled. She hopped toward us with exaggerated wiggles, happy to play along.

The whole thing would've been cute if I weren't dying of second-hand embarrassment.

Pausing halfway, Juniper downed both the beers she'd been clutching and promptly belched into the sunny afternoon air. The crowd of flannel-wearing, barbecue-devouring people that populated the yard cheered. After tossing the empty bottles, Juniper grinned and hiked up her massive, blue ball gown. Shiny black cowgirl boots poked beneath the lifted hem. With an air of importance, she continued to hop the rest of the way toward us, eating up her fiancé's smile with a happy shimmy.

Alex was a silent shadow behind her.

He didn't hop.

He didn't speak.

Simply content to observe his sister with obvious fondness. His eyes even had the audacity to *sparkle*. This was a side to him I hadn't seen at the airport, and I tried not to be affected by it. To be honest, I was relieved to have his focus off of me.

It didn't take long for the siblings to reach us, or for that feeling of relief to evolve. When they arrived, pausing on the other side of the table, I sat up taller, fighting the urge to shrink and run, or crawl under the table to hide.

Please, please, please don't mention Neil, I begged—though knowing my luck, the plea would be fruitless.

During that short walk, something…changed.

The heat in Alex's eyes was gone.

He was…cold.

Which felt odd, considering how doggedly he'd pursued me while on the plane. It was almost like I'd imagined the whole thing. He barely looked at me, before his attention moved back to his sister. She leaned over the table, dark silken hair a wild mess as Roderick rose to smack a kiss right on her mouth.

Pulling back, Juniper grinned at the both of us.

"You must be George." She turned her full attention to me. "I've heard a lot about you."

My cheeks heated, eyes flicking to Alex as my earlier worries came back full force. "Good things, I hope?"

"Oh, definitely."

That was better than the alternative, right? That Roderick, and potentially Alex, had been talking shit about me. Though, it also didn't mean Alex hadn't told her about the dildo during their drive over here.

Speaking of Alex…his expression was guarded, lips pressed into a flat line. Juniper elbowed him, but he didn't flinch, nor did he greet me.

Was this a game to him?

"Juniper, right?" I scrambled to find something to say. I was aiming for polite, but I wasn't sure I exactly nailed it, distracted by her brother and his hot-to-cold switch-flip.

"Yessiree." June bobbed her head.

A beat passed. No one said anything, including me. I glanced at Alex again, even more confused. Why wasn't he *reacting* to seeing me? Was he not surprised? When his gaze finally met mine, his expression was still closed off.

Like there was a wall of ice between us.

"Congratulations on your pending nuptials." The words spilled out before I could stop them, directed at June, but pointed in Alex's direction. Roderick laughed, the sound breaking the awkward mood that'd settled.

Alex's mouth twitched.

It was the first sign that the man on the plane hadn't been an apparition.

"He said that to me too," Roderick told June.

"Thank you." As she spoke to me, she turned her attention Alex's way, frowning at where he stood beside her, a silent shadow. "We're happy you could make it."

I nodded, cheeks still hot.

"It's been an eventful trip, that's for sure." Understatement of the century.

Alex's mask cracked a little more.

June's gaze was hawk-like as she observed her brother. "I feel like there's a story there," she teased. "A story that you didn't tell me. Care to share with the class?"

Alex didn't hesitate. "It wasn't all that interesting."

My dildo had *literally* hit his shoe.

He'd certainly found it interesting earlier. What the fuck was his problem? Was he *trying* to antagonize me? And if he was, why wasn't he *looking* at me? The emotional whiplash was confusing as hell.

I forced my face to remain blank, even though an uncomfortable pit had formed in my stomach. I'd thought he was different. That he was forthright in a way Brendon never had been. Maybe I was wrong. Maybe Alex was just as manipulative as Brendon.

"Then why did you say there was definitely a story?" Juniper looked confused.

"Stories can be boring," Alex replied.

Boring?

Why did that hurt?

I didn't care what he thought of me. At least…I hadn't *thought* I did. Clearly, I'd been wrong. Because Alex calling me boring felt like an ice pick to the heart. I swallowed the bile climbing up my throat.

Was I really…a *joke* to him?

Fine.

This was fine.

Two could play that game.

If he wanted to act like an ice prince, so could I. There was no way I was letting him know how badly he'd dug beneath my skin. If he *was* making fun of me, he was about to realize how futile that effort had been.

There would be no punchline.

I would survive this.

I would escape with my reputation and what little self-confidence I had intact.

I wouldn't forsake my mom's pride just because Alex had hurt my feelings.

When Alex wasn't flirting, it was almost too easy to ignore him.

Questions bubbled up inside me, but I shoved them down, turning my focus onto Alex's sister. She was watching him the same way I had, like she was trying to figure him out.

"I was just telling George about Alex," Roderick hedged, obviously attempting to end the unpleasant silence. He addressed me, "Didn't you have something you wanted to ask him?"

"I did," I shrugged.

"You did?" Alex sounded surprised. Which was fair. I had actively done my best not to participate in conversation on the plane. I certainly hadn't asked him questions.

"I'm no longer interested in hearing the answer," I replied to Roderick, not Alex.

Another pause.

"Why not?" Alex's brow furrowed. He turned those clever, pale eyes on me. I shrugged again, not bothering to answer. It didn't matter anyway. After this turn of events I was more than done with him. I rose from my seat, offering Roderick a smile.

"Congratulations again," I said, figuring I could part ways now that this troublesome encounter had reached its natural conclusion. "It was good to see you again, Roderick."

I should've known escaping wouldn't be that easy.

Because apparently, ignoring me was fine, but the second *I* ignored *Alex*? Yeah. He did not fucking like that. His entire focus lasered in on me, the heat of his attention palpable. I froze, stuck halfway out of my chair only to sit right back down.

"I'm confused," Roderick said.

"We've met before," I answered, meeting Alex's gaze head-on. "Which is *why* I know I'm not interested."

"You've met?" Roderick only sounded more perplexed. Immediately, visions of Neil's cerulean blue surface wiggling in the middle of the air assaulted my senses.

"At the airport," Alex explained.

Alex is going to tell them.

Oh fuck.

My entire body exploded, red-hot and itchy with fear.

"That was my fault." Juniper wiggled in excitement like she hadn't just confessed to a despicable crime. "I'm the one who bought the tickets. His mom and I thought, you know…all things considered, it'd be nice if they could get to know each other before they arrived."

"Why didn't anyone tell me?" Roderick frowned. "I'm a member of the club, too." I barely heard his words, too focused on what Juniper had said. Suddenly… my mother's involvement in buying my ticket made a lot more sense.

This had been an elaborate ploy to set us up.

Jesus Christ.

What a goddamn shit show.

And Alex had known.

Of course he'd fucking known.

The whole. Entire. Time.

Why hadn't he said anything?

Another manipulation.

"That's how you knew my name." The words were out before I could stop them. "Not because of the backpack. Because your sister—and my family— set us up."

I needed to calm down.

But I couldn't.

"Correct," Alex's eyes flickered. He was still studying me. The longer our gazes locked, the more the ice in his eyes faded, bit by bit.

"And you couldn't have *led* with that?" I knew my voice was strained, but I couldn't make it stop. "I literally *asked* you. There was a perfect opportunity to tell the truth—and you lied to my face."

Calm down, George.

Calm—

"It was more fun that way," Alex grinned, proving that he was a total dick.

"This is *fun* for you?" Vibrating with rage, it took everything I had not to start yelling. I could tell I was getting louder, loud enough we'd definitely attracted attention—but I couldn't seem to stop. He was cracking my perfect persona. Snapping it right down the middle so that everyone here could see the mushy, broken man beneath.

And I *knew* he was doing it.

But I couldn't stop myself from responding.

Couldn't stop the fissure from growing as my wrath burned hotter.

Goddammit, I really should've walked away—but now I couldn't. Not when Alex was *smirking*. Smirking like he thought creeping beneath my skin and outright lying to me was funny. It wasn't funny. None of this was.

69

"Definitely fun, yes." Alex's smile grew brighter. He leaned in to mock whisper across the horrible Christmas bauble-themed tablecloth at me. "You're a *very* fun man, Georgie."

Aware we had an audience, but unable to stop myself, I retorted. "Well, *you're* a fucking dick."

Roddy gasped.

Juniper gasped.

The crowd gasped.

Everyone else stopped talking. What'd been a small group paying attention became the whole fucking party. Roderick's family. My family. Alex and Juniper's. Adults and children alike. Most notably, my mother—apple fritter halfway to her mouth as her attention moved from the woman she'd been chatting with over to us.

The weight of their perception made me feel small and miserable.

Instead of backing off, Alex pushed again.

"A fucking dick?" Alex mused. "Huh. I'll defer to you. Seeing as you're more familiar with those than I am."

There was no way anyone else would understand the innuendo.

But I did.

I snapped.

Suddenly, the table between us became a *massive* problem. It was the only reason I wasn't currently strangling him. Fuck it. The thing was older than I was anyway.

I'd buy Mom a new one if it broke.

Exploding out of my seat, I launched across the table at Alex. Roderick was too shocked to try and stop me. By the time I was on solid ground again— the table miraculously still standing—my chest was heaving.

Crack, crack, my "golden boy persona" splintered even more. The crowd was eerily silent, making the sound of each great, angry gulp of air that whooshed into my lungs impossibly loud. Alex was a few inches taller than me, but that didn't prevent me from glaring down my nose at him as I stepped into his personal space. I could taste the mint on his breath.

The smug bastard leaned closer, entirely unfazed by my fury. If I didn't know any better, I'd think he was egging me on. That's certainly what it *felt* like he was doing. Like he was inciting my wrath on purpose—offended by my feigned disinterest, even though *he* was the one that was blowing hot and cold for no fucking reason.

"Is that *Versace?*" Alex's voice was husky.

"W-what?" The question was so out of pocket it nearly shocked me out of my rage.

"Your cologne, Georgie. Keep up. Is that *Versace?*"

"No," I snapped. Of course it was *Versace*.

"*Liar*," Alex's minty breath fanned hot against my lips in an annoyingly sultry way. He shifted imperceptibly till his toes bumped mine, making himself at home in my personal bubble—like he had every right to do so.

Alex's eyes were prettier up close, and that thought only made me more bitter. How dare he be so...so *smug*—and so attractive, at the same time. I wanted to wipe the smile off his face.

When he looked at me like that, his dark lashes fluttering with each blink—his lips curled up, dimples flashing—it felt like the rest of the world disappeared entirely. Our audience was gone. There was only him, and me, and the electricity between us.

His eyes said, *pay attention to me.*

They said, *I need it.*

Hands moving before I could stop them, my fists clenched in the front of Alex's t-shirt. Soft, slightly sweaty fabric brushed against my palms as I yanked Alex an inch closer—close enough our noses bumped. His pupils dilated, nearly swallowing the icy blue.

"*George*—" Roderick tried to interrupt, but he might as well have not been there at all.

"Alex started it," June replied, looking inappropriately excited about Alex's reaction to me. "Let them finish."

This was out of character for me. In all my life, I'd never gotten physical like this—even when I was at my most upset. I could see why he was concerned.

But there was simply something about Alex that pushed all my buttons.

And he did it on purpose.

Like he was a kid in an elevator, jabbing every last one just to see them light up.

Shame—due to our audience and the scene I was causing—made my throat feel tight all over again. Squeezing, squeezing, as each labored breath puffed against Alex's lips. I did my best not to be unfairly affected by how very hot Alex's body ran—or the way his expensive scent made my cock perk up.

He'd pushed me to my breaking point, but oddly enough, he didn't back down. Even though he knew first-hand that I was the kind of man who followed through with my threats.

My nostrils flared.

"Guys, seriously?" Roderick once again played peacemaker. I refused to look away from Alex. Not for a single fucking second. "Alex was teasing. Right, Alex?"

"*Right*," Alex agreed, his black gaze caught on mine. "I was *teasing*, Georgie," he purred, pink tongue flickering out to wet his lips. "Listen to Roddy. Be sensible. There's no need to get *physical*."

Despite his words, he sounded pleased. Cold turned hot. His apathy was gone. Was this another trick? Confusing. He was so fucking *confusing*.

Judging by the hungry look in his eyes, Alex wanted to get far more physical with me than this. That thought sent another fizzle of electricity zapping between us.

"Right!" Roderick agreed, bless his heart, not recognizing the innuendo.

"You're so adorable when you're mad," Alex whispered, quiet enough only I heard. "You know that right? Makes me crazy."

Which one was I? Boring, or adorable?

Christ.

My head had begun to hurt, the weight of the crowd's attention burning-burning-burning.

Alex's body was solid against mine. Sweat beaded at the edge of his collar, glistening at his temples, making his dark hair stick to his forehead. He'd been damp at the airport too, because of the rain. This was better, somehow.

Pressed tightly to Alex's deliciously full, muscular chest, it was impossible to think about anything other than sex. One push and our cocks would align, for god's sake. Alex looked like the kind of man who liked to get rough. Who liked to shove and bite and fuck. Who wasn't afraid to take what he wanted.

Alex wasn't frightened of my anger, or the crowd's opinions.

And no matter how hard I pushed, and snapped, and hissed—he didn't cow. I knew, realistically, at the moment he was being an asshole. But…for the sake of being fair, I was the one who'd stabbed him earlier. I also knew that all I'd done since we'd met was bite his head off—even after he'd been kind enough not to mention the dildo incident.

We were both acting ugly.

So why…did fighting with Alex feel good?

Because there was no denying that it did.

I'd never been like this with anyone else. I'd always been reserved, eager to please—a peacemaker, like Roderick. A people pleaser. A perfectionist. Docile and fake—so terrified of losing the affection I craved that I'd do anything to keep it, even compromise myself.

But not with Alex, apparently.

With Alex, I spoke my mind.

Even when it shattered my image.

"*Alex*," Juniper sighed, exhausted. "Enough."

That was it.

Two words.

Alex *laughed.*

And god, it was a pretty laugh.

Loud and unrepentant.

A riotous, wicked thing that immediately cooled my boiling rage to a simmer. My anger dissipated. I was struck by the beauty of the wrinkles by his eyes as he tossed his head toward the fluffy white clouds above.

Man, God really did have favorites.

When Alex's guffaws softened into a honeyed chuckle, I had no choice but to concede defeat.

The tension between us was gone. It was impossible to stay angry when he was looking at me like that. Like he didn't realize how awfully he'd just fucked me over.

Our tiny group of voyeurs settled. Juniper shook her head in amusement. I wasn't sure what the look she leveled our way meant, or that I wanted to know.

"Well, that was uncomfortable," Roderick said, obviously as relieved as the rest of us that no fight was going to break out.

"I can practically taste the chemistry," Juniper cackled, and then to herself added, "Damn, I'm good."

"Jesus Christ, June," Roderick snorted, though he didn't disagree.

The crowd was still watching, though luckily for me, they began to disperse. Without my anger as fuel, I had no choice but to acknowledge the mistake I'd just made. There was no denying that I'd just shattered my "perfect son" persona. The one thing I'd fucking wanted desperately to protect. My carefully constructed reputation ripped to shreds.

Regret.

That's what this was.

"I like you, Georgie," Alex told me, awe laced inside his tone. His voice was as quiet as it'd been when he'd called me adorable. Like these words were mine, and mine alone. There was a hint of surprise there too—surprise I didn't understand.

Confusing. He was so fucking confusing.

"Well, I don't like you," I hissed in reply.

"Yeah?" Alex dipped his head again, eyes dancing. Our noses brushed, reminding me of how close we were to kissing. Immediately, I released his shirt. As though burned, I took a step back and put some much-needed distance between us.

Before he could manipulate me into tarnishing my reputation even more, I stalked off to lick my wounds in private.

This time, when I ran away, I played it cool. I should've done that earlier—before the fight. I had no idea why I hadn't. I wished I could turn back time, but that wish was futile.

My body would not stop tingling.

Calm down.

Having a lovely laugh doesn't make up for how infuriating he is. He's messing with you. He doesn't actually like you. Don't let him win.

That was the conclusion I came to.

If I had to deal with him for another second, I was going to explode again. Once was bad enough. I could still feel my mother's eyes on me—the frown on her lips causing shame to burn white-hot through my body.

So, yeah.

Avoiding Alex, despite everyone else's meddling, was my new mission in life. How hard could it be, really? We'd be off to Hocking Hills tomorrow. And I could spend the week leading up to the wedding in the woods with my family. That'd been the plan to begin with. It wasn't as though anything was changing because he'd be there too.

I piled up a plate of potluck delicacies and retreated to the sandbox near the porch. Sitting below where Dad and Joe were grilling, the scent of charred meat wafted through the air as I settled beside the only person who hadn't paid attention to my earlier outburst.

Mavis.

My darling, lovely, slightly-older-than-toddler-age niece.

"Unca George," Mavis greeted me from behind her sandcastle with her huge brown eyes. For the first time since I'd left for the airport that morning, I finally relaxed.

"Hi."

"Why is your face red?" she asked. "You look weird." I waved a hand at myself, fanning the heat from my cheeks as I shrugged.

"It's summer."

"Okay." She gave me a dubious look. "*My* face doesn't do that."

"Then you're lucky," I replied, tucking into my food with gusto.

The unnamed cousin-kid with a bat peeled across the yard toward us with a squeal. His bat was held high as he paused by our quiet nook, before moving on. Kid was going so fast he was going to hurt himself. He'd looked at me like he expected me to jump up and yell at him. And once again, shame coursed like acid in my veins.

The pickle on my plate was another reminder of what a disappointment I was. Mom had bought these for me. She'd been so excited for me to come home. So excited to show me off to her friends…and I'd…

Christ, she was probably so embarrassed.

I felt horrible that I'd let her down. I'd cracked the facade I tried so fucking hard to protect, and everyone here had seen.

"*I* like pickles," Mavis interrupted my spiral of self-importance. She was obviously eyeing my plate. Taking the hint, I offered her my pickle. I didn't have much of an appetite anyway, even if they were my favorite.

"Thanks." Her chubby little fist was covered in sand. She accepted my humble offering and brought it close to her face. As soon as it had passed inspection, she took a thoughtful bite.

"Good, right?"

"Good." Her words were muffled around her mouthful, but she did grace me with a tiny-toothed grin that made my heart throb. Snorting, I did my best to hide my responding smile behind my hand, lest she see it and think I was laughing at her—even though I was.

After thoroughly wiping the remaining pickle juice off my fingers, I grabbed my sandwich. Not a burger—for obvious reasons. Simple cold cuts on white bread. Mom always provided it, because she knew better than anyone how heinous Dad's hamburgers could be.

I was lucky they'd had napkins at all.

Mom tended to forget that.

Across the yard, she was chatting with Roderick. I shrank behind Mavis, using her as a shield in the hopes that no one would look at me. I hated this—feeling small. And I was so fucking pissed at Alex, because he'd proven to be just as much of a dick as Brendon was.

Turning my attention back to my niece, and my sandwich, I tried to ignore the fact I had no idea where Alex had ended up. It was difficult, but I managed. Mostly. Wayward worries plagued me—my food like sand on my tongue.

Mavis was surprisingly excellent company—very distracting.

She thought my suit was "good".

She let me know when my face wasn't "ugly" anymore.

She asked if I liked building castles.

All while pilfering half the food on my plate. Which was *impressive*. She was a tiny, precious garbage disposal with one pigtail loose. For nearly an hour, I licked my wounds in private, ignoring any and all adults, deliberately hiding as far away from the crowd as I could. Eventually, my food started to taste like food again, and the pit in my stomach disappeared.

Which, of course, was when Alex found me again.

Seven
George

I HADN'T SEEN ALEX approach. Sneaky bastard came from behind. Like a coward. He disrupted my peace, like always, and I was halfway out of the sandbox before he could fully settle next to the spot I'd just vacated. Immediately, his hands were out, held placatingly.

"I just want to talk."

He looked vulnerable sitting on the ground while I loomed above him.

I considered it. It would be the adult thing to do. Mature. I had no idea what had happened between our earlier fight and now. Clearly something— if he was approaching me with a white flag raised.

But I simply wasn't interested.

"C'mon Mavis, let's go find your mom," I said instead of acknowledging him. Alex blinked, obviously surprised. Mavis ignored me, even going so far as to wiggle to the other side of the sandbox so she could build another castle away from us.

"George—" Alex tried.

"I'm not talking to you." I cut him off. Half in the box and half out, I was at a crossroads. This was not a conversation I wanted to have with Mavis around. But then again…she acted as a buffer. Forced him to behave, at least somewhat.

Unless Roderick had been lying when he'd said Alex liked kids.

"Look—"

"No, *you* look." I jabbed a finger at him, honestly so fucking done with this entire fucking day. Hushed enough Mavis wouldn't hear, I spoke again, enunciating every syllable. "I haven't been home for eight *fucking* years. Eight. *Years.* And after the shittiest year of my life, all I wanted was to come here—to see my mom—to get to pretend for one fucking *week* that my life isn't a goddamn shit show."

Alex's eyes were wide. He looked caught in a way he hadn't before.

"And *you…*" I sucked in a breath, then deflated. "Jesus. I'm not going to pretend like I wasn't at fault too, but we both know you were fucking with me—why? I have no idea. And frankly, I don't care." Surprisingly mature, I know. "I can't be around you. I don't want to talk to you. I don't want to make peace with you—if that's why you're here. In fact, I want to be as far away from you as fucking possible for the rest of this goddamn trip."

Alex was quiet.

Uncharacteristically quiet. Like until that moment he hadn't realized how far he'd pushed me. He opened his mouth, blue eyes swimming with complex emotion. "I…" He sucked in a breath. "I'm sorry, George." There was a lot packed into that simple apology. "I didn't mean to."

It caught me off guard how much I wanted to believe it. But I didn't have it in me.

"Yes, you did," I said in reply. "Now will you please just…leave me alone?" And then, because I was making a point, I plopped back down into the spot I'd abandoned.

Alex rose from his seat, folding that big body up, then straightening. He blocked the setting sun from view as he shuffled in front of me, dark brow furrowed like he didn't know what to say. Our positions were mirrored. In a way it felt poetic.

That was fine.

"I…" Alex trailed off, awkwardly standing there. For the first time since I'd met him, he looked off-kilter. The spark in his eyes was missing entirely. "Okay. Sure. Whatever you want." His hands clenched at his sides, big fists squeezing anxiously, once, twice, three times.

And then he left.

Like I'd wanted.

And I could breathe again.

He didn't go far, flirting with one of my mother's friends in the center of the yard, and then my mother herself. I kept an eye on him—for insurance. But even I could tell the flirting was half-hearted. There was a droop to him that hadn't been there before. And he kept giving me these sad puppy eyes. Way fucking worse than when I'd left him alone on the plane.

I was tempted to storm over there and separate him from Mom, but I didn't. Not when she looked at him fondly, nodding along to whatever he was saying—even going so far as to reach out at one point and lay a hand on his arm. I had no idea what he was telling her. Something stupid, no doubt. Even if…judging by her expression, it was sincere.

Alex knew my family.

Maybe better than I did, considering how far away I lived.

It pissed me off to no end how attractive he looked. And also? It wasn't fucking fair that seeing him talk to my Mom ignited a flurry of butterflies in my belly. Butterflies I squashed as quickly as they appeared.

I hadn't been lying when I'd told him I was done with him.

And I was…kind of proud of myself. I'd only ever stuck up for myself once before, when I'd broken up with Brendon—and that had been after a panic attack or two, and actual real physical evidence that proved he was a goddamn liar.

So, it was odd that with Alex, I'd managed it so easily.

How was it fair that the only man I'd ever been fully honest with was such a fucking dick?

And what about him made me feel safe to speak my mind?

None of this made any sense.

Breaking my bubble of peace, a screech filled the air. It was the most sincerely heinous thing I'd ever heard—at least since the last time Mr. Pickles had needed a bath. The horrible wail rattled my ear drums. Mavis slapped her sandy hands over her ears, scowling toward the kid with the baseball bat—the culprit behind the noise.

Apparently, he'd injured himself.

His mom, a woman I didn't recognize, was consoling him, but it wasn't doing much. Due to the commotion, the festivities were at a standstill. Mom frowned, a tenseness around the corners of her mouth, and immediately, I rose to my feet to help.

"Is he okay?" I called, crossing the yard, ignoring the weight of Alex's gaze as I did so.

"He scraped his knee," she said, smiling at me, before turning her attention back to her child. "It's just a scratch, baby. You're okay—" I could hear the kid's mom's reassurances, but her words were soon drowned out by his anguish once again.

"There's so much *blood*—" Baseball-kid wailed, clutching his injured leg like it was broken—when in reality, it was barely scraped.

"There's a first-aid kit in my backpack," I promised. "Give me a second to find where my brother stashed it on the porch and I'll grab it for you?"

The kid sniffled as he nodded. Relieved, I swiveled to face the porch where I knew Joe had wandered with my bag. Only...apparently Dad had overheard. Because he was no longer manning the grill, and with abject horror, I watched through the gaps in the railing as he bent over to retrieve it.

Shit.

Shit.

He better not open it.

Oh my god.

No.

No.

If my dad opened the pocket, he'd see Neil. He'd see Neil. He'd see—

No.

No, no, no, no, no.

This could not be happening!

Murphy's Law was a sad, vicious bitch.

Dad reached for the zipper, but before I could protest, or throw up, Alex was pounding up the steps to the porch. He was fucking fast for such a large man. Agile. Which I suppose made sense, considering how active he'd said he was when we'd chatted on the plane. I was right below, and therefore could hear and see just fine when Alex yoinked my backpack out of Dad's hands with a blurted, "I got this!"

Somehow, this was even *worse*.

I didn't know what to expect.

Had Alex seen an opportunity to humiliate me again?

Was this his way of getting back at me for not forgiving him when he'd apologized earlier? I'd been the one who hadn't wanted to bury the hatchet. It would be the perfect revenge for him to yank my bag open, grab my dildo, and wave it around for the whole world to see.

My life flashed before my eyes.

Visions of shiny silicone hell nearly blinded me as a cold sweat broke out across my forehead. Frozen still, unable to even react, my cry of panic stuck in my throat. There was nothing I could do to stop Alex. I was simply too far away.

This would live in infamy at every family gathering for the rest of my life.

I could see my future now. George-Arthur, the size queen, exiled from his hometown for bringing a dildo to a barbecue.

I grimaced, waiting, *expecting* him to open the bag.

But…

He…didn't.

Instead, Alex jogged down the stairs and to my side, big chest heaving. "Here," he said softly, handing me my backpack before surreptitiously stepping in front of it to block it from view. "I got you."

I remained frozen, shocked. Just like at the airport, Alex had come to my rescue. I…didn't know what to do with that.

So I did what I did best.

Ignored it.

I was careful not to jostle Neil as I pulled the first-aid kit out and quickly zipped up the bag. My heart was pounding, an unhealthy flush on my cheeks as I offered the kid's mom the kit, and Alex stepped out of the way.

He hovered, but didn't speak to me again—even though I could feel the weight of his gaze like a brand on my face. I looked away, unsure of what to do with the ache of gratitude that filled my heart.

Alex had saved me.

Again.

The kid blubbered as his mother murmured softly to soothe him. She was gentle as she cleaned the, frankly, *tiny* scrape.

"It hurts!"

"I know, bud." Alex made a soothing sound, crouching down by the kid. Now bandaged, the child lay on the ground like a dead fish. The silence had drawn on too long, and I opened my mouth to offer the kid something— anything—to distract him, but…once again, Alex beat me to the punch.

"Wanna hit me with your baseball bat?" he asked, smiling down at his splotchy, tear-streaked, ruddy cheeks. "Would that cheer you up?"

"How many times?" Baseball-bat-kid sniffed suspiciously.

"As many times as it takes for you to forget about your knee."

"Deal." The kid launched to his feet, thoroughly distracted by the promise of violence. He tugged Alex away by the wrist, hunting for the inflatable bat he'd abandoned prior to his minor maiming. Alex gave me one last lingering glance over his shoulder before he turned away again.

And I genuinely did not know what to think.

Not about him, or about all of this.

Not about his apology, or the fact that he'd come to my rescue.

I simply couldn't wait for the day to end.

After the party had wound down, and I'd helped clean up, Mom awarded me with a kiss to the cheek and the command to go rest. I didn't argue. I was way too fucking tired to do anything other than nod and follow her upstairs.

Hours later, I lay awake on my twin bed, tucked into the same sheets I'd had in high school, freshly washed—courtesy of Mom of course. Through the window, I could see the lights on at Roderick's house across the street. They were all still preparing for the campout the following day.

Tonight was the only night I'd be spending in Chesterton. After that, it was seven days in the wild—a fact that absolutely horrified me.

My mom was also awake. I could hear her downstairs ordering Joe and Lacey about—both of whom hadn't said a single word when Mom had exiled me, even though it meant they had to do my work too. Maybe I'd looked as wrung out as I felt.

Either way, they'd offered me some grace.

Mom's yells were intermittent, scattered between bouts of silence as everyone worked to pack up the food and kitchen supplies we'd need to host a large group for such a long period outdoors. Mom was in charge of the food. Not because she was officially a caterer, but because she'd insisted it was her wedding gift to Roderick to take care of him like she had when we were kids.

It was no surprise that even well past midnight, Mom was bossing our entire household around like she was their sergeant and Roderick's wedding was war. She took her promises seriously. She always had.

I'd missed her.

I'd even missed her nosiness.

She was—*incredibly* nosy.

"You and Alex looked cozy in the sandbox," she told me as she'd been making my bed for me a few hours earlier. I'd offered to do it myself, and she'd looked so offended I'd shut up. "Maybe you can ride with him to the venue tomorrow."

"Cozy" was a stretch and she knew it.

"Ha. Very funny," I replied, too exhausted to say much else.

"It's not a bad idea to clear the air," she gently prodded. I could still remember how massive Alex had looked towering over her, a contrite expression on his face.

"What did he tell you?" My heart skipped a beat. "Whatever it was—was most definitely a lie. He's a manipulative lying son-of-a—"

"He told me not to blame you," Mom cut me off, tucking the sheets around the corners of the bed. "That he'd provoked you, and not to hold it against you."

I blinked.

A beat passed, silence echoing between us.

"He said that?"

"He did." She moved to the other side of the bed, working at the other corners. "He wanted me to know he was to blame for the entire argument." With a grunt, she straightened up, turning to look at me. There was a knowing glint in her eyes I wasn't sure I liked.

I was surprised, to say the least.

Confused, mostly.

I didn't know what to make of any of this.

"I'm not riding with him," I replied, because I had no idea how to confront… any of that. Shame sat like lead in my stomach at the reminder of how I'd let her down. "And I'm…" I sucked in a breath. "I'm sorry about earlier."

"You didn't do anything to be sorry about," Mom shook her head, quirking a brow. "Flirting is not a punishable offense."

I flushed. "I wasn't flirting."

"From where I was standing, you were."

So apparently I hadn't offended her like I'd thought I had. That was good. Even if it was embarrassing.

"I'm not riding with him," I reiterated, because she'd ignored that bit.

"Mhm." Mom did not sound convinced.

"I'm not."

"We'll see."

"Mom," I cut her off, shuffling from foot to foot as she turned back to the bed to tuck in the comforter. "Please tell me you're not also trying to hook me up with Alex?" I already knew she was. Juniper had confirmed it earlier, but playing dumb was the easiest way to confront her.

Mom's silence was all the answer I needed.

"I don't need you, or Joe, or god forbid, *Roderick* to set me up. I'm perfectly fine on my own."

She sniffed, "I never said you weren't."

"I don't need a boyfriend."

"Of course not," she replied noncommittally.

More silence.

"*Mom.*" And now I was whining, like a petulant child.

"It's been a year since you broke up with Brendon, George." Mom peeked up at me through her off-center, overly glued false eyelashes. "Besides…Alex is *nice.*"

"Uh-huh. *Sure.*" I tried to hide my smile, but I couldn't help it. "And I'm a leprechaun."

"You could do a lot worse," she wheedled.

It didn't take a genius to understand the implications of that statement. Mom had never liked Brendon. Ever. I knew what she'd wanted to say. She'd wanted to say, "You've *done* a lot worse," but had been too kind to outright call me out.

She looked cute when she was guilty. Like a naughty pug. Her figurative tail was between her legs, her face scrunched up, and her skin was flushed splotchy. Huh…I was now realizing that it was probably genetic.

"I'm riding with Mavis," I reiterated.

"Fine, fine." She sighed, giving up on me. She paused, her blonde hair bouncing. It was clear she was debating whether or not to speak. Braving my ire, she added on, "But you can't blame me, can you? I worry about you, that's all. And that ex of yours was a real piece of work."

Her face did the scrunched-up pug thing again, and I hid my smile against my shoulder, shaking my head.

"You just want more grandbabies," I accused to lighten the mood.

"*George!*" She slapped my arm, but then her face twisted into a wry grin. Her blonde hair bounced again. Like Jell-O.

"You're not as sneaky as you think you are," I teased as I leaned down to kiss her cheek.

"So *you* think," she said, though she did pull me into another hug, showing me that we were okay. It'd been so long since I'd felt this warmth, I almost didn't know what to do with it. Her meddlesome kind of care was as welcome as it was foreign. The perfect edges of the sheets she'd folded were another reminder of how deeply Mom loved me.

Deeply enough I couldn't be angry—not when she so obviously only wanted to see me happy.

I figured the whole thing was resolved.

I was wrong.

Eight
Alex

AS I SETTLED ONTO the too-firm mattress in the guest room at Roderick's parents' place later that night, I couldn't help but feel off-kilter. I'd slept in this same bed more times than I could count—and never once realized how unyielding the surface was. Like every spring poked into me, a constant prickle of unease I couldn't shake even if I wanted to.

Over the course of their six years together, June and Roderick had made a habit of auto-inviting me to a variety of different activities. Camping trips, day-dates, and movie parties—among other things. I'd never minded. Nor had it ever felt odd to spend so much time with my sister. Lord knew, aside from her, the only friends I had were the guys on my recreational hockey team—the very same team I'd met Roderick on, before I'd hooked him up with my sister.

June and I were close.

We always had been.

Even for twins.

Sometimes it felt like we each had half of the same soul.

And though our personalities could clash on occasion, at our core, we always aligned.

I'd taken a liking to Roderick right away.

He was a boring guy. Plain, honestly. He wore long socks with his sneakers, only ever replacing them when they were full of holes. He only knew what hair gel was because I'd shown him. And I was pretty sure he thought that Gucci was a kind of cheese.

Suffice to say, he was perfect for Juniper. A girl who'd grown up in the suburbs, fallen into money in her teens, and spent the last decade warding off people who wanted to use and abuse her just to get to her wallet.

Roderick wasn't like that.

Which was why I felt remorseful that I'd caused a commotion at his party earlier. Though, if I were being honest, Roderick's feelings about the barbecue were the least of my worries. No, what was keeping me up wasn't the too-hard bed, but guilt over the face I'd caused George to make.

Shame, because my actions had caused him pain.

And even though I'd set out to prove we weren't compatible—something I figured we were in mutual agreement about, considering his apparent lack of interest—instead, all I'd managed was to genuinely hurt him.

"I haven't been home for eight fucking years. Eight. Years. And after the shittiest year of my life, all I wanted was to come here—to see my mom—to get to pretend for one fucking week that my life isn't a goddamn shit show."

His words haunted me.

He wore his heart on his sleeve, face so expressive that if you paid close enough attention, you could almost read his thoughts. Which was how I knew I'd fucked up. Because before George had even opened his mouth to tell me off, I'd seen the tremble of his lower lip, the glassiness in his eyes, the way his hands shook at his sides. And instead of backing off, I'd pushed him over the proverbial cliff.

He'd looked terrified.

Of me, maybe.

Terrified I'd rope him into another uncomfortable situation.

There was no taking back what I'd done. The damage had been dealt. I suppose…until it happened, I hadn't realized how badly I abhorred the idea of being a person that George disliked. The thought that he was hating me— even now, from across the street—made my skin feel too tight.

This was the first time in my life I'd felt this way.

George wasn't the first match June had set me up with that I'd sabotaged. But he was the only one that I regretted. He hadn't deserved the way I'd treated him. And like we were goddamn magnetized, even after I'd sworn I wouldn't flirt—wouldn't react, wouldn't put fire to the kindling June had stacked—I still hadn't been able to help myself.

Not when he'd acted so…unaffected.

I don't know why it bothered me so much. But it did. I was used to people liking me. And between his reactions on the plane and at the barbecue, I'd… lost control.

I'd pushed too far.

Simple as that.

I didn't blame George for not accepting my apology, even though it had been sincere. I understood better than anyone how important it could be to maintain a facade of perfection when one felt rotten beneath the surface. I'd cracked his, like he was an egg, and I'd splattered his yolk all over the party.

In my defense, I'd set out to leave him alone. But I couldn't bring myself to do that. Couldn't ignore him, or the way he made me feel. It ate me up inside seeing him sit beside Roderick looking somewhat content when all my efforts to put him at ease on the plane had only resulted in more tension—and a goddamn pen in my leg.

I couldn't believe how torn up I was over George. It didn't make sense.

Interrupting my thoughts, a knock on the door sounded.

"Come in," I called with a sigh.

June pushed the door open, and I flashed her a smile. Normally, I'd tease her. Say something off-putting to make her laugh, but I didn't have it in me right now.

But I was glad for a distraction, even if I knew why June was here, holding her phone. Every time I talked to our dad, all I could see was his bruised face. All I could remember was the hours in the waiting room, head in my hands, June's cheek on my shoulder. The *beep, beep* of the heart monitor. And the fear, and subsequent relief, when we found out he'd be alright.

We'd almost lost him.

It was the scariest moment of my life.

"Dad wants to video chat," June said.

She hadn't said anything about the party since we returned.

Which, honestly, spoke volumes.

"Right," I agreed, sitting up and scooting over to make room on the bed for her to sit. It was late. We'd stayed at the Milton's till well after dark, but Dad was a night owl, so I was unsurprised he still wanted to talk.

June sat beside me, legs spread wide. She took up a huge amount of space for someone who was basically a big-boobed hobbit (her words, not mine). She was quiet as she held up her phone and hit dial. In companionable silence, we waited as the call connected.

"S'up, old man," I said as soon as Dad's forehead came into view. His forehead. Even though he was a fifty-plus-year-old business-savvy mogul with his thumb in so many profitable pies I'd lost count—he acted ancient when it came to tech.

I'd explained FaceTime to him about a hundred times, and still, most of the time it took him a solid five minutes to realize we were conversing with his eyebrow, or his forehead—or one memorable time, the inside of his nose.

"How was the party?" Dad asked, not bothering to respond to my teasing.

"Fun." June was quick to reply before I could. "Alex wouldn't stop flirting with Roddy's ex."

Dad knew all about George-Arthur Milton.

Of course he did.

Roderick was a blabbermouth and he'd spent the better part of the last five years informing all of us about every one of his exes, George included. No one had ever *asked*—but no one had wanted to make him feel bad by shutting him down. Hurting Roderick would be like kicking a puppy.

It was just wrong.

"Which one?" Dad asked.

A fair question, considering.

"George-Arthur," we both said in unison.

"Well, that's a mouthful," Dad chuckled. "Are his parents fans of British Aristocracy?" he asked, poking fun at the origin of the name.

"Not that I know of," I said, pleased that we'd gotten far enough off-topic that I wouldn't have to admit that I liked him. At least…not yet. "Mr. Milton doesn't seem like the kind of man who'd appreciate tea." Tall and severe-looking, the Milton patriarch would look downright hilarious sipping a cuppa over his morning paper.

Not to judge.

"How tit-tea-lating," Dad giggled. He finally figured out his camera, swearing a little as he pulled the phone back far enough we could actually see his face. Dark eyebrows greeted us, as well as twinkling brown eyes. He sported the same shit-eating grin and black hair that June and I shared— only Dad's was full of gray now, at his temples, by his widow's peak, and all throughout his beard.

"Hardy har har," June snorted. He looked frail in his silk robe, tied tight enough to strangle, so the only bare skin visible was his throat. I wanted to wrap him in bubble wrap so he could never be injured again.

"You said tit," I pointed out, only for Dad to huff and glare at me.

"I did not," he sighed, pinching the bridge of his nose. He was smiling, though. I loved it when I made him smile. Behind him, I could see the mahogany wood walls of his office, leather-bound books lining the shelves along the back.

"You kinda did," June smirked, to which I responded by high-fiving her.

"Why're you working?" I frowned, glancing at the time. "You're supposed to be resting." Dad wasn't allowed to be doing *anything* in that damn office.

"I'm not going to keel over and die because I fill out a damn paper." Dad rolled his eyes.

"Too soon," I said, because it was.

"The doctor okayed me for light exercise."

"Since when is working exercise?"

"Exercise of the *mind*, Alex." Dad looked far too pleased that he understood the meme I'd just referenced. He was a regular old "meme king". Spent an hour on social media every day so that he could drop random references in conversation, all because he wanted to look "hip." His words, not mine.

The man was a riot.

"Maybe you should put that on my gravestone," Dad said. "Alexander James. Father. Philanthropist. And then below that, in cursive, *too soon*. Maybe with a picture of that cat. The mean one."

"Grumpy Cat?" June said dryly.

"No. I don't think that's right."

They argued about memes for another five minutes before Dad finally forced us back on track enough to hear about the party. But June and I could tell his energy was waning, so she didn't heckle me more or bring up George again. I made sure to remind him to go to bed and that pushing himself was not the answer right now—and he agreed—but we had no idea if that meant he'd actually listen.

When we hung up, the mood was bittersweet.

The car wreck that'd broken his ribs, leg, and left arm had left June and me untethered. It'd been a close call. A reminder of mortality that neither of us had been prepared for. Especially when Dad's concussion had been so severe he was disoriented for a few days, and neither of us was sure he even recognized us.

June's phone sat silent and black on the bed between us. She leaned into my side, one of her arms wrapping around my middle, cheek smooshed against my bicep. We didn't speak for a long time, letting the silence mend the fractures left behind by my father's absence. Dad's bruises had healed, but we hadn't recovered from seeing him battered.

"Alex?" June said eventually as I lay my cheek on the top of her head.

"What?"

"I feel like such an asshole…" June's voice cracked. "I should've had my wedding closer to home. Made it easier for him, you know?" She sniffed. "It feels so selfish that I didn't."

"Dad would be pissed if he'd heard you say that," I admonished. "He wants you to have your dream wedding."

"I know."

"And if that dream wedding is…a camping trip in the mountains? Then that's what you're going to get."

"Maybe I should cancel…" June was still spiraling, and I hated it. "Or postpone? We'd lose the deposit…but…" If she did that, months—hell, a fucking year of work I'd put into this damn thing would go right down the drain. And yet, that wasn't why I spoke up. It wasn't me I was worried about

"Don't cancel," I replied immediately.

"But he—"

"The doctor said Dad's fine to escort you down the aisle. Everything else has been taken care of. All *you're* supposed to do is enjoy the shit I've spent the last—*infinity*—planning for you. All any of us want is for you to be happy. Dad, me, and your fiancé included." I wasn't sure if I was getting through to her. Her expression was sad. "Besides. You're like…the least selfish person I've ever met. The fact you'd even *consider* postponing your wedding proves that."

June sniffed, a wobbly smile twisting her lips. "You're only saying that because it would mean a lot of work to reschedule. Fuck. Maybe I'd need to elope? I don't want to put you through that agai—"

"Fuck you." I rolled my eyes. And then, I put on my "sincerity hat" with a grimace. "Look. You deserve to have this day be exactly as you envisioned— *when* you envisioned it. You've both waited long enough, and it took for-fucking-ever for the cabins you wanted to rent to be available. If we push it back, it could be a year or more before everything aligns the way you deserve." I'd already had enough problems with the cabin situation to foresee *that* being a nightmare and a half.

June had been looking forward to this damn thing for what felt like centuries. She was so excited. So fucking excited.

She'd had a binder when we were kids, full of pictures she'd hacked out of magazines and slapped inside—pages and pages of inspiration. June's dream wedding had simplified somewhat since then. There were no unicorns, for one thing. And the festivities she was most excited for involved basic camping activities—like the "Wedding-Lympics" and the day at the lake that she'd rented wave runners for.

But still.

My tone softened, "Don't you think you've waited long enough?"

"You're sure I'm not..." June trailed off, but I filled in the gaps.

"You're not being selfish," I repeated. "No one thinks that."

"Okay." She was still quiet. And though I could tell she felt somewhat better, I knew there was only one thing I could do right now that would legitimately cheer her up. June wasn't selfish. But she was, in some ways, a sadist. I winced, already knowing what I was about to do was going to be painful.

"You were right," I admitted. Her silence was unenthusiastic, despite those words being something I rarely said. "About George."

"Yeah?" June perked up, twisting out of my grip to gape at me. "For real?

No bullshit?"

"For real, no bullshit." I shrugged, trying to force away how uncomfortable this amount of honesty made me feel.

"And?"

This was a direct mirror to the conversation we'd had earlier, but I couldn't even be mad. My sincerity hat was still on. Now was good-brother time. Distract-my-sister time. Even if it meant cracking my heart open and revealing the black hole inside it.

"And I really do like him. Not just because he's fun to poke. But because he intrigues me. On a level that is not purely physical." George's eyes intrigued me most of all. His earlier distress transfixed in the back of my mind.

"This is a first for you." June looked pleased with herself. "You're a chronic fucker."

"I don't know what that means."

"You know." She made a crude gesture with her hands. "Wham bam, thank you ma'am. You get someone to occupy your bed, then forget they exist the second your dick's not wet. You don't do feelings. Not since…you know."

"Gross." I grimaced, but she was…right. Even if I didn't like to be reminded of why exactly I'd decided relationships weren't for me. It had been a decade since the last time I'd had more than a one-night stand. "I already fucked it up, though." Just saying those words out loud made me sick to my stomach. "He said he doesn't want to talk to me."

June made a sympathetic sound. "Did you apologize?"

"Yes."

She blinked, surprised. "Really?"

My cheeks went hot. The fact that I'd immediately tried to make amends was more telling than openly admitting my feelings to her. "He didn't accept my apology."

She laughed.

Which was just *evil*.

"Well, you probably didn't deserve his forgiveness." She shrugged. "Words don't mean shit, Alex. It's actions that count. You know that."

She was right, so I didn't argue.

"Besides," June continued, "George isn't like the other people you interact with. He's a *Milton*. He can't be bought, charmed, or manipulated." June nodded up and down, cheerful again, her tears forgotten. Mission accomplished. "If you're going to get on his good side, you're going to need to be more creative. And also stop playing games. Miltons don't like games."

"I know." I didn't *really* know. How could I? I'd only just met him. But… it was true that no one in his family had ever treated either of us differently because of our background or our surplus of money. They were no-nonsense by nature, and because of that, the Miltons were the fairest people I'd ever met—aside from Roderick's parents. Hell, they might as well have been his second set, considering how often I interacted with them.

It made a cosmic amount of sense that George would need more than flowery words. Something tangible, maybe? An apology gift?

My thoughts spun.

"I have a good feeling about him. Plus, I've never seen you act the way you did earlier today, even if your flirting totally bombed," June said, interrupting my plotting. "Call it intuition, but…I think George would be good for you. "

How the hell could she possibly know that? She'd spoken to him less than I had, for god's sake.

"You had a good feeling about Paris, too. And we ended up getting mugged—and our tickets to Madonna were counterfeit," I pointed out.

"Still." June's smile only grew. Her eyes were shining. "I know setting you up with him is a little…unconventional."

"Considering he's your fiancé's ex? Yeah. I would think so."

"But Roderick has only ever had nice things to say about him. That he was a total fucking sweetie when they dated." June's hands expanded, fingers fluttering as she ticked off each fact by closing a finger into her palm. "That he was incredibly loyal. A *fierce* friend. That he was honest. That he was never afraid to be who he was."

"Thanks for the TED talk."

"It didn't work out with them for good reason," June continued, on a roll now. She clapped her hands together. "*Obviously*, their personalities didn't clash romantically. There was no sexual chemistry." She waggled her eyebrows. "Not like what Roderick and I—"

"Ew. No. Do not finish that sentence."

It amazed me that she could say any of this without a single ounce of jealousy. *Most* people would feel threatened if their partner spoke so highly of someone else. *Most* people wouldn't talk about the sexual chemistry their fiancé had with his ex—or lack thereof. But not my June. Her heart was disproportionately large for her tiny frame. And the only petty bones she possessed were borrowed from me.

"They were too different and too young—and now that they're older they're even more incompatible. But *you*..." June sucked in a breath, eyes lighting up. "Maybe you guys could mesh? The way they didn't. You could be...uh."

Oh jeez. Here came one of her signature metaphors.

"You could be the peanut to his butter."

That was even worse than usual. Didn't even make sense.

"Maybe," I conceded. "I still don't know him."

"But your chemistry is off the charts."

"True."

"So, maybe...apologize again tomorrow? *Show* him you're not an asshole all the time. Stop playing games with his feelings. Drop your guard a bit. " I balked at the suggestion. "Just a little!" She was quick to interject. "You could see how it goes. See if there's *something* there to explore," June urged. "Even if the arrangement is only temporary. How are you ever going to know if you don't try?"

She was right.

But I'd been hurt so badly before, it would take a lot of courage for me to agree. I'd have to push aside that pain. Think outside the box. Figure out how to break through George's icy exterior. Flirting hadn't worked, nor had words, and unbidden my mind cycled back to the idea of a gift. It was a solid option. A symbol of my remorse. A way to show George that I hadn't meant to ruin his trip home—even though I had.

That was when June let me in on her plan.

Apparently, June, Joe, Roderick, and Mrs. M had all hatched up this hare-brained scheme to make George ride with me to Hocking Hills—to "clear the air". It felt like a bad idea. A super bad idea. For so many reasons. George would be less than thrilled to spend the afternoon alone with me.

I hadn't realized what today meant to him. I'd been blinded by my own agenda—and failed to empathize. Failed to see what was right in front of my face.

In my defense, I hadn't had all the pieces until he'd given them to me.

Maybe George and I were more alike than I'd realized.

I still had no idea why he'd been away from home for so long, or why the last year had been the "shittiest of his life," but…I couldn't leave this be. I had to try to make it right, one final time. I owed it to him. Besides, we'd both benefit from burying the hatchet, so to speak. I doubted spending this trip avoiding me was what he'd wanted when he'd booked the flight home to be with family.

Even so, what June was proposing was…intimidating to say the least. In order to prove to George that I wasn't the total dick he thought I was, I would have to lower my guard more than "a little".

And that was…

Petrifying.

"Fine." I agreed, heart thumping erratically at the thought of being alone with George again. "I'll try."

"That's good enough for me."

I'd accept whatever fate George chose for us.

If he never wanted to talk to me again, I'd respect that.

I could put aside my pride.

I could accept this sliver of grace for what it was.

A second chance to make things right wrapped up in one terrible, awful, bad decision. Even if I had to *earn* that second chance by embarking on the most uncomfortable road trip in the history of the world. That was a small price to pay for an opportunity to earn George's forgiveness.

Nine

George

THE NEXT MORNING WAS a shit show of epic proportions. Between the packing, the yelling, and the inevitable havoc that broke out whenever all of us were home, it was no wonder I forgot about my mom and her matchmaking.

At least…until it was time for me to claim my spot inside Lacey's van next to Mavis, and I realized in my haste to be helpful, I'd made the mistake of dropping my guard. All it took was one glance after yanking the door open to understand that I had been betrayed.

Again.

My seat was already occupied. Roderick smiled at me, glasses glinting as he offered me an unapologetic wave. I was so surprised to see him that I did a double take. Mavis was unconcerned, sitting obediently with a stuffed lion tucked protectively in her lap, its mane almost as matted as her own hair. I'd watched Lacey comb it that morning, so it was a mystery how she'd managed to get it that messy that quickly.

Kid magic.

"What are you doing in Lacey's car?" I asked, already anticipating the answer. "I assumed...you would be riding with Juniper? You know...your fiancée?" Maybe he'd forgotten. Perhaps this was a fluke and he'd hop right out and thank me for the reminder.

"Your mom invited me."

"My mom...*invited* you?"

"Yes. When I told her all the other spots were full of coolers."

"Jesus." Mom had packed ten coolers herself. I knew because I'd helped. One of them had been entirely filled with bacon.

Roderick appeared benign, but he was far from innocent. "So here I am!" Roderick's jazz hands were awkward as hell. Fingers still wiggling, he offered me the same cheeky grin that had made me weak-kneed in high school. Now it just made me want to pull my hair out. Or stab him. Or both. "Don't worry. We made sure you had a ride."

"You made sure that I..." My sentence was cut off when I felt a familiar wall of heat at my back. A shadow fell over me, slipping along the sun-sanded surface of the paint on the hood of the van. The scent of designer cologne filled my nose.

No.

No.

No.

"I've got a free spot in my car." Alex's voice was cheery. "Not to worry, my pretty little friend." I was not his friend, nor was I little. Height-wise. He did have a considerable amount of bulk on me. And probably a few inches in the cock department. But still. Nothing that would constitute him calling me...me *that*.

I tried to ignore my arousal, but found that impossible. Especially when Alex's fingers curled around my shoulders, thick and strong, and steady. In a dominating way that made me feel like a melted pile of goo, he steered me away from Lacey's minivan of death, and marched me across the street to his car.

I didn't dare say anything biting, worried about causing another scene. The last thing I needed was to embarrass my mom again. Once was enough.

It felt like everyone was watching us.

Maybe because they were.

Juniper was halfway out the front door of Roderick's house. She paused, not at all subtle when she gave Alex a thumbs up, and then aimed one toward Roderick in the back seat of the van. My mother, who had just strolled onto our porch in a floor-length, bright red, monster of a dress, smiled smugly when she saw who had abducted me.

Saboteurs.

Saboteurs everywhere.

"What did I do to make your sister hate me so much?" I whined under my breath. Alex's throaty chuckle sent a shiver down my spine.

"I wonder that myself every fucking day."

Alex drove a black Mercedes. Which did not surprise me in the slightest. The paint was shiny and recently waxed. In comparison, how well-maintained his vehicle was made Lacey's van look like it'd been pulled right out of a junkyard.

This car was all sleek lines and paint so new it was practically a mirror.

"Do I really have to do this?" I grumbled as one of his hands slid to the nape of my neck. Collared, I had no choice but to stumble—then melt.

"Yep." Unrepentant as ever, Alex's voice crackled with heat.

I heard a clicking sound, felt a bit of wind, but was too distracted by the palm holding me steady to do more than breathe.

"In you go," Alex urged, using his grip on my neck to gently push me down into the passenger seat. Leather. Real leather. The smell tickled my nose. Surreptitiously, I sucked in a deep, greedy lungful. Alex's car was as ridiculously good-looking as he was.

The thing probably cost the same as a small country, judging by all the dials and buttons it had.

Across the street, my sister, Lacey, eyed us with interest. She was climbing into the front seat of her minivan with Mavis's unicorn backpack tucked protectively in her arms. The only member of my family that wasn't actively torturing me.

Thank god.

Alex opened his door, having crossed behind the vehicle. I mouthed *help* Lacey's way. I even widened my eyes to show how dire the situation was. But she didn't immediately jump to my rescue. Instead, my no-nonsense, asshole fast-track-to-district-attorney sister's lips pulled into a smirk. And then she turned to face the garage and completely ignored me.

Traitor.

When Alex slid into his seat I had no choice but to accept my fate. His door shut with a resounding click. I shrank, glaring at him through my lashes—aware that I was well and truly stuck.

He smiled at me.

It was a sweet smile.

Softer than the ones yesterday.

I didn't trust it one bit.

Not.

One.

Bit.

The nice thing about riding with Alex? I was sitting in the front seat. The not-so-nice thing about riding with Alex? *I was sitting in the front seat.* Which made it very difficult to ignore him.

I was a mess of jumbled up feelings.

Did I find Alex attractive? Yes.

Had he saved me from immense embarrassment? Yes.

Had he taken the heat off of me yesterday, going so far as to outright find my mom and "make things right"? Yes.

All of those things *normally* would've made me more inclined to like him. But nothing about this situation was normal.

My saving grace was the fact that Alex's particular brand of playful teasing never slipped into a category that was actually abusive. I'd had ample time to reflect on yesterday's events. Without the hurt clouding my judgment, I'd come to the conclusion that the only time Alex had come close to crossing that line had been at the barbecue when he'd brought up Neil—and even then, he'd been careful not to speak openly enough to cause me real embarrassment.

Even his provocation was mindful.

I wasn't sure if that was another manipulation or not. Truthfully, I didn't know what to make of him. The fact he'd spoken to my mother in itself was unexpected. Brendon would've never done something like that. Ever. Aside from the odd hot-and-cold behavior he'd exhibited yesterday, nothing about Alex reminded me of Brendon.

I knew logically, I should dislike Alex—and part of me did. Simply because I had not accounted for his presence when I'd taken off work to visit. He was throwing a wrench in my plans. Which was something I had always hated.

However...

I could tell he wasn't totally awful.

And objectively speaking, I could understand why my family—and his— were trying to push us together. On paper we were compatible. Not to mention that neck grabby thing that he'd done to get me in the car had been...*fuck*. My skin was still tingling from it. In a good way.

"So..." Alex started as he pulled out onto the street. I truly had no idea what was about to come out of his mouth. Nothing good. The CD player kicked on, a song beginning to play that sounded kind of like one of the musicals I loved. Alex quickly hit the off button. "You and Roddy, huh?"

I sighed, frustrated that I had no choice but to respond. "A long time ago."

"High school?" he asked, arching a brow.

"Briefly." I could tell he was going to keep pushing, so I figured I might as well go ahead and tell him to save us both the headache. "We were never all that compatible." Alex made a sound, and I continued. "When I went away for college it seemed logical to end things. We knew it wasn't working. The breakup was amicable."

"Did you love him?" Alex's voice was subdued.

"I've loved everyone I've dated," I replied.

"Huh." I'd never seen Alex's face look so broody. Alex gathered his thoughts and I soaked up the sun that hopped between the trees planted along the road. Almost perfectly spaced. Shadow, light, shadow, light. "I've only loved one person," Alex confessed. "Romantically," he added, as though that hadn't been clear.

"And did it end amicably?" I inquired, honestly curious.

"No."

Now it was my turn to stew. I wasn't sure why we were having this conversation at all. But as I glanced through my lashes Alex's way I couldn't help but come to the conclusion that he was…maybe possibly as damaged as I was. At least, if what he'd just said was true, and the expression on his face wasn't fake.

"What happened?" I knew I shouldn't ask. I certainly didn't want him prying into my private business. I could only assume that feeling was mutual. We were strangers. But…well. He looked…

He looked *sad*.

A furrow between his brows, his lips pressed into an unyielding line. The muscle at the corner of his jaw jumped as he clenched it tight. "He was a liar," Alex said simply. It was a small admission, but it was enough.

Immediately, I thought of Brendon. Of his dark eyes. His brown hair. Of the smile he'd given me every time he'd told me *soon, soon, soon*.

Soon we'd go public with our relationship.

Soon we'd move in together.

Soon we'd get a dog.

Soon we'd start our family.

Soon.

"Liars are the worst kind of people," I agreed, bile climbing up my throat. It seemed Alex and I had found some common ground at last.

"I'd drink to that, but I'm driving," Alex laughed, some of his usual cheer back already. "And I—"

"Don't have a drink," I finished for him, because he was nothing if not predictable.

"Cute," Alex's lips curled into a smirk. I shrugged, ducking my head to gaze out the window again. The seat was soft. The leather clung to my ass in a way that was somewhat erotic—and should not at all be the design of a vehicle. It was slutty. Just like his t-shirt had been yesterday. Just like his Armani suit.

"Ha, ha."

We were silent for a few minutes. Out of Chesterton and on the road toward our destination, it was easier to breathe. It was only one car ride. I could survive one car ride. Wasn't like it was going to be a life-altering experience.

I didn't hate Alex anymore.

But that didn't mean I wanted to chat.

"George—" Alex said.

"The small talk is unnecessary," I cut him off. "Let's get this over with." I'd been a smidge…harsh yesterday when I'd told him I didn't want to talk to him again. But still. It was beneficial for all of us if I stuck to that. It would minimize potential contention.

"Right." Alex was quiet for another minute, hands flexing on the steering wheel.

I couldn't help but stare.

They were lovely hands.

I'd thought so before.

His knuckles turned white from tension, the sound of his breaths coming a little faster, a little louder. If I didn't know any better, I'd say he was nervous.

Clench, clench, the veins on the top of his hands rippled as he squeezed.

"I…" Alex started, then stopped. He made a frustrated noise as he glared at the road. The trees that dotted the edge of the street grew wider apart as we drove. Soon enough, they'd disappear entirely, replaced by farmland once again.

I waited for him to finish his thought, but he didn't.

Squeeze, squeeze, Alex continued to strangle the steering wheel.

Up ahead, the "Hell is Real" sign came into view. Black and white, it'd been a landmark that'd reminded me I was home for most of my life. Growing bigger by the second, I waited for the words to blur as we sped by. But they didn't. Because instead of continuing toward our destination Alex slowed down. I frowned, turning to look at him as he pulled over onto the side of the road, wheels crunching on gravel.

"What the fuck?" I managed as he got out of the car. Concerned, I watched him stalk around the back to the trunk. Had we hit a nail or something and I hadn't noticed? Was he fixing a tire?

Why was he—

The trunk closed, revealing Alex once more, holding…*pickles?*

A giant jar of pickles.

When he rounded the vehicle to my side and pulled the door open, I wasn't sure what I expected. To be kicked out? Told to walk because I hadn't wanted to chat with him? To be beaten over the head with the jar and tossed into the corn?

"Here," Alex said instead of murdering me.

His chest was heaving, shallow little pants as he shoved the jar of pickles toward me. I took them, bewildered.

"You…stopped us on the side of the road…to give me *pickles?*"

Alex looked panicked.

It was the most unsure I'd seen him yet.

"They're…um." He scratched the back of his neck, big shoulders flexing in a way that was far too distracting than it had any right to be. "They're apology pickles."

"Apology…pickles…" I echoed, staring down at the jar. It was the brand I favored. My favorite. The same kind I'd lost my appetite for the night before. "I'm confused."

"Because I was a dick yesterday," Alex tried to explain. "Words didn't feel like enough. I wanted to *show* you that I'm not an asshole." The more he spoke, the faster his words came out. "I wracked my brain all night trying to figure out the best way to do that."

He'd worried about this all night?

"After talking to your mom I figured this was the best way to prove my sincerity."

"With…*pickles?*" I confirmed. The glass was cool to the touch, slightly warmer where the wrapper lay. I rubbed the edge with my thumb, so confused by this new turn of events, it took me a second to realize my anxiety had fled.

Laughter bubbled up.

The horrible kind.

The kind that made me feel like I was choking. It spilled free, these awful wheezes escaping as I clutched my apology pickles close.

Alex was startled at first, his eyes wide, like he didn't know what to do. Then his unease melted away, broad shoulders relaxing. He cracked a smile. If I didn't know any better, I'd think he looked proud of himself.

When I finally stopped choking on air, I wiped tears away from the corners of my eyes and shook my head. "This has got to be the stupidest, sweetest thing anyone has ever done for me," I told him. "Apology pickles. Wow. Just…*wow.*"

Alex grinned, wide and unrepentant. The sun glazed him in gold, highlighting the bump on the bridge of his nose, and the curve of his jaw. "I'm glad you liked it."

I shrugged. "Hard not to like pickles."

Alex laughed, this elated, sharp burst of breath. Then he sobered. He was nowhere near as rigid as he'd been previously, however. Just stiff enough I knew to expect another wild card. Proving me right, Alex dropped to his knees on the gravel in my open doorway. The car continued to run, and I held tighter to my pickle bottle.

"I was an asshole," Alex said softly, holding his hands palms up. It was a sign of surrender. The same gesture he'd made the day before when I'd rejected him.

"Mmm," I agreed, because he had been. "I was too."

"I was worse," Alex replied. "I…" He sucked in a breath, and then, because he was full of surprises today, he was honest. "You're the fourth person June has tried to set me up with for her damn wedding. I'm not looking for a relationship. Not fucking interested. I was…frustrated that she was pushing this on me, prepared to treat you the same way I've treated all the people she's tried to make me date." He paused, refusing to look at me. "But then I *met* you."

I arched a brow.

"You didn't like me." Alex's voice caught. "I…fuck. This is hard. I don't normally talk openly like this."

"Why do it now?"

"I want to make things right."

Another pause.

"I'm used to everyone liking me." Alex grimaced. "I know how that sounds. But it's true. I've been…a mess since yesterday. Not sure how to talk to you, or…what I even wanted. To push you away? Get June to stop setting me up? Or to feed into this…because you weren't at all what I expected. This is the first time I've been even remotely interested in one of her matches and that was fucking with my head a bit, all things considered." He took in another breath. "I shouldn't have ignored you at the party. I shouldn't have pushed you when you were clearly uncomfortable."

My heart skipped a beat.

"I should've left you alone when you told me you wanted me to," Alex added, staring at the pickles in my grip. "But…I figured you deserved answers. I didn't want things to be weird between us. Didn't want to ruin more of your trip," Alex murmured, turning his pale blue eyes on me. Puppy eyes. Again.

"Okay?" My voice was oddly soft.

It was hard to process everything he'd just said but I tried. Maybe he wasn't manipulative like I'd thought. Maybe Alex was simply off-kilter? I could understand that. I didn't know what to make of him either. Maybe I'd misjudged him.

Alex's smile was sad. "I really am sorry, George. Seriously, *genuinely* sorry. And I swear if you forgive me—even though I know I don't deserve it—I will make it up to you. I'll be honest from here on out. I won't play games anymore. Not with you, and not with myself. As crazy as it sounds…I think we're kindred spirits."

I'd forgiven him the moment he'd brought out the goddamn pickles. His explanation was nice though, and appreciated. No one, in all my life, had ever apologized to me so sincerely. And so…endearingly pathetically? Like a kicked puppy. And like he really, actually cared what I thought.

What a trip.

"You were flirting with me as a joke?" I confirmed, because he hadn't addressed that. "Because I didn't like you, and you thought it was funny."

"*No.*" Alex shook his head. "The flirting was all real. It was the…other shit that wasn't."

"Huh."

I frowned, processing this.

"So, do you—" Alex bit his lip.

"I forgive you."

He sagged, giant frame collapsing forward. The rocks had to be digging into his knees, but he didn't seem to notice. "Thank god."

"I don't know why you care," I said, pickles still clutched close.

"Honestly? I don't either." Alex reached a hand out, hovering it over my knee before retracting it. "All I know is the idea that you might hate me makes me sick to my stomach."

"I don't hate you," I reassured. Maybe I had, a little, but it'd been fleeting and before the puppy eyes.

"Yeah?" I swear to god if he'd had a tail it'd be wagging.

"You gave me pickles."

"I did."

"You're hurting my knees just looking at you," I grimaced. "Please get off the ground." Alex was on his feet before I could blink, blocking the sun again. He smiled down at me, golden and sweaty.

I didn't understand why he would flirt with me when he wasn't looking for a relationship. Maybe he found it fun? Like a psychopath. I suppose it didn't really matter. It wasn't like I was looking either.

Alex shut my door for me, jogged around the back of the car, then slid into his seat. I studied the "Hell is Real" sign thoughtfully, deciding what to do now that we'd reached a tentative truce.

"It wasn't that I didn't...like you," I confessed.

Alex's presence alone made the inside of the car several degrees hotter.

He let the AC blast, but made no move to pull back onto the road. Twisting to look at me, his eyes were swimming with intelligence. Every ounce of his focus was on me. It made me feel bare, and I wasn't sure how to react to that.

"I've just...never been treated that way. And I was...embarrassed. For obvious reasons," I said.

Alex made a soft sound. "Treated what way?"

I rolled my eyes, self-conscious. I glowered at the cornfields outside the window. "You wouldn't stop paying attention to me. *Flirting* with me. It was confusing."

"Confusing how?"

"I've never...experienced that."

"You've never been flirted with?" Alex sounded appalled. I hummed noncommittally.

"My recent ex wasn't particularly…open with his affections." That was the understatement of the century. "We were together for a very long time."

"He didn't pay attention to you?" Alex's voice was full of disbelief. "How is that possible? Have you seen your legs? And your face?"

I flushed.

"He wasn't like you. His affection was difficult to earn, and only offered behind closed doors." I picked at the label on the pickles as I spoke. The pit in my stomach returned. "You saw my…Neil, and you continued to talk to me. I thought you were making fun of me."

"Fuck no." Alex sounded so adorably angry, I had to turn to look at him. He looked pissed off on my behalf, which was…flattering. "I mean, yeah, it's a pretty wild choice—to bring a dildo on a—"

"I didn't."

"You didn't?" He blinked. "But you—"

"My roommate packed it. Not me."

"Oh. Well. That makes sense." Alex's smile was apologetic. "No offense, but you give off a kind of sexually repressed vibe. If I hadn't seen it with my own eyes, I never would've believed you'd bring a sex toy with you like that." His smile morphed into a grin. "So, what? She snuck it in there without you knowing? Won't she miss it?"

I gagged. "It's not hers."

Sexually repressed?

I'd bet anything I'd practiced more kink than he had.

"So it's…" Alex blinked. "So it *is* yours?"

"I never said it wasn't. I only said that I wasn't the one who packed it."

"Right." He nodded up and down. His eyes were on my body. My chest, then my hips. His pink tongue flickered out to wet his lip. "And you…use it?" His hands twitched, almost like he wanted to reach out to measure my waist—to see if someone as slight in frame as I was could really fit a cock that big inside.

"That's a very inappropriate question," I admonished, cheeks hot.

"Right, sorry. I'm just…" Alex inhaled sharply. "*Fuck*." He squeezed his eyes shut, trying to redirect his thoughts, probably. Horny bastard. His lips were still slick, and they looked…even more kissable like this, when he wasn't smirking and smarming and taunting.

Honesty was a good look on him.

"Suffice to say," I mirrored his earlier words. "I didn't know what to do with you. Being *wanted* is unfamiliar."

"That's a shame," Alex said, eyes opening again, his pupils flooded black. "A serious shame."

I shrugged. "I'm used to it."

"So, you've never had a boyfriend who showered you with affection?" Alex echoed, finally putting his hands back on the steering wheel. "A guy who couldn't keep his hands off you, no matter how hard he tried?" He shifted gears, pulling out onto the road. It was a relief not to hold the entirety of his attention any longer.

"Never."

"Not even Roddy?" Alex said.

I quirked a brow. "We weren't like that."

"Right." He shifted in his seat, chewing over our conversation as the world blurred by. It was too hot, so I reached over, pointing the cool air my way. The pickles jostled, but I managed to keep them from falling to the floor. "Would you…want that?" Alex asked, voice uncharacteristically breathless.

"Want what?" I inquired.

"A boyfriend who showered you with affection," Alex clarified.

I paused with my fiddling. Now it was my turn to chew over his words. Scowling, I settled back in my seat. "I…" Imagining that hurt. Someone to love. To care for me openly. To be proud to parade me around. To touch and hold and pamper me. Someone who thought I was enough. "I would."

"Okay." This silence dragged on longer. I didn't interrupt, certain there was a purpose to it. Alex's expression was contemplative as he watched the road with unseeing eyes. We passed over a railroad track, wheels thunk, thunking.

"*Okay*," Alex said again, a bit louder, like there hadn't been a pause at all. "I have a proposition for you. And it's going to sound unhinged—"

His expression softened as he glanced my way.

My heart rattled in my chest.

"How would you feel about a practice boyfriend?"

Ten
Alex

"A...PRACTICE BOYFRIEND?" GEORGE looked charmingly miffed as he clutched his jar of pickles close. He hadn't let go of them since I'd handed them to him. Like he was worried they'd grow legs and walk off if he didn't hold them tight.

"Yeah!" The more I thought about it, the more it made sense. "*My* practice boyfriend." I nodded, oddly elated by the prospect. June had said the arrangement didn't need to be anything but temporary. That, paired with what George had said about wanting an affectionate boyfriend, had given me the idea.

"Like fake dating?" George sounded dubious at best.

"Yes and no." I tapped my fingers on the wheel, getting hyped up the more I thought about it. "It wouldn't be fake. Just...temporary? Assuming you're as uninterested in your family's matchmaking efforts as I am with mine." Mrs. Milton had been way too excited when I'd asked her what I'd need to get back into George's good graces.

Like a hairspray-obsessed kid on Christmas.

"I'm not looking for a boyfriend," George huffed.

"See? Neither am I! It would be perfect."

"I'm not looking for a *practice* boyfriend either," George scowled, guarding his jar of pickles like a blond goblin hoarding treasure. "I'm thirty-three. Feels juvenile."

"You sure?" I couldn't help but feel disappointed. "You'd get all the attention you could ever want. More even." This was perfect. I was a genius. A goddamn genius. This could be the best of both worlds—everything I'd ever wanted for long enough I could savor it. Things would end before George got sick of me. It'd be *perfect*. "It'd get your family—and mine—off both our backs." I could please June, attend the wedding with someone, and get to spend time with George, without pressure. He wouldn't see beneath my cracks. I could be a perfect boyfriend for seven days. Fuck yes, I could. "And it'd be fun! A week of affection, no strings attached."

George eyed me distrustfully.

I continued, "I've never had someone to spoil before." I'd never had the opportunity to be the kind of boyfriend I'd always wanted to be—too afraid of being too much, too afraid of scaring whoever I was dating off with my "intensity." Too afraid of being rejected when they realized what was beneath my polished exterior.

George tilted his head to the side, the light in his eyes warming. "You... *want* to spoil someone?"

"Oh yeah," I bobbed my head. "So much. More than anything." That was the most honest I'd ever been. I couldn't believe how easily the words had come out, considering how closely I'd guarded that secret.

"I'm not having sex with you," George scoffed. "If that's why you—"

"Sex is optional," I was quick to reassure. I meant that. "Totally optional, and totally up to you."

"Hmm." George leaned back in his seat. My sincerity was evident. "I'll think about it."

"That's good enough for me." It was tempting to try to sell the idea to him more. But...I'd been in sales long enough to know that at this point, that wouldn't help. If George desired what I had on offer, he'd take it. And... maybe like June had said, the best way to convince him would be to show him what he'd be missing if he said no.

George was baffled but pleased when I took us to a diner for brunch. The place was darling, a mom-and-pop joint that looked straight out of the seventies. I made sure to pay for his food, finding great satisfaction in the way he ate.

These tiny, dainty bites.

I wanted to poke fun, but I was on my best behavior at present, and figured that wouldn't get me any extra points. I got the door for him too, grinning when this little perplexed wrinkle formed between his brows as he stepped outside and into the sun.

It caught on his hair, making it glisten like spun gold. He was dressed more casually today. A tight-fitting white t-shirt that clung to his lean frame. Dark denim that highlighted the length of his legs and the bounce of his ass. His biceps were toned, if still skinny, like he spent a lot of time doing cardio, with a side of lifting, not in the gym, but in his everyday life. An effortless sort of strength.

I tried not to ogle.

But failed, spectacularly.

My phone vibrated in my pocket, and I groaned. Caller ID said it was the florist. Normally, I'd ignore it—but with June's wedding only a week away, I was constantly on edge, worried something was going to go wrong. Unfortunately for me, my intuition was right.

"You go ahead," I urged. "Here." I tossed George the car keys, not wanting him to be stuck in the heat while I dealt with this. "I gotta take this."

George caught the keys. Only barely. They bumped off his fingers, and he scrambled to try and snatch them before they fell to the ground. He didn't ask any questions as he moved to the car and gracefully climbed inside, folding those long, long legs into the space.

I licked my lips, then forced my mind out of the gutter.

"Hi, Miranda," I answered the call, aiming for cheerful—as I knew that was the best way to deal with this particular employee. She was a sweetheart. I could tell she hadn't had much praise in her life, because every time I told her what a good job she was doing, she perked right up.

It took fifteen minutes to get her off the phone after we'd come to the conclusion that I'd need to go in person to approve the bouquets. Something had happened with the original shipment, and that meant a new headache for me—and her.

When she hung up, I received another call—this time from the venue we'd booked. So it wasn't like I could ignore it. This one took even longer. Nearly half an hour. By the time I returned to my car and the blond I'd left inside it, I felt wrung out.

"Sorry," I apologized, slipping into the driver's side. I was relieved to feel the blast of AC—especially because that meant George hadn't been in here roasting. "We had a problem with an overbooking issue, and I—you know what? It doesn't matter. I fixed it. I'll need to go into the city to deal with the florist, which again, I apologize for. It's a last-minute…uh." I stopped talking when I saw George's face.

He didn't look annoyed.

He looked sleepy.

Like he'd been out here napping. Maybe his night had been as sleepless as mine? I grinned, unable to help myself.

That was a new face.

I'd never seen him relaxed. It felt like disturbing a tired kitty, all comfortable and safe. I wished I could go back in time. Wished I could enter the car quieter, so I could let him nap longer. That or pull out my phone and snap a picture. I got the feeling George-Arthur Milton didn't let his guard down often, if ever.

"How far are we?" George asked, voice huskier than before. He was trying to pretend like I hadn't caught him napping.

So cute.

Fuck.

"From the campgrounds?" I clarified. Now that we'd been honest with one another, things were…easy. Effortless. I didn't overanalyze why that was. Or why even though he'd refused my offer I still felt hopeful.

It felt weird to talk to him without flirting or arguing. But it was nice too. The underlying electricity between us was still there—no doubt the sexual chemistry that June had called us out for, but…it was softer somehow.

George nodded slowly. A lock of blond hair fell onto his forehead, the wavy strand sticking to his skin. I had to squeeze the steering wheel tight so I could resist the urge to reach over and tuck it back into place.

"Not long. But…I've got a few things I have to do before we head up, if you don't mind tagging along," I added. "That was what I was on the phone about."

"Do what you must," George sighed, in the most dramatic way possible, eyes drifting shut.

His peace didn't last.

Unfortunately for both of us.

His phone buzzed, and he frowned, pulling it out of his pocket with a couple dazed blinks. He sobered quickly, his entire body going rigid. The air in the car felt colder as George's good mood disappeared. There was a haunted look about him as his lips pressed into a thin, wobbly line, his body curling in tightly, as small as he could make it.

Like he hoped to disappear.

"What's wrong?" I didn't have any right to be nosy. But…fuck. He'd lost all the color in his cheeks in a matter of seconds. I wanted to fix it. I *needed* to fix it.

"It's nothing." George's tone was biting. The screen on his phone went black. "I don't want to talk about it."

"Okaayyy." I didn't press, even though I wanted to. Maybe the text had something to do with the ex he'd mentioned? The one he'd said wasn't open with affection.

Was that George's way of calling him a dick?

Why didn't he just outright say it?

He'd called me that yesterday.

George didn't speak for an entire minute.

And it was the most excruciating minute of my life—second only to the minute I'd had to wait for him to accept my pickle-apology.

I didn't dare pull out onto the road. I could tell he wasn't done yet. And that he might—*possibly*—need more support.

I'd always had a talent for reading people. It was what made me good at my job. And it was also why I knew how unpalatable I was. The look in people's eyes when I did something "too much" was telling enough, even without them having to outright say.

George's eyes stormed. A hurricane of a thousand different emotions, swirling, ebbing, rioting in the depths of his gaze.

"You know…if that's your ex and he's not leaving you alone…" I kept my tone carefully neutral. "I can help."

"I didn't say yes to your hare-brained "practice boyfriend" scheme."

"Pro-bono," I promised. "On the house. No schemes attached."

"Doing your civic duty?" George sighed, fingers tapping anxiously on the lid of his pickle jar.

"Offered in good faith," I swore. It was difficult not to reach out and yoink his phone out of his hand so I could see what had ruined his mood. I managed. But only barely.

"And if I were to accept your…no-strings-attached offer…" George frowned. "What would that…entail?"

"Depends on the severity of the infection." I paused. "Or should I say… inf-ex-tion?"

George rolled his eyes, but he was amused.

"You'll have to let me see your phone so I can properly diagnose." I held a hand out. A beat passed as George glared at my palm like he expected it to grow teeth and bite him. Then…with an anxious puff of air, he handed the phone over.

"The password is 102219," he sighed. I arched a brow. "My cat's birthday."

"Right." It was even more difficult not to laugh. But this situation called for the utmost seriousness, so I schooled my expression as I typed in the code. The main screen was a photo of what had to be the ugliest—and cutest—cat I'd ever seen. All white fur with blue bug eyes, and what I guessed to be a permanently annoyed appearance, much like his owner. "What's his name?"

"I'm not telling you," George growled.

"Why not?"

"You'll laugh."

"I like laughing."

"Yeah, well. I don't like being laughed at." George's hands twitched, like he was about to yank his phone back, so I stopped teasing.

"One sec." I opened his texts. There were four unopened messages from a guy simply called "Brendon." The ex, presumably, seeing as they were the only texts in his entire phone that were untouched. It was difficult not to snoop. The most recent text, aside from Brendon's, was right there—to a woman named Missy, and all it said was:

George

I hate you.

I could only assume Missy was the dildo-planting roommate.

Opening the texts from Brendon, my good mood vanished. Scrolling,

scrolling, I passed hundreds and hundreds of thinly veiled pleas for attention. Insults. Backhanded jabs. The occasional outright abusive statement. Things that made my fucking blood boil. They evidently worked together, as interspersed between each biting remark were work-related questions.

My grip on George's phone tightened to the point of pain, and I had to take a second to calm down before I snapped the damn thing.

I may not know George well, but no one—and I mean no one—deserved to be treated like that.

"Seems to me like he can't let go," I said after a tense minute of silence. "How long have you been broken up?"

"A year," George answered. He'd wilted, head back against the headrest, his eyes on the pickle container on his lap. Well that answered my question about why the last year had been shitty.

"Have you ever shown anyone these?" I asked, trying to keep my voice calm.

George shrugged. "Why would I?"

"Because it's...fucked up, George. Especially if you work together. He shouldn't be sending you this shit."

George shrugged again. "It doesn't matter."

"Of course it fucking matters." I bit my tongue. He looked small enough as it was. The last thing he needed was to be chewed out. My anger wasn't directed at him, but at the creep he'd used to date. "Okay." I blew out a breath. "Does he follow you anywhere? Social media? Anything like that?"

George nodded.

"Where?"

"Picstogram." George was sounding more despondent by the minute. Dissociating maybe? I dunno. I was quick to pull up his account, and didn't even have to ask for Brendon's username. George's profile was full of pictures of the same ugly cat on his phone screen, as well as a few book reviews, mostly anime comics. I didn't recognize any of them. The anime I watched was action-oriented, and George seemed to favor romance.

On every post, he only had a handful of likes.

Joe_Milton95 was one of his bigger fans, as well as MrsMiltonDoesHair. The only person who liked each post that wasn't family, was a guy with no profile picture, and a username with more numbers than words.

Okay…so Brendon liked to keep his footprint online anonymous.

He spent a lot of time following up with George, given the fact that he'd reacted to every fucking post since they'd broken up. Sometimes he'd even comment. Like a creep.

I could handle that.

"Did you ever post him on your account?" I asked, even though I could see that George hadn't.

"No," George sighed. "He didn't want me to."

"Even better."

"What?" George turned his attention back to me, that adorable little grimple on his chin returning. "Why would that—"

"Because. There's only one way to deal with assholes like this. He won't leave you alone because in his fucked head, he thinks you're available."

"But I *am* available." George wasn't getting it.

"Not to him." I turned on his phone camera, aimed it at one of his long, deliciously limber thighs. "You can say no, but let me just…" I licked my lips, floored by how fucking bad I wanted to bite his thighs. "Can I touch you?"

I hadn't asked earlier when I'd touched him.

But…maybe I should have.

George deliberated before he nodded, a quick up and down.

When I lay my hand on his upper quad it nearly enveloped the whole width of it. I groaned, unable to help myself as I fanned my fingers out, stroking along the denim of his jeans.

"How is groping me going to help with—"

"Hold still," I aimed the camera and shot a picture of my hand on his leg. The pickle jar was in it, but only a bit—enough to cause intrigue but not detract from the possessive grip I had on him. And fuck, was it possessive. My fingers digging in, holding him in place like it was my right to do so. "There." Reluctantly, I removed my hand, flipping the camera around to show him. "Post that. Maybe it'll get him to back off."

George stared at the photo, his eyes wide. He licked his lips, pupils expanding as he saw what I saw. How fucking good we looked together. My ring and watch catching the light, tan skin against dark denim. Our size difference evident in the way I dug my fingers in just right.

"You really think this will work?"

"Believe me. It'll piss him the fuck off. But—" I nodded. "He'll get the message."

George studied the picture for a minute longer. I couldn't read his expression, and I didn't want to rush him. I figured it was his choice—and as big as I talked, I wasn't entirely sure my plan would work.

I could only hope.

"Fuck it." George decided. Then he opened Picstogram again and began the uploading process.

"Caption it…" I said, hovering over his shoulder, my breath tickling his ear. He jumped, but didn't scoot out of my space. "Big hands are good for opening jars…among other things."

"No." George scrunched his nose. "Absolutely not."

"Fine. Something less sexy." He shivered, and I fought the urge to blow on his ear directly to see how he'd react. "How about, I like my pickles like I like my—"

"You're really bad at this," George laughed. It was way calmer than the charming choking noises he'd made earlier. Another expression to add to my collection.

"I can't help it if my brain thinks in innuendo."

"I'm going to caption it with an emoji," George decided. "A sun. Because it's summer."

"Is there a pickle emoji?"

"Yes." I was not surprised he knew that. I'd never met another person whose favorite food was pickles. It suited him. Considering his sour disposition and penchant for phallic-shaped objects.

"Oh. Add a heart. He'll hate that," I tacked on.

"I'm not trying to make him jealous." George scowled. "I just…want him to leave me alone."

"I know," I replied, even though I hadn't. And now that I did, I felt something almost…pleased settle over me. It was good to know how little interest George had in his ex. Really good to know. "Do it anyway."

"Fine." George selected a blue heart, then hit post. He didn't check that it'd gone up, simply closed out of the app. Immediately, his phone buzzed. A text. From Brendon.

I snatched it away before he could read it.

"Wh—"

"It doesn't matter what he has to say," I said, deleting the message. "We don't care."

"We don't?" George looked to me for guidance. God, was that heady.

"No."

"Oh." He glared at his phone. "Okay." And then stronger. "We don't."

"Our point has been made. Anything he says from this point onward is going to be bullshit to try and hurt you." Another text came in, and I deleted it also. "You know what? Why don't we turn your phone off?"

"But—"

"I know you can't block him." They worked together. "But if he can't reach you, he can't bug you. Right?"

"Right," George repeated. I waited to see what he'd say next.

"You have a choice here. Off or on. Your pick. I'll do it for you so you don't have to see anything."

"But what if…" George made a frustrated noise. "What if there really is something work-related?"

"Funny, I thought you were on vacation. You know… To spend a week away from the shit show back home?" I raised a brow, challenging him. George's eyes widened. The sound he made was incredulous but resigned.

"Okay. You're right."

"Off or on?"

"Off." George sounded firm. Which was good. His earlier indecision, his earlier ice gone. I turned his phone off and handed it to him.

"You can put it in my glove box for safe keeping if you want. That way you don't need to worry about it getting lost."

"Oh, but—" George plucked at his hair anxiously. "Missy is watching Mr. Pickles. What if she calls—or needs me, or—"

Mr. Pickles.

His cat was named Mr. Pickles?

It took everything I had not to laugh.

George paused, seemingly realizing what he'd said too late. His hand dropped back to his lap. "Oh, fuck off."

"I didn't say anything."

"You didn't have to." He smacked my shoulder, harder than necessary. "Stop looking so pleased." I pressed my lips together so I wouldn't outright grin.

"I'm not pleased," I countered, "I'm—I mean. I'd ask *why* you named him that, but I already know the answer."

"I'll tell my mom to let Missy know she can reach me through her phone," George ignored me. "That way I won't have to see his texts, and I can still be reached."

"Mhm, good plan." Mr. Pickles, Mr. Pickles, Mr.—

"I will strangle you," George warned. I doubted his bitty little fingers were strong enough to cut off my air supply.

"Okay, okay." I backed off, turning my face away from him, feigning like I was checking the mirrors when in reality I was hiding my grin. "No more smiling or good humor. None."

"Thank god."

"One miserable Alex coming right up."

"That would be preferable."

We pulled out of the parking lot, and it wasn't until we'd hit the open road that I lost the battle with my laughter. Only, despite George claiming he hated being laughed at, he was the one that looked pleased. There was a smile on his lips, a private one, aimed out the window at the rolling fields of corn and the endless blue sky, not at me.

But it was my smile regardless.

Which was why it wasn't fair.

Wasn't fair at all—as I toted him around on the rest of my last-minute errands before we headed to the camp—that he hadn't said yes to being my practice boyfriend. Because after one day I already knew I'd do anything to see that smile again.

Eleven
George

"SO..." NOW IT WAS my turn to push, apparently. "Why is your sister hell-bent on setting us up?"

We were on the way out of Columbus, having finished all our errands in record time. When Alex wasn't pushing, poking, or playing ice-prince he was surprisingly good company. And it was…oddly attractive to see him in his element, arranging, talking, and charming the vendors we visited into giving him what he wanted.

"You're one to talk. Joe's nearly as much of an instigator as she is," Alex interrupted my thoughts with a laugh.

"And my mom."

"Too true." Alex shook his head, amused. "Honestly? I think June thinks we'd be good together, as naive and silly as that sounds." Thus far, we'd avoided the topic of Brendon. Not since the Picstogram post—which I was resolutely refusing to think about.

"June doesn't even know me." I frowned. "How could she possibly know that? It makes no sense. Shouldn't she be...I don't know...jealous or something? Most people would be pissed an ex was invited to their wedding—not trying to set him up with their brother."

"June and Roderick are very odd people," Alex admitted fondly. "I don't think either of them have a jealous bone in their body."

That...made sense.

When we'd dated, Roderick had been nothing but smiles. Sometimes I'd wondered if he had the capacity to feel anything but happiness. He never raised his voice, never got mad, never jealous. It was that lack of passion that made us so fundamentally incompatible.

Unlike Alex. Alex, who had big hands, and a big temper, and became pissed off on my behalf—despite the fact he had no reason to be protective of me at all.

Alex, who wanted to *spoil* people.

Alex, who was apparently...kind of sweet—even if he was still frustrating.

"It's too bad I've sworn off men entirely. Otherwise having this many matchmakers would be useful," I sighed, gazing out the window as we passed by even more cornfields. I swear to god I'd seen enough over the last two days I was drowning in them. Because Alex hadn't pushed, and he'd already seen more of the way Brendon treated me than anyone else, it felt natural to open up.

"Brendon was..." It was challenging to sum him up in a single word. And even now, a year after I'd broken it off, it was difficult to speak about him. Like I was being disloyal. Like I expected punishment for the infraction. "Brendon is...hard."

There.

That was accurate, wasn't it?

Hard to please. Hard to be around. Hard on me. Hard-handed. Hard-headed.

"Not that you should care. But..."

"I care." Alex picked up speed, the roads barren of anyone but us. "Of course

I care. I'm not heartless. You seem like a good guy. And for what it's worth, I'm sorry that Brendon—" God it felt weird to hear Alex say his name, "sucked enough that you'll never give another man a chance again."

He was poking fun. But not in a mean way. Simply pointing out how silly my statement had been. I supposed it did seem rather…depressing.

"You know what the best revenge is after a bad breakup?" Alex continued, taking the exit that would lead us southwest toward Hocking Hills.

"What?"

I knew where this was going, but…didn't stop it.

"Being blissfully, happily in love with someone else."

I snorted, rolling my eyes. Again, Alex was nothing if not predictable. "Not posting pictures with handsy men online?"

"That too—" Alex laughed. "But, seriously," he added. "*Look*. I'm not trying to manipulate you into accepting my offer—and also, to be totally honest, as someone who is still hung up on what *my* shitty ex did, I am far from qualified to give advice—but don't you think cutting off all possibility of happiness with someone else would be exactly the kind of thing an ass like Brendon would want you to do? He'd want you miserable. The texts he sends you make that pretty clear."

Oh.

Fuck.

"I guess I never thought of it that way."

"Food for thought," Alex replied.

We were quiet for a few tense minutes as I processed what he'd said.

"I'm still not having sex with you," I teased, because again, it was jarring having him be so nice to me. Alex was the kind of man that kept you on your toes.

"Sex is optional!" Alex chuckled. "Buuuut…for the sake of my promise to be honest, I feel it imperative I inform you that what I've got downstairs would be on par with your tastes."

"Jesus."

"Size queen."

"I really will strangle you."

"I'm driving." Alex said, like operating the vehicle gave him immunity. "Mutually assured destruction."

I glared at him, but there wasn't any real heat to it. "Are we at a truce now?" I asked because I was curious. "You apologized. I accepted. You helped me. I went along with you on a thousand and a half errands."

"I want to say no," Alex replied. "Because if I say yes that means we can't fight anymore."

"Something is wrong with you."

"Don't pretend you don't like it too!" Alex's head tossed back as he chuckled. A dark lock bounced on his forehead as his grin turned wicked, sending a frisson of heat down my spine. Before he could open his mouth and say something flirty, I cut him off.

"So, not a truce. But…maybe sometimes we can be this too."

"Amicable." Alex bobbed his head. "Two guys who find their families' meddling endearing but obnoxious."

"Too true."

"Two *fellas* who may or may not become practice boyfriends," Alex waggled his eyebrows in a way that was supposed to be enticing, but was more dorky than hot.

"*Maybe*," I huffed.

"Glad to know we're on the same page. I'm enjoying our enemies to lovers arc far too much to end it now." If I hadn't known he was into romance novels the comment would've felt out of place. But I did, so it wasn't.

"Are we even enemies?" I arched a brow at him. "There's debate among the book community that in order to be a true enemies to lovers plot line you have to actually *be* enemies."

"Romeo and Juliet?"

"Kylo Ren and Rey," I countered.

"*Star Wars* nerd?" Alex's eyebrows shot up. He looked way too giddy.

"A bit."

"*Lord of the Rings*?" he inquired, excited. We weren't talking about enemies to lovers anymore, but I didn't mind. For the first time in a long time, I was simply content to chat.

"Obviously. Anyone with taste loves *Lord of the Rings*."

"Pick a favorite hobbit."

"Bilbo," I replied.

"From *Lord of the Rings*," Alex said.

"Bilbo is in the *Lord of the Rings*."

"As a side character."

"Still." It was difficult not to laugh too.

"Fine, pick a hobbit from *The Fellowship*," Alex tried again.

"Bilbo is in that too."

"*George*," Alex admonished.

I squinted, mulling it over. "Frodo."

"Hmm," Alex cocked his head to the side as he processed this. "I can see that." If he was trying to psychoanalyze me based on my hobbit preferences, who was I to stop him?

"Now you pick one." I waited expectantly.

"Sam." Alex was quick to answer.

Huh.

"Really? I thought for sure you'd like Merry or Pippin."

"Because of my merry attitude?"

"Because you're *chaotic*. Like a demon," I replied, and then, "Why Sam?" This was way more fun than I'd ever had talking to anyone else.

"He's steady," Alex replied. "Honest. Loyal. And dependable. I admire those qualities."

"And he can cook," I tacked on.

"Which is a *great* skill. I can't cook for shit."

"I can cook."

"Really?" Alex's eyes drifted over to me, only long enough for a fizzle of heat to burn between us before his attention returned to the road.

"I make a mean steak," I added, not sure why I was still talking about my cooking prowess. Was I trying to impress him? Is that what I was doing? Jesus Christ.

"I'm a big steak fan," Alex purred. "I like meat in general. Don't care what kind or size." Was he talking in innuendo again? "And I really like to eat out. Probably my favorite hobby."

"Eat…out?"

"Mhm. I bet you like to be eaten out—I mean—" Alex coughed, a healthy flush decorating his cheeks. "Sorry. Got distracted by my own…" He cleared his throat, shaking his head. "I'm trying to be good."

"You're failing." I laughed. I couldn't help it. And once I started, I couldn't seem to stop. For the second time that day he'd cracked through my exterior. "You…" I covered my face, snorting into my hand, embarrassed by how loud my laugh could be. "We were discussing hobbits! And now you're talking about eating my…I mean—"

Oh geez.

Visions of just that assaulted my senses.

Me with my pants around my knees, bent over a kitchen island after I'd cooked Alex a nice steak dinner. Those big, tan hands pulling my cheeks wide enough they stung, as his slick, clever tongue slid inside my hole. He'd be able to keep me in place, hold me open. The memory of the picture he'd taken of his hand on my thigh proved that.

Alex would be greedy about rimming me.

That much was obvious.

Alex would push and lick and suck. He'd use his teeth to make me sob. Shove his tongue in deep—add a finger, then two. Not because he was rushing to fuck me, but simply because he liked the sounds I made when I was full of him.

"Fuck," Alex swore. Evidently, we'd both been thinking the same thing. I shifted, grateful my jeans hid my arousal fairly well. Alex was not so lucky. His joggers clung to his cock, thick and trapped against his thigh. One of his hands drifted from the wheel to give it a squeeze.

I was tempted to lean over, pull his waistband down, and take it into my mouth.

But...I didn't.

I wasn't a one and done type of man.

I was a serial monogamist.

This was flirting, and flirting only.

"What about non-hobbits?" I asked, breaking the silence for a second time. Again, something that was entirely unlike me. "Gimli is my favorite—"

"Legolas," Alex blurted. "God. Those *legs*. I'm a leg guy for sure." He blinked. "Leg and ass—oh, fuck. His name's pretty on point, isn't it?" Again, he glanced at me, but this time his gaze scraped over my thighs. "Blonds too. I love blonds."

"Is everything that comes out of your mouth filthy?" I sighed, pinching the bridge of my nose.

"Mostly."

We chatted for another fifteen minutes, trading barbs back and forth. I learned that Alex was a secret nerd. Not even his sister knew about his anime obsession. A fact that immediately made me like him more, as I was a big fan of manga— Japanese comics—myself. I had a giant shelf at home dedicated to my *BoysLove* collection that no one had ever seen—not even Brendon. It was the one thing I hadn't wanted him to ruin for me, as he'd ruined most other things.

Eventually, we settled into comfortable silence.

I stole a few glances Alex's way. And in return, he was touchier than before. Simple, tantalizing brushes of his fingers along my thighs, across my shoulders, as he unnecessarily checked my seatbelt after we stopped for gas.

My stomach growled when we were getting close to the turnoff leading into the mountains. No doubt Mom was already at the cabins cooking up a storm. Despite this, Alex turned off the main road and headed in the wrong direction.

"Where are we going?"

Alex didn't explain himself. He smiled, dark brows twitching upward as he pulled into the parking lot of a local diner. After he flipped the ignition off, he twisted to look at me, that peculiar air of gentility hanging between us.

It was...addicting.

And I wasn't sure that was a good thing.

"You're hungry," Alex said, not giving me a chance to protest before he was out of his seat and heading around the car. To my surprise, he opened my door, gesturing magnanimously for me to head in front of him.

"You didn't have to open my door for me," I protested, my cheeks pinking up.

"True." Alex's eyes danced with mirth. "I did it because I *wanted* to." And then, because he couldn't help but ruin everything, he added, "After you, your majesty."

"Your...majesty?" I echoed, confused.

"You know. King George. King Arthur? Take your pick."

I laughed, unable to help myself.

Alex groaned, a hand slapping over his chest like he'd been shot. "*Damn*, you've got such a nice laugh." It was the exact same thought I'd had about him the day before.

"You're such a liar." I just glared at him, settling into our playful routine like it was second nature. When I exited the car and headed toward the cafe's front door, I resolutely did not look Alex's way. And if I smiled as I stomped through the parking lot, that was my business and no one else's.

Alex whistled appreciatively from behind me, trying to inspire another laugh. "Hate to see him leave, love to watch him go," he called, voice a silky rumble.

I flipped him off.

My secret smile remained.

The food was tasty. Greasy, but tasty. I enjoyed my fries a little too much, hiding my chewing behind my napkin as Alex demolished a massive mushroom Swiss burger. He wiped up the leftover sauce with one of the fries he'd pilfered from my plate, grinning at me as I rolled my eyes.

I ate slower than he did by a fair margin. My bites were normal bites, and his were gigantic.

"Like a baby bird," Alex cooed, leaning his head on his hand as he watched me. Heat simmered between us. But this time it felt more intimate. Alex's gaze was darker than before, assessing, like he enjoyed having dinner with me as much as I enjoyed sharing it with him.

A revelation for sure.

Alex's watch gleamed in the sunlight that streamed through the window, and I glared at him, frustrated it had taken me so long to come up with a comeback.

"Shut up. I do not eat like a bird."

"What?" he teased, his leg brushing against mine. "I never said it was a bad thing." He was messing with me again, his blue eyes flashing. "It's cute."

"I'm not a bird," I repeated.

"Chipmunk then?" Alex perked up, no longer resting on his hand. "I could see that. Though…there's another kind of nut I'd like to see you stick in your mouth."

I kicked him.

Hard.

He cackled like a hyena, reaching down to rub his shin as his dimples flashed. He sat back up. "There it is. My favorite Georgie face. Look at that little chin dimple—"

I slapped a hand over my chin, violated.

"So grumpy. So cute. God, I wanna bite you so bad." As he spoke, his fingers fiddled with his watch band, metal catching the light. The dark gunmetal color had a stark contrast with his tan skin. The waitress, who had been walking over to refill our drinks, paused, turned around, and walked back the way she'd come.

"You're terrorizing the employees."

"Giving them a show, is all," Alex replied, back to his regular bullshit. "Nothing to worry about, Prissy-Mc-Leggy-Legs."

Prissy-Mc—*what?*

"I'm not the one who's wearing a designer watch on a camping trip." Ha! Take that. I couldn't wait to see what he said in reply. I expected Alex to quip back, to flirt again, to smile—anything.

Instead, he clammed up, his eyes growing cold and far, far away. He slid his feet back to his side of the table. No longer within comfortable kicking distance. An invisible wall rose between us.

That same icy wall I'd met at the barbecue.

It wasn't until it was in place that I realized how open we'd been before it.

I swallowed the lump in my throat, regret pulling at my heartstrings.

What had I said wrong?

The...the watch?

What was so special about it? It was nice, yes. Designer, like I'd said. But upon closer inspection, it looked rather old. Chips in the glass, and if I didn't know any better, the time was incorrect.

I suppose it didn't matter, though.

Because I'd obviously fucked up.

This was far from comfortable. And way too close to the way I'd felt when I was with Brendon. I drew into myself, staring at the table, willing the chill in the air to dissipate.

"Sorry," Alex said, his voice less stiff than before. A pause. "Can I...touch you?"

I nodded. "You don't need to ask."

He certainly hadn't earlier.

His hand found mine. His skin was colder than before. I relaxed a bit, finding the courage to lift my gaze from the crack in the table I'd been looking at. The ice in Alex's eyes melted by the second.

"It's not you," he whispered, the reassurance helping immensely to soothe my panic. "You didn't do anything wrong." Alex observed me, a frown on his lips—not because of my comment this time—but because of the way I'd reacted to his displeasure.

I knew I'd shown my cards too obviously.

My fear of retaliation.

He was observant.

He'd seen.

His thumb swiped steadily along the back of my knuckles. A shaky smile spread across his lips. "The watch is a sore spot," he confessed. "Wasn't your fault. You didn't know."

I nodded, a sharp, jerky motion.

I wanted to ask him *why*, but I didn't. One good afternoon didn't make us any more than strangers. We certainly weren't friends. And if a single mention of the watch could turn flirty, chatty Alex into a block of ice, then asking him outright about it would be inappropriate.

I'd called him brain-damaged. I'd stabbed him. I'd taken everything he'd given me and responded in kind. But…I didn't actually want to *upset* him or make him uncomfortable.

If the swipe of his thumb and his reassurance were any indicator, that feeling was mutual. He'd snapped himself out of whatever had struck him, just to comfort me.

"I won't bring it up again," I promised, my voice far weaker than I liked it to be.

"You can," Alex said immediately. "I really am sorry. I didn't mean to scare you."

Had I been scared?

I…

Fuck.

"I wasn't scared," I lied.

Alex saw right through me. He gave my hand a tight squeeze, heat back in his skin and bleeding into mine. "I won't scare you again."

I wanted to believe him.

And I resolved myself to try.

As much as I complained, I actually kind of liked the way he messed with me. It made me feel alive. Like I was desirable. Not a broken husk of a person who didn't know who he was anymore.

Alex released my hand so I could finish my food. I missed the contact immediately. The waitress came over with the bill shortly after, and I quickly procured my wallet so that I could slip her my card before Alex gave her his.

He paused, card in hand, hovering.

"Split or together?" the waitress asked, tucking my card into her clipboard, waiting for Alex's as well.

"Together." I hurried to reply. Alex's gaze bore a hole into the side of my head. He studied me with an unreadable look on his face.

"Treating me on our second date? How traditional of you," Alex teased, lips tipping upward. Second date? When had our date first been? Brunch? The last of the lingering tension I'd been carrying since I fucked up slipped away.

"You wish."

We were the last of the main group to arrive at the cabins. There were four buildings, all knit together in a clearing surrounded by trees covered in leaves as pale as Granny Smith apples. The buildings were fairly large; though, despite that, it was clear the housing situation was going to be more complicated than I'd realized.

Especially as we pulled into the parking lot, and I was shocked to note that Roderick's family had begun to set up tents along the border of the meadow at the front of the central area.

"Tents?" I asked.

My tone had apparently betrayed my alarm because Alex took pity on me and answered without his usual teasing. "There were supposed to be six cabins, but the listing got double-booked. I had to switch locations last-minute, and this was the biggest place I could find."

"So, who exactly is going to stay indoors…?" I wasn't sure I wanted the answer to my question, but I asked it anyway.

"The wedding party. Bridesmaids, groomsmen, the older guests, including your parents—and Roderick's—as well as all the kids."

"And the rest of us?"

Oh fuck.

I did not like where this was headed.

"We're in the tents." Alex did not look disturbed by this at all. Though he did narrow his eyes at me, taking in my rapidly paling skin with curiosity—and dare I say it, concern?

Mortified to be so caught out, I gaped in horror at the nylon—tents were made of nylon, weren't they?—sweat-box monstrosities at the bottom of the meadow.

"I want to go home." I decided immediately, turning my attention back to him. "Take me back, Alex. I'll pay for gas. Hell, I'll pay for your time too. Think of it like being a Ryde driver."

"A *Ryde driver?*" Alex blinked. Then he laughed, that same lovely sound that had charmed before. "That's a new one."

His eyes said, *you're delightful.*

They said, *don't worry.*

They said, *I promise you'll be okay.*

His eyes were liars.

"It's really not that bad." His mouth was a liar, too. "Didn't you ever go camping as a kid?"

"Yes." I glared at him. "That is exactly why I know I'll hate it." I didn't actually want to leave and go back home to New York. It felt like admitting defeat, plus facing Brendon right after I'd posted that picture was a recipe for disaster. But the idea of staying here was just as unpalatable.

"It'll be fine." Alex's voice was a soothing rumble. He reached over to squeeze my shoulder, this time without asking permission. I was glad. It was unfair how the heat of his grip made me melt.

Stop it, heart, you traitorous whore.

"Why do you hate camping?" Alex asked, instead of dismissing my fears and forcing me from the vehicle.

"The bugs. The animals. The dark. The...*dirt*. It's all so...unpredictable." It didn't help that I'd lost my luggage and therefore only had like two outfits. Doing laundry would be a lot more difficult if I wasn't staying in the main cabins.

Alex's eyes narrowed as he drummed the steering wheel thoughtfully with the hand that wasn't turning me into goo. "Even though we'll be in tents, we still get to use the showers—so the dirt problem is easily solved. I've got bug spray if you need it, and the yard is fenced off to protect us from rogue critters. I think you're safe."

"What about snakes? Snakes can go under fences."

"How about this? If you see a snake, all you need to do is yell, and I'll come running." He was teasing me again, that humorous twinkle in his eyes. His confidence that we'd be okay was as reassuring as his words.

"Do you mean that?" I blinked, fiddling with my seatbelt. "That I can actually come to you if I...you know, need to?"

"Of course I mean that, Georgie. You have my word. If you need someone to take care of any big, bad creepy crawlies, I'll be your guy." Releasing the steering wheel, he held out his hand, his pinky extended. I narrowed my eyes at it, unsure how to proceed. "What? You've never done a pinky swear before?"

"Of course I've pinky sworn," I huffed. It was just…this felt intimate. Very intimate.

I swallowed, my heart fluttering as I reached out tentatively to lock our pinkies together. He smiled, clasping me tighter before releasing.

"What if your tent is way far away from mine?"

"Knowing our families? I don't think that's going to be a problem."

It wasn't until we were hauling our stuff from the car that it became abundantly clear that there were not enough tents for everyone to have their own. I hoped I didn't get paired with someone who snored. Or…god… someone who didn't use *deodorant*.

My family, I trusted to have good hygiene.

Roderick's? Not so much. I'd grown up with them, after all.

I went to find my mom, figuring she was the one who would know which tent I was in. Alex disappeared, flagged down by his sister and her gaggle of cowgirl boot-wearing bridesmaids. I couldn't help the way a flare of jealousy twanged inside my chest at the thought of a flock of women fawning over him.

Which was silly.

He'd flirt with a rock if given the opportunity.

Besides, it wasn't like Alex was mine to be jealous over.

Neither of us was looking for a relationship.

I didn't want him.

I didn't.

Not even as a practice boyfriend.

Shut up.

I found Mom knee-deep in blankets, arranging them over the cots in the cabin that was reserved for kids and grandparents.

"Do you know where I'm sleeping?" I inquired.

"Well, hello to you too, dear." Mom laughed innocently, like she wasn't a saboteur-ing saboteur. She gestured at the blankets. "Grab a few of these, would you? I can't reach the top bunks without climbing the ladders."

I was grateful she'd asked for help.

She was getting old enough that scaling up and down a bunch of rickety wooden rungs wasn't a good idea. Luckily for both of us, I was tall enough to reach without having to do any climbing at all.

Nodding, I obediently did as I was told. As I gathered bundles of blankets and placed them up high, she tackled the bunks below. After each bed, I glanced over at her, nervously awaiting her answer to my earlier question.

Maybe she'd forgotten?

Or maybe she was waiting until we finished to speak.

Because it was my nature, I fretted the whole time.

Hopefully, they'd pair me with Joe. That wouldn't be so bad. I loved Joe. It'd be brotherly bonding. Even Lacey and her phone addiction would be preferable to one of Roderick's stinky cousins. Perhaps I could convince everyone to let me sleep on the floor in the kids' cabin?

I could stand watch over them—protect them from…bears.

Or something.

The grandparents were too old to fight a grizzly.

It didn't escape my notice how ironic it was that I was debating signing myself up to be a defender against animals, when only half an hour previously I'd practically begged Alex to do the same for me.

Mom took eons to reply, waiting until I finished setting up the last of the bunk beds. Uncomfortably sweaty from all the reaching and tucking, I offered her a nervous smile.

"I think you already know who you're staying with," she said.

The color drained from my cheeks.

"No."

"It'll be good for you."

"Mom—"

"He's a nice boy."

"Yes, I know, but—" I shook my head.

"He'll take care of you." She reached out to rub my back. "I even made sure he had one of those little lamps so you don't have to be alone in the dark."

Fuck.

Fuck.

Fuck.

I walked from the cabin in a daze, my feelings at war. Was I relieved? Kind of. Was I horrified? Absolutely.

An entire week.

In a single tent.

With Alex.

Could I survive that? I mean…the car ride had been pleasant. And he *had* promised to protect me from snakes. So really, it was…convenient. But it also meant we'd be biting each other's heads off soon enough. And—and—*flirting*!

Oh dear.

Oh dear, oh dear, oh dear.

I had no idea which tent was ours, so I stood in front of the line of them, twitching every time something rustled in the distance. Snakes. Bugs. Creatures with maniacal, dirty little hands. Just dying to get their grubby paws all over me.

I might as well have a heart attack right now.

The trees shook as a gust of wind danced through the leaves, and I shuddered, my ears tucked into my shoulders. I shouldn't have come here. I should've pushed Alex harder to take me back. Why did I agree to this? What had I been thinking? Had it really not occurred to me that I might end up in the wild? *While camping?*

How stupid could I be?

"C'mere." Alex's voice rumbled warm and increasingly familiar as he sidled up to me from whatever dark pit he'd been summoned. His hands closed tight on my tensed shoulders just like they had earlier that day. He kneaded them as we walked. A bolt of lust shot through my body. "I'll show you to our bed."

"O-our bed?"

"Oops. Our tent. My bad." Alex's voice quaked with mirth. He was just as unsurprised as I was to discover our families had put us together. Despite my anxiety, I relaxed some. Oddly enough, I trusted Alex to keep to his word.

He'd pinky promised.

Twelve
Alex

I DIDN'T RECOGNIZE THE way George made me feel. Like a teenager but worse, because simply being in his vicinity inspired me to act in ways that were downright juvenile. I couldn't help but pull his proverbial pigtails. I also couldn't stop the surge of protective energy I felt when I thought about him and Brendon, or the apprehension that'd flickered when he'd mentioned all the things he didn't like about the great outdoors.

It said a lot about him that he was here despite this.

That he'd chosen to spend a week outside—doing activities he abhorred, more than likely—so that he could reunite with his family. I didn't know why exactly it had been so long since he'd been home. I still felt guilty about the watch incident and wasn't going to press for answers from George when today had already been stressful enough.

Protectively, I held his shoulders tight as I herded him toward the tent we'd be sharing. Though June had let me in on her evil "carpool" plan, the tent had been unexpected. Funny, seeing as I was the person that had planned the whole damn event.

She had tricks up her sleeve.

Wily, sneaky, evil tricks.

Luckily for me, somewhere between the "Hell is Real" sign and the florist we'd visited in Columbus, I had reached the conclusion that I no longer minded her meddling. As mortifying as my apology had been, it had done wonders for the uncomfortable tension between George and me.

I emphasize uncomfortable, because there was certainly still tension left behind—but the sexy sort. The kind that made my skin feel buzzy, and my dick half hard.

George remained stiff despite the way I rubbed circles into his tense shoulders. He was genuinely freaked out. Anxious puffs of air escaping. Wide eyes. His chest barely moved with each shallow breath. Part of me was tempted to take him back to Chesterton. Or maybe to my house? Where I could tuck him into bed, force him to watch *The Hobbit*, and order us steak.

But this was June's wedding.

And I wanted to be here.

Besides, I got the feeling that George didn't *actually* wish to go. He was the kind of man that didn't mince words. He took action. If he really didn't want to be here, he would've found a way to leave, with or without my help.

When we arrived at our destination, I pushed those thoughts aside. Mournfully, I released George's shoulders and leaned around him to unzip the tent door. Our tent was fairly large. Yellow, thick-walled, with a see-through panel in the ceiling to peek at the stars at night. It definitely had enough room for two people, though not much else. I'd bought it when June had made it her mission in life to trick me into going camping with her and Roderick on the weekends. Even considering our long legs, George and I would have plenty of space to stretch out. Sure, we'd be somewhat pushed together, but that was only part of the thrill.

A fact I'm sure had fueled June's decision to commandeer our sleeping arrangements. I swear to God she was getting ideas straight out of the books we'd buddy-read.

"You first," I said, forgetting for just a moment what a jumpy little rabbit he was.

George turned alarmed eyes on me, his lips wobbling as he pressed them in a thin, distressed line.

"You want me to go *first?*" The deep, throaty quake of his voice had my cock instantly perking up, despite how inappropriate that was. My mouth went dry. *Fuck.* For such a slight thing, George's voice was wildly deceiving. Low and delightfully melodic. You'd never expect a sound so deep to leave a man so delicate.

"You're right—I'll go first," I said immediately, stepping through the open flap and inside the dark tent. *Stop acting so horny,* I chided my dick in the privacy of my own mind. *He needs comfort.*

After checking the darkest corners for bugs or animals, and concluding the tent was safe, I turned back to the open flap where George was lingering.

"No snakes, bugs, or creatures of any kind," I reassured. "Come on in."

To hopefully put him at ease, I adopted an air of casual indifference. With a grunt, I flopped onto the camping mattress I'd set up while George had been off with his mother. It gave beneath my weight. Like I was coaxing a wild animal closer, my lips twisted into a friendly smile—that unfortunately felt like a leer despite my best efforts.

George didn't move.

I patted the space beside me in a way that I hoped was inviting.

After some tense deliberation, George finally reacted. He ducked his head in through the flap, his steely eyes narrowed on me and the surrounding space. He studied the tent's interior with his brows drawn into what could only be described as a suspicious scowl. He didn't step a foot inside, obviously still holding some reservations.

Okay, so patting the bed hadn't worked.

Maybe he needed more reassurance?

"I promise it's safe," I said, raising my pinky and wiggling it to remind him of our earlier pact. I wasn't about to go back on my word. Clearly, George trusted me well enough, because it was the pinky wiggling that finally broke through his fear. Stiff as a board, the long line of those oh-so-sexy legs slipped through the gap in the fabric. He stood just inside the tent with his back to the open flap, eyeing the interior distrustfully.

George looked two seconds from bolting.

His hands were twitching, his nose scrunched up in disgust as he eyed the musty sleeping bag his dad had foisted off on me in preparation for the night. The thing looked like it'd seen better days—scratch that...*decades*, really. All torn at the bottom, and stained, from years sitting on a shelf in his basement.

My own sleeping bag was easily twice the size of his, practically brand new, and perfectly clean where it cushioned my ass from its position on top of my mattress.

I was a lot more prepared than George's family had been. Not that they'd neglected him per se. He had a pillow too. Equally as old as the sleeping bag.

I suddenly wished I'd had the forethought to buy a second sleeping bag. Why I would have done that? I have no idea. My own setup was a lot more pleasant. The "nice" kind of camping mattress. The aforementioned six-hundred-dollar sleeping bag I'd bought because of its glowing reviews. Three puffy memory foam pillows, and a wireless space heater.

"You planned ahead," George accused, even though it wasn't my fault that everyone had opted not to warn him about the sleeping arrangements.

I couldn't say I was sorry he was stuck with me for the foreseeable future.

"This is not..." George trailed off. His expression shifted into something forlorn as he turned back to the still-open tent flap and the cabins outlined in shadows at the top of the hill. Several yards away, I could hear one of my cousins—Martin maybe?—arguing with his wife over how to properly put stakes in the ground.

Their voices were muffled despite being loud, so I knew if I kept my volume down, we weren't likely to be overheard.

"I know staying in a tent with me isn't what you expected." It was obvious he'd anticipated staying in the cabins. "I'm sorry." I felt guilty. If the original booking hadn't fallen through, he wouldn't have had to deal with any of this.

"It's…fine. I suppose." George bit his thumb, whittling away at the skin as he focused his attention back on me. The weight of his gaze was heady. It made something hot and fizzy quiver low in my belly. Like arousal, but softer.

He was still on guard.

I had no idea if it was me or his surroundings—either way, I figured a distraction was in order. He'd feel better if he got his mind off the animals lurking outside the fences surrounding the property.

Tomorrow night, there'd be a bonfire. It was going to be a big deal— s'mores, music, the works. June had requested a playlist of almost entirely country—gross—and I'd acquiesced. She was the bride, after all. Tonight was slower. Everyone was too exhausted from setting up to do anything but take it easy. Cousins, aunts, and uncles—nephews and nieces—all were still arriving and would be late into the night. Most of June and my family lived in the Columbus area, so it wasn't like it was a massive trip. A few, however, were flying in, just like George had.

The vast majority of the guests planned to attend the week-long festivities, but a handful, like my parents, were only going to be there for the rehearsal and ceremony.

Rising to my feet, I closed the distance between us. George's pulse jumped, and I had to bite back the urge to lick his throat as I leaned around him, reaching for the zipper. Our chests brushed. More butterflies filled my belly. I could practically hear the rapid thrum of his heartbeat. As I lingered, George was a deer in headlights, a panicked breath escaping his lips.

Like he wasn't sure what I was about to do.

His throat bobbed.

He was so cute.

Jesus.

I wanted to bite him so bad. To mark that pretty, pretty neck. To feel him swallow beneath my tongue, Adam's apple shuddering.

George's eyes were accusatory, questioning.

Right.

I was supposed to be doing something other than looming over him.

"Just shutting the door, Georgie Porgie," I explained. I took my sweet time, lingering where I probably shouldn't. He didn't push me off, though he did scoff at the new nickname as my fingers dragged the zipper down. "Gotta protect his majesty from all the bad, bad bugs."

"Bad, bad bugs," he repeated, like he agreed that they were evil and out to get him—even though I'd been joking. My face was level with his shoulder, then his stomach, then his crotch as I pulled the zipper into place.

Licking my lips, I forced myself back up, even though I desperately wanted to shove my face against his pelvis and breathe him in. Wanted to mouth his cock through the denim. Wanted to distract him for real—with my tongue, and my throat, and maybe a finger or two if his little hole could take it.

I didn't do that, though.

I was good.

Not entirely good—because I couldn't stop myself from hovering my hand over the back of his neck like I had earlier. "This okay?" I confirmed.

"I already told you that you don't have to ask," George sighed, annoyed.

Permission granted, I closed a hand around his nape and gave it a tight squeeze.

He smelled fruity. No Versace today. Was it because I'd pointed it out and made him self-conscious? I hoped not. Either way, his scent was delicious. There was a sharp citrus note to it that reminded me of lemonade.

George melted incrementally, sinking into my grip as his lashes drifted shut.

It was leagues away from how relaxed he'd been in the car, sleepy and dazed—but I'd take it.

I'd take whatever he wanted to give me at this point.

Practice boyfriend or not.

The rest of the night went by in a blur. I helped George ensure his sleeping bag was bug-free, and we spent a good hour in our tent decompressing. Not that I really needed to, but every time I rose to go, he'd get this frantic look in his eyes, and I'd quickly sit back down and play it off like I hadn't been about to leave at all.

June texted me a few times.

June

**Soooo? How's it going? Did you apologize?
What happened?**

We'd chatted a bit when I arrived, but it had mostly been logistics. I'd needed to set up my tent, and she'd given me hardly any time—considering she'd known all along that George and I would be "rooming" together. "Tenting" together?

Whatever.

Me

He accepted my pickles with grace.

June

!!!!

Me

Stop texting me. He's right here and it's rude.

June

Okay, okay.

Fine.

Second dinner was delicious. Potatoes in tin foil with mystery meat I was pretty sure was beef. He sat down at the table across from me with his family. June kept sending me sly looks, but was wise enough not to pry when we were within hearing distance.

Throughout the meal, Mrs. Milton asked George a plethora of questions. About his roommate, his cat, and about work. She seemed to be particularly interested in that. No doubt, so she could brag about him when she went back to work at the hair salon after the wedding had concluded.

With their freshly styled 'dos, the women in Chesterton would be returning home for the next six months with new "Golden Boy George" stories.

George was reserved as he spoke—going on and on about a campaign he was working on for a big-name company that he wasn't "allowed" to disclose. Mrs. M ate that shit up, obviously. As did I. But for different reasons. It was somewhat surprising to discover that George was creative. I couldn't tell if he worked in marketing, advertising, or design—but he seemed to know what he was doing.

Which was sexy.

Almost as sexy as his scrunchy, grumpy face.

Or his Type-A personality.

Apparently, he'd had to scramble to finish the project before he left. And when she oohed and ahhed, and Joe offered him a set of little brother heart eyes despite the lack of open expression on his face, I could see why George had been so desperate to come home.

Not once did he mention Brendon, or his creepy-ass texts.

Nor did he complain about his roommate, or the "shittiest year of his life."

If he hadn't outright said that to me, I never would have expected that he'd been having a rough time. He was the perfect older brother. Even Lacey looked impressed—and she was a tough nut to crack. The way his whole family hung on his every word fascinated me. He blossomed, practically glowing with pride at the positive attention.

It was pretty fucking cute.

And I could certainly appreciate how well loved he was.

Mr. Milton didn't ask any questions, but that was unsurprising. I'd heard him speak maybe five words in the entire time I'd known their family. He too listened intently to what George had to say, even if his interest was silent.

When the sun had gone down and everyone else had retired to their respective sleeping arrangements, I steered George toward our tent. He'd found the bathrooms on his own, and I'd caught him exiting, hair damp from a shower, golden waves soft and free of gel. He was wearing the most distracting shorts in the history of the world but I kept my thoughts to myself. Careful to keep my grip on his shoulders firmer now that it was dark, I breathed him in. His mother had told me that he had a thing about being alone at night. I didn't want him to feel scared. Especially not when I was around.

I'd already gotten ready myself—catching up with June and her gaggle of bridesmaids in the cabin that was reserved for them. They ate me up. They always did. Asking about my work, the wedding plans, and my hobbies—a never-ending ploy for attention.

June found it funny. She'd smirk at me every time someone would grope one of my biceps. It'd taken far too long to escape their clutches after liberally brushing my teeth and borrowing their shower. I was a bit worried I'd find one of them trying to sneak inside the stall with me, and made a mental note not to use that cabin's bathrooms again for the duration of my stay.

The groom's cabin would be less disastrous, but…I wasn't sure I wanted to try.

Besides…George was using the one delegated for the campers. It was a separate building, all wooden logs on the outside like the others, but fully updated inside. Clean too. Clean enough to pass even a "George inspection." I had a far better chance of catching a glimpse of him shirtless if I stuck to that one.

Back inside our tent with the flap zipped up, again—after a fair bit of innocent chest bumping on my part—I gave George's nape another, reassuring squeeze. He fit so good beneath my palm. An odd thought to have, yes, but no less true.

"Try to get some rest," I urged, directing him to his sleeping bag.

It felt wrong to leave him on the floor when I had a mattress. But when I opened my mouth to offer to share my bed, he glared at me like he knew exactly what I'd been about to say.

"I'm fine," he grumped. "Don't baby me."

"Wouldn't dream of it." I wanted to baby him, though. Really fucking bad. Which was confusing. Part of me wanted to just go ahead and do it. But…he hadn't consented to my earlier plan. And therefore, we were in this odd state of friendly-but-not-quite-what-I-wanted limbo.

There were lines I couldn't cross without him crossing first.

I'd rather not get lumped in with Brendon. Just thinking about him made me want to pummel something. His face preferably.

Climbing into my sleeping bag, heater turned on low, I twisted to watch George get ready.

His hair was still damp, curling across his forehead in slightly darker than usual blond clumps. He pushed it back in frustration. Bent over his sleeping bag so he could double-check that no creepy-crawlies had climbed in while we'd been helping everyone set up, the locks kept falling into his eyes.

"Everything okay?" I asked, only for him to level me with a glare.

"Stop asking."

Yikes.

Best leave him alone then. Though, that felt…really impossible.

It was going to be difficult to sleep knowing he was uncomfortable next to me. Eventually, after fifteen minutes of him fussing, George finally lay down. He pulled the sleeping bag up to his chin, closed his eyes, and feigned sleep—like he could fall unconscious through strength of will.

So adorable.

Fuck.

Even though I desperately desired to climb on top of him and lace kisses along the scratchy corner of his jaw, I didn't. I'd bet anything the stubble that'd formed would be gone in the morning. Which was…such a shame, really.

"Let's get some rest," I said, because I wanted to hear him talk again, and I wasn't sure what else to say.

"I can't."

"You…can't?" I frowned up at the dark ceiling before remembering—like an idiot—the lamp his mother had given me. I was quick to rise, hunting for it, and flicking it on. With it in the back corner of the tent, its soft, unobtrusive glow was enough to chase away the shadows.

"Better?" I confirmed, climbing back into bed.

"I hate that she told you about that," George muttered to himself. Deliberately, he shuffled around so his back faced me, obviously embarrassed.

"I'm glad she did."

"You're probably making fun of me in your head." He countered grumpily, his shoulders tense, the hair at his nape slightly more dry than the longer waves up top.

"I can promise you I'm not."

George didn't speak again. Not even to complain about his sleeping bag, or the cold, hard ground, or the fact that his pillow was flatter than a pancake and covered in water damage.

"Here." I tossed him one of mine. It hit his back, and he made the angriest little noise in the world, snatching it up and launching it right back at me.

"Baby, it's for your neck." The pet name slipped out before I could stop it. It was no surprise George didn't catch it, though. Instead, he assumed I was making fun of him.

"I *told* you not to baby me," he snapped.

"That isn't what I'm doing and you know it." Damn, he was stubborn.

There was just…something about George that made me want to treat him right, even if he was resistant to such care. So I chucked the pillow at him again, harder this time. He caught the pillow before it hit him in the face. "Throw this at me one more time and I'm going to strangle you in your sleep," he hissed.

"You know, you throw that threat around a lot," I hummed. George made an annoyed sound. "I'm starting to think without a pen to stab with, you're all talk."

"Alex." The way he said my name sent another fizzle between my legs.

Softening my tone, I wiggled like a giant caterpillar to the edge of my mattress so that we were only a few inches away from one another. "I can't rest if I know you're down there stiff and uncomfortable."

George's long, elegant fingers strangled my pillow, like he was imagining it was my neck.

"*Please?*" My voice dipped silky low. Woah. I don't think I'd ever begged. Especially not for something as silly as this. "Take the pillow. Get some *real* rest. You'd be doing me a favor."

He deflated, clutching the pillow tight and nodding. And then, like a grouchy cat, he beat it into submission beneath his head. When he'd decided it was abused enough, he turned on his side away from me, and settled down for the night again.

This time, he was far less stiff.

"Thanks," he said, voice quiet. Quiet enough that I wasn't sure he'd meant for me to hear at all. "For the pillow. And for…you know, earlier."

I hadn't expected gratitude. My heart tripped as I stared at his back, hands sweaty. I felt as off-kilter as I had the night before when I'd lain awake, desperate to figure out how I could get on his good side. "You're welcome."

Listening to his breathing made me relax. Despite myself, I dozed, the steady puff of George's breath soothing me. It'd been a long time since I slept beside someone else. Hook-ups were gone when the deed was done. It was a line I'd set for myself, so I'd never get my hopes up.

This was…nice.

So close to what I wanted, even if it wasn't.

Some time later, I was startled awake by the brush of cold fingers against my shoulder. The muted whirr of the space heater buzzed in the background. Outside the tent, crickets chirped, and the wind whistled through the trees on the edge of the property. Above, the mesh panel showed the stars above.

It took me a moment to figure out what was happening, groggy as I was.

"Alex?" George's voice was tight, trembling.

"Hmm?" I twisted to face him, blinking the sleep away from my eyes. George's silhouette in the dark was illuminated by the faint orange glow of his night light. My eyes were gritty, but I forced them open with a grunt.

"I think I felt something inside my…um…my sleeping bag." George sounded scared. I sobered. My brow furrowed. Immediately, I unzipped my sleeping bag enough that I could sit up. George hovered over my mattress.

"*Something* as in…?"

"Maybe…" George's voice was small, his bottom lip wobbling. "A bug? Or…"

Jesus.

He was adorable when he was freaked out. I was a *very* bad person for thinking that. Being self-aware didn't make it better. But I couldn't help the way I reacted to him. I ached to fix whatever was causing his current expression.

"Will you walk with me to the cabins? I think I'll sleep there. Maybe on the floor?" George sounded defeated. Mortified. Like the last thing he wanted was to appear weak in front of his family.

I latched on to his wrist, surprised by how cold his skin was. *Jesus.* How long had he been sitting on top of his sleeping bag before he'd decided to wake me and ask for help?

This wasn't like him.

The shivering man beside me was vulnerable.

Small.

The same man who'd frozen up after reading a text from his ex.

"Alex?" George frowned, clearly confused by my lack of answer. I gave his wrist another squeeze then gently tugged him toward me.

"Get in."

"*What?*" he squawked, but didn't fight very hard as I grasped his hip with my other hand.

"Jesus, you're freezing," I hissed as the cold night air nipped at my fingers, the skin on his hip just as chilly as his fingers and wrist had been.

"What are you doing—" George's voice was high-pitched as I yanked him where I wanted him. He tumbled onto my mattress with a startled huff. Quickly, I unzipped my sleeping bag the rest of the way. When it was open, I grabbed his slim waist and hauled him inside it.

"There," I hummed, pleased. "Better?"

George was a block of ice beside me. Slowly, he nodded, eyeing me warily like he wasn't sure what to expect. This way he wouldn't have to feel vulnerable in front of anyone but me—a thought I liked, maybe too much.

Half-asleep, I felt like a caveman.

Possessive over him, especially in his rawest form.

Once he was settled, I reached around him to zip us inside. He was shivering. I ignored my own discomfort, pressing so close to his chilly body, that I knew he'd warm up in no time. I arranged his limbs, his back to my chest, allowing him to keep his facial expressions private.

My bare pecs brushed the soft cotton of his t-shirt—I wasn't even sure when

I'd discarded mine—and my nose tickled the fuzzy strands of hair above his ears. I wanted to nibble on them—badly—but I managed not to through sheer force of will. An impressive feat, considering I was still in caveman mode.

"Get some rest," I said for the second time that night. "I've got you, Georgie."

To my surprise, George didn't protest. He stayed stiff as a board though, and I respected him enough to not cross that distance, even though the chill of his body against my chest made me want to rub some heat into him—in more ways than one, if you get what I mean.

This time, George was the one who fell asleep first.

Exhausted by his own nerves, George's body succumbed to sleep. His shivers settled. I made a mental note to crank up the temp on the heater the next night.

Like this, two peas in one pod, the scent of George's shampoo was even stronger. Fruity and as sharp as he was. Sweet, too. I shifted to get comfortable, very aware of the sleeping man cushioning my chest—and my uncomfortably hard cock that I was doing my damndest not to touch him with. Apologizing to my balls—which were about to become blue—I reached into the tight space between our bodies to grind the heel of my palm against my aching dick.

It didn't help. Unfortunately.

I just wanted George more.

Wanted to press my hips into his ass, catch my cock between his cheeks, grinding till his pajamas were sticky with sweat and cum and that pretty hole was clenching.

I wouldn't do that.

Of course not.

Not without his consent.

I refused to hurt George again.

I wanted to protect him.

The glimpses I'd seen of how…skittish he could be only made that desire more prevalent. I had the feeling that his ex had been more than "hard" to deal with. Made me so fucking angry. But I pushed the thoughts aside, doing my best to get back to sleep given the current circumstances.

Eventually, I did manage to pass out. Unfortunately for me—maybe karma? I don't know—my dreams were plagued with slick tongues and eager red cocks. With tight, wet little holes, and chin dimples. And sticky white streaks of cum. When I woke the next morning I discovered my hard dick pressed against the swell of George's supple ass.

Mortified? Guilty? Yes.

Surprised? No.

Fuck.

George made the sweetest noise as his hips hitched back into mine. As I stayed impossibly still, frozen, George's ass cheeks parted, and my cock slid right where it'd so desperately wanted to go the night before. It was a practiced movement. Like in his sleep he'd already done this exact motion countless times. Judging by how sticky my boxers were, it could've been going on for ages.

George pushed his pelvis back again, seeking friction. I could hardly breathe, terrified of moving now that my dick was effectively trapped, held hostage. His body was inviting me to rut into the tight, hot space—but it was simply that, his body. Not him. Despite wanting nothing more than to lose myself against him, I practiced self-control.

Yay for me.

Pulling my hips back so he couldn't reach, my dick pulsed in mourning.

The last thing I was going to do was betray his trust. Especially after he'd come to me for comfort the night before.

"George." My voice was lower than normal, scratchy from a combination of sleep and arousal.

George stirred, his long limbs stretching, his body loose and soft as his slutty ass shuffled back, hunting for my dick again. I had to grab on to his hip to stop him. Which ended up being a mistake, because his t-shirt had ridden up, and he was so fucking warm, all naked, soft skin. And my pelvis twitched forward of its own accord, a primal need to fuck rising to the surface.

"*George*," I repeated, strained. My hand spasmed on his hip, and he frowned.

When his eyes drifted open, all that sleepy relaxation fled. His cheeks blazed a ruddy, splotchy red. He glared at me, the sweet, scared man from the night before gone with the last dregs of indigo sky.

Horror dawned on him, his eyes widening the moment he realized he'd been the one grinding on *me*.

"I didn't—" I started again, unsure what I wanted to say. "I *wouldn't*. I stopped you. Not because I don't want to but because I—George, it's okay. It happens—it's—"

George was unzipping the sleeping bag before I could blink, or finish my sentence. His gorgeous ass was right in my face, sticky patch from my precum on the back of his shorts, as he crawled toward the tent flap. I groaned, salivating after him, before I shook my head to force my brain back on track.

"Wait, wait—it's okay—don't be embarrassed!" I attempted to reassure.

George ignored me, shoving his feet inside his sneakers as quickly as he could. He had nice feet. Bigger than you'd expect, lovely arches. Strong but delicate, even in the slutty knee-high white socks he apparently favored. God, what a nerd.

Sexy nerd.

Who could make a mean steak and loved *LOTR*.

"George, wait!" I tried one last time to no avail.

Without a single word, George disappeared out of the tent flap and into the crisp morning air. He left the door open, and I groaned, palm sliding down my face. I'd royally fucked that up.

He'd looked embarrassed.

Probably because he'd made such a point to tell me that he was not having sex with me—and yet, he'd been the one all up on my—

Stop thinking about that.

Or you will cum like a teenager right in your goddamn pants.

I was in no place to judge.

All night I'd been dreaming of how tight his little hole would cling to my crown as I drilled into him. The sugar plum fairy had graced me with visions of breeding his mouth, his ass, his hand—any part of him I could stick my dick into.

My thoughts were far from innocent.

I wasn't mad at him for touching me. He'd been unconscious for god's sake. I grunted, rising to my knees and crawling over George's abandoned sleeping bag to watch him go. Through the gap in the fabric I could see him striding confidently across the meadow toward the main cabin where we'd had dinner the night before.

Aside from the barely perceptible mark I'd left on his ass, there was no sign that he'd been grinding on me all morning.

Left reeling, and alone, with my dick pointing right at him, I had no choice but to retreat to my sleeping bag till my cock went down. I'd never been the kind of man who overthought. But I found myself doing so now, replaying the previous night—and this morning—over and over and over to try and figure out how I could have done things better.

Maybe I should've grabbed him? Forced him to listen to my reassurances? No.

That would've been rude.

Turning onto my back with a sigh, I reached up to scrub my hand over my face again.

When George thought of touching me I didn't want him to feel shame.

"Fuck." No matter how I played it, I couldn't think of something I could've done different. I'd just have to talk to him later, when he wasn't surrounded by his family or mine.

I tipped my head toward the still-open tent flap and my dick gave an overeager throb. When it stopped misbehaving, I got dressed in silence.

I didn't search for George, opting to skip breakfast to give him space as I headed off to find my sister.

With the morning sun came the promise of a new day, and I couldn't wait to see what it would bring with it. June was in her cabin, unsurprisingly. She was catching up on the book we were buddy reading—as she'd been six chapters behind me—with a plate of food that Mrs. M had apparently gone out of her way to deliver.

"Oh my god, *finally*," she said when I entered. And then, "What's gotten into you?" I stabbed her waffle, stealing a single, solitary bite before she beat me away with a growl. "Go find your own fucking food, gargantuan."

"Stingy," I sniffed, resolving myself to go hungry on the hike later today. I hadn't been sure I was going. Not until I realized it was the last place George would be—and I figured he could use the extra space. "I thought hobbits were supposed to be generous."

"My wedding, my waffles." June wagged her fork at me, ignoring the hobbit comment. "Now, fill me in. Mama needs her daily dose of drama."

I rolled my eyes.

I kept a lot of details out. Namely things I felt were too private to share or would embarrass George. And by the time I'd finished talking, June's smile had grown from happy to something so gleeful she belonged in a horror movie.

More attempted breakfast theft was dealt with by threats of death. June's mood had certainly improved now that we were out in the woods. None of her earlier moroseness remained, like a switch had been flipped, and only mania could exist during the middle of her wedding festivities.

She didn't talk about postponing again.

I was grateful.

And as I pushed aside the events from that morning, fending off bridesmaids and their handsy hands, I did my best not to dwell too hard on the fact that I'd swiftly moved from "not looking for a relationship" territory to "desperate for Georgie" in less than a day.

Thirteen
George

OF COURSE, BECAUSE EVERYTHING was just fucking *fantastic*, when I arrived to help with breakfast at the main lodge shit hit the fan. Not immediately, though. First, I served plates of food to children—strange ones and familiar ones—and plopped heaps of reheated pancakes on massive, hairy adult men's trays. All the while pretending like I hadn't woken up actively molesting Alex's dick.

It was hard to forget that last tidbit.

The guilt, shame, and confusion I felt made my cheeks permanently flushed. And even Roderick's cousin's lack of hygiene could not pull me from my thoughts.

Gaggles of people filled the long tables that took up the majority of the main log cabin that'd been delegated for meals and crafts. Most of the children were still sleepy, some of them even laying their tiny faces on the tables to nap while their parents chittered back and forth. Everyone was dressed in various pajama sets, but all were plowing through the food my mom, my siblings, and I had prepared.

Speaking of my wayward mother, she was currently heating a frankly terrifyingly massive amount of hot chocolate in the kitchen. I'd walked past her to get a refill for the bacon, and been momentarily floored by affection the second I saw her.

Her dress that morning was an eye-fuckingly bright neon yellow. Covered in tropical birds, her dress was nearly as obnoxious as the colossal pile of blond hair on her head. I swear to god it was somehow even taller than yesterday's beehive.

Mom was singing to herself as she stirred the pot, looking like an evil witch with her cauldron of sugar. The scent of cocoa was so strong I wouldn't be surprised if she accidentally summoned an Oompa Loompa. The current sight reminded me of an ad campaign I'd done once for a Halloween-themed cereal company.

Nostalgia warmed me from head to toe.

Every time we'd gone camping with Roderick's family when we were kids, the first thing we did in the morning was heat up a huge jug of cocoa. It was tradition—which made it less than surprising that she'd opted to include that particular treat for Roderick's wedding.

It shouldn't have been a big deal.

And it wasn't.

Until I was reassigned—no longer on plating duty—and relegated to the freshly set up "hot cocoa stand". There was a sign and everything on a small black chalkboard, Mom's handwriting effortlessly pretty, the words written in swirly white. She'd always had excellent penmanship, something that had inspired all of her children to follow in her footsteps. We were hellions growing up most of the time, but at least every last one of us had a passable signature—even Joe, and his massive-ass hands.

Atop the table was a giant thermos of the cocoa I'd watched her heat.

Running its length was a plethora of small glass jars full of a myriad of toppings: marshmallows, sprinkles, peppermints. Beside the jars sat enough whipped cream bottles to feed a small army. Which...I supposed we kinda were.

Between Roderick's family, June and Alex's, and all the randos, the place was positively packed. I'd say I was surprised by the turnout, but that would be a lie. June and Roderick were obviously adored.

Anyway, Mom didn't trust the teens and children to serve their own cocoa—which was fair—and meant that it was my job. At the front of the line was a group of rowdy teens. Judging by the dark hair, I figured they were probably from the James's side.

Pre-teens maybe? No. Some of them were too tall for that.

They were giggling, and as I settled into the repetition of filling mugs, my thoughts wandered. Back to the tent this morning. Back to how sleep-scratchy Alex's voice had been. And god...his dick. His dick had been so fat and thick and insistent—just as large as he'd hinted it was. Easily the same size as Nei—*fuck!*

Fuck, ow!

Fucking fucking fuck stick. Jesus Christ. Mother*fucker.*

That hurt!

When I glanced down, I realized I'd somehow—like a total idiot—poured near-boiling cocoa all over my fingers. Ah. Jeez. Fuck. *Ugh.* I wanted to swear, to stomp, to—to—*something.* But I didn't. Young ears were listening. After what had happened at the barbecue I refused to cause another scene. And cussing up a storm was a sure-fire way to do just that.

Shaking, pain making my vision fuzzy, all thoughts—okay, most thoughts—of Alex fled.

"H-Here you go," I managed through gritted teeth as I shakily handed the first teen his cup.

"Thanks, dude!" he said, stepping out of the way so the next teen-person could take his place. I grinned and bore the pain. Cup after cup, far more carefully, I finished my task. By the time the line had diminished, the pain in my fingers had morphed into a dull numbness. Which…unfortunately meant that the burn was worse than I'd initially thought.

But even then, *that* wasn't when the shit hit the fan.

No.

It hit when Joe came bounding into the mess hall, his arms held high in triumph, a gaggle of bobble-headed faux alpha-males trailing after him wearing…*hiking* backpacks. I vaguely recognized some of them from the barbecue, and also from serving them this morning, but not well enough to recall names. The hiking backpacks were a dead giveaway that something terrible, horrible, awful was about to happen.

Oh god.

No.

No, no, no.

Roddy was right behind Joe at the front, pleasant as ever. He fit in with my family better than I did. My chest gave a dull throb as I watched Joe herd him in Mom's direction. Which also just so happened to be *my* direction, as the breakfast table was adjacent to the cocoa one. I'd been lucky she'd been out of the room when I'd burned myself, or she would've caused a fuss.

"Mrs. M." Roddy was grinning, all cheesy and earnest, like he had when we were sixteen and he'd asked me if I "might like to dance with him at the prom?"

"Roddy!" Mom beamed at him, moving around the table to pull him down into a hug. She'd done the same to me when I'd walked in this morning. I knew firsthand how back-crushingly lovely her hugs were. Roderick laughed, returning the hug before releasing her and standing straight. "You're too skinny," she said as she moved back behind the table, dishing him up a heaping plate. "Here."

It was the same thing she'd said to me at the barbecue.

I had to cough to hide my amusement.

"Ha!" Roderick said good-naturedly, patting his stomach. "I don't know about that."

"Oh, posh." She'd been watching way too many *Great British Bake Off* episodes lately. Picking up the lingo. "Here." His paper plate was piled high as she shoved it toward him. There were definitely extra strips of bacon on there beside his eggs and pancakes.

"Thanks," Roderick beamed, accepting the food. The men behind him waited patiently. "Gotta keep my strength up for the big hike today!"

"Smart boy," Mom winked.

"You know it!"

"Are you going too?" Mom asked, turning her attention to Joe. He nodded, a short up and down. "Why don't you bring your brother? He could use some sun."

"I don't know about that," I replied quickly. I'd been wanting to spend time with Joe today, but hiking? Ugh. No thank you.

"Honey," Mom twisted to look at me, and my cheeks flushed anew. "Go have some fun! That's why you're here, right?"

Ha.

As if any of this was fun.

My thoughts—because they were assholes—slid back to the car ride with Alex and how much I'd enjoyed it. Also the pillow fight the night before. His apology pickles. And his big hand on my thigh—

Fuck.

Okay.

Maybe hiking would get my mind off of him? Hell, that was not something I'd ever thought I'd say. At the very least, it would keep me away from him until I had a chance to calm down. It might even…be a good thing. Then I wouldn't start panicking the next time I saw him. And I could slip in some solid big brother, little brother bonding while I was at it.

Win-win.

Alex's offer to be "practice boyfriends" continued to weigh on me. There were five days left till the wedding. Five days. And he'd be impossible to avoid even if I never said yes.

There was…a lot on my mind.

Maybe Joe could distract me?

"Okay," I finally conceded. Mom beamed. Roderick's eyes twinkled like he knew something I didn't. They shared a look that was less than subtle, but I was forced to ignore it for the sake of my own sanity. "Fine."

"Hell yes!" Roderick gave me a thumbs up, plate clutched in his other hand. "We're leaving in twenty. Meet outside cabin two. Wear a hat! And bring sunscreen."

"Will do."

Joe smiled at me.

Smiled.

I had no doubt that if the table wasn't between us, he'd try to break my back with another of his bear hugs.

"See you in a bit, buddy," I promised. He nodded, and the light in his eyes made it a lot easier to swallow the fact that I'd just agreed to go on a hike. My burns stung, and I ignored that too, focused instead on what I'd need to do to get ready.

Luckily, I'd packed a shirt with long sleeves. Unluckily, the fabric did nothing to conceal the burns on my fingertips. I pulled the sleeves down, trying to slide my fingers beneath, but that only seemed to make the fact I was hiding something obvious—so I stopped.

The numbness was still there, which made it easier to ignore, a blessing and a curse. It felt strange, like the really burned bits were all sensationed-out, but the parts of my skin that hadn't literally boiled off were still smarting.

I kept an eye out for Alex—but he was not in our tent or the bathrooms when I hurried to dress for the day. I debated treating my wounds, but didn't want to draw more negative attention to myself. If people saw them, what would they think? That I was inept as well as volatile. Brendon's voice was as loud as ever in the back of my mind.

You're too fussy.

I left the burns alone.

Luckily for me, I'd packed a few sets of shorts in my backpack along with a single pair of jeans, so I could be more comfortable as I moved. I'd run out of clothing soon, but for now I was covered.

I hadn't seen Alex at breakfast.

Which of course had made me begin to stress.

He's not avoiding you.

He's with his sister.

The bride.

Because that would be logical, I told myself, even though part of me still remained worried.

I was supposed to be avoiding *him,* not the other way around.

Maybe he was off managing…something? Like he had when we'd run errands together. All effortless confidence and poise. Alex always seemed to know exactly what to say to get what he wanted. I'd watched him charm the florist out of a mental breakdown.

Empathy was not something he lacked. Nor was it possible to ignore how good at social engineering he was.

Which only served to remind me how embarrassing last night had been.

He'd probably seen right through me.

Thinking about how stupid I'd looked squirming into his sleeping bag because of a fucking *bug* made my skin crawl. There were *so many reasons* to stay away from him I was beginning to lose track.

Which was why I was shocked-horrified-elated to discover Alex waiting at cabin two for the hike with the rest of the dude-bros. He offered me a grin that I did not return.

Fuck.

There went my plan to avoid him.

Right down the drain.

Honestly, why was I surprised? Nothing on this trip had gone to plan. Not my backpack, not my suitcase, not our sleeping arrangements.

Half an hour later, the sun had climbed high enough it dripped through the trees. Bursts of heat passed over my skin every time I stepped between the shadows. I was the slowest in the group, which was unsurprising, but I was content to linger at the back.

Avoid, avoid, *avoid*, that was my new motto.

Joe stuck to my side. He was as stoic as always, thick and silent as the trees we passed. Every so often, he'd point out a bird in the trees, and I'd jump, terrified of the great outdoors and all its perils.

"Magpie," he grunted when a black and white bird hopped along a log to our left.

It was…admittedly beautiful. A lot less intimidating than most other wild creatures, that was for sure.

Animals weren't afraid of Joe. They flew in close—one time, so close, I was worried a robin was about to land directly on his head. Like he was a Disney princess.

I asked him questions to fill the silence. About his farm fund. About his hunt for land. About whether or not he was interested in living anywhere but Vermont. To which the answer was maybe.

Apparently, there were a lot of birds there.

And farms.

And our…second cousin? Baxter Baker lived there. Not that I'd ever met the man, as Mom said his side of the family—aside from him and his daughter—were not the nicest people.

Which made it enticing.

"I want to be like you," Joe said, blue eyes caught on the branches above. "See the world. Expand...horizons."

He thought way too highly of me.

"I'm not all that great," I confessed. Joe shook his head like he didn't believe me. Without skipping a beat, he moved on. Eventually, even Joe, with his blank-faced patience, grew tired of slowing his pace. He left me to fend for myself at the back, working his way to the front, ahead of Roderick to scout out the trail.

I was relieved not to have the pressure of his attention, but I missed it all the same. Especially because now, without him to distract me, every fucking noise made me jump.

Alex was also ahead—no surprise there.

He hiked along in the noon sunlight, like climbing this goddamn never-ending hill was child's play. Wearing another pair of frankly delicious black joggers, his ass flexed with each confident step. A backpack was slung easily over his broad shoulders, sweat building at his nape and spine, making his white cotton t-shirt stick to his skin, translucent in some places.

This was like...hiking porn, honestly.

Alex cackled at something Roderick said, their familiarity obvious. His head tossed back, thick throat exposed to my starving eyes. He acted as though they'd done this hundreds of times. Like they were brothers already. Alex threw an arm around Roderick's shoulders, tugging him in close as one of the unnamed dark-haired cousins joined in the teasing. Alex's t-shirt slipped up a few inches, revealing tan skin at his lower back, the dimples above his ass framing his spine.

Stop ogling.

I moved my gaze upward again, somewhere safer as I huffed and puffed along, dodging small craters in the earth that looked suspiciously like rodent homes.

Or worse.

Snake holes.

Alex wasn't the only one sweating up a storm by the time the men leading the pack of stragglers decided we deserved a break. I was moist. Which was *not* a feeling I liked. My thong had been riding up the entire fucking hike and I hated myself a little because somehow I hadn't predicted the underwear would be an issue on top of everything else.

Worse? My nipples felt chafed.

Paired with the wheeze of my lungs and the burning in my legs, I was having a hard time remembering why I'd thought coming on this hike was a good idea.

Joe had wandered off.

I hadn't gotten away from Alex.

I had not reached emotional clarity.

I was sweaty and miserable and…lonely, despite being surrounded by people.

There was a creek up ahead. I could hear its tinkling babble as I collapsed onto a boulder just off the trail and shook out the pins and needles in my feet. I hadn't worn hiking shoes. The only shoes I'd had were my loafers from the airport. They were not outdoor shoes. I was lucky my mom had had a new pair of tennis shoes in my size laying around. She'd claimed they were an old Christmas gift she'd forgotten to give me.

They were new, not even close to broken in—and definitely not meant for hiking on uneven terrain. I swear to god it felt like I was going to roll my ankle every five seconds.

Stretching out my legs, I mourned the fact I was not with Mom back at the tables in the main cabin, helping the kiddos with arts and crafts.

I hated this.

I hated it so much.

A bee buzzed by my head—or maybe it was a wasp?—and I startled, swatting at it. Wait. I froze, realizing that swatting was *exactly* what would incite the heinous creature's wrath. A very unhappy noise squawked its way out of my throat.

"Fuck off you buzzy bitc—"

Which was, of course, when Alex finally decided to grace me with his presence, all shiny white teeth, and dimples. The wasp flew away, thank God. My shame remained.

"You good?" he asked, studying my red face and wide eyes. He was probably already regretting his choice to approach me.

I almost lied and said I was fine, but then I remembered how much he said he hated liars and figured the truth would only cost me a bit of pride. I'd abused him enough for one day and it was barely lunchtime.

"There was a bug," I sighed.

"Ah." Alex bit his lip, obviously trying not to smile. "Sneaky little things, huh?"

"I didn't see it coming."

Alex clucked his tongue, his amusement only growing. "What kind of bug?"

"A…*buzzy* one." Wasp or bee. I wasn't sure. "Murderous, probably."

"Probably." Alex lost the war with himself and laughed. Except it didn't feel like he was laughing at me, more like laughing…with me? Or…at the very least, finding joy from my particular brand of fussiness. "I have bug spray in my backpack if you want some. Won't help you against murderous-buzzy ones, but will make sure your cute ass doesn't get bit by mosquitos."

"Mosquitos?"

"Because of the lake, Blondie. Didn't you read the itinerary?" Alex sat down beside me on the boulder, his thigh pressing into mine.

"Do I look like the kind of person who doesn't read itineraries?" I sniffed. "I didn't receive one. I would've read it if I had."

"I can find one for you somewhere if you want," Alex offered.

"That's unnecessary."

"Suit yourself."

His body was warm. As warm as it'd been this morning when I'd—no no no. Stop thinking about that. Sneakily, I glanced down at Alex's legs and the python he had hidden between them. It'd felt big. Really big.

Fuck.

My mouth watered.

"Water?" Alex asked after rustling around in his bag. He waved his fancy insulated metal bottle at me. It was name-brand. Because of course it was.

I hadn't brought one, even though I knew Mom had a cooler full.

Like an idiot.

"Thanks." I took the bottle because as much as I hated relying on him—again—I was, in fact, rather parched. I popped the cap open, then paused, realizing with a flicker of heat that Alex had just put his mouth on this. Which meant if I put mine there, we'd be sharing germs.

Like…an indirect kiss.

"I don't have cooties if that's why you're hesitating."

"Shut up," I scoffed. Kiss or not, I was thirsty. I took a long, languorous sip. Didn't want to take too much, so I left it at that, the cool water spilling across my tongue, wetting my dry, dry throat. I sighed when I finished, reluctant to give the bottle back because the chilled metal felt like heaven on my sore fingertips.

"I figured you would've stayed behind," Alex said, rustling around some more, presumably for the bug spray. "I didn't take you for the hiking type." His words rankled but he said them in such an open-minded, non-judgemental way that I couldn't really take offense. It was simply a fact, not an insult.

"I'm not."

"Then why come?" Alex found the bug spray, and I reluctantly handed him back his water bottle so he could tuck it away.

"I'm here to spend time with Joe."

Alex glanced around pointedly, the lack of Joe in my surroundings evident.

"You sure you weren't out here trying to avoid me?" Alex quirked a brow, and I hated that I'd already decided not to lie to him. Because I definitely wanted to.

"Maybe a bit."

"You know, this morning—"

"Let's not talk about this right now," I cut him off, cheeks red. "*Please*. People could hear and—and—"

"Yeah, okay." Alex agreed easily. "Later, then." He didn't push me, which was weird but nice. Just like his behavior last night had been, and the day before. "When we're alone."

Oh god.

I was going to have to be alone with him again, wasn't I?

We shared a tent.

"Roll up your sleeves," Alex urged. "I'm gonna get you covered in no-no bug juice."

"No-no bug juice?" I arched a brow. "What are you, five?"

"Apparently." Alex smirked. "Got you to smile, didn't I?"

"Oh."

He was right.

I *was* smiling.

Huh.

"Whatever."

I glared at him.

Then I did as I was told, rolling up the sleeve on my right arm. I was careful not to allow him to see the burns on my fingers, lest he judge me.

Alex was, as always, very handsy as he helped spray me for bugs. He dealt with my left arm, pushing up the fabric so he could get at bare skin, fingers firm and sure. Somehow his touch was even more electric than before. And his scent—Christ, his natural musk made me feel like I was going crazy every time I got a whiff of it. All clean sweat and sunshine.

He had to have some crazy pheromones because I had *never* in all my life been more tempted to climb on top of someone and rub myself all over them. I knew firsthand what it felt like to be squashed up against all that bulk. Strong. Squishy in all the right places. Hard in others.

I swallowed, once again distracted.

Get your mind out of the gutter, George.

Change the subject.

"Do *you* like hiking?" I asked as I tipped my head away while he sprayed my exposed arms and legs. The smell was awful. Which was unsurprising. I tried not to breathe it in.

"What gave me away?" Alex winked. I narrowed my eyes at him, and seeing my ire, he elaborated. "I didn't get to do this a lot. Dad was busy when we were growing up, so June and I didn't branch out much with our hobbies till we were adults. We've tried a lot of things together since. Travel. Et cetera. But camping and hiking are her favorite—hence why she wanted me to rent out a glorified summer camp for her wedding. She drags me out all the time with her and Roderick."

"You spend a lot of time with each other?"

"Oh, yeah. She's my best friend." Alex said this with no hint of self-consciousness whatsoever. He fanned a hand over my arms to dry the bug spray. "Right out of high school, we went backpacking together. Spent a few days in Utah climbing through Zion, some time at the Redwoods, and Yellowstone. Went to Central America at the end, hiked Machu Picchu. We don't go nearly that wild anymore—both of us are mostly homebodies—but we find time to hang out even when we're home."

"Wow." Very outdoorsy then. That paired with his admission on the plane that he liked sports, and I was swiftly realizing that Alex was more unhinged than I'd hypothesized. I mean…who chooses to do any of that? Insane people, that's who.

"You don't have to look so disgusted," Alex teased. I hadn't realized my nose had been scrunched up until I forced it to relax. His skin was hot as he rolled my sleeves back down when I was sufficiently dry.

The innocent touch made my skin tingle.

"I'm not disgusted, I just…" I shuddered. "I don't see how you could voluntarily put yourself in that position."

"In the position of going outside?" Alex was obviously trying not to laugh.

"Yes."

"Almost like you're doing right now," he pointed out.

I elbowed him.

Hard.

Alex chuckled, the sound rolling over me. He leaned into my side, and I felt the tickle of his dark hair against my ear as he spoke. "I don't mind that you're not outdoorsy, Georgie. For the record, I like that about you."

I didn't know what to say so I just said, "Fuck off."

This wasn't fair.

I wasn't supposed to find Alex charming—or to enjoy talking to him.

And what the hell had happened to my irritation? That was more rational than the riot of butterflies in my stomach.

Alex booped my nose playfully.

Which was violating.

And also…begrudgingly *adorable.*

My heart was wobbly, which was not at all comfortable.

Maybe I really was going to have a heart attack out here in the woods.

"Thanks for the no-no bug juice," I joked, surprising myself. "And the water."

"Anytime, Georgie Porgie. Was my pleasure." Alex really looked like he meant that, too.

"Why don't you go find someone else to terrorize?" I grimaced.

"Worn out my welcome?"

"When were you ever welcome?" I snarked. Alex laughed, tossing his head back, his throat bobbing. Not to compare, but it was an even sunnier laugh than the one he'd graced Roderick with earlier.

"Touché," he replied.

And then he was gone, rising from the boulder and loping away just as quickly as he'd arrived. Even though I'd been the one to banish him, I kinda missed his grin as I rose to my already sore feet. Joe was at the front, gesturing Alex and Roderick forward. Apparently, our break was over and it was time to torture ourselves some more.

Except…the hike didn't feel nearly as horrible now that I knew Alex and I were okay. He hadn't seemed weirded out or uncomfortable. He was his usual, insufferably endearing self. Ew. Endearing? When had I started to think that?

I still needed to apologize for this morning.

But that could wait until we didn't have an audience.

I picked up the pace, no longer dragging my feet as we made our way to the creek. Maybe this hiking thing wasn't so bad?

Famous last words.

Fourteen
George

THE BABBLING CREEK WE needed to cross was as beautiful as it was intimidating. Lined with foliage, the shore dotted with sandy pebbles, I should've been stunned by its beauty. But instead, all I could think about was how embarrassing it would be if I fell in front of all of these people.

Or god forbid—a water snake leapt at me as I crossed.

There was so much that could go wrong. The rocks that had been used to create the stepping stones that spanned the width of the creek were fairly close together—and large enough it should be easy to step on them—but that didn't mean that I was going to *successfully* do it.

Especially not with an audience.

Lingering at the back of the group, I could feel my apprehension growing with every person that leapt across the water. Joe was at the front, stalking forward like a hound on a hunt. He didn't stumble, blue eyes focused on the path.

By the time it was my turn to cross the creek I could hardly breathe, I was so stressed out.

Don't fall, don't fall, don't fall.

Waiting till last had not been the smartest idea. I'd attracted far too much attention standing frozen, letting the gap between me and the person ahead of me grow wider and wider. Across the water, Joe's adoring eyes found mine. He gave me a thumbs up. A gesture that I'm sure was supposed to be encouraging, but wasn't.

It only made the pressure climb higher.

I was a grown-ass man well into his thirties—this should not be so hard for me.

I was so fucking frustrated with myself.

The creek was only ten feet wide. And at most was three to four feet deep. I could swim. And even if I couldn't, standing on flat feet on the creek bed would easily keep my head and even my chest above water. And though logically I knew this, fear still wrung its fingers tight around my throat, compressing my airway.

What if I slipped?

What if I fell?

What if I didn't go at all, and proved to everyone—including myself— that I was a coward? Fuck. Why had I decided to come on this goddamn hike? There was no choice I could make that would save me from potential mortification. And the only person I could really blame was myself. Sure, Mom had urged me to come, but I'd been the one who said yes. I knew she wouldn't have actually forced me to.

At least...I hoped?

Anyway.

There was nowhere to go but forward. Steeling my nerves, I took a big breath.

"You've got this!" Roderick yelled, sincere but humiliating. I wasn't a kid. I didn't need encouragement.

Alex was already on the other side, having been one of the first to make the journey. He didn't yell or give me a thumbs up like Joe had. And when I made the mistake of meeting his gaze, I could see real, genuine concern flickering in his pale blue eyes.

Maybe that's what made me finally move.

The fact that—and I hated to admit this—I had the feeling Alex would make sure I was okay by the end. He'd pinky promised.

Besides, I *could* do things.

Even though my brain sabotaged me sometimes, I'd survived every one of its treacheries.

"One step at a time, George," I murmured before taking a deep breath. "Just move forward." The first rock was easy enough, barely half a foot from the shore, and not slippery in the slightest. The second was just as effortless. The third was less flat, but ultimately not horrible. Halfway across the creek, my spirits began to lift.

This isn't so bad.

I can do this.

"Hell yeah! Go, Arthur, Go!" Roderick yelled, another misguided attempt to be supportive. Unfortunately for both of us, his words startled me, and I wobbled. Shit. Without thinking, I glanced up at the crowd, which turned out to be another mistake.

Ten feet away on the other bank, Alex was watching me like a hawk. A lock of dark hair had slipped onto his forehead, sticking to the sweat beaded there like he was stocky-Clark-Kent. Expression creased with concern, Alex took a hesitant step toward me. His gaze dropped to the water and his eyes went comically wide, eyebrows shooting up.

What was he—

I followed where he was looking, terrified of what I might find. I'd definitely never seen Alex make *that* face before.

There. In the water.

Gliding smoothly near the surface with its head poking out about a foot from the rock I had been about to cross onto.

A snake.

Distantly, I recognized it as one of the ones my dad had taught me about when we'd gone camping when I was younger. He'd called it…a northern water snake? Or something like that. Said it was non-venomous, even though the bands on its body often tricked people into thinking otherwise.

They liked to sun themselves on rocks. We'd seen a few before—and I was sure that was where this one was headed. Right to the stone that I was headed toward.

I froze.

Even my lungs stopped working.

For a moment, I might have even blacked out.

"George!" Alex called, keeping his tone even for my sake. The smooth timber of his voice should've soothed me but instead, it just proved that I was *not*, in fact, seeing things. There really was a snake blocking my path. The exact creature I'd been terrified I'd encounter.

And there it was.

I had to go back.

There was no way in hell I was going forward.

But I couldn't seem to get myself to move.

The tinkling of the creek did nothing to distract me from the danger ahead. *I need to go back.* I had to. I had to, I had to, IhadtoIhadto.

Realistically I knew that snakes weren't evil. They were animals, just like cats or dogs or even birds. Not nefarious. Hell, some people even kept them as pets, willingly. I knew all of this—but that didn't change the way my body reacted.

"What's going on?" Joe called, giant himbo that he was. "Why isn't he moving?" This was directed to Alex, or Roderick? I wasn't sure who. Without waiting for a response, he shouted, "Why aren't you moving, George?"

I couldn't answer.

My words were as frozen as my body was.

I couldn't stop watching the snake with naked fear.

Alex said something, but I didn't catch it, my gaze caught on the wiggly creature that had just innocently made its way up onto the rock itself.

Slither, slither, slither.

"Jesus Christ," I gasped.

"Georgie!" Alex's voice was louder now, but I didn't turn to look, entranced by my would-be assassin. He was pretty, I could admit that. All shiny, water-dotted scales. "You're okay, baby. He can't reach you. You just need to go back the way you came, okay? It's going to be fine."

Right. Alex was my snake-champion.

My woodland protector.

He'd get me out of this mess.

He'd *promised*.

Except—what had he said? That I needed to…I needed to holler? I couldn't holler. I couldn't—I—

"It's alright." I must've breathed or something equally alarming because Alex sounded relieved. "Just breathe, sweet pea. In and out. Remember our promise?" I nodded jerkily. "I got you."

He kept saying that.

It was like his catch phrase.

And I believed him every fucking time.

The rest of the crowd faded away, my brother included. There was only Alex's disembodied voice, the snake, and me. The snake simply stayed where it was, innocently existing on the rock like it didn't plan to attack at all.

I sucked in another breath, then forced it out in a whoosh.

"That's so good," Alex praised. His voice sounded closer, accompanied by sloshing. "You're being so brave, Georgie." The praise sent a shiver down my spine. Or maybe that was the terror? Hard to tell. "Breathe again for me, okay? In and out, nice and easy." I breathed. "There's a good boy."

Warmth flooded my limbs.

Another shiver.

This one was maybe—probably—because of Alex.

"Now, I'm gonna keep my eye on the snake, okay? I just want you to move back one stone, okay? Just one."

"But what if he doesn't like it?" I hardly recognized my own voice it was so brittle.

"He doesn't mind," Alex reassured. "He's just taking a nap, don't you worry." I knew he couldn't possibly know that. Wasn't like he was a snake mind-reader, but the reassurance still helped. Even though it was illogical. I breathed again with Alex's urging. "You've got this. Just one stone, okay? Just one. I believe in you, Georgie."

I believe in you, Georgie.

I wasn't sure anyone had ever said that to me aside from my parents. It certainly hit different now that I was an adult. It'd been a very long, very lonely decade since the last time someone had said something that sweet to me.

"Just one?" I echoed, shaking so hard I had no idea how I'd get my body to move.

"Just one," Alex promised. "That's all I'm asking."

His voice was even closer now.

There was a loud splashing noise to my left that sounded an awful lot like a giant fish was disrupting the water. Alarmed, I twisted to look only to see Alex himself—the fish in question.

He was half-submersed, the water up to his belly. Only five or so feet away, and far enough from the snake not to disturb it. Why was he…*why was he in the water?* That splashing noise sounded again as he pushed forward.

"You're okay, I'm almost there." Alex's voice was a comforting rumble. It made my cold, shaky hands clench. I was so stressed I couldn't even feel the burns on my fingertips anymore.

Looking at Alex had been a mistake.

Because when I glanced back at the rock with the snake, he'd moved. A high-pitched horrible noise escaped me. "It moved. Oh my god, oh my god."

"He's just getting comfy for his nap," Alex reassured. Why did this not rankle? He was babying me, just like I hated. But it felt so…so good in my current fragile state.

His eyes said, *trust me.*

They said, *I'm going to keep you safe.*

They said, *I don't lie.*

Finding my courage, I forced myself to move.

I kicked a foot backward, searching with my toe for the stone I'd vacated. I couldn't look away from the snake again—not when it'd moved the last time I had. When my foot met solid stone, I exhaled sharply, settled my weight, and moved the rest of my body. With more distance between me and the snake, it was easier to breathe.

"Do you want me to hold your hand?" Alex asked, now right beside me. I hadn't even noticed he'd arrived. "To help keep you steady."

I nodded jerkily, holding a hand out blindly for him. His skin was wet when it found mine, and yet despite that, his hand was as hot as ever.

"You did so good, sweet pea," Alex coaxed. "We just need to do one more, okay? Just one. I'll be with you the whole time." I wished the rocks were big enough for him to climb up here with me, but I knew they weren't. His hand was nice though. Firm and steady. I held it so tight I was fairly certain he'd bruise.

"Just one more," I repeated, cottoning on to his trick, but not calling him for it because it was *working*.

"Easy peasy," Alex agreed.

I whined, a sharp, brittle sound, because nothing about this was easy. I could feel the crowd looking at us, and I kind of wanted to die. This was worse than the airport. Worse than Neil out in the open. Worse than the matchmaking— and the scrutiny my fight at the barbecue with Alex had incited.

"Don't you worry about them," Alex said, as though he could read my mind. "You just pay attention to me, okay?" It wasn't a suggestion, it was a command. I nodded jerkily. "Good boy," Alex said for the second time that afternoon. "The only person you need to pay attention to is me. I'm going to take such good care of you."

"O-okay." More warmth settled over me, helping to ease some of the frigidity in my limbs as Alex directed me onto the next step. It was hard to do so backward, but I wasn't ready to look away from the snake yet.

"One more," Alex urged, predictable as always. "Squeeze my hand. That's right. There you go. Lift that pretty foot up—yep. Perfect. Damn, look at those sexy legs go," he was teasing, and it worked.

A startled laugh escaped me.

"Well, that was gorgeous. You have such a pretty laugh, you know that, right, Blondie? The prettiest. Like an angel or some shit. Okay, there we go. Now settle your weight. Damn, you're so good at following orders."

"Shut up." I didn't want him to shut up. I didn't want him to stop. Everything was so much easier and better when he was talking to me.

"One more," Alex promised, ignoring my reprimand. "Where's that cute foot—ah! Hell yeah. Okay. Back we go. Back it up—" I glanced down, and he waggled his eyebrows at me. I laughed again. "Last one." Alex urged as I settled. "Then we're home free."

He was soaked, water up to his belly. His white t-shirt was totally transparent. His eyes were the same crystalline blue as the creek below. Alex's reflection rippled, dotted sunlight painting him like a god of mercy.

I lifted my leg up, stepping back just as I had the previous times. I strangled his hand tight, tight, tight with my own. And then—because even with Alex's help, I was apparently incapable of escaping unscathed—my equilibrium shifted. Distantly, I recognized that I'd missed the step but…it didn't hit me what that meant till cool wind whipped my cheeks and my body smacked the water with a distinct splash.

Snakes.

I should've been thinking about how cold the water was, or the fact that I was drenched—or all the diseases I could get from getting my wound wet with unfiltered water—but instead, the only thing I could think about was *snakes*.

As I scrambled to figure out which way was up, all I could do was panic.

I hated myself a little then, but…that feeling wasn't new.

Before I could accidentally drown myself in the shallows, strong familiar fingers wrapped around my wrists, dragging me up, up, up. It wasn't far, but it felt like miles and miles of endless water.

When my head popped free, my eardrums were clogged. I spluttered, and my blurry gaze met the glacial blue of Alex's dark-rimmed eyes. He looked tired—something I hadn't noticed until now—like he'd had as rough of a night as I had.

"I've got you," he promised like he had last night. "Up you get."

Part of me wanted him to carry me away from all of this. Rescue me like a damsel in distress so I didn't have to think about how humiliated I was about to be—or the fact that the snake was still slithering away behind us, possibly coming closer.

But the other part of me recognized how helpless I already felt. Weak in the face of my own short-comings. All I had left was my pride, and even that was as flimsy as a rubber-necked dog toy.

Alex slung my arm around his broad shoulder and bodily dragged me out of the water and up the steep bank. The silt was slippery beneath my feet, covered in algae and muck. I tried not to think about things like leptospirosis or giardiasis—both waterborne diseases—as Alex murmured reassurances in my ear until our feet hit solid dirt.

Water dribbled cold down the back of my legs as my shorts clung to my thighs. I could breathe some better now. Maybe because we were away from the snake? Or maybe because Alex was a solid, protective wall of heat against my body.

"You guys okay?" Roderick hollered, but I ignored him, my face red, my hands shaking. "George? You good?" He sounded stressed, which was cute—

but unnecessary. Mostly.

Embarrassed, embarrassed, embarrassed.

I'd looked like an idiot, pinwheeling my arms like that, nearly drowning in the shallows. Quaking, I didn't reply, too cold to do anything but let my teeth chatter.

Alex would do the talking if I stayed quiet. Again, it was strange that I trusted him so much, and so quickly. It didn't make sense. But I couldn't seem to stop, even after acknowledging how strange my reaction to him was. As much as he pushed me, I just…couldn't believe that he would hurt me.

Besides, if I opened my mouth, I'd start swearing. Or crying. Both?

"We're fine!" Alex called. "We're gonna head back. Get some dry clothes. Maybe find some lunch before you fuckers return and eat it all." He sounded way too cheerful for a guy who had just been dunked in ice water. He gave Joe and the rest of the party a jaunty wave. "See you later!"

I knew he was doing this for my sake. And as the crowd laughed at his joke and Roderick flipped him the bird, no one looked at me. Alex had officially stolen their attention. To save me. Again.

"George—" Joe growled in question. I looked up at him, touched when I realized he was concerned. "Should I come?" He glanced toward Alex, a silent question. I still wasn't sure how much of the matchmaking he'd been involved in—maybe not as much as Mom, if he was offering to accompany us.

"You keep going. I'm fine." I was surprised the words came out loud enough he'd be able to hear over the babbling creek. He nodded, a knowing glint in his eyes.

I was not going back with Alex because I wanted to be alone with him, dammit.

And then Alex was leading me away, our soaked bodies clinging together as we headed back down the path the way we'd come. He was sturdy at my side, supporting me even though I didn't need it. We left a trail of water droplets in the dirt—like fucked up Hansel and Gretel.

Alex didn't stop right away to ask me if I was okay, somehow understanding that treating me like I was fragile in front of everyone else would only make me feel worse. I was already a one-man train wreck. The last thing I needed was to bring more attention to myself.

Instead, he simply helped me along the trail. When we were out of earshot and no longer visible, hidden behind a swath of green-leafed giants, he slowed the pace. Alex shifted gears swiftly. His muscles flexed as he quite literally hauled me back to the boulder we'd occupied when we'd taken a break earlier.

The sun had made its surface even hotter, the dry scratch of stone under my ass centering me in the present. Dripping and miserable, I allowed Alex to manhandle me where he wanted me. Which was sitting legs squeezed tightly together, my weight off the ground.

I glared at him because if I stopped glaring I was pretty sure I'd cry.

I didn't want to hate myself even more, so that wasn't an option.

Now that the shock of what had happened was wearing off, it was hard not to admire the specimen of a man in front of me. The truth was, Alex was gorgeous always—but wet Alex? In a see-through shirt? Jesus Christ. This was another thing entirely. Better than porn, really.

God, I was such a perv.

Alex was as drenched as I was, but he wore it like an underwear model and not a bedraggled rat. His joggers stuck to his shapely thighs, highlighting his quads. The same quads I'd repeatedly drooled over.

Unbidden, my eyes drifted upward—only to be assaulted with a view of his lovely flushed nipples. They were hard, pushing against the fabric of his shirt where it clung to the thick swell of his pectorals. I wanted to nip them. But not as much as I wanted to lick the water that dripped in rivulets down his ropey forearms. He looked cold, hair clinging to the tan, gooseflesh-dotted skin. His watch glinted, just as soaked as the rest of him, and immediately guilt cinched tight around my throat.

His watch had been submerged.

Because of me.

But he didn't complain.

Instead, Alex's chest heaved as he sighed. It was a long, gusty sigh, like he was as relieved to be away from the group as I was. Then with no warning at all he shoved my thighs apart with his knees, crowding into my personal bubble without a care in the world. Like it was his favorite place to be. I couldn't help but be reminded of one of our first conversations—

"I like your personal space," Alex had said on the plane ride to Ohio, and that statement had never proved more true than it did now. My stomach fluttered nervously. I unconsciously wanted to snap my legs back together to preserve my dignity—but that was silly. And besides, having Alex between them like this was…Christ.

"Your watch—" I panicked.

"Broken," Alex shrugged. My eyes widened in horror, I clenched my hands tight, then gasped in pain when the pressure exacerbated the burns on my fingers. "No, *no.* Not by you. Or this. It's been broken for years."

Why the hell did he wear a broken watch?

Quickly trying to cover up the sound I'd just made, I tipped my head back to meet Alex's gaze. Confused, turned on, and mortified all at once, I recognized that not all of those things were Alex's fault. Though…it would almost be too easy to slip into old habits and blame him anyway.

He'd like it.

I'd push, he'd push back.

We'd banter and fight.

I'd storm off down the mountain, running from him and what he made me feel.

But…

Alex didn't look like he wanted to tease, or play, or fight right then.

Not with his lips drawn into a thin white line. There was a lovely wrinkle above his brows that I'd never noticed before. Worry lines. Alex's tongue was bright pink as it flickered out to wet his lips.

All I could think about was what that tongue would feel like against mine.

I had no doubt that Alex was a good kisser. He had a silver tongue, had made it clear he enjoyed eating people out, and was cocky enough there was no way he didn't have the skill to back it up.

Would his lips be soft?

Yielding?

Or hard and commanding? Like he knew better than I did. Like he knew how to take care of me. How to push me to the edge, and lift me over it. Like he knew how to catch me when I fell. Like it was a pleasure to carry me.

Did I…want him to kiss me?

His mouth is so close.

It would be so easy to cross that distance.

Alex's eyes were full of concern. Pale and gorgeous, rimmed with shadows cast by his unfairly thick, black lashes. Without panic blinding me the dark circles beneath them were even more apparent. He hadn't slept well. It was written all over this face. Why? Because of me?

The thought made a pit form in my stomach.

"Lemme see," Alex commanded.

"Let you…"

Apparently I was too slow, because Alex wasted no time reaching for my cheeks. He held my face as he tilted my head this way and that. At first I had no idea what he was doing, my mind still unfortunately in the gutter. He inspected me liberally, behind my ears, my throat, my arms. I watched the way his chest moved with each breath.

"What are you doing?" I asked, but Alex didn't answer at first.

"I'm making sure you're not hurt," he finally said after he'd finished yanking at the neckline of my shirt to hunt for bruises.

"Oh."

Minutes passed as Alex took the time to part swathes of my wet hair, searching for injuries I already knew he wouldn't find. It wasn't like I'd fallen all that far, or been in the water for all that long. But still…I appreciated his concern.

Brendon had never done anything like this for me. Never worried over me. Never taken the time to fawn and fuss.

"I'm fine," I reassured, my eyes hot for a new reason.

It wasn't until I'd felt the inverse of the way Brendon had treated me that I truly realized just how little he'd actually cared. We'd been a couple for eight years. Eight fucking years. And not once could I ever recall feeling this…important.

This cared for.

It was the same with the stepping stones. The way Alex had supported me, the way he'd encouraged me, the way he'd…he'd…taken *care* of me. I…I'd never had that. I hadn't known how badly I needed it until he showed me what it was like.

Was this a taste of it would be like to become Alex's practice boyfriend?

Shaken by my own thoughts, I didn't even realize that Alex had moved on.

Now he was feeling around my back for bruises. It wasn't until that moment that I realized his inspection was going to lead to the discovery of my burns.

I winced.

"Does that hurt?" Alex inquired, concerned.

"It's fine." I shrugged. With every touch of his sure, confident fingers my pulse kicked up a notch and my traitorous stomach danced with butterflies.

No one had ever looked at me like this before.

Ever.

Alex continued to explore, and I let him, too dazed to do anything but obediently bend to his whims. By the time he found my burned fingers my fear of discovery had somewhat faded. I'd known this was coming. It was inevitable.

What I didn't expect was his response. I figured he'd do more clinical back and forths, maybe tell me I needed some Band-Aids—or even ignore my burns entirely since they weren't anything serious.

But he didn't do any of those things.

Instead, Alex's voice went quiet.

Dangerous.

"George." There was no room for argument in his tone. "What happened?"
He squeezed my wrist. With long tanned fingers, he pulled my injured hand up
so I could see the blobby little burn bumps. I shrunk back. Alex gave my wrist
a reassuring squeeze. "When you sat on the boulder you made a sound. *This* is
why," he rightfully deduced. Like the whole reason he'd been hunting my body
was because he'd heard that tiny fucking noise and couldn't leave it be.

"I burned myself."

"When?"

"This morning?" I tried to pull my wrist back but he didn't let me. I felt
like a naughty kid. "When I was helping with breakfast. It was just hot cocoa.
Nothing to worry about."

"Why didn't you treat the burns?" Alex's eyes were stormy.

My toes curled in my soggy tennis shoes as I shook my head. My cock, of
course, decided now was a great time to twitch despite the cold. I glanced
away, horrified. A grasshopper buzzed by, and I jumped.

"*Why?*" Alex questioned.

I squirmed.

A new kind of shame bubbled up inside me. Shame that I hadn't taken care
of myself. Shame that I'd been more concerned about what people thought
of me than my own health. Shame that I had a first-aid kit and hadn't used it,
simply because I was worried the bandages would attract too much attention.

Once again, when I tried to snatch my wrist away, Alex held tight. His free
hand rose to cradle my face. He tipped it gently toward him until I had no
choice but to meet his gaze. The storm in his eyes had softened. And beneath
that, all I could see was genuine worry.

Again, I didn't know what to do with that.

It made me feel small and large at the same time.

"I...didn't..." I stalled, unsure what I was trying to say. Surely I wasn't about to admit the truth?

"You didn't, *what*, George?" God, even now he sounded gentle, despite the edge in his voice. George. Not Georgie. That's how I knew this was serious.

The truth spilled free before I could stop it.

"The bandages are too noticeable. I didn't want to be 'fussy George' again. I wanted to slip under the radar. I wanted to be…normal. To…to fit in. I didn't want to be seen as high-maintenance."

"Fussy George?" he trailed off, processing my words. Even though he'd just been repeating me, hearing the old nickname on his tongue made me flinch. I knew Alex didn't *mean* anything by it—but fuck. I'd heard that term so many times from Brendon that it physically hurt to hear it out loud again. Like a knife had sliced directly into my heart.

Clearly I'd outwardly reacted because Alex's softened. "You don't like that," he stated, his thumb rubbing a soothing circle across my cheekbone. "That name upsets you."

I bobbed my head in agreement. "Brendon used to—It…it doesn't matter."

"Okay." Alex exhaled sharply. He debated with himself before he gave my cheek one last swipe with the pad of his thumb and released me. "I won't make a big deal about the burn, but I want you to let me treat it when we get back to camp. I understand why you did what you did—but I'm not going to allow you to remain in pain. I'm not Brendon—your *health* is what matters to me. Besides, anyone who thinks you're 'high-maintenance' because you got hurt is a fucking asshole. If someone bothers you I'll take care of it. All you have to do is say the word."

I melted a little, warm despite my chilly clothing.

He was right.

Of course he was right.

"We can use the first-aid kit in my backpack," I whispered. "I'll let you help."

"Good," Alex softened. "No complaining, George. I mean it."

I nodded again, echoing him, "No complaining."

"Good boy." The praise warmed me from head to toe. Alex ruffled my hair, messing it up even more than it already was. I scowled at him, but his sunny smile was impossible to resist. Especially when he called me *good boy* like that. Still though, I reached up to smooth my hair down with my uninjured hand, attempting to fix the rats nest on my head.

When I was done, Alex tugged me to my feet. I stood there awkwardly, dripping. When he turned his back to me, bent over, and patted his shoulders expectantly it took me a second to figure out what he wanted.

"My fingers are burned, I didn't break my leg. I don't need you to carry me," I huffed. Now that we were no longer within make-out distance my mind had already wandered back to snakes and other creepy crawlies. I was a bit jumpy after the creek—but I felt like that was justified, all things considered.

"You'll feel better if you're not worrying about all the critters out here."

I blinked.

Okay, mind reader.

"I'm heavy."

"Not for me," Alex replied immediately, still waiting. His ass was pushed out, and my gaze slipped to it, a small groan spilling free. Apparently, Alex thought the groan was because I was annoyed, because he spoke again, in that firm tone that made my knees feel like jelly. "I'm not going to ask again. Get on my back, Georgie. *Now.*"

Georgie again.

Good.

"Okay." I didn't fight him this time. Instead, I obediently wrapped my arms around his neck and hopped up. Not gonna lie, it was surprising how easily he took my weight—even though he'd reassured me he could.

"This way you can relax," he added, and I could hear his smile in the words. "Rest those grumpy lil eyebrows. Give your grimple a vacation."

"My grimple?" I repeated, belly flip-flopping as Alex stood straight.

"Grumpy-dimple. Grimple." He readjusted me, and I squeezed tight, a gasp exhaling against the back of his tan neck. Unlike me, he was not lobster-red from the sun. Though, he did have a tan line that looked particularly kissable. A drop of water wandered down his nape and it was so…so tempting to lick it.

How the hell was I supposed to relax like this—with my wet body clinging to all his supple, equally drenched muscle?

Knowing me, I'd get a boner any second. It was Murphy's Law. Worst-case scenario always. Gah. And now that I was thinking about boners it was almost impossible to stop my mind from wandering again like it had earlier that day when I'd been serving breakfast.

Fuck. Alex smelled good.

He always did. But today was even better than yesterday.

I resisted the urge to bury my nose in the back of his neck, but only just. Maybe if I nuzzled him a bit he wouldn't notice? We could chalk it up to forced proximity and the steady thud of his footsteps.

"I know what will help you relax," Alex said after a brief pause. We'd gone a dozen yards or so, which I still felt was quite a feat considering how much I weighed. I was slim, but denser than I looked.

"What?" He could probably feel how stiff I was.

"Close your eyes."

"And let the creepy crawlies sneak up on me? No thank you."

"That's why I'm carrying you," Alex reminded me. "So no creepies can get to you."

"Right." Huh. Okay. So that argument was out the window.

"Close your eyes, Georgie," Alex urged. It wasn't a command this time, merely a suggestion, but I followed it anyway. Against my better judgment, my eyes drifted shut. Every time we stepped into a patch of sun my lids would turn a brilliant red. I waited for a minute, expectantly.

"Okay," Alex said. "Now listen."

"Listen to what?"

"To the woods."

"This is stupid," I huffed.

"Georgie," Alex laughed, fed up with my bullshit but amused regardless. "Just do what I say."

"Fine." I breathed in. Another sunny red puddle. More shadow. Chirping. Rustling. The crunch of Alex's feet on the path. A bird sang somewhere high above. Maybe one of the ones Joe had pointed out? Unconsciously, I felt myself begin to relax.

"What do you hear?" Alex asked after several minutes of silence.

"Nature," I responded stupidly. "Birds. Um. The wind?"

"That's my favorite," Alex replied, voice soft and almost wistful. "Sometimes when I'm overwhelmed it's the only thing that calms me down."

"Oh." I peeked an eye open to look at his nape again, then swiftly shut it, letting the noises of the forest wash over me again. This time, I didn't speak for a longer period. I absorbed every chirp, enjoying the whistle and woosh of the branches shifting above. "It's…"

"Nice, right?" Alex murmured. I got the feeling he was listening too.

"Your eyes aren't shut are they?" I worried.

"No." Alex laughed and it rumbled through his back, vibrating through me. I squeezed him tighter and he hopped a little to adjust me again.

"Maybe nature's not so bad after all," I conceded, giving him an inch because he'd been nothing but lovely today and he deserved it.

"Maybe I can teach you to love it," Alex said thoughtfully.

"Fat chance of that," I scoffed.

"Fine. Maybe I can teach you to hate it less," he corrected himself.

"Maybe." I didn't tell him that he just had. That for the first time in my life I could kind of understand why someone would willingly come out here in the woods. It was…peaceful. The rest of the world faded along with my worries. Brendon and my past felt so very far away at present. And the birds, the squirrels—the forest was near.

It was a simpler place.

Softer.

Alex and I didn't speak again for the rest of the trek back to the campground. At least not about much. On occasion, I'd point out a bird I heard, and he'd murmur his pleasure and tell me he'd heard it too. But aside from that, we simply enjoyed the woods for what they were. And that horrible, awful, mortifyingly embarrassing event at the creek didn't feel so horribly awful anymore.

Alex's steps never stuttered, even if they did squelch.

He never dropped me.

And as I listened to the steady thump of his heart, my cheek pressed to his back, I couldn't help but think that maybe…just *maybe* our matchmaking families were onto something, after all.

Fifteen
Alex

THERE WAS NO DENYING that George and I had reached a turning point. It hadn't taken long—the close proximity we'd shared since we'd met had definitely helped. He didn't react to me the same way he had the first day—like he expected me to hurt him. Now…his glares were softer. A silly thing to say about a glare, yes. But still true.

Like he was wary, rather than uncomfortable.

In my book, that was a win.

I'd set George down before we'd entered the meadow, of course, well aware of how bruised his pride already was. I doubted he wanted anyone else to see him vulnerable. And though he stood tall and strode forward with his head held high, George stuck close to me of his own free will—my new adorable, soggy, leggy shadow.

George was silent when I'd taken him back to our tent to gather dry clothes and his first-aid kit.

The majority of the wedding party was out on the hike, and the children and the remaining adults were in the main lodge doing arts and crafts until lunch was ready, which meant that George and I had the communal bathroom all to ourselves.

Made up of logs—like everything else was—the bathroom itself looked like something out of a catalog. Fancy tile. Multiple sinks. Everything was impeccably clean. The back wall housed a line of separated shower stalls that *actually* had hot water. And the toilets were in a separate building entirely at the back. Which meant, no one had to listen to anyone else shit while they got themselves clean.

"You need help?" I inquired, setting our dry clothes and the first-aid kit by the sink. I was careful not to inflect too much concern into my tone. I didn't want my head bit off. But more than that, I didn't want to ruin the tentative truce between us. George had asked if that was what it was, and I'd been lying when I said it wasn't.

As fun as I found pushing his buttons—and boy, wow, *was* that my new favorite hobby—the last thing I wanted was to make him feel unsafe. There were invisible lines I didn't cross. And I was grateful for my natural people skills as it was intuition and intuition alone that was keeping me from accidentally hurting him.

Our conversation in the woods kept replaying in my mind. Believe me, that was surprising. It would've been easier to focus on how sexy George had looked with his shirt soaked through, and his hair slicked back. Instead, I thought about the way he'd flinched when I'd said the words "fussy George"— like it physically hurt to hear the name out loud.

It was obvious that mentioning Brendon was painful.

I'd never wanted to punch someone more.

I didn't intend to bring it up again.

There was a glob of toothpaste in the sink—from one of the kiddos if the stepping stool still placed in front of it was any indication. I stared at it, so I wouldn't ogle George through the glass. It took him a second to reply to my question, another indicator that he was still feeling wrong-footed. I could hear him rustling around, probably checking the showers for bugs. Or pulling his soaked shoes off. Maybe both.

"I've showered without your help for thirty-three years," Georgie sniped. Good. If he was getting snippy it meant he was returning to normal. "I think I can manage with a few little burns on my fingers."

"Holler if you change your mind," I replied, not taking the bait. "It's no trouble at all."

"You just want to see me naked," George muttered under his breath, quiet enough he probably didn't think I'd heard him. But I had.

"Ha, ha, touché." This time, I did look at him. I was grinning as I found his reflection in the mirror. Just as I'd suspected, he was inspecting another shower stall, working his way down the line so he could pick the best one. "I'm serious, though. If you decide you need—"

"*I don't need help,*" George rebuffed for a second time. And then, like a disgruntled rabbit, he stomped his cute foot and marched into the stall he'd picked fully clothed. He shut the door harder than was necessary—which I only knew was an accident because he immediately called out a shy apology, totally at odds with the way he'd stormed off.

We were lucky it was a hot day in the summer, or a dip in the creek could've been a lot more dangerous for the both of us than it had been. Hypothermia could be deadly for someone as lean as George. I was pretty sure there wasn't an ounce of fat on him—not that I was one to speak, given the intensity I trained in the gym and how anal I was about my diet most days.

My physique was born from hard work, mental illness, and deep insecurity. George's appeared to be genetic.

He looked like his sister, Lacey. They were both tall and lean like their father, whereas Joe and their oldest sister, the one I'd only seen pictures of but never met, resembled their mother's natural width.

George tossed his clothes with a wet *plop* over the shower door. A flare of heat curled low in my belly at the thought that he was naked and only a few feet away. A single door without a lock separated me from all that damp, lovely skin. My fingers itched with the urge to tear it open, press George into the chilly tile, and distract him the best way I knew how.

Blowing out a breath, I glared down at my dick, willing it to stop being such a horny bastard for once. It went against everything I was to admit this, but…I could honestly say the last thing I wanted to do was fuck Georgie right now.

I know, I know.

Shocking.

I just…I knew he needed comfort—and a friend. And I couldn't really do or be either of those things if my dick was shoved so far up his ass I could feel it in his stomach.

Ugh. *Man.*

I really needed to stop thinking about that or I was going to get in trouble.

Now that George was taken care of, it was time for me to worry about myself. Which was difficult when my dick was hard. As I entered the stall right next to George—because I was a masochist, apparently—I swear I could hear the soapy swish of his hands as he cleaned himself.

Stop it, stop it.

I turned the water to ice cold in the hopes it would make my dick go down. My clothes were already drenched, why should I care if they got even more wet? I bit back a gasp as the water hit. The warmth felt good on my chilly body. I spent a solid thirty seconds calling myself an idiot in my head while I struggled to wrangle my sopping shirt off.

Even considering my idiotic move to drench myself again, I managed to shower faster than George did. I had no doubt it was because he was as meticulous with his personal hygiene as he seemed to be with everything else. Not that I wasn't—because I was.

June made fun of me constantly for that. As if it was a bad thing, when it was the opposite.

"Checking for leeches?" I teased, a towel slung low around my hips. I'd already dried off, so now I just needed to retrieve my new clothes so I could change. It would've been convenient if there was a covered shelf inside the stall or something for them, but alas, despite being nice, the bathroom was not *that* fancy.

George exited his stall a second later, and I paused, the bundle of clothes I'd just retrieved tucked in one arm, abs tightening at the sight of all that creamy damp skin. He had a cute belly button. Christ. And his hip bones—there was a freckle on one that begged to be bitten. It'd look so pretty framed by teeth marks. Flat belly, almost concave, prominent ribs, and perky pink nipples—

I licked my lips, suddenly parched.

My cock perked up. It tented the front of the towel, pointing right at George.

"Put that thing away," George sighed.

"I can't help it." I laughed, embarrassed. When I glanced up at George's face, he was smiling. Ah. So not all that offended then. In fact…he even looked, dare I say, flattered?

"I need to…" George made a gesture to his pile of clothes—that I'd been blocking.

"Sorry." Like an idiot, I jumped out of the way.

He had the upper hand. I hadn't meant to give it to him. But he didn't abuse it. He didn't even admonish me again as he stalked past me to grab his new outfit, and immediately retreated right back into his shower stall to put his clothes on.

I mourned the loss of all that skin, but shoved the thought aside. Shaking my head at myself, I mirrored him and headed into my shower stall to change.

This time, when we exited, we were fully clothed and my dick had decided to behave somewhat.

A miracle.

"Fingers," I said, because I needed to get my mind back on track. "I need to take care of your fingers."

"They're fine," George waved me off. In response, I closed the scant few feet between us and caught his wrist. It was frail so I held him gingerly, careful not to squeeze too tight. George's eyes went wide before they darted away and a healthy flush covered his cheeks.

"They're not fine. I thought I made it clear that I was helping you. You agreed." I tipped his hand toward myself, studying the swollen digits with concern. "You don't need to pretend it doesn't hurt for my sake. Hell, I'd rather you cry than fake being okay."

George opened his mouth to argue. He was reluctant to admit just how bad they actually hurt—like it was difficult to accept help, even when he needed it.

"I'm not going to judge you," I promised before he could, needing him to know that he didn't need to be perfect when I was around.

"Everyone judges everyone. It's human nature."

I supposed he was right, so instead of fighting him about it, I nodded. "Okay. Fine. But I'm not going to judge you for *this*."

George's eyes met mine again and a war waged between us. He did that a lot—stared into my eyes like he could read my mind through them. I wondered if he could. If he could see my intentions as plainly as I could see his discomfort.

Maybe so.

Maybe Brendon had been unpredictable.

Maybe George read people the way I did. But where I used that skill to keep people at a distance, George used his to stay safe.

Two sides of the same coin.

"Fine," he acquiesced verbally, though he still looked mildly uncomfortable. "You can help me."

I relaxed, grateful now that we'd come to an understanding. George was quiet as I worked, his ass on the counter between sinks, his hand in my grip.

Wasn't like I knew a shit-ton about first aid or anything, but I'd been alive long enough to learn how to treat a basic burn. Besides, I'd been a Boy Scout—and I figured whatever courses I'd taken to earn my first-aid badge would kick in when I needed them to. Like learning to ride a bike.

"How's that feel?" I asked when I was finished and George's fingers were covered in white non-adhesive bandages. I'd done a pretty damn good job, if I did say so myself. The bandages looked neat, all perfectly spaced. And most importantly, they were protected. The heavy layer of burn ointment I'd coated them with was trapped inside where it could do its work.

"Better," George admitted. Some of the tension in his frame had eased. Maybe he'd been extra prickly because of the pain? That would make sense.

Now that he was taken care of I was tempted to address the elephant in the room—this morning and the cock-against-ass debacle—but I didn't want to make his hackles rise again, so I stayed quiet.

I'd finally gotten on his good side.

At least...I *hoped* I'd gotten on his good side.

"Let's get food," George said, surprising me when the words came out almost like an invitation.

"Really? Together?" I blinked.

He nodded, sliding off the counter and out of my personal space. The whole walk back to the tent George held his pile of wet clothes away from his body, refusing to get damp again. I did the same, so I didn't blame him. We were quick to abandon the clothing, and even quicker to zip the tent up behind us, back in the midday sun once more. George put his loafers on so his sneakers could dry. He looked ridiculously darling in a new set of long socks, loafers, and shorts.

The shorts were a revelation.

God's gift to mankind.

I'd nearly choked on my tongue the first time I saw them. I'd had to force myself not to stare, just like I was doing now—resolutely looking ahead so I wouldn't drop to my knees and start licking from his knees up his thighs.

George didn't touch me, but he also didn't shy away as I laid my hand on his lower back and urged him toward the main lodge. Lunch was being served, and my stomach was a cavernous empty hole.

"Are you hungry?" I asked. I was curious why he'd invited me to spend more time with him. I'd assumed he'd run as far and as fast from me as possible— just like he'd done every other time he'd been vulnerable in my presence.

"No," George said. I frowned. His back bunched beneath my hands, the ripple of muscle tantalizing. "But *you* are."

How the hell had he known that?

I must've side-eyed him because he answered my question without me having to ask. "You didn't come to breakfast. And you went on the hike with an empty stomach. You're probably starving," George explained.

Huh.

I paused, honestly floored. No one ever paid attention to my needs. I wasn't used to it. For a second, I didn't know how to process what he'd said at all. And then just as quickly, I forced my feet to move again, my heartbeat oddly fluttery. "You noticed that?"

"Of course I did," George quipped. "That's not healthy, you know. If we're speaking about health—" I grimaced, knowing he was right. "Especially if you're going to be doing something as strenuous as hiking. You need to eat a solid meal for fuel beforehand. You're a big man. Big man equals big fuel."

"Big man also equals big di—" I flirted, but George kept going like I hadn't said anything at all.

"Considering your muscle mass and overall size I have no doubt you need to eat more than the average person even on a normal day."

He was right. And god, was he cute when he was chewing my head off.

"I'll do better," I promised, not bringing up the fact that I hadn't gone to breakfast because I'd known he was there and didn't want to crowd him. A single bite of stolen waffle did not "big man fuel" make.

"Good." George blew out an irritated breath. "Take better care of yourself. You're a grown-ass adult. You shouldn't be going hungry. Not when there's food readily available. It's poor planning."

He was the most charming hypocrite I'd ever met.

"You're right," I agreed, gently compelling him forward again. We were halfway to the main lodge, and I desperately wished it was farther away. I wanted to prolong this conversation for as long as possible. No one had ever been so righteously indignant on my behalf before—or cared so much. Not my ex, or any of the randos I'd dated in my early twenties.

George fussed over me the entire walk and I enjoyed it far more than was healthy. By the time we entered the building, George's ire had dissipated a bit and I was grinning. Of course, because fuck my life, June was already sitting down for lunch. Her shit-eating grin told me that she'd definitely clocked my smile for what it was, but I was too pleased to squash it, even knowing the teasing I was about to endure.

Despite his injured hand, and my protests, George insisted on gathering my food for me. He pointed across the room at the empty places on the bench beside my sister, arched a brow, and flared his bossy little nostrils in a silent command to sit and wait.

"Do you have any allergies?" he asked before I could follow my adorable orders. "Dietary restrictions?"

"Ah, nope. None. Don't like Brussels sprouts, but I'll eat them if I have to."

"Noted." George's lips twitched like he was trying not to smile—then he remembered he was being a Bossy-Mc-Cutie-Pie and scowled at me all over again. Swiveling on his heel, George stormed off toward the kitchen where his mother was lurking.

Cheeks already flushed from the teasing I knew I was about to receive, I worked my way to my evil twin. The closer I got to her table, the more diabolical she looked. Like that scene from *The Grinch* when his smile curls and curls and curls.

Now that she was out of her pajamas, June was dressed in another puffy gown, this one in the colors of the trans flag. Had she not been knees-deep in her makeup trial, she'd have joined us on the hike that morning.

June made kissy faces at me as I slid into the seat across from her.

"Oh, shut up," I griped. Her pale eyes danced.

"Someone's looking cooozy," June cooed like the asshole she was.

"You're a bitch."

"But I'm *your* bitch, Alex." June batted her lashes, and I groaned, sliding my hands down my face to hide my flush. Not that it helped, she'd already seen it. "Your *favorite* bitch," she added. "Because I introduced you to Geooorgieee."

"Don't say his name like that. Or at all." I was the only one that was allowed to call him Georgie. It was the law.

"I've never seen you with heart eyes before," June continued, like she wasn't killing me one comment at a time. "It's so disgusting." Her voice told me she didn't find it disgusting in the slightest. "I'm very proud of myself and the fact that this is all my fault. You should buy me a present. I'm thinking flowers? Oooh, actually, no. I want dinner. Dinner for me and Roddy. Somewhere fancy, with candles. We could make it a double date! Oh my god, I'm a genius."

I couldn't even deny her accusations. I really did have heart eyes. Which made me feel itchy and hot and embarrassed. And half-inclined to run. "The whole thing is temporary, June."

"That's what *you* think," she waggled her eyebrows. I rolled my eyes.

I doubted that these new, bubbly, fluttery feelings were mutual. I wasn't even sure if I wanted them to be. That was why I'd come up with the "practice boyfriend" scheme in the first place. Low risk. That was safer. I turned my attention to the back of the room where I knew Georgie would reappear.

"What was he telling you when you came in?" June asked. "He looked so grumpy."

"He was mother-henning me." My smile was disgustingly soppy and way too big to properly hide. June stared at me like I was an alien.

"Mother-henning you?" She tossed her head back and cackled. "God, you would like that, wouldn't you?"

I did like it.

Way too much.

"It's fucking cute," I breathed in excitement, forgetting for a moment that I should probably play it cool. "God, it's even better than when I was pissing him off on purpose."

"You, my friend, are actually smitten. Never thought I'd see the day." She grinned wider. "So he said yes, then? To your little 'fake boyfriend' scheme?"

"*Practice* boyfriend," I corrected. "And no. Not yet. But…"

"But?"

"I'm hopeful."

"Good. For. You." June clapped her hands for emphasis.

I genuinely liked George.

Which is probably why I was still holding out hope that he'd accept my proposition. He deserved more pampering than anyone I'd ever met in my life. And the fact that we were on a timer? Even fucking better. That way it was a guarantee I couldn't overwhelm him. I could be as open and wild as I wanted.

"George likes *Lord of the Rings*. Did I tell you that?" I gushed without prompting.

"You did."

"And he can cook steak."

"A good trait to have when your boyfriend is a carnivore." I ignored the 'boyfriend' comment.

"He reads—"

"*You* read." June looked elated on my behalf.

"We have a lot in common."

"True, true."

"Plus, have you seen his ass?"

"Oh, definitely." June looked unrepentant in the slightest. I snorted. Then a weird twinge of jealousy and possessiveness flared through me and I glared at her. That only made her laugh, looking somehow even more delighted than before. "Oh my god, you are so fucking whipped, Alex. I never thought I'd see the day."

"Shut up. Ah! He's coming." And he was. George strode toward us, less hunched in on himself than he usually was. Now that he had a mission to accomplish, it seemed there was less room for self-consciousness in his brain. I worried about his hand, but didn't want to push too hard as he slid the tray down on the table, and sat gracefully in the seat beside mine.

"Ham and cheese," he said immediately, so focused on his task he hadn't even greeted June. My sister simply smirked, watching him with glee. "You like ham and cheese, don't you?"

"I do."

"Good. I also grabbed some potato salad with extra egg for protein." George nudged the tray toward me, waiting for inspection. I nodded along, my heart squeezing tight in that new-scary-good way as I noted the three sandwiches that took up a majority of the tray.

Three. Christ.

And lord, right next to them was possibly the largest pile of potato salad I'd ever seen. There were so many pieces of hard-boiled egg I figured he'd hand-picked them. That was probably what had taken him so long. He'd been on an egg hunt.

Ohmygodhewassocuteiwantedtobitehim.

"That was very sweet of you," I said, instead. It was taking every ounce of my self-control not to squish his cheeks and smooch the hell out of his grumpy little face.

George slanted me an unimpressed look, though his skin was flushed, betraying how much he'd liked the compliment. "If you're going to do something, do it right," he said. I wasn't sure who he was quoting. His mom, maybe? There wasn't a shadow on his face like when he talked about his ex.

"God, you're adorable." The words slipped out before I could stop them. Immediately, I stiffened, worried I'd scare him off. The last time I'd called him adorable had not ended well. He was like…a stray cat. You had to feed it treats from a distance for a while before coaxing it forward. Especially… if you were an idiot like me and had thrown multiple stones its way the first few times you'd met.

George didn't storm off, or get mad, or glare at me. He just…kind of froze? Like he hadn't been expecting the compliment, especially while he was mid-rant. He blinked, his flush growing splotchier and redder as he ducked his head shyly.

June, to her credit, didn't say a single word.

As much as she liked to tease me I knew she was far too loyal to mess this up for me. Even her chewing was less loud as she glanced away to give us the illusion of privacy.

"You don't mean that," George wavered, avoiding my gaze as he stared shyly down at the table.

"Oh, I definitely do." I angled in close enough that my lips skimmed his ear, and he jumped. "Thank you for taking the time to prepare lunch for me, George." He shivered. "And thank you for worrying about me."

"You're, um. You're welcome." George didn't move, but he was back to being stiff as a board so I shifted out of the way to give him space to process. Our dynamic had evolved in the last few hours and it was jarring. He hadn't expected sincerity. And given what I was beginning to suspect about his past relationship, I highly doubted George was used to it.

Hell, neither was I.

I didn't normally interact with people without a mask in place.

"What did you get for you?" I asked him, leaning an elbow on the table so I could watch the production that was his face. So many emotions flitted across it. *Gotta catch 'em all,* the Pokemon theme played in the back of my mind.

"I'm not hungry."

"*Georgie*." My voice dropped in warning, and he sighed.

"I'm really not, I had a big breakfast. And my stomach is…" he trailed off, eyes darting to June who was still politely observing us from the other side of the table.

"Your stomach is?" I pushed.

George scooted in, closing the distance I'd just created between us, clearly embarrassed. "I'm still feeling anxious. My stomach's in knots."

"Oh." My heart gave a squeeze for an entirely new reason. The fact that he'd admitted that to me at all showed how far we'd come in such a short amount of time. I really didn't want to fuck this up. I had no idea what I was doing. "How about we save one of these for later?" I grabbed one of the three unnecessarily large sandwiches. "That way, when you're feeling a bit more settled, you can eat it."

George sagged, the strain in his shoulders bleeding away as he nodded. "That would be acceptable, yes."

So fucking cute.

"Do you want a couple bites of my potato salad?" I offered after setting his sandwich to the side for safe-keeping. "Might help."

"I…maybe." George glanced at the plate, plucking anxiously at his hair before he caught himself and dropped his hand.

"Just try one. Like the stepping stones." The potato salad was less intimidating than the sandwich and I hoped that once he got a bite down he'd realize he was hungry enough to manage another. George nodded, reaching for my fork—the only fork he'd grabbed—before hovering it above the food.

"I'll need to get you another fork," he informed me with a frown.

"We can share. I don't mind Georgie-cooties."

At that, June made a noise. I glared at her, and her eyes went wide and apologetic. She clearly hadn't meant to react—it had simply slipped out. Luckily, George was too busy having a stare down with the salad to have noticed.

Don't, I mouthed with a glare.

I'm not, June mouthed back.

My attention was quickly stolen by George again as he violently stabbed a potato. I didn't dare tease him, worried I'd break his concentration. After he'd swallowed it, a small smile tugged proudly at his lips. Without prompting, he went in for another bite.

I grabbed my first sandwich and took a big bite out of it, wagging my eyebrows his way encouragingly. What started out as slow-paced tiny bird bites turned into average-paced tiny bird bites. George ate a quarter of my potato salad while I tried to pretend like I wasn't staring.

Apparently I failed, because he glared at me. "Stop staring."

"I'm not—" I lied, quickly turning my attention to June because I totally *had* been staring, and we both knew it.

"How was the hike?" June asked, probably figuring enough awkward silence had passed for it to be time to break it.

"You didn't miss much," I shrugged, playing off the snake misadventure for what it was. The last thing I wanted was to poke George's open wound.

"How come you're back earlier than everyone else?"

"It's hot as balls outside. I decided to take a swim in the creek," I answered, a half-truth. "Needed some dry clothes after."

"Idiot." June laughed, amused. I grinned back. "Man, I wish I could've gone. My boob sweat has boob sweat. A dip in the creek sounds lovely."

George choked.

She'd find out the full story later when Roderick returned, but I refused to hurt George's feelings by bringing it up. The last thing he needed was to be put under a microscope when he was already feeling vulnerable and anxious.

"There's a sunrise hike tomorrow," I reminded her as if she hadn't been the person who'd written the entire itinerary herself. "Same trail." She had a horrible memory. Like a fucking goldfish. "That can be your redo. I recommend packing a swimsuit." I'd have to warn her about the snakes if

Roderick didn't.

"Oh, right! I forgot about that." I rolled my eyes fondly. "Roddy and I are going," June beamed, excited. "Are you?"

"After the bonfire tonight?" I frowned at her like she was out of her mind, because she was. "Hell no."

"Huh." June blinked, frowning, like I hadn't repeatedly told her this during the initial planning phase.

"Dad and I pointed out how sadistic that choice was, like six times."

"Okay but—"

"I know, I know. It's *your* wedding and *your* plan and blah blah *blah—*" I changed the cadence of my voice to mimic hers. "*No,* Alex. You don't understand. It's so *romantic!*" I took another bite of my sandwich, shaking my head with amusement before dropping my impression of her to play my own role in this conversation. "But June, don't you think it's a bad idea to do both events consecutively? Shouldn't we break it up?" I had my Juniper impression down to a T—had since we were kids, a fact that caused her a lot of ire. "No, no. Ugh! You're *such* a boy. You just don't understand. It's the only day that could *possibly* work."

No reaction.

None.

Not even a smile.

"Do you think the others won't want to go?" June asked without acknowledging my teasing, brow furrowed. "On the hike I mean. Because of the bonfire."

"I would bet my left ass cheek the only people waking up at sunrise are you and Rod."

June processed this. I had no idea why she was acting so shocked. This had been a point of contention between us the entire time we'd been planning. I'd told her it was a bad idea, and she'd refused to hear reason. "You know what? I actually don't care." June's smile came back. "In fact, even better! Romantic sunrise stroll alone with Rod? Hell yeah."

"You enjoy that," I said, finishing my first sandwich with a little sigh. I really *had* been hungry. And though at first I'd judged George for bringing me this much food, I was grateful for it now as I plucked open the wrapper on the second sandwich and began to devour that too. "I'm going to enjoy my nice cozy tent. And the fact I get to sleep in. Because this is technically a vacation. And I am expecting to be hung over," I managed around my mouthful.

Tomorrow I'd be right back in wedding-task mode, and I figured I at least deserved a solid night's rest before lake day. I didn't have a lot of opportunities to relax, given I was in charge of everything. I planned to take advantage.

"Speaking of alcohol—" June began. For a solid fifteen minutes, we discussed the plans for the bonfire that night, and all the while, George nibbled on my potato salad, content to eavesdrop.

It was nice.

He smiled a few times when June and I would quip at each other, but otherwise, didn't weigh in. It was…comfortable in a way I'd never expected. And the one time George spoke up to tease June, it made me grin so hard it felt like my face was going to break.

I didn't end up getting Georgie-cooties.

Because he finished the potato salad all on his own.

And when he tried to apologize when he'd realized what he'd done, I simply shook my head, offered him the third sandwich, and felt proud. Because somehow, someway, I'd been able to set George at ease enough that he'd been able to eat despite all that he'd been through today.

I'd taken care of him.

Just like he'd taken care of me.

And I had never felt more accomplished in all my life.

Or more terrified of why that was.

Sixteen
Alex

GEORGE AND I WERE inseparable after that—a fact that only caused me immense joy. He nagged me all day, trailing behind me like a lost kitten. We ended up eating during the same early dinner rotation, and Mrs. Milton roped the both of us into prepping for lunch for "lake day" after we'd finished. No one said a word about the disaster of a hike, for which I was genuinely glad.

It was satisfying to witness George slowly, but surely, dropping his guard when I was around. I didn't think he realized it was happening. But his iciness was decidedly less icy. Which meant I was privy to some rather fascinating sights and observations as the day wore on.

Every breath George took was captivating, and every twitch of his mouth was something to be celebrated. I loved the way he moved, all clipped and focused. Loved how his default expression was guarded annoyance. Loved the way he so clearly adored his mother. He lit up when she walked by. And those dark blue eyes told me he thought she was *sunshine*, especially as he puttered around the kitchen doing her bidding.

George kept glancing at her dress, this pleased curl to his lips that told me he loved it. Which in itself was a miracle—because while Mrs. Milton had many qualities, fashion sense was not one of them.

Every time I'd attended one of the Milton-Quil—Roderick's last name—summer barbecues, she'd been in something gaudy and eye-catching. She wore her creativity outwardly, the patterns of her dresses as loud as her voice could often be. Despite her no-nonsense tone, Mrs. Milton was a soft, kind woman. Her heart was overflowing with love for everyone she met, me included. She hugged as a greeting. And every time she squeezed and squeezed me, all my years melted away. Like she was hugging the little boy I'd been, not the jaded man I was now.

She was a mother, through and through.

I hadn't really had one of those. My mother was really only that in name. She'd be coming to the ceremony, but it was more than likely only for a few minutes before she jetted off on her next adventure, far, far away from us.

I could see why George loved his mother.

And he *did*.

Even when she was acting ridiculous, or pinching his cheeks, or bossing him around. The affection in his eyes never wavered. When he'd catch me looking, he'd glare at me, though the look was far from intimidating.

"What happened to your hand?" Mrs. Milton fretted when she noticed the bandages. George gave an excuse that didn't even make sense, and she sighed, then enveloped him in a back-breaking hug. He wheezed, and she chortled, before directing him to the far end of the room, away from the knives—as if the last thing she was going to do was have her injured son handle anything sharp.

"You too." Mrs. Milton wasted no time whipping my ass with a towel to get me moving. "Many hands make light work." Yelping, I scurried after George quickly, unable to hide my laughter.

George and I were on sandwich duty. Which meant a whole lot of mayonnaise. Magnanimously, I let George take care of that part while I plopped cheese and meat into the pre-cut rolls.

"Disgusting," George muttered under his breath when he spilled a glob of the sauce on his wrist. I handed him a napkin and he flashed me a smile in thanks before returning to his task. He worked with quick efficiency. George was good with his hands, despite being a jittery guy, and it was almost hypnotic the way we fell into a rhythm. Open, spread, slide. Plop, close, seal. Rinse and repeat.

"Did George ever tell you he's a senior designer at his company?" Mrs. M said conversationally. She was like June, always with an agenda.

"He did not, no," I replied, glancing at him curiously. "I bet he's good at that."

"I'm a perfectionist," George grunted. "Comes with the territory." He was embarrassed to be talked up like this. He kept shooting his mom looks, like he was begging her to stop.

"He was top of his class in school too," she added, undeterred.

"This isn't a job interview." George glared at her.

"Of course not, honey," his mom nodded, smiling serenely. "Just making conversation."

And then five minutes later…

"Did you know George was a cheerleader in high school?"

And.

"Did you know George graduated with high honors and a 4.0 GPA?"

And.

"Did you know that George—"

By the time Georgie and I had finished prepping lunch for the following day, the bonfire had already begun. Mrs. Milton shooed us out of the kitchen. She promised to handle clean-up so long as we "had fun" and also "behaved ourselves."

To which I replied, "How can I have fun if I'm behaving myself?"

"*Aleeeex*," George whined under his breath, but Mrs. Milton just laughed, and laughed, and laughed. Like she knew something we didn't. And then she'd *winked*, and that sent us both running before our asses could get whipped by her all-knowing towel again.

I made a mental note to ask her for pictures of cheerleader George later.

I highly doubted he would be wearing a skirt.

But a man could dream.

I could hear the chatter of the group gathered at the fire pit before we reached it. Behind the main lodge, there was a large, flat dirt area. Maybe a half dozen yards wide, the space was populated by a plethora of large log benches. They sat in a haphazard circle around what had to be the largest fire pit known to man. Inside it, flames roared, the heat casting the yard in an inviting yellow-orange glow.

Even well into my adulthood, the sight of a flickering fire and s'mores could move me.

I was careful with what I ate normally, but June and I'd had multiple talks about me enjoying myself without guilt while we were here. The last thing she wanted was for me to get stuck in my own head or worry about what I looked like when I could be making memories instead. I'd promised to enjoy myself, so I fully intended to.

And if I went home a little heavier than usual, my personal trainer would simply have to deal with it.

The group of adults, and some children—already roasting marshmallows— were enjoying the bluetooth speakers Roderick and June had bought to set the mood. Something peppy and country strung through the air between the notes of laughter.

Not that I liked country.

But I could appreciate the ambiance.

"I hate country music," Georgie sighed to himself, reminding me that he was there—not that I'd ever forgotten. That was fundamentally impossible, even distracted by the fire and the promise of treats as I was. As stupidly romantic as it sounded, when George was nearby I could *feel* him, even if I couldn't see him. And when he wasn't…I could feel that too. The absence of his presence like an open wound.

"Me too," I agreed with a snort. "Never been a fan."

"Blasphemy, I know. Given I'm from the country." George perked up, looking delighted to once again find common ground. "You and your sister are very different." It was an observation, nothing more. "I mean…she picked this, didn't she?" George frowned. "Would you play country music at your wedding?"

"This isn't her wedding. It's her bonfire party," I teased. "And no. Absolutely not."

George was far too relieved for someone who had zero stakes in what kind of music I decided to play at my hypothetical wedding. As though he was… testing me, in a way. I'd passed, if the way he relaxed was to be believed.

"You know, this could've been me?" He shivered, like the idea of marrying Roderick was truly heinous. I got what he meant. I couldn't picture that. George and Roderick together was fundamentally wrong. Just thinking about it made my skin itch, and a frankly inappropriate amount of jealousy nearly overwhelmed me.

"No," I said softly. "You and Roderick aren't good together."

"Oh, I know." George shrugged, proving he didn't care in the slightest. "I just…when I was younger and we were dating I would've agreed to this. Even if I hated it. Simply because I liked him."

"*I* would never make you get married in the middle of the woods," I replied, my jealousy swirling tight like a noose around my heart. "You'd get somewhere fancy. No bugs. A live orchestra. Caterers. Anywhere you wanted, no budget constraints at all. It would be what *you* wanted. Not me."

"Hmm." George's eyes took on a faraway sheen like he was picturing what marrying me would be like. Which was far preferable to him thinking about marrying *Roderick*. I grinned, proud of that particular redirection.

Good.

Imagine me in a tux, Georgie.

I would look *fantastic.*

Way better than Roderick, that was for sure.

And theeeeen I felt bad. Because why the hell was I comparing myself to my future brother-in-law, anyway? He was marrying June. There was no need to be jealous that he and George may have possibly bumped uglies when they were—no, nope. Best not to think about that or I was going to go find him and punch him, man-of-honor title be damned.

That's what June had dubbed me. Man-of-honor, instead of maid-of-honor. She thought it was funny, and it was her wedding, so I hadn't argued. Truthfully, when she'd asked me, I'd been honored even if I had been unsurprised. It was only right that I support her on her wedding day. I knew she'd do the same for me one day if I ever decided to trust again.

I offered George my hand. He was so distracted by his thoughts that he simply accepted without complaint. Tugging him toward the fire, I tried to figure out how best to keep his mind off any of his many, *many* annoying exes.

Fine.

There were two that I knew of.

Two.

But two was two too many.

Christ, what a mouthful.

"June and I have a lot of varying tastes," I said. "We're twins. Which meant that growing up we often got lumped together. People pretty much assumed we were the same person. And that we liked the same things simply because we shared a womb." George listened intently as I hunted the log benches for a spot close enough to the flame that we could make some marshmallows of our own. "They were right in some ways—we can be frighteningly similar. Especially when we were kids and our dad dressed us in matching outfits. He stopped doing that when we hit…ten, maybe? And that was when our differences became more apparent."

"Huh."

"June always liked country music, and I *hated* country. I loved football, June hated football. June started playing piano, I refused to learn an instrument. When I picked hockey, June picked figure skating." There. Perfect. I tugged George to a seat on the free bench I'd found. The scratchy wood clung to my joggers as I sat down, spreading wide so that I could press our legs together. I liked the feel of him. Slightly chilly, his thigh only a fraction of the width of mine, but still comforting when it was pressed close.

He had nice quads. I was tempted to smooth my hands up them from knee to hip to see if they felt as firm as they looked, but I didn't. With him in the same dark jeans he'd worn yesterday, it was difficult to control myself.

"We're less contrary now," I shrugged. "Neither of us care like we did when we were younger. Especially now that we look as different as we do. But still. Some habits are hard to stop when they're so ingrained into who you are."

"I understand that," George admitted. "I still refuse to watch the second *Lion King* just because Lacey bugged me about it so many times. Siblings make things complicated." He didn't move away, in fact, if I didn't know any better his leg was pushing harder against mine. Like he wanted to feel me as much as I wanted to feel him.

Wishful thinking, maybe.

But maybe not.

Because his eyes were swirling pools of blue-black ink, and the way he was looking at me made me feel like I could climb a mountain. Or maybe the Empire State Building? Put him in a pretty dress, hold him in my hand, and pound my chest like Kong.

"There are exceptions to my blind hate for country," George added guiltily— as though he expected the genre of country music would be offended by his blind, blatant hatred. "Like…um." His brow knit as he mulled over his own thoughts, trying to remember the exceptions he'd just claimed existed.

I didn't mind. I just liked looking at him.

Loved the little dimple on his chin, not grumpy presently—but thoughtful.

For an entire minute, I was mesmerized by the way the crackle pop of the fire illuminated the play of emotion on George's face. And then the silence broke, and with triumph, George began listing off an entire list of songs he liked that fit within the country genre. Even better was the fact that George actually took the time to explain *why* he liked them. It was usually for a sentimental reason, like a "good storyline" or because "he thought it was romantic."

More curiously, George *loved* sad songs.

A fact that I found incredibly charming.

"I just like to *feel* something, you know?" George told me. I wasn't sure how long we'd been roasting our asses by the fire, but my knees felt hot from its proximity, and sweat had built at my temple. I barely noticed. I did, however, notice a damp lock of George's blond hair when it slipped free and stuck to his pale forehead. He pushed it back with an angry motion. My hands twitched when it simply fell again.

I wanted to fix it for him.

But I was having so much fun talking to him, I didn't dare move. We were caught in a spell I didn't want to break. Hell, I hadn't even gone hunting for the skewers and marshmallows like I'd wanted, as absorbed as I'd been in his rant.

"I know what you mean," I echoed. "That's why I like anime." George blinked. I elaborated. "Some of the plots can be super devastating. They make you feel things. Especially the more long-winded series. It feels like you grow with the characters. They become your friends."

What an embarrassing thing to say, Alex.

George nodded along like he didn't think it was embarrassing at all.

When I checked my phone nearly an hour had passed. I'd been so captivated by him, chatting back and forth as though we were old friends, I hadn't realized. It was peaceful and companionable in a way I'd never expected, especially after how we'd met. George poked fun at me whenever he could and I was just as merciless in return. We enjoyed each other. And at some point, I'd slung my arm around his back, and he hadn't pushed me off.

It was an effortless sort of friendship.

Easy.

The way only conversing with June or my dad had been before George and his dildo came along.

Most of the time, when I interacted with people it left me drained. I was good at talking, but that didn't mean that social interaction didn't take a toll. Work was easier than personal relationships. I found gatherings like this more tiring than my job, even if I used a similar skill set during both.

When friends had parties and I had no excuse not to attend, I always knew before I went that I'd be wiped out afterward. All day in preparation, I had to ration my energy to ensure I could last. Maybe it was a product of coming into money early in my life—or late, depending on who you talked to—but I had never quite figured out how to survive the social cost of being wealthy.

There was always something you were expected to do. A party you were expected to attend. A new trend you were expected to know. Keeping up was endlessly exhausting.

Talking to George didn't feel like that.

It was easy.

And not once during our conversation did I ever feel like he was judging me, or growing bored, or lying to keep me on the hook. It was honest and genuine. The kind of conversation I had grown starved of the higher up I climbed in my father's company and the more money my family accumulated.

At some point, we were swarmed by George's nieces and nephews, as well as a few of my cousins. We got roped into helping them with their marshmallows, which wasn't exactly how I'd expected the rest of our night to go—but was also better somehow. Because watching Georgie with children was…Christ. He was gorgeous.

Patient and stern and kind.

He listened intently to everything the children had to say. It didn't matter how serious, or mumbled, or incoherent. George found a way to validate and reply, all while creating some ridiculously sad, undercooked s'mores.

The kids didn't seem to mind though, and one by one they scampered off with their treats. The line dwindled. Eventually, there was only one kid left for each of us. I split my attention between Patrick, the toddler, and his surprisingly hefty weight on my lap, and George and his niece, Mavis. As I stuffed a toasted marshmallow between a set of graham crackers, I smiled at Patrick, but kept an ear on George, eager to hear more of his quiet crooning.

He was so much softer with children than he was with adults.

Still his acerbic self, of course. But gentle too. Like it came more naturally and he could drop his guard. He didn't expect them to hurt him. And why would they? Children, though sometimes accidentally brutal, rarely did things out of malice.

It was why I liked them too.

They were honest and innocent.

And they loved so very fiercely.

"See?" George said softly to Mavis, who could be most accurately described as a tiny blonde menace. "We want it just right, like I made yours. Not burnt." George's stick drifted too close to the coal and before he could pull it back, it burst into flame. "Oops." He frowned, quickly pulling it out of the fire and next to his mouth. His pink lips parted, a gust of air putting out the flame. Obviously, I had a problem, because the gesture was nothing but innocent, and all I could think about was rubbing my dick in marshmallow and making him blow on it too.

"And if we get too close, that's what happens. It goes *boom*!" Mavis cheered, like George had just performed a magic trick. Which I suppose he had.

"I want *my* shmallow to go boom," Patrick, the three-year-old cousin on my lap, immediately blurted. Cousin maybe wasn't the right descriptor. Second cousin, maybe? Whatever meant he was my cousin's kid. Either way he was cute.

"It doesn't taste as good that way," George warned him.

"I beg to differ," I argued, deliberately sticking my stick right next to the coal so it would catch aflame. "The more char the better. Black like my heart."

"That's because you're apparently a pyromaniac," George retorted. "With bad taste." To which Mavis gleefully agreed. "See? Even Mavis thinks so."

"Mavis doesn't know what that even means," I teased back.

"I don't." Mavis giggled her head off.

"See?" I grinned, and George glowered. His lips were twitching though, betraying his own amusement. Mavis and I had interacted a lot over the last few years. I remembered when she was still round as a baby seal and unable to do more than make noise. I wasn't friends with her mom or anything, but Roderick's and George's families were close—which meant by extension I had spent a lot of time with most of them, children included.

It was probably why they were all on board with the matchmaking subplot.

Maybe they could see how damaged he was too.

Maybe they'd known I wouldn't hurt him.

"Have you ever even *tried* a burnt marshmallow? Because if you haven't you have no leg to stand on," I teased, steadying my roasting pole and watching George do the same.

"Unca George has legs." Mavis was already sticky with her own treat, so I knew the one George had—in his words—"ruined" was his own. She frowned at me.

"You're right, my bad," I replied. Patrick was eyeing the marshmallow I'd melted for him like he was fully prepared to chomp it right off the stick.

"Why the hell would I do that?" George inquired as though I hadn't just been cut down by a toddler. "When I already know I'm right?" We reached for graham crackers simultaneously, and George unwrapped an extra piece of chocolate, handed it to me without being asked, and turned back to his own task.

"If you're as right as you say you are, then you have nothing to lose," I nodded toward the charred lump of sugar at the end of his stick. "Put your money where your mouth is, Blondie. Try it. Then tell me I'm wrong. Hell, we can even make it a wager."

"You don't have anything I want," George muttered. I arched a brow at him, and his cheeks went bright red. Apparently I did, in fact, have something he wanted. I got the feeling it wasn't something that was appropriate conversation for the present toddling company.

I licked my lips, and our eyes locked, before George's gaze darted away.

Something had changed between us today.

He felt it.

I felt it.

We allll felt it.

Like a switch had flipped.

"Try it," I urged, pinching the marshmallow on the stick between the cracker and chocolate I'd set up. I pulled it free, the white sugary substance sticking to my fingers. The graham cracker slid a bit as I passed it to Patrick, but he didn't mind. One-track mind, that one. His dark skin gleamed in the firelight as he munched on his treat, lapping sugar off his fingers like it was his mission to devour every bite. "Here." I offered him a napkin and he took it, clutching it tight in his chubby fist.

"I don't know…" George dutifully mirrored my movements and made his own s'more, despite his protests.

"Wanna share?" It was a pretty delicious-looking snack, if I did say so myself. The marshmallow oozed out the sides, and without overthinking, I angled my head toward it, mouth open expectantly. Without protest, other than a pinched expression, George brought his own dessert to my lips.

I hadn't actually *expected* George to let me take a bite. I was pushing him, like was normal and natural between us. But he had surprised me. He was constantly surprising me. A fact, in itself, that should've meant I should not be surprised.

Parting my lips, I clamped my teeth down, my heart skittering. I was so close to his fingers, if I wanted, I could've licked them. But even I knew that wasn't appropriate. So instead, I focused on the food. Crunching through the graham cracker, I sighed happily, eyes drifting shut. Okay, fine. I was going to tease a little.

But just a little.

Licking the sticky, melted marshmallow from my lips, I groaned. "So *fucking* good." When I pulled back, opening my eyes, George was staring. And fuck, was that gratifying. "Okay, now it's your turn. C'mon. Prove me wrong."

"But you just bit it," George protested, squinting at his contaminated food with a frown. "Alex cooties." He was making fun of what I'd said earlier. I snorted. Oh, well. Who was I to judge if he wanted to hand me the rest and make himself a new one?

Of course he wouldn't want to put his on there t—

Oh.

George tentatively brought the s'more to his lips, expression tentative. He hesitated, blond brow furrowed, his eyes trained on the flickering fire. His free arm was wrapped firmly around Mavis, keeping her steady as he became lost in his own thoughts. And then, because he was nothing if not unpredictable, George took a bite.

He chewed.

He swallowed.

George's eyes went wide, sticky white smeared across his lips as he turned from the fire to look at me. Christ, what a mouth it was. So pretty. Especially when sticky.

"Seeeee?" I urged. "So much better."

George chewed deliberately, reaching up to brush the crumbs off his lips. "I never thought I'd say this—but I think you're right. The...um. The texture is better."

"See?"

"It's not...even burnt tasting?" George was shocked, obviously. "And it's softer."

"Right?" I beamed at him. "Now you know why I like my men like I like my s'mores."

"Oh Jesus, not in front of the kids."

"They don't even understand what I'm saying," I muttered with a laugh. "And they're not paying attention, even if they did." It was true. Both kids were too absorbed in their own food to care what we were doing.

"Fine."

I waited.

George sighed, his s'more still clutched tight in his grip. "How do you like your men, Alex?"

"Melted and sticky."

"That wasn't even good," George snorted. "Was definitely not worth the build-up you gave it."

I shrugged, leaned in close, and opened my mouth expectantly again. I was pushing my luck. Especially after my terrible joke, and I knew it. Chances were, George would shove me off, or smash his s'more against my face. I was...strangely okay with that.

I liked my odds.

In response to my wagging eyebrows, George sighed. With *deliberate* extra grumpiness, he gently pressed the treat to my lips so I could take another bite. "Why don't you make your own?" George grouched. "Rather than mooching off mine."

"That's not the only thing I wish I was mooching off of," I muffled around my bite. George's whole face scrunched up with disgust, so I didn't speak again until after I'd finished chewing.

"What?" he said, confused.

"Sorry, I meant smooching. My bad."

"Oh my god." George grabbed a napkin, smearing it across my lips more roughly than was necessary to clear them of crumbs and chocolate. It was oddly domestic, and seriously fucking cute. Patrick ruined the moment by belching.

I chuckled, flicked my tongue along my teeth to make sure they were clean, then opened my mouth expectantly again.

"Make your own," George grumbled, already feeding me another bite despite his protests.

I swallowed, then grinned. "Why would I? When the way yours tastes is better."

"We're using the same ingredients. They'll taste the same," George glared at me, clutching the rest of his s'more close to his chest like he worried I was going to snatch it right out of his hands.

God, he was so cute.

And stingy.

And generous, all at once.

"But *you* made this one," I argued. "Therefore, it's better."

"Do you want me to make one for you, too?" George asked. I had no doubt he would do it. But I shook my head. The real joy had come from sharing with him and the fact that he was willing to indirectly touch mouths with me.

Gave me hope that the spark between us could lead to him accepting my offer.

Though, I forced that hope aside as quickly as it came.

I didn't want to be disappointed.

"I'm good," I said. "I had enough. But thank you." I licked my lips deliberately. George *stared*. "You're very generous." He blinked, then shook his head quickly, like he was dazed.

"I'm not—I mean," George's face went bright red. He stuffed his s'more into his mouth to shut himself up. I adjusted Patrick on my leg, and tried not to ogle. But that was impossible. Because George was fucking adorable with his cheeks puffed up. Pretty little chipmunk.

"C'mon, Mavis. Let's go find your mom," George urged when he'd finished eating. He cleaned himself off meticulously, then rose to his feet, effortlessly slinging Mavis into his arms. She clung to his side, sticky chocolate fingers leaving a smear on George's shoulder. He didn't say anything, even though I knew for a fact the shirt was expensive.

I had one just like it back home.

Before I could ask if he was planning on coming back, George saved me the trouble. "If you want…" he trailed off, cheeks ruddy. In the flickering orange firelight it was impossible to tell just how flushed he was, but I knew his face almost as well as I knew my own by this point. I'd certainly spent long enough committing it to memory. So I noticed. "I can come back? After I find Lacey."

He didn't need to explain.

But I recognized this for what it was. Nervous rambling. To cover up his second olive branch of the day. It seemed George-Arthur Milton wanted to be away from me about as much as I wanted to be away from him. And wasn't that a heady thought?

"I'll find Patrick's dads." I agreed. "Meet you here in like twenty?"

"Hopefully." George bit his lip.

I was pretty sure my smile was bright enough to blind, but George didn't complain when he finally looked at me. "I'll be back then," he said, side-stepping away. "Soon. And we can…"

"We can chat some more," I replied, still grinning.

"Or…whatever." George rolled his eyes at himself, but his lips twitched into a small secret smile.

"Or whatever," I repeated.

He stood there awkwardly for another minute, studying me.

I kept smiling, curious to see what he was waiting for.

"Okay, bye," George waved one of Mavis's tiny hands. I waved back.

"Bye," I teased.

"Bye!" Mavis beamed at me, then turned her attention back to George. He took a few steps away. Before Patrick and I were fully out of earshot I saw Mavis's little head tip up and heard her innocent question. "Do you like that boy, Unca George?" George made a choked sound. "Mama says that sometimes boys are mean when they like you."

"That's horrible advice," George scoffed. "No one should be mean to you *ever*. Especially if they like you."

Mavis sounded confused but agreed.

I snorted out a laugh, then called out, "Hypocrite!"

"*Alex!*" George admonished over his shoulder. His cheeks were still bright red when he stalked off. Pleased, I turned my attention back to Patrick, who had started to doze. Sugar crash without the high. Brutal. His head was drifting forward, ebony curls catching the firelight.

"C'mon, little dude," I said. "Let's find your dads so they can get you to bed."

I tucked him close, making sure my hands were free of marshmallow so I wouldn't leave sticky bits in his hair. Patrick curled against my body, letting his weight settle as I picked up our mess and shoved the napkins into my pockets to discard them. When I'd finished, the last thing I expected was to see George again, Mavis still in his arms, waiting right at the edge of our log.

I jumped.

"You okay?" I asked, immediately concerned.

"Yes." George's throat bobbed. He looked indecisive. Nervous. Staring at a whorl on the wood, he refused to meet my eyes again.

"Are you su—"

"I was just…I mean. I could go by myself—to find Lacey," George said quickly. "But I was just thinking. Maybe…if you wanted to…we could go together?"

Oh Jesus.

Sweet, anxious, adorable *baby*.

I wanted to kiss that cute-as-pie worried face.

Worried I wouldn't want to go with him? Christ. Impossible. Since the day we'd met, all I'd done was worry about what he was doing. I'd accept any and all clinginess he exhibited with the utmost gratitude. It saved me the work of hunting him down. The reality was, I was simply desperate to exist in the same vicinity as him.

"Of course we can do that," I said immediately, butterflies flitting in my stomach. Apparently, George was as reluctant to be away from me as I was to be away from him. "Tag team it?"

"Yes." George nodded, a short, jerky thing.

So fucking cute.

"Mission: Find The Adults, commence!" I teased, moving toward him slowly so as not to startle him. This…was a vulnerable thing he'd just done. I knew that. He'd gone out of his way to spend more time with me. Again. I wasn't sure if it was because I'd promised to protect him from the snakes, or if it was because he simply liked my presence. Either way, I was happy.

"Idiot," George's lips tugged into a smile—which was exactly the reaction I'd been hoping for. I was only a foot away now, and I marveled at the difference in our sizes. Standing, I was the perfect height to admire the pale curl of his lashes. Tipping his chin up, George's eyes finally, *blissfully* met mine.

I'd related them to poetry once.

That complicated, fathomless blue.

Years of chaos, of hurt, of love tangled inside their depths. Georgie came across as the kind of man who took what he wanted, when he wanted it. The kind of man who had the confidence to succeed. He knew exactly who he was.

At least…that's what I'd thought when I'd first met him.

This man before me was someone else entirely. Not the suit-wearing, pen-wielding, dildo-carrying maniac from the line at security, but a person who had been beaten badly—so badly that when he'd finally gotten back up again, his feet didn't understand whether or not they were on solid ground.

How could one stand steady after their face had been shoved in the dirt? When up wasn't up anymore. When bruises on the ego, on the skin, on the heart were more familiar than affection.

George's eyes were honest now in a way they'd never been before.

He was vulnerable.

And I knew, had I been a worse man, I could've taken advantage. I could've seen his affection for what it was—his olive branches, his tremulous smiles—and I could've wrapped him around my finger, wound so tightly he never even realized he was being strangled.

Had that been what Brendon had done?

Is that why he'd said he'd sworn off men? Because deep down, he couldn't help but worry that all men were vipers. That they would bite and strangle and hurt the second they were given an opportunity.

I didn't want to be another person that hurt George-Arthur Milton.

And as I fell inside his eyes, aching to reach out, to close the distance between us and feel the puff of his breath, the warmth of his skin, the thrum of his heart, I saw the secret messages he often hid climb through the darkness to the surface.

George's need to be loved was obvious.

His eyes said, *I'm scared to let my guard down.*

They said, *I want so badly to trust you.*

They pleaded, *don't hurt me.*

I hoped the answer in my own gaze settled him.

I hoped he understood it, because I certainly didn't.

This unfamiliar surge of protective energy was unreal. Foreign in a way. But...it wasn't *bad*. Only new. I was learning to skate for the first time, my feet skidding on ice. It was hard to find my balance.

"Alex?" George's voice was hushed as we made our way to the cabins where Lacey was waiting. I hummed noncommittally, still lost in my thoughts.

His eyes, dark as the sky above, sucked me inside their orbit.

"Yeah?" My heart skipped a beat.

"Is the...offer of being your...um...practice boyfriend—" George stumbled over the words, rushed and bashful. "Still on the...table?"

It seemed George had another surprise up his sleeve, after all.

Seventeen
George

THE STARS DANCED, PINPRICKS of light that peeped through the branches above as Alex and I returned to the bonfire. After helping the kiddos find their parents in the cabins, I certainly had not expected this. What had previously been a family-friendly gathering had evolved into chaos.

Now that I'd officially accepted Alex's offer, I'd had it in my head that we'd spend an hour or more chatting peacefully by the fire, maybe sharing another s'more—before retiring to our tent.

I'd never had so much fun just talking to someone.

That, combined with Alex's care and attention, had been what finally tipped me over the edge. Or maybe it had been the way he'd held Patrick, aware of his own strength, and yet…gentle, despite it.

Suffice to say, nowhere in my plans had I expected to spend my first night as Alex's not-boyfriend at a full-blown frat party.

June and Roderick had set up two entire kegs, both on opposite ends of the fire pit. Red solo cups populated the fists of the cluster of adults gathered. Some were dancing, some were howling with laughter, and an ambitious few were deep into the s'more-making process with drunken determination.

That has to be a health hazard, I swear to god.

A giant bowl of mystery punch had been deposited at the end of a log bench. Made of glass, and clearly bought for the wedding reception, the thing was almost ridiculously fancy-looking. Currently, Joe bent over it, filling his cup liberally from the spout. His large body was pretzeled in a way that did not look natural so that he could reach. When he saw me, he raised his cup with a slosh.

I waved. Joe spilled, scowled, and stumbled toward where June and Roderick were elbow-deep in a pair of giant black and yellow bins full of miscellaneous party items. There was a jump rope, for some ungodly reason, as well as bondage rope. I really…did not want to know why they'd brought that here.

Shifting my attention back to Alex, I discovered that he was *amused*, and not at all disturbed by the depravity of his cousins grinding on each other while listening to country twang—or the skunky scent of weed in the air. He thrived in the chaos.

Like a demon.

I wasn't sure *who* was smoking—I couldn't see the source of the smell, even though I'd definitely looked—but it was safe to assume it was one of Roderick's brothers.

I was wrong.

Apparently, eight years away from home had changed a lot about my parents. Because the closer we got to the group of sixty-plus-year-olds leaning against the back of the cabin, joints in hand, the more difficult it became to rationalize what I was seeing.

That's right, the people currently getting high were my *parents*—and Roderick's—puffing away like a gaggle of misbehaving teens.

Mom smiled at us. It would've been impossible not to approach, even if Alex hadn't been dragging me. Like watching a train wreck—only that train wreck was my own mouth and what was going to happen if I couldn't keep it shut.

Mom's giant blonde hair practically glowed in the dark, like it was its own source of light, reflecting the moon and the stars.

"Are you having fun?" she asked when we halted, only a few feet away. She passed the joint she was holding to my dad. It was still lit, a plume of smoke escaping. "I told you to have fun," Mom reminded me.

My *dad*. My no-nonsense, trucker dad. All long and skinny, wearing the flannel he'd dubbed "the good one" when I'd barely been old enough to remember, was holding a joint.

A joint.

"I'm having…uh—" I was distracted, and therefore did not know how to get my mouth to work to answer my mother's question. At my parents feet was a frankly obscenely large pile of snacks, primarily cookies. All were in plastic packages, and only a few had been opened. I recognized the brand.

"George is having *so* much fun!" Alex replied, with what could only be described as sadistic glee. Again, the cartoon villain was back. He eyed the snacks. Little Debbie cakes. Brownies. A variety of different kinds of E.L. Fudge cookies. Mom bought those in bulk when they went on sale. She liked to save up coupons and fill the entire pantry. Now I knew why.

Because munchies.

"Mrs. M, are you by chance interested in charity work?" Alex batted his lashes in my mother's direction. His gaze darted to the mint chocolate cookies that were sealed in their package at my parents' feet.

"Charity work?" Mom echoed, amused.

"Feeding the youth," Alex clarified.

"*The youth* can take what they'd like." Mom giggled. She jerked a shoulder toward her overflowing snack stash. Judging by the way her eyes sparkled, she found Alex's flirty bullshit charming. "Lord knows we don't need it all."

"Speak for yourself." Dad—tall, skinny, wheezing dad—narrowed his eyes at her like she'd just sold his puppy to the devil. It was always jarring hearing his voice. Sometimes I forgot he had one. Alex looked as surprised as I was that he'd spoken.

Mom did not respond to Dad's declaration, she simply gestured toward the cookies magnanimously before flicking a returning glare his way. Roderick's parents giggled amongst themselves, too absorbed in their own plume of smoke to care that Alex was about to rob them. Alex, with no remorse whatsoever, ducked down to grab a few packs of cookies.

"Thank you!" he said cheerfully. "Your sacrifice is greatly appreciated."

"You boys enjoy yourselves," Mom waggled her eyebrows.

"Oh, we will!" Alex sounded way too sure of himself—considering the fact that I was still as a statue beside him and certainly no longer having fun.

There was a knowing glint in my mother's gaze that I didn't want to think too much about. The wicked smirk she sported as Alex looped an arm around my shoulder and steered me away made me feel violated. Like I was naked out in the wild for all to see. It wasn't nearly as bad as how I'd felt at the airport with Neil out in the open, but it was close enough.

My head was fuzzy.

Maybe it was shock?

Or maybe I was high now, too.

"You're not high," Alex chuckled, squeezing me even closer.

What the hell?

"Did you just read my mind?" I gaped. Alex was slightly damp, the summer air muggy enough to affect even someone as perfect as him. The way his body brushed mine with every step was riveting.

"Ha! I wish. *No.* But you're pretty predictable once a guy knows what to look for. You barely breathed that entire time." How the hell had he noticed that? He'd been flirting cookies out of my mom? Wow, that sounded weird. "At most, you'll get a small contact high, but I doubt it."

"You sure know a lot about drugs." I wasn't judging, except for the fact I was.

"Weed isn't a drug." Alex arched a brow. "It's a plant."

"Yes, well. I've never thought all that much about it, plant or not." I didn't pay attention to where Alex was leading us, too absorbed in my own thoughts. Had my parents always smoked? Had I simply never noticed? Or was this a recent development? Maybe it was...fun?

"It's not that serious," Alex rumbled softly against my ear. "Nothing to stress over, I promise you." For a second, I'd zoned out enough I'd forgotten we'd been talking at all. Alex's body heat was almost as comforting as his words, even if his close proximity also managed to light a fire low in my belly. "If it makes you feel better, my dad smokes. For medical purposes. It's normal. Not anything to have an existential crisis about."

"My parents were definitely not smoking for 'medical purposes'," I snorted, though I appreciated him trying to...I don't know, comfort me?

Maybe I looked distressed.

"That's true," Alex shrugged. The motion rustled his cookies, and me, and it should've been annoying but I liked it. Liked the way he pressed into me solid and sure—possessive, almost. Liked how human he felt, especially when we touched.

I shivered.

"Cold?" Alex inquired, proving once again how very closely he paid attention to me. I wasn't cold. But I nodded anyway, because it was easier than admitting how much he affected me, even when he wasn't trying to.

"A bit," I lied. A white lie. Nothing to offend his sensibilities.

"Mmm," Alex's hand was just the right amount of scratchy as he rubbed it over my shoulder and arm. Calluses on his palms. From what? I didn't know. Weight-lifting maybe? Considering his physique. Or hockey. He'd said he liked hockey. I shivered again, and his pale eyes flickered with heat. Sinking into him, I let the atmosphere suck me in.

The crackle-pop of the fire a dozen yards away, the hoot-hoot of a lonely owl, and a cricket's song, somehow loud enough it could be heard over the rowdy crowd gathered between the kegs.

It wasn't that I was dissociating or anything.

I was…distracted—but only by the present. The scent of Alex's sweat beneath his cologne sucked into my lungs with every breath. He was solid and sure against my body. Proving to be a surprisingly pleasant companion despite how much he chatted with the people we passed by, and how many items he acquired along the way.

I was simply happy to go along for the ride.

To be the pretty thing on Alex's arm, silent and content.

Even if that wasn't where I'd thought the night would go.

It was a testament to how much I'd grown to like him that I didn't mind all the people-ing.

It wasn't until Alex had run out of space for his loot that I realized just how deftly he'd managed to flirt, wheedle, and trick his way through the crowd. By the time we had abandoned the bonfire and headed into the dark alongside the main cabin, Alex had been forced to let me go because his arms were simply too full to cling close.

He'd stolen a blanket from June—after she'd tried to smooch him.

Stolen a new bottle of wine from Roderick—who had also tried to smooch him. They'd been setting up a picnic of sorts near the back of the fire, which definitely should've been a clue—in hindsight—but it hadn't been.

My head had been far too fuzzy to pay attention to the details.

Just like now—fuzzy, out of it, dazed as I stared up at the sky and let Alex take the lead.

Alex weaved us through the cabins, and then up a hill at the north end of the camp site. I wheezed as we climbed, calves burning, mind a thousand miles away. Alex simply chuckled, finding joy in my pain like the little shit he was.

He didn't offer any explanation for our impromptu midnight trek through the dark—other than a wink, and then his open hand after he'd dumped his plunder once we'd reached the top of the hill.

I didn't take the offered hand.

I didn't know *how* to.

I didn't know how to deal with *any* of this.

Away from the party, with the music and frivolity far enough it was barely an echo, I was in even more uncharted territory. The stars were so very bright above us, clearer now that we were away from the fire. We'd climbed high enough that even the trees couldn't block them from sight.

"You just keep standing there looking pretty. I'll get everything all set up," Alex teased, not offended that I'd inadvertently ignored him.

"Sure," I didn't look at him, still drinking in the stars. They really *were* beautiful. I'd missed nights like this. New York's skyline was too polluted to truly see them even when the weather was clear.

"Get what set up?" I questioned belatedly.

Alex didn't reply.

He continued to rustle around, grunted, and swore a few times. A few minutes later, when he'd gone quiet, his fingers brushed against my wrist, snagging my attention.

"Your Majesty," Alex said, "your feast awaits." Kneeling in front of me, Alex's head was tilted back. He looked at me the same way I'd just been staring at the stars. Like I was something worth admiring.

Realistically, I should've seen this coming.

Alex James was a lot of things, but subtle wasn't one of them.

And he'd made it clear that if I accepted his proposal he was going to "spoil" me. I just…hadn't expected it to be so soon—or…so…cute?

"You…made us a picnic." I was honestly flummoxed. The picnic he'd set up was interesting to say the least. Alex knee-walked to the side so he could gesture at his hard work with a flourish. "Does it please, His Majesty?"

Jesus he was so fucking cheesy.

"Dork," I snorted.

The blanket was a patchwork monstrosity, threadbare, and as old as I was. The snacks piled on top of it consisted of an eclectic mix of items—mostly sugary—with the exception of a block of cheese Alex had charmed away from his cousins.

Sitting front and center, the package of cookies that Alex had scavenged from my mom's stash had been torn open. Beside the cookies, the wine bottle—pink moscato—had accidentally tipped to the side on the grass. Luckily for us it remained capped. Capped and not corked. Our only saving grace as even Alex, with all his foraging skills, would not have been able to score a bottle opener from the crowd of half-drunk adults.

Fuck.

My eyes burned.

"I…" I didn't know what to say.

He was joking in an attempt to make me laugh, or smile or…something. But I had the strangest, *horrible* urge to cry instead. My throat went tight. My numb hands were so very lonely without him holding them. I was supposed to be smiling. To be teasing him back—but instead…I simply…stared.

Stared and stared and stared.

Stared at his clumsy picnic—at this sweet, unfamiliar gesture—and did my best not to fall apart. My earlier calm was gone, drowned by loss and loneliness and gratitude all at once. I squeezed my arms tightly around my body to keep myself from falling apart.

Thirty-three years of my life had taught me to expect disappointment. That I wasn't worth the effort. *This* was effort. Effort to please me. To…I don't know—clichely get me to like him more? Romantic and clumsy, but… perfect all the same.

Alex had said it wasn't fake. That this was real. Just temporary.

And I took that to heart, as I beheld the most lovely, heart-achingly romantic gesture I'd ever received.

And I didn't…know what to do with it.

"Hey…" Alex's smile, once bright, was gone. "George—" He was in my personal space before I could blink. Limber for such a big man. Huge hands cupped my face. The pads of his fingers tickled my temples. Alex's breath was minty, somehow. He probably carried mints with him. Or mouthwash. The slut. But even *that* thought couldn't make me smile. "What's wrong, George? You don't like it?"

"It's not that."

"You not a wine guy?" Alex's pale eyes flickered with emotion. I wanted to yell at him. Wanted to push him away, to storm down the hill, and escape. But even more than that…the shriveled, lonely part of me wondered what would happen if I didn't. What might happen if I stayed? If I didn't run—if I let myself accept this for what it was.

If I let myself *trust* again.

"I like wine," I murmured numbly. "Sometimes."

"If you don't like sweets I've got the cheese." Alex was trying to make me laugh again. And it just…it wasn't fair. Why was he doing this to me? Why was he being so nice? In fact, why had he been so nice all day? It was confusing. Confusing and sweet, and…and…intimidating.

He'd said sex was optional—and I truly believed him. It was a big reason I'd said yes to his scheme. Because I didn't think he'd stop being kind to me if I didn't. And for the first time in my life, I wanted to know what it felt like to be wanted by someone who didn't also want to hurt me.

I had wanted to taste what it felt like to be enough.

But this was…God.

This was *so much* more than that.

"No one's ever done anything like this for me," I choked out, heart thundering. "I don't…I don't know what to do. *Why would you do this?*"

"Oh, Georgie," Alex's voice dropped low. "Because I *like* you. Obviously. It's our…third date? Yes. Third." The two meals we'd shared before totally didn't count, but I let it slide. I couldn't get my mouth to work as I processed his words. "Our first *officially*-unofficial one, now that you've accepted your fate."

Because I like you.

Simple as that.

"'Accepted my fate?' Jesus. You sound like a Bond villain."

"Does that turn you on?"

"Fuck off."

Alex laughed, not deterred whatsoever. With him clutching my cheeks the way he was there was nowhere I could hide. There was no pity in his voice, only understanding. "If it makes you feel better, this is a first for both of us."

That did help.

And again, it felt like he was reading my mind.

Could we really be that in-tune?

I must've relaxed some because Alex's next words were huskier. Throaty and full of pride. "There you go, that's it," he murmured. "Relax, Georgie Porgie."

I hated that damn nickname.

One of Alex's hands slid into the back of my hair, then down to squeeze my nape. I melted. "You know it's okay, right? That this being your first picnic has nothing to do with you."

We weren't talking about picnics specifically. He knew that. I knew that. But I appreciated the euphemism.

"If it has nothing to do with me, then why has no one ever done something like this for me before?" My lip wobbled. "My ex—"

"*Brendon.* The asshole," Alex finished for me, tone darkening. I made a stifled sound in amusement. He grinned. His pale eyes were even warmer than his hands. It was difficult not to melt when he held me so close.

"He…he never did anything like this."

"Yeah?"

"Eight years and he never…" My voice wavered. "I thought it was my fault. That I wasn't worth the effort? Or maybe it was just *normal* to feel lonely, even when you were with someone." My chest squeezed so tight it made it hard to breathe.

Alex continued to hold me safe, his eyes full of understanding. He didn't speak, letting me continue as if he knew just how badly I needed to get the words out. These horrible, awful words I'd never spoken aloud, not even to my therapist. Shards of glass that'd been stuck inside my throat for almost a decade.

"But you…you've only known me two days," I continued.

"Nearly three," Alex interrupted. I snorted. His smile was even brighter this time, crinkles by his eyes and everything. Dimples too. The same smile I'd admired when he'd been dappled with sunlight in my parents' backyard. The same smile that had charmed me on the hike earlier that day. The same smile that I'd received when I'd eaten all of his potato salad, after promising him I wouldn't.

There was a lump in my throat I couldn't seem to swallow.

"Three days…" I didn't argue, "and you've already done more for me than he did." It was true, he had. Alex had been nothing but a constant irritation and source of strength. He'd been a pillar of kindness, even when he'd teased.

"Isn't that…I mean… Doesn't that make me pathetic?" My voice cracked. "I stayed with him, Alex. *Voluntarily*. For a long time…I think I knew, deep down, it wasn't right. But I stayed anyway. I stayed even though staying *hurt*. Because I hoped one day…I'd be…enough? That we'd be happy. That I could be what he wanted if I just folded myself small enough."

"I don't think that makes you pathetic," Alex answered, voice firm. We were whispering. There was no need to be loud when we shared every minty breath. I scoffed, trying to duck out of Alex's grip—so I could escape what I'd just admitted—but Alex's grip was unyielding. Squeezing me a little, his strong hands held me immobile. When he spoke again, I had no choice but to gaze at his mouth, then his nose, then his eyes—drinking in his every word, desperate to know what he thought.

"You're loyal."

"I'm…loyal?"

"Yeah." Alex looked at me like he was seeing me for the first time. Like he'd never understood me as clearly as he did now, standing in the dark, with only crickets and the stars for company. "You loved him." He said that simply, even though my love for Brendon had never been simple. "You wanted things to work out. That's the *opposite* of pathetic. If anything…that's pretty fucking admirable. At least, I think so."

When I blinked, my lashes were wet.

"Loyal like Sam," I responded, voice rough.

"Exactly."

My smile was wobbly. Not at all as confident as he was. Not snappish and irritated as I often was when he was nearby. My walls had dropped, and in light of Alex's high opinion of me, it was near impossible to pull them back up again. A reflex, nothing more. It could be trained away given time, if I let it.

I wasn't sure I should.

This was just for practice, after all.

"I'm going to hug you now," Alex warned. "Because you look like you need one. And hell, I could use one too, all things considered."

I didn't protest as he dropped my face and neck and pulled me in tight to his chest, tight enough my feet lifted from the ground and his back popped as he squeezed. "You're a sweetheart, George-Arthur Milton," Alex promised against my hair as I pushed at his chest, playfully fighting him to put me down. "I am honored to be yours."

"Temporarily," I reminded him.

"Temporarily?" he teased. It was a safety blanket. One that told us both what we were. That laid a line for us not to cross, so we wouldn't be hurt again. "I thought you were a full-time sweetheart." That hadn't been what I was addressing, and he knew it.

But I played along.

"I'm not," I countered, my ire softened by the smile I couldn't seem to hide.

"You totally are," Alex replied, squeezing me tight enough it was my turn to have my back pop. "Such a fucking sweetheart. So fucking cute, man. It's ridiculous honestly."

"All I do is snipe at you," I replied, confused why he'd think any of this given the facts.

"Because you care," Alex replied back. "And because it's fun. Believe me, I get great joy out of sniping right back."

Alex set me down but didn't let me go. My chest was tight again, but this time, it was because he was still holding me close. Squeezing my bones together. It was easy to forget Brendon then, wrapped up in Alex as I was.

"If you ever stopped I'd think you'd been replaced by a pod person."

"Or an alien."

"Yeah, that." Alex snorted, gave me another squeeze, and then released me. I didn't even have time to mourn the loss of his sticky, summer warmth before he was flipping me around and steering me toward the picnic. "Now, stop ignoring all my hard work and thinking about other men—"

"Jesus."

"And enjoy your goddamn picnic, I swear to god."

"You're such an asshole," I griped, smiling despite my best efforts as Alex walked me onto the blanket and then shoved me down. Stumbling, I flopped onto my ass, tipping my head back to observe him. Towering above me, the grin on Alex's face did nothing to soften the heat in his eyes. He liked me below him. There was no denying that.

"Yeah, yeah. An asshole who cares," Alex replied, falling into our usual bickering to set me at ease. "And who also wants to beat your ex with a baseball bat."

"*Alex!*"

"Full of nails." He flopped down beside me and immediately went for the bottle of wine. "You know, I usually don't eat any of this stuff," he said. I was grateful for the change of subject, not sure how to respond to his threats of violence.

"Really?" I asked, amused when he fought with the wine bottle for a moment before getting it open.

"No. My PT—personal trainer—has me on a strict macro-nutrient based diet plan."

I stared at him dubiously. "But all I've seen you eat is junk."

"Yeah, because I'm on *vacation*." Alex reached over to boop my nose. I glowered at him and he laughed, undeterred. He offered me the wine bottle with a waggle. "Some of us know what that means." He arched a brow my way. "Want some? I don't have cups. Forgot that part, ha. But! I mean, we've already shared cooties a couple times today. What's the harm of a few more?"

I grimaced but accepted the bottle. "I don't normally drink." For the sake of fairness, I offered him a concession of my own.

Alex tried to take the bottle back but I fought him for it.

I won.

"Fuckin' rabid raccoon. Fine. Keep your damn bottle." He snorted and shook his head. A dark lock of hair fell over his brow as he eyed me curiously. "Why don't you drink?" he inquired, instead of asking why I was hell-bent on keeping the bottle despite this.

"I don't like feeling out of control. Or unsafe."

"Baby—"

"Stop *babying* me."

"I'm not!" Alex rolled his eyes heavenward. "It's—you know what? Never mind. You weren't this prickly when I was snuggling you like five seconds ago. Biting my head off, goddamn."

"I don't—" I started, flushing a bit and ignoring his grumbling. "I mean...I don't feel unsafe with...you...though." Alex's eyes lit up, like I'd just offered him a winning lottery ticket.

"Yeah?" His smile softened, face slanted my way as he leaned back on his hands, the picture of relaxation. He spread his legs in the cocky way he always did, thigh bleeding heat into mine. I clutched the wine bottle tighter, the chilly glass smooth against my fingertips.

"I would drink with you," I told him, cheeks flushed. "I think…I think it might even be fun."

"Wow," Alex's voice was teasing but the look in his eyes made it clear that he was flattered. "You know you don't have to though, right? I didn't know you didn't like alcohol. If I'd known I could've brought something else."

"You're not listening."

"I actually am, though."

"I *want* to drink with you." To demonstrate my point, I tipped the bottle back and took a long, messy chug. Messy, not on purpose, but simply because the nature of drinking directly out of a wine bottle made it difficult. The taste was musky sweet, not overly cloying, but enough that it didn't feel like chugging battery acid.

Setting the bottle back between my legs, I swiped a hand over my mouth, waiting for Alex's reaction. He was definitely watching me. In particular, my mouth. His pale eyes had darkened, a groan escaping him. Why the hell he was getting turned on by me chugging wine, I had no idea. But I wasn't about to shame him for it.

Okay…maybe a bit.

"If you get hard because I wrapped my lips around the bottle I am going to scream."

"It's a big bottle," Alex teased. I smacked his shoulder. He laughed. So I smacked it again. "Okay, okay. I believe you. You want to drink with me. Because you trust me." Having Alex's attention was addicting, especially when he talked to me like that. He yanked the bottle right out of my grip like it was easy. "Sharing is caring, Georgie. Didn't your mama teach you that?"

He stared at the open lip of the bottle, like he was picturing the way my mouth had pressed to it. "Christ, I am going insane," Alex muttered to himself, so quiet I hardly heard him. And then he licked around the rim of the bottle like he was chasing the memory of my lips there.

"Did you just *lick* it?" I asked in disbelief. "Because my mouth was on it?"

"I could lick something else if you want." Alex waggled his eyebrows, tipped the bottle back and guzzled. Too flustered to do anything but laugh, I turned to his pile of snacks and let the tingle of the alcohol settle syrupy in my limbs. We passed the bottle back and forth until it was mostly empty.

At one point, we ended up on our backs, half-eaten snacks lying in a mess around us. Alex found my hand. I wasn't sure when—the alcohol made it hazy. His skin was…so fucking warm. Always. Like he was half inferno. His thumb did this incredibly distracting thing, gliding back and forth, back and forth over my skin as we giggled and chatted, eyes on the stars.

We chatted for a very long time.

"Pretty, huh?" Alex asked after a dip in the conversation.

A small white blip flitted across the sky. Shooting star maybe? Or plane.

"Yes," I agreed. He clutched my hand tighter.

"It's quiet out here," Alex murmured. "Peaceful. Easy to forget the rest of the world."

I squeezed back, understanding a little more why he'd chase moments like this, bugs be damned. "Only peaceful because the wasps are in bed," I replied, words sluggish and far more freely given.

Alex chuckled. "Yeah?" He twisted to look at me. His shoulders were so broad when he lay on his side he blocked my view of the woods behind him. I wiggled to match him, blinking slow, because it felt nice every time my lashes brushed my skin. "Do they have a set bedtime, Georgie? Nine o'clock. Oh shit! Gotta get my twelve hours."

"Twelve hours? Why would wasps need twelve hours to sleep?"

"I dunno. Why would they have a bedtime?"

"Because nature, Alex. Obviously."

"Right. Nature." Alex's eyes danced. His lips looked very soft. Very, very soft. Had they always looked so soft? So…inviting? "Because you know so much about it."

"Like any adult with anxiety I spend a lot of my free time watching *Planet Earth*."

"I'm not sure those two things coincide, but okay."

"I'm surprised you even know that word," I taunted.

Alex leaned in close. "Co-in-cide." His nose brushed mine.

It was…distracting. As distracting as his eyes were up close like this. There was a smudge of chocolate on his bottom lip and I wanted to lick it clean for him. You know, because I was generous.

"I know a lot of words. Way bigger words than that," Alex laughed, breath tickling my lips.

"Do you like cats?" I asked instead of sticking my tongue in his mouth like I wanted.

"Cats?"

"Yes."

"They're growing on me." Alex's lashes looked as ridiculously long as ever. Some people were just blessed and it was unfair.

"What do you mean?" I didn't understand.

"I kinda adopted one." Alex's nose brushed mine again, rubbing back and forth. I found myself mirroring the motion just like I'd mirrored his position on our sides. It was nice, this sleepy, drunken nuzzle.

"How do you *kinda* adopt a cat?" I said, attention diverted.

"Think about it."

It took me a second, but realization dawned fairly quickly. "Are you saying you adopted me? And I'm a cat?" I frowned.

"Yep." Alex's eyes were drooping. Not because he was tired. But…something else. The heat inside his gaze simmered, his breathing picking up. "One of the white ones—like Mr. Pickles but prettier—"

"Hey—"

"With a diamond collar. And a pedigree. Like from that movie—with the kittens. What's her name…*Duchess*. That's you."

"I don't have a diamond collar." I wasn't a cat either, but for some reason, that was the thing I latched on to.

"I'll buy you one," Alex promised, his eyes drifting shut. "I'll buy you whatever you want."

"You're drunk."

"I'm not," Alex countered, nuzzling, nuzzling away. "I haven't been drunk since you told me you think that Lego Batman and Joker should've been together in the movie. That sobered me right up." I didn't believe him, so Alex reassured me again. "I'm *really* not, Georgie. Unless you count being drunk on you? Because if you do, I totally am."

"Stop flirting with me." I wasn't drunk anymore either. The wine had run out long ago. So I couldn't even blame intoxication for my next words. It was all me. Like an idiot. "Shut up right now or I am going to kiss you."

"If you don't, I might *literally* die. Right now. I am being so…so *good*." Alex's voice was quiet enough I could hardly hear it over the thundering of my own heart. "I want you so fucking bad it's driving me crazy. You have no idea how difficult it's been to hold back."

"Then why don't you make the first move?"

"Because I respect your boundaries. I told you sex was your choice to make. I won't betray your trust. If you want more then you can have it," Alex replied immediately. "But you have to *want* it."

His eyes opened, and I met his gaze, shuddering. The hand that had been holding mine slipped free, a single finger tracing up the back of my forearm. I found it incredibly difficult to decide where to focus my attention, his mouth—or his hand. "I don't think you were given choices in your last relationship. And I don't think people listen to you enough. You deserve…better."

"And *you're*…better?"

"If you'll let me be," Alex replied. His fingers climbed higher, dipping into the inside of my elbow, then skimming up my bicep. "I didn't mean to pressure you—to say anything," he added. "But you just…your mouth. Jesus, George. I swear to god you have the prettiest mouth I've ever seen. And I just want to—"

I kissed him.

I kissed him and the world didn't end. I didn't explode. Didn't burst into flames. I did, however, die a little. Because as Alex's lips parted, and a needy sound escaped him, I realized just how stupid I'd been. I should have been kissing him all this time. For *three* days I could've had his mouth on mine. For three days I could've—

"Stop thinking," Alex chided. "C'mon, Georgie. Please. I just—" His mouth firmed, lips growing hungrier, still soft, still careful. "Just feel me— Feel how much I need you."

"Mmm," I was the one who deepened the kiss, let my mouth go slack, let my lips part, let my tongue sneak out to tease along his lower lip, chasing the taste of chocolate cookies. Alex made another hungry sound, his teasing fingers turning into the scrape of his palm as he dragged his hand over my shoulder, then my collarbone, finally settling at my neck. He squeezed. My Adam's apple bobbed beneath the touch, pulse skittering.

Alex was a greedy kisser. Once invited in, he never seemed to want to leave. He licked everywhere, these hungry swipes of his tongue that set my toes curling. If I didn't give him what he wanted *exactly* the way he wanted it, he had no qualms about tugging my chin down with his thumb and forcing my mouth to open wider for his enjoyment. It felt like being fucked. Thoroughly. Completely. Lewd in a way I wasn't sure kisses had ever been designed to be.

Despite how voraciously Alex devoured my mouth, palm on my throat, he never initiated more. He respected the unspoken boundaries I set as though it were easy to do so. Like he didn't mind at all.

Content to be blue-balled for the duration of our short relationship, if that's what I chose.

He acted like this kiss was a gift.

Like it was worth something.

Priceless, honestly.

I'd never been valued as highly as Alex valued me. Never been treated so softly. Never had someone pay attention to me the way he did. Never had someone to protect me, or coddle me when I needed it, or allow me to coddle back.

He let me need him and he didn't get angry.

It was no wonder that I'd initiated this.

That I wanted this.

It was as inevitable as the moon rising high in the sky.

We kissed for a long time, eons probably. Soft, then harsh, then soft again. Alex was on top of me for more than half of our impromptu make-out session, the hot line of his body between my legs, hands on my face, holding me still and open for his tongue to plunder.

At one point, I ended up in his lap, fingers in his hair, his hands clutching tight at my lower back. He let me lead then, but only for a few minutes before he gave up trying to control himself and devoured my mouth again.

He was a little sloppy, and I liked that.

It felt honest.

By the time we'd stopped kissing, we were both breathless and spit slick. Alex's cock was a hard, insistent line in his joggers, but he made no move to do anything about it aside from reach down and give it an apology squeeze with one of his big hands. I wasn't sure how much time had actually passed. An hour? Maybe more.

Before this picnic, I'd never…kissed someone just for the sake of kissing. I'd never desired another person so much that the brush of their lips made me feel like I was shaking apart. Even when I'd been a horny teenager I hadn't felt like one. I certainly did now though, still ogling Alex's cock, my own dick pulsing in my jeans.

I sucked in a breath, and Alex groaned. He tipped his head back, the long line of his throat bobbing as his dark lashes drifted shut. "You are killing me, Duchess," he murmured. "If you don't stop staring at my dick I am not going to be held responsible for my actions."

He was all talk.

"Don't call me that."

"It's Duchess or baby, you pick."

"How about George?"

"Boring." Alex made a sound like a buzzer going off. "Try again."

"Do I really have to?" I pouted, and Alex's responding chuckle was smooth as honey. He was on top of me again a second later, pinning me to the grass with his bulk. We'd rolled off the blanket, and the grass was chilly at my back. He was heavy. I liked it too much.

"No. You don't. But I'd like it if you did." Alex's hand slid into my hair, pulling it taut. He tipped my head back to inspect the single, slutty hickey he'd left just behind my ear before I'd caught him and told him off. "I like giving you silly nicknames. Makes me feel like we're close."

"We're literally as close as two people can be right now," I countered, my hard dick aching. If he lowered his hips, we'd...oh god. Best not to think about that. I was half a second from cumming already, I didn't need my imagination to help.

"I can think of a way we could be closer." Alex's voice dropped an octave, breathy as tingles shot down my spine. He leaned in, lips skimming my ear. "You like to be fucked, don't you, Georgie?"

I whimpered, hips twitching up, searching for friction.

What a...what a lewd thing to say!

"I've seen the kind of toys you enjoy," Alex added. "Long. Thick." He nipped the shell of my ear and I squirmed, embarrassed. For a minute there, I'd almost forgotten about Neil. "Do you know how distracting that is? That I know you like your ass pounded? Can't even fucking sit beside you without thinking about your cute little face pinching as you sink down on a big, fat cock."

Apparently, horny Alex had a mouth on him. I...was not complaining. Not at all. This was spank bank material for the next century, even if it was mortifying to be so thoroughly called out.

"If you like *big*, Georgie, I can give you big," Alex promised, breath teasing my ear. "I can fill you up nice and full. Wanna see?"

I nodded, heart stuttering.

To emphasize his point, Alex reached down, seeking out my hand. I let him guide it, knowing exactly where it was headed before it even reached his destination.

Alex laid my hand right over his hard cock. It was even thicker than I'd realized, and pulsing inside the soft cotton fabric of his pants. He gave my hand a squeeze, then released me, but I didn't let go. Instead, I fanned my fingers out, curling them around the length of him, measuring his dick with bated breath.

Christ, he really was big.

As big as Neil.

Which was a tall order for a dick that wasn't made of silicone.

Sliding my hand lower, I measured his length just like I had his width. All the while, Alex's breath came hot and heavy, his big chest heaving. He was obviously affected by me. When I twisted to look at his face, his dark brow was furrowed and his eyes were scrunched shut—like it was taking everything he had not to buck into my hand.

"Nngh," Alex made the frankly most pathetic—but sexy—sound I'd ever heard when I tightened my grip right at his tip. I swear to god the fabric was damp.

"I like to be fucked," I confessed, shy but sure at the same time. Something came over me, a confidence I'd never had. It was his desire that brought it to life. Like being wanted gave me the courage to be honest. Alex's hips rutted of their own accord and he swore softly, widening his stance like that would help him keep in control. "I like it *hard*, Alex. Raw. No barriers."

"Christ."

"I like to be split wide."

"Ohmygod." Another flex of his hips.

"I like to feel it when I sit down the next day—" It was impossible not to egg him on when he was like this. Even if the filth coming out of my mouth was as foreign as the cock in my hand. It wasn't a lie though. It was the truth—a truth I'd never felt safe to tell anyone else.

"You would, wouldn't you? Jesus with those legs and that ass—you're made to be pounded into." I squeezed Alex's dick in reply and he made another pitiful sound, bucking into my grip. He'd been under the impression he had the upper hand when he really did not.

My hand slipped lower, cupping his sac overtop of fabric. Alex made a sound like he was dying. I'd never felt more powerful in all my life than I did then, holding Alex by the balls, literally.

"I like to be bred, Alex," I added, voice shaking—because I'd never admitted this out loud. "Like to be fucked full and leaking."

"I'd put a baby in you so fucking fast," Alex blurted. "Jesus, I'd keep you pregnant twenty-four-seven if I could."

Now it was my turn to whine.

Apparently, Alex and I shared kinks as easily as we shared wine bottles. My own hips canted up, and Alex made a hungry sound as my hand tightened on his sac. "If we're not having sex, I need to know like *right* now," Alex gasped out. "I didn't mean to initiate this—I meant to respect your boundaries. But holy fuck, Georgie. You're like goddamn ecstasy or something."

"Again with the talk of drugs."

"*George.*" Alex's voice snapped. It wasn't angry so much as it was a warning. I'd never heard Alex do that and it was shocking to say the least. Maybe it should have upset me, or scared me—because Brendon had been dominant that way too, but it didn't. Instead, a little thrill zinged through my body.

"*Alex,*" I drawled, softening my grip on his dick.

His nostrils flared, and our gazes met.

A beat passed as a silent war waged between us—and then Alex's lips were on mine, somehow even hungrier than before. I slipped my hand inside his pants, fumbling beneath the elastic as he swore against my mouth.

"Condom?" I croaked.

"I'm good. Are you?"

"I am."

When my fingers finally wrapped around his bare dick it took everything I had not to cum. He was just so…fucking *huge*. Jesus Christ. Easily the biggest I'd ever been with. Now I knew why he always spread his legs when he sat down. This thing was a goddamn monster. Thick and throbbing and sticky at the tip. Like he'd been leaking the last hour, leaving a wet patch in his underwear.

"Ohmygod," Alex gasped, spreading his legs before flexing his hips into my grip. It was a bit dry. Of course it was. Neither of us had brought lube up here, but Alex didn't seem to mind. His precum slicked the way enough, if the grunts against my mouth were any indicator. He enjoyed the snug scrape of my hand as I stroked him from root to tip, doing my best to smear the precum around.

The damp patch on his boxers where his cock had touched kept brushing my hand. Normally, that was something that would bother me. At least, with anyone else. With him, I found I didn't mind, so engrossed in getting him off that the only thoughts in my head revolved around how fast, and how soon I could get this fucking monster inside my ass.

Alex's hips bucked forward, grinding into my grip as he dropped his head, his breath puffing against my throat. "I'm not going to last," he managed, riding my hand. The drag of his velvety skin tickled the pads of my fingers, making me feel frenzied. I wanted to see him. Didn't want to simply touch. "Jesus Christ, you're perfect."

No one else had ever called me *perfect* before.

And I would've basked in it if I weren't so eager to make him come. *Snap, snap, snap,* went Alex's hips, fucking into me with a brutal grace that belonged in the wild—not here, in the relative safety of the campgrounds. He snarled, head tossing back, teeth bared.

I tightened my grip, his crown nudging against my palm—and then he was coming, spilling all over my fist and the inside of his pants. Alex losing control was a sight to behold. His head tossed back, big chest quaking with every desperate breath. His eyes, normally so full of mischief, were a flat, hungry black.

He rode my hand a few more times, slippery crown rubbing at my skin before I pulled my hand free of his boxers with a grimace. My wrist kind of hurt from the angle. And my palm was messy—not at all pleasant. Especially as his cum began to cool.

Alex caught my wrist before I could wipe myself clean on the grass. "*No*," he said, voice like gravel.

"*Alex*," I said, glaring at him. "My hand is—"

"You're going to lick it up." Alex sounded so sure of himself I automatically wanted to argue.

"No, I'm not," I huffed. But I didn't protest whatsoever as he forced my hand toward my mouth. There was a question in his gaze. It was clear he didn't want me to actually follow through if it bothered me. But… Christ.

It didn't.

Grimacing, I flattened my tongue along my palm, scooping up the ribbons of cum.

"Oh my fuck." Alex's hips jerked forward like he hadn't just come and was ready for round two. His eyes were trained on my tongue, on my face—like watching me lick up his pleasure was the single sexiest thing in the entire world. "Stick your tongue out, let me see it."

I felt ridiculous, but I also felt…I felt gorgeous, too, as I stuck my tongue out as instructed, Alex's cum sitting inside its curl. It was bitter tasting and salty—but I didn't mind so much. Not if it was his.

"Now you *really* have Alex cooties," Alex smirked. I scowled at him, mouth about to snap closed, but he stopped me. One of his hands gripped my jaw, forcing my mouth open wider as my tongue began to tremble with the effort of staying out. "Keep it out like that," Alex commanded, voice throaty and soft. "Lemme just…"

And then he was sucking around my tongue, cleaning it up with the filthiest, most delicious slurping noises. Eating his own fucking cum right from my mouth like it was a normal thing to do. Like it wasn't dirty or lewd at all. When he pulled back he looked pleased as fuck. His hair was messier than I'd ever seen it, and that ravenous look in his eyes was still there.

Alex very slowly, very reluctantly released my mouth, allowing me to shut it, though his hand remained on my chin. "Jesus, I bet you'd let me spit in your mouth if I wanted to."

"W-what?" I whined.

"Fucking filthy, baby. You're so fucking sexy." Alex sucked in a breath, rerouting his thoughts, his eyes just as hungry as before. Determined, he spoke again, "But I'll save that for another time. Right now I'm going to suck your cock, Georgie," he informed me. "If you want me to."

Jesus Christ. Was he really going to make me say it out loud? I whined, and Alex had the audacity to look amused. He was a sadist. Worse than I was. Because he struggled back onto his knees, staring at me with evil glee. Staring at the way my cock tented my pants, at my flushed cheeks, at the way I couldn't fucking stop squirming like it was a goddamn reward.

"Maybe you don't want it," Alex sighed—obviously fucking with me.

I made another sound, but apparently that wasn't good enough because he acted like he was going to climb off of me.

"I want it," I said in a rush.

"Huh." Alex cocked his head, eyeing me up and down. I'd never felt more naked in all my life and I was currently fully clothed. "I'm not convinced."

"Alex—"

"Beg me for it."

"I'm not—I won't. I'm not going to *beg*." I growled at him, and his eyes danced.

"Fine," he replied. "Then ask me. Nicely." His shit-eating grin made me want to punch him—and also shove his face between my legs so he could make good on his promise. "You have good manners. Not with me—obviously. But I've seen it. C'mon. Give me the Georgie everyone else gets."

"I hate you so much."

"Sure, sure." Alex waited. He could tell how much I liked this, which was seriously unfair. My entire world had narrowed. Even the party, still raging, could not steal my focus. I wasn't even worried about bugs, or the dark, or random passersby seeing us in a compromising position.

There was only Alex and his mouth, and how badly I wanted to be inside it.

"Alex…" My voice cracked.

"Yes, Your Majesty?"

Jesus Christ, he wasn't going to make this easy.

"Will you please…" Oh god. This was so embarrassing. Why did it make me so goddamn hard? Something was wrong with me.

"Yeees?" Alex's grin only grew wider. Like he was the fucking Cheshire Cat or some shit. "I'm listening."

"Will you please…" *C'mon George. You can do this. It's only one little request. Sure, it's mortifying, but you've survived worse. You dropped Neil at the airport, remember?* "Will you please suck my cock?" There! I'd done it. Surely Alex was going to end my suffering. He wanted this as badly as I did, right?

Wrong.

"Duchess or baby?" Alex's voice was a teasing rumble.

"Oh Jesus Christ, not again."

"You want your dick sucked? Pick a nickname."

"This is coercion."

"You can safe word out at any time. Red, yellow, green." Alex ticked off, somehow already aware that I was familiar with the stoplight system. How the hell had he known I'd understand that? "Lucky guess," he said, reading my mind for what felt like the millionth time.

"Alex." I squirmed some more. Why was the fact that he'd had me pegged so effectively so attractive?

"I'm not going to ask again." Alex's voice took on that low tone. No teasing. A simple, effective command made even more effective by the fact that he hardly ever dropped his playful attitude.

I gulped, cheeks flushed.

"Duchess," I finally replied, the word ripped right out. "Or baby."

"Both?"

"Yes."

"You like both," Alex confirmed, pleased as fuck as he bent close. "Don't you?"

"Y-yes."

"Good boy." A pleased shiver ran up my spine as Alex laced a tender, almost apologetic kiss against my mouth. "Alright. You gave me what I wanted. Now I'm going to give you what you want."

"Please, please, please—" Wow. I had not meant to say that. I had apparently been whittled down to nothing. Instead of teasing, or finding triumph in the fact that my walls had shattered, Alex's smile grew soft. *Proud.*

"What a good boy you are, Duchess," Alex murmured. "Being so very sweet for me, aren't you? So patient, playing my games."

I had been patient.

So patient.

And my dick hurt—and I just—

"You're going to need to be quiet," Alex purred against my ear. I nodded eagerly, my knees pinching together as my cock pushed insistently against my jeans. "Someone could walk by—it's a risk."

"I know," I managed, because I did know.

"Are you drunk, Georgie?" Alex questioned, sliding down my body, slow and sure. "Don't you dare lie to me."

"No. I already told you I'm not. I haven't been since…since before the kissing."

"Good." Alex slipped lower, lower. His breath ghosted my abs where my shirt had ridden up. "Just making sure. And you want my mouth on you?"

"Y-yes."

"Even though we're out in the open—where anyone could see?" Fuck. How the hell did he know that turned me on? I could hardly breathe I was so fucking hard. Stars swam as I pinched my eyes shut and nodded.

"I want it."

"Quiet," Alex reminded me. "Put your hand over your mouth." I did as I was told, belatedly realizing the hand on my lips was the cum-coated one. Grimacing, I forced back my initial reaction, instead letting the heat of my current bad decisions simmer between my legs.

I spread my legs a little, and Alex's fingers worked my button free, then my zip. By the time he'd shoved my jeans down enough my briefs were showing, I was already whining up a storm behind my hand.

"That's not very quiet," Alex admonished, fingers slipping along the waistband of my underwear. My hips jolted up, and he clicked his tongue in reply. "Maybe this isn't a good idea." I couldn't tell if he was teasing again or serious, so I was quick to shake my head, hand still firmly over my mouth.

"Are you shaking your head in agreement or disagreement?'"

It was definitely not a good idea. Not at all. As he'd pointed out, we're out in the open. We could get caught at any moment, and while slipping my hand in his pants could be easily concealed, his face full of my dick could not. It was a bad choice. A bad decision. Stupid.

But I wanted it.

I wanted it so fucking bad.

I lowered my hand, lips trembling and glossy with his cum. "I want it," I said. "I can be quiet."

"Mmm," Alex replied, hot breath against my hip bones as he looked up at me through his dark, dark lashes. "I guess we'll find out if you're telling the truth."

Eighteen
Alex

GEORGIE WAS A GODDAMN mess. The sexiest, cutest, most enticing mess in the history of the universe. He would not stop shaking. So fucking desperate to be touched that he quaked with every breath.

I kissed his left hip bone, then his right, and he made a pitiful sound behind his hand. It was muffled, yes, but nowhere near quiet, like he'd promised he'd be. "That's not very good, sweetheart," I admonished, just to watch the way he shuddered. Like my reprimand was getting him off.

Christ.

My dick was at half mast already. And that shit hadn't happened to me since I was in fucking high school. He was seriously...the most attractive person I'd ever met. All nervous and quaky and needy all at once. Not afraid to fight me. But eager to lose.

"Try harder," I said to test the waters. George's lashes fluttered, and his hips flexed up, proving my hypothesis correct. He liked me a little mean. He liked me firm. At least…in bed. Worn thin with his heart on his sleeve and no walls to conceal it, George was so eager to give up control it was addicting.

I hadn't been lying when I'd told him I could tell. Sure, I'd exaggerated a bit—you know, to match the mood. But exaggeration wasn't a lie.

"Remember, *quiet.*" I slipped my thumbs under his waistband and tugged his briefs down a few inches. I tucked them beneath his sweet balls, mouth watering as I took in the majesty of George's little cock.

And it *was* little.

Maybe max three inches?

And so fucking sexy I could hardly breathe. Pulsing and red, the poor thing looked fit to burst. All it'd take was one suck and he'd be spilling. I almost wanted to tease him some more to see how long I could make him last.

But…he really had been good.

And he was shaking, those dark blue eyes swimming with tears.

He probably didn't even know that he was crying. He'd be mortified if he did. George was easily embarrassed. Even when it wasn't fair to react that way. He was as prickly as a cactus, and charitable to everyone but himself.

I had never met someone who deserved pleasure more.

Though I'd never outright dommed before, I was familiar with the concept. Blame my choice of reading material. I had a big imagination, and I could admit over my years soaking up smutty page after page, I'd grown…curious. Not to say that I'd ever particularly felt the drive to actually scratch that itch—because I hadn't.

But I had also never been with someone like George.

And he…fuck. He made me want to take charge of every aspect of his goddamn life. To make sure he ate right, to tuck him into bed on time, to fuck him when he acted up—and needed release. To bully my way into every aspect of his life so that I could ensure he was well-maintained and happy. To put that same dopey, *needy* look on his face like he was sporting now, all flushed and turned on—embarrassed by his own nature, but desperate to let go. Like I was the only thing that mattered.

Like I was his world.

And he was trusting me to take care of him.

"A-Alex?" George lowered his hand to speak. I hadn't realized I'd stopped moving, lost in thought as I was. That wouldn't do. I didn't want that softness to flee, replaced by fear that he'd done something wrong when he really, truly hadn't.

"You're doing so good, baby. So fucking pretty." The praise came easily. It wasn't an act. Or forced. It was natural. This was a lot more personal than I ever got during sex, and because of that, the intimacy only felt heightened. "I'm just taking my time admiring your sweet little cock."

George squirmed like he was embarrassed, and I smirked.

"You like that?" My voice went even lower. "You like me calling your dick little?" He made a sound—mortified and turned on, obviously. "Yes or no?"

"Yes." George's admission was barely a whisper.

"You like all the nicknames I give you," I deduced. "Every last one." Seemed I was going to need to get even more creative moving forward. "Okay, enough teasing. You just lay back and relax, gorgeous, I'll take care of everything."

It was time to cease torturing him.

He'd waited long enough.

When I wrapped my fingers around the root of his cock, George gasped. His entire body went rigid. "If you want me to stop, tap my head three times," I told him. Oh— "And keep your mouth covered. I don't want to share you with the rest of the goddamn camp."

George's eyes widened.

Realistically, he was still way too loud for that to *actually* help, but he seemed to like the illusion of it anyway. The secrecy most definitely. Struggling to be silent despite his pleasure. Breaking the rules. The threat of *discovery* only heightened each sensation.

This was the kinkiest I'd ever been with another person.

I usually fucked in, and out, and left when the deed was done.

I sated the physical and social urge like it was another task on my to-do list. And as someone with an overactive libido *that* happened often. I never allowed myself to be anything other than a glorified sex toy. I needed more, but I never let myself have it.

I certainly never experimented.

That took trust.

I found, as I settled into what felt like my natural role, George looking to me for guidance. George only looking at me, I'd definitely been missing out on how intimate sex could be. It certainly helped that for the majority of the day I hadn't censored myself. I'd been fully me, in all my "overwhelming" glory, and George had still chosen to take me up on my offer.

George had seen my stupid-romantic picnic and he'd loved it.

He'd wanted to kiss me.

He'd been the one that wished to touch me first.

For him, I hadn't been too much.

At least…not yet.

When I sucked George down to the root, it took hardly any effort at all— he was so small.

Obviously, I had never been harder in all my life.

His tiny cock barely tapped the back of my throat even with my nose buried in the golden hair at its base. The *sound* George made wasn't human, this garbled choked thing that made my own dick throb. His hips flexed up, feigning like he wanted to gag me, even though that was frankly impossible. I pressed them back down, forcing his pelvis against the grass as I swallowed around his twitchy length.

Because his hips were trapped, George's legs jumped next, like an anxious rabbit kicking out—so I had to restrain those too, using my bulk to keep him immobile. Pinned like prey, George was the prettiest fucking thing I'd ever seen. He struggled for a minute, wiggling and jerking, and then—

Like magic.

He gave up.

Sagged into the dirt, all the tension in his frame bleeding away.

I watched his eyes grow glassy with a primal sort of satisfaction.

I'd done that.

I'd caused this.

A few tears slipped down his red cheeks. Dazed and submissive, George still wouldn't stop quaking. His nipples were hard enough they poked his shirt. It was only my delicious mouthful and the fact that I was using every limb I had to keep him still that stopped me from leaning up to bite them.

George's hair, usually styled, was this *horrible* wavy mess, sticking up in clumps and spikes. Debauched already, and I'd only just gotten my mouth on him for the first time.

More.

I wanted more.

Wanted him to keep making that face.

Wanted him to lose himself entirely.

To forget about everyone and everything but me.

Wanted to silence his noisy thoughts.

Wanted to give him peace, hand in hand with his pleasure.

I swallowed around his cock, spit slicking my lips and leaking into the golden curls at his base making them sticky. George's Adam's apple bobbed like he was drooling as much as I was.

There was no denying he liked this.

Hand over his own mouth, me between his legs.

Entirely at my mercy.

Was he sniffing my cum on his hand right now? Was his sweet tongue chasing my taste from his fingers as he cried and cried and attempted—to no avail—to hump my mouth?

There was something so gorgeously addictive about the way George submitted. His lean frame twitching, the width of his shoulders pressed into the dirt.

Someone as high-strung as he was, reduced to gibberish and sobs—*man*.

This was so fucking hot.

And the hottest part was that I'd caused it.

He'd given this to me.

Trusted me.

Chosen me.

Forgiven me.

Determined not to let him down, I swallowed again, slurping around his length as his dick pulsed against my tongue. I could practically feel his heartbeat through it as I pulled up and down, shifting the soft skin back and forth with deliberate precision.

George's chest heaved, these anxious, broken breaths wracking his frame—followed by another fruitless attempt at a kick. Simply reflexes. He was nothing if not predictable. It was easy to thwart his efforts. As leggy as he was—and surprisingly strong—he was no match for me.

He could kick all he wanted and it wouldn't do a damn thing.

However, one of his hands did find its way to my shoulders. And his nails were a different story. Though as perfectly groomed as the rest of him, they dug in hard enough to sting. The pain only heightened my pleasure, making me sink into him with a groan. Scratching, digging, scraping into my skin with gusto, clinging tight.

When I pulled off his dick after a few minutes of back and forth sucking, I dragged my tongue along the vein on the underside. I could still feel the skip of his heartbeat there, the steady thrum of it as I held still and watched him squirm. I paused, the crown of his cock still suckled gently between my lips.

George's nails sank in again, a new line of scratches forming as he tried to encourage me to take him deeper again.

He was so responsive.

It was *intoxicating*.

Pulling off with a pop, I arched a brow at him. "You're kinda a slut, you know that, right?" I teased, keeping my tone light so he'd know I wasn't criticizing him. "If I let go of your hips you'd be fucking my face right now."

George choked, eyes widening. Despite being foggy-headed and pleasure-drunk, he *still* wanted to deny what I was accusing him of—even though we both knew I was correct. He attempted another fruitless kick.

"If you keep that up, you're going to have bruises on your hips and leg tomorrow," I warned. "And it's lake day. So everyone is going to see." I had no doubt George was going to wheedle his way out of swimming, but that didn't mean I couldn't tease—or that he wasn't going to be wearing trunks.

I didn't mention the scratching, worried that if I brought attention to it, he'd stop.

I didn't *want* him to stop.

He may be too shy to wear the marks from tonight, but I wasn't.

George gave up protesting.

Instead, he sank into the grass again, somehow even softer than before. This time, his head tipped far enough back that I could no longer see his face. Which was a shame. There was nothing sexier than watching his expression while I sucked his twitchy, red cock.

"Look at me," I said, lips pressed to the tip of his needy dick.

George convulsed, even his arm trembling as he tilted his head down to peer at me again.

Obedient.

He was so fucking obedient like this—totally at odds with his usual personality.

His teary eyes peered down at me from above the delicate line of his fingers, still strangling his mouth. "There we go. That's just what I wanted," I purred. "I need to see your face when I make you fall apart."

George's brow pinched, and then relaxed as I took his cock back into my mouth with gusto. His crown was tight and slippery beneath my tongue, slit weeping as I dug the tip of my tongue inside it, chasing the flavor of his pleasure. Salty, and frankly delicious. Because it was George.

George's musk I was smelling.

George's taste on my tongue.

George's most personal, private parts—vulnerable inside my mouth.

Though short, George's dick had a decent width. Proportionate. Not enough to even get close to choking me, of course, but enough that when I tightened my lips at the base and slid all the way to the tip, my jaw began to ache.

Up and down, I abandoned my need to tease him in favor of giving him what he needed. Just like before—except this time I had every intention of sending him right over the edge.

All the while, I watched his face, enjoying the pinched furrow his eyebrows performed every time I sank low enough his balls tapped my chin. Enjoying the way the hand over his mouth tightened till his knuckles went white when I nibbled on his tip. He was so fucking sticky. Covered in spit, in precum, skin spongy and wet as his curls tickled my nose.

George didn't last long just like I'd suspected he wouldn't.

A fact that pissed him off, judging by the angry grunt he made when he came—breaking through his obedient sprawl. It was flattering to taste the evidence of my effect on him. Salty and a bit sweet—stronger than what he'd been leaking before—George's cock began to spurt after a particularly snug glide up and down.

I was careful not to swallow, cupping his seed safe in the curl of my tongue as I rose from my spot between his thighs and climbed up his body with slow, deliberate movements.

George's nostrils flared, his blue eyes—nearly black with lust—wide enough I could see the whites. That dazed look in his eyes was still there, though slightly more alert. Like his guard wasn't back up yet. He was present, still processing his orgasm.

I grabbed his wrist, squeezing the bones and pulling his hand away from his face to see what lay beneath it. His mouth was bitten red and raw. They were so fucking enticing. Swollen and wet, like the entire time I'd been sucking on his tiny dick he'd been biting and rubbing his lips behind his fingers.

Or maybe that was from before? From our kisses.

Christ, that was even better.

With an arched brow, I waited, giving his parted, glossy lips a pointed look.

When he didn't understand what I wanted, I helped him along. I released his wrist—which he dropped at his side in the grass—and used that same hand to cup his jaw. My thumb skimmed his bottom lip, dragging it open. The flash of teeth made my dick jump, but I ignored it.

This wasn't about sex.

This was about *him*.

About asserting dominance over him—the way we both craved.

About allowing him to let go of his worries and simply feel.

And I knew exactly how to do that.

George stared at me. He didn't say a word. He looked half drunk, even though he'd sworn to me that he wasn't. Maybe he was as drunk on me—on us—as I was? His nostrils flared, alarm written all over his face when he *finally* seemed to realize where this was headed.

George knew his safe words. But I still waited to give him time to use them. When he didn't, I *groaned*. My cock twitched, cupped in sticky fabric. He parted his lips on his own, holding his mouth open submissively—and I…fuck.

I wasted no time.

Slow and steady, allowing us to really feel the moment, I leaned in close. For a beat, we just observed each other, blue on blue. And then…I opened my mouth and fed him his own cum.

George jerked at the initial taste, but I held him still by my grip on his chin. My tongue slid deep inside his expressive mouth, urging him to swallow every last drop. Still struggling, despite having consented to this, George whined.

His jaw tensed, like he was going to snap it shut, right on my tongue.

But then…he did the most beautiful thing.

He stopped fighting.

He relaxed.

And he did as he'd been urged, his mouth convulsing with my tongue still inside it as he swallowed his own seed like a fucking champ. Every last drop.

Jesus Christ.

He was such a kinky little shit.

Holy fuck.

So surprising.

After I was sure he'd taken it all, I gave his lips one last parting lick before pulling back. His mouth didn't look any different now that he'd just eaten his own cum. Still pink and puffy. But simply *knowing* what I'd put in his belly made me feel feral in a way I never had.

So many kinky, wonderful possibilities.

A world I'd never tapped into at my fingertips.

I only hoped I could keep up.

"Good boy, Georgie," I murmured, watching as his lashes fluttered with pleasure in response to the praise. "You're such a *sweetheart*, aren't you?" George's breath quickened. I peppered soothing kisses across his lips, his jaw, and up his cheek. "You did so well, baby. *Perfectly.*"

He gasped.

Fuck.

He really liked that.

Really liked being called perfect.

"You're such a perfect little slut for me." George jolted, proving my point. His hands sank into the back of my t-shirt, clinging to me as I praised and comforted him. The marks he'd left on my back stung, but I ignored them. Wore them as a badge of honor.

For several long, glorious minutes, I told him how gorgeous he'd been. Told him how *much* I *loved* his obedience. How he'd been so pretty with his cock in my throat. Told him I'd never seen a prettier man in all my life.

Never been with a better lover. Never seen anyone look so goddamn earth-shatteringly riveting when they lost control.

I spoiled him the way I'd always wanted to spoil someone.

George ate it up.

He softened with every word, clinging, clinging—like he didn't know how to let go of me now that we'd crossed this line together. Like he was scared the second he did, I'd abandon him.

I didn't.

I wouldn't.

Even if we weren't literally sharing a tent, there was no way I was letting him out of my sight tonight. This had been…a lot. I definitely hadn't intended the picnic to lead to sex when I'd set it up—but I didn't regret anything.

I liked being close with him.

And discovering what he looked like when he actually let his walls down was ridiculously enthralling.

Had Brendon done this for him? Brought him high, high, high—and protected him from the subsequent low?

Somehow I doubted that. Based on how George responded—like he'd never been praised before. Like this was his first time receiving any sort of care after sex.

It pissed me the fuck off.

But I pushed those feelings aside.

Instead, I focused on him. On bringing him out of that foggy headspace. On kissing his grimple, the corners of his mouth, and that sweet scrunchy nose.

"Alright, baby, up you go," I said several long minutes later. George was less shaky now, the glassy look in his eyes having faded into something more aware, though still soft. He huffed at me, which was a good sign—his ire returning. "I'm gonna let you rest on the blanket while I get our mess cleared up."

George didn't protest, even when I half-carried him back onto the fabric and laid him down. He didn't get mad when I kicked the snacks off of it and bundled him up like an adorable, grumpy little caterpillar. He just watched me, those dark blue eyes full of emotion.

Mouth still slick.

His own cum still in his belly.

"You just stay there and look pretty," I said for the second time that night. "I got this."

I said that a lot when he was around, but I couldn't help it. Couldn't help but want to take care of everything for him. It felt right. Like all my life I'd been wandering, and only now found the place I was needed.

Stop thinking like that, Alex.

George glared at me—which was another good sign that he was coming back to himself.

Christ, he was so *cute* all swaddled like that. I clenched my jaw, nearly overwhelmed by cuteness aggression.

Do not bite him.

No biting.

I resisted the urge to pick him up and do just that—but only barely. And only because it felt imperative I get everything in order so we could brush our teeth and climb into bed.

It was late, and even though there was no way in hell I'd be waking up for the sunset hike the next morning, that didn't mean I didn't have stuff to do, despite what I'd told June about being on vacation.

Now that I'd discovered what sex with George was like, there was a lot I needed to figure out before the next time we did anything like this.

And we would be—doing something like this, I mean.

At least, if I had anything to say about it.

As always though, the ball was in his court. I'd have to see how he reacted in the light of day. And I really did need to figure out how exactly to…do this again. Maybe experiment? More kinks would be fun. And being in control of George had been the first time in my life I'd truly felt needed. With his eyes on me, looking to me for guidance—it was like nothing else mattered.

Not the thoughts in my head.

My insecurities.

My fears.

I'd brought him peace, but he'd brought me peace too.

He gave me somewhere to focus my boundless energy. He gave me purpose. Release.

And I wanted that again. I just…wanted to make sure I got it right. Not like Brendon, who I assumed was as much of an asshole in bed as he'd been outside it. There was no telling whether or not he and George had dabbled in a more… kink-oriented relationship? Just thinking about that made my blood fucking boil, honestly. But regardless, I doubted he gave George what he needed.

And I intended to do just that.

I'd do it the right way, too.

No going in by halves.

"You doing okay?" I checked in when I was nearly done packing up the picnic. We'd eaten a lot of the things I'd gathered so it was mostly trash I had in my arms. George grumbled in reply, which I translated to mean that he was fine. Once finished, my arms full, I debated the best course of action.

I could dump the trash off and come back for George? But I wasn't sure his legs were working properly, and the idea of leaving him alone in the dark—given his fear of it—made me uneasy. I was lucky enough he'd been so distracted tonight he'd not once brought up the snake incident again.

Maybe…I made him feel safe?

The thought was almost too much to handle.

Too close to what I wanted.

Too close to something that would cross the line from "temporary" to "permanent."

I shoved it away quickly, terrified of its implication.

Think, Alex. Think.

What to do…what to— Oh.

Perfect.

"Alright." Plan decided, I knelt beside him. "I'm gonna need you to be in charge of carrying the trash." George responded with an affronted look. I laughed. "Because I'm going to carry *you*."

"I don't need you to carry me," he huffed, speaking for the first time since I'd had his dick down my throat. His voice was hoarse, his vulnerability evident in every rusty syllable. He was eyeing me warily—like he thought that now that I'd had him, I'd lose interest.

Ha.

Yeah right.

"Of course you don't. But I'm going to do it anyway." I grinned. George was too tired to protest again. Or maybe he didn't mind being babied as much as he let on. Because soon enough the blanket was off of his shoulders and rolled up neatly in his grip along with an arm full of trash. "Cutest little raccoon I ever saw," I cooed, enjoying the way he growled at me as I looped an arm around his back, and one beneath his knees, and hefted him up.

Trekking down a somewhat steep hill with a fully grown man in a bridal carry was easier said than done. I was glad for all my training in the gym as I was pretty damn sure if I'd been at any less than peak physical health, George and I would've ended up on our asses at the bottom.

We didn't though.

Miraculously.

I didn't want to lose my "cool guy" persona just yet.

The closer we got to the cabins, the more George stiffened up. He glanced this way and that—as though nervous we were going to get caught. Which was hilarious, given the fact that he'd been far less concerned when he'd had his pants open and his cock out. Apparently, getting caught being cuddled was exponentially worse than being caught having sex in George-Arthur-Milton-Land.

Damn he was adorable.

Seriously so fucking adorable.

Do not bite him, Alex.

My stomach gurgled so I made a detour toward the main cabin to drop off the trash and grab a snack. Sex always made me hungry, and carrying George certainly didn't help. By the time we entered the empty kitchen, George was wriggling and struggling in my grip, so I set him down. Not because my arms were burning or anything, of course.

"I could hear your stomach growling the entire walk," he huffed, mother-henning me again as he stomped to the fridge and began pulling out a handful of items.

"Sex makes me hungry," I replied, and George glared at me.

"Of course it does. *You* didn't eat anything."

I'd eaten plenty of snacks. What did he mean—

Oh.

Oh. Naughty, naughty Georgie.

It took George a second for his words to catch up. He paled, then reddened, then stormed over to the counter. Running away was his go-to when he was overwhelmed. I let him have it. Especially because it looked like he was about to make me a bomb-ass sandwich.

Peppers, turkey, lettuce.

Far more sophisticated than the ones we'd made together earlier that day.

"Are you saying I'm hungry because I didn't swallow your cum, George?" I teased, stalking after him with a sly grin. I leaned into his personal space and kissed his blanket-covered shoulder, just because I could. He shook me off, hands full of deli meat, his brow furrowed.

"*No.*"

"Really? Because I think that's exactly what you're saying." Christ, he was irresistible when he was annoyed. Part of me had wondered if sex would change our dynamic, but it hadn't. I was glad. I'd never had more fun with another person in my life.

There was, however, a new layer of intimacy between us.

Like a cushion.

Soft and unobtrusive. Like it should've been there all along.

"Stop talking about cum, and eat your sandwich." George was apparently an olympic level sandwich maker because I hadn't even realized he'd finished. He shoved the food against my chest, mayo—ugh—smearing on my shirt.

"You didn't make one for you?" I took a bite, talking around my mouthful.

"Don't talk when you're chewing." George's face scrunched with disgust.

I swallowed, then smirked slyly. "Not hungry, huh? Belly full of—"

"I will *literally* stab you, I swear to god."

I shut up. Because as much as I liked to tease him, the kitchen was full of knives—and I'd learned the hard way that George followed through with some of his threats. He looked incredibly pleased with himself as I finished my sandwich in silence.

Comfortable silence.

The kind of comfortable silence that should not come after a threat to stab someone, but it did. Because I was with George, and when we were together, even the quiet was pleasant.

"Thanks," I said when I was done washing my hands in the sink. I took my time like I always did, and George watched me soap up like it was foreplay. And then, because I remembered just how much he'd lit up when I praised him, I added, "Best goddamn sandwich I've ever had."

"You're just saying that," George waved me off.

His ears were red, betraying him.

George had already cleared up the mess we'd made and was waiting eagerly, his blanket draped over his shoulders like a cloak. He really did look regal like that. Regal and dorky. My own personal elf.

"C'mon, Legolas," I urged. "Time to get that sexy ass ready for bed."

George scoffed as I slung an arm over his shoulders, leading him back out of the kitchen and off to the tent to grab our hygiene stuff. He griped at me over how much toothpaste I used, but aside from that, was content to remain in silence at my side as we got ready for bed. Despite his chatter, it was clear how much George liked my meticulous routine.

"I knew he had a clean mouth," he muttered to himself, thinking I couldn't hear. I gargled more mouthwash, trying not to laugh. Of course he, of all people, would appreciate that.

Zipped up in the tent, with his nightlight on, and both of us dressed down, neither of us seemed to know what to do next. I wanted to offer him my bed again—to save him from the bugs—and steal a cuddle or two, but had a feeling, especially after how vulnerable he'd been during sex, if I offered he'd refuse.

I was wrong.

George surprised me once again.

"Alex...?" George's voice was small—like it had been the night before when he'd tapped me with his cold fingers and put aside his pride to ask for help. He didn't look at me, arms stiff at his sides, minute trembles shaking his sexy hands.

"Yeah?"

"Do you think I could...maybe—"

"Of course." I didn't make him finish the question, instead striding over to my mattress and sleeping bag with purpose. "I'll double-check it for bugs first, okay?" I promised, even though I doubted anything had snuck inside there.

"Thank you." George watched me as I worked, checking every nook and cranny. Because I'd remembered how cold he'd gotten the previous night, I made sure to turn the space heater on a bit hotter before returning to the freshly inspected sleeping bag with a smile that I hoped was enticing.

"You want to be little spoon or big spoon?" I offered.

George didn't reply; he just climbed onto the mattress and slipped inside the sleeping bag, wiggling all the way toward the edge. He faced away from me, which I suppose was his answer to my question. Pleased, I snuck in behind him, twisted to zip us up, then settled at his back. It felt second nature to sling my arm over George's torso and pull him in close. He shivered when I nuzzled the back of his ear, lacing a few unassuming kisses there to show him just how much I appreciated his vulnerability.

"Georgie?" I said after a few minutes of comfortable silence. He'd gone lax in my arms, his breathing deep and easy. Not asleep yet though, if the way he was absentmindedly playing with my fingers was any indication.

I didn't want to wake him up, but I figured I needed to know.

"When you were with…asshole-Mc-fuck-face," I began. George made that high-pitched noise he only did when he was trying not to laugh. "Did he… you know…" I paused, realizing that was the wrong question. "Was he your Dom?" There. Better.

"Yes." George's voice was quiet. It was all the answer I needed.

"And that's something…you want? Not because of him, but because—"

"Yes. I want it."

"Okay." I sucked in a breath, thoughts whirling. I wasn't surprised. In fact, I felt validated. Validated that what I'd assumed was reality. That I'd read him correctly. But that didn't change the fact that this revelation proved Brendon's abuse had run far deeper than surface-level. He'd taken George's trust and he'd…

He'd crushed it.

At least…if the way George talked about him was any indicator.

It made me so fucking angry. So goddamn livid—that anyone could take such a gift and twist it into something so—

"Go to sleep," George replied, still playing with my fingers. "Stop worrying so much."

My swirling thoughts stilled. The anger fled. Just like that.

It was funny. He was such a cute little hypocrite. Telling me not to worry— when that was all he ever did. But…it worked, despite this.

Because George was here in my arms, not with Brendon. George was *safe*. George was cared for, cuddled, and pampered the way he deserved to be. There was no need to waste what little time we had together chasing apparitions.

I hid against the back of his hair. It was soft. *So soft.* Tickling my nose as I nuzzled into it, inhaling the scent of his cologne greedily. Or maybe that was his shampoo? Either way, he smelled amazing. He always did.

"I'm not worrying," I lied, realizing—belatedly—that we hadn't addressed the elephant in the room from this morning. Specifically, the way he'd run away from me, *worrying*. "I'm just…ruminating."

"Ruminating about what?" George said when I didn't finish my thought.

Now I felt guilty for what I was about to say, simply because I was teasing him again—and here he was being adorable and grumpy and sleepy in my arms. I held him tighter, debating whether or not to open my mouth.

George sighed. "You're going to say something stupid, aren't you?"

"You know me so well."

"Spit it out," he replied with amusement that he tried to hide. "So that we can sleep."

"Okay…" I grinned, something fizzy and bright buzzing in my stomach. Not between my legs this time, but higher up. Like butterflies were actually a thing, and I had a whole colony dancing around in there. "I was just going to promise…not to run away if I wake up tomorrow morning with a boner."

George froze.

I waited, eager.

He was either going to elbow me or smile—either would be lovely.

Instead, he laughed, once again defying expectations.

His whole frame shook with it. Another one of his choking, snorting fits. My favorite. My favorite thing in the whole goddamn world. Like he couldn't get a breath in, he was so overwhelmed with joy.

I joined him, chuckling against his shoulder, unable to help myself, because Georgie's happiness was contagious.

Like the flu.

"Shut the fuck up," George wheezed between snorts. "That is not—that's just. That's *mean*—"

"I'm just saying—" I spoke over him, seeing how long I could drag this out. "That getting a boner while being in bed with a handsome guy is a *totally* normal reaction. And in *my* world a little grinding is always welcome."

"Ohmygod. Good*night*, Alex." George continued to giggle and I did too.

When we finally fell asleep, we both had smiles on our faces.

Tomorrow, we could worry about what the future held for us. I could worry about the wedding. About learning. About being a better temporary partner than Brendon had ever been as a permanent one. I could worry about the timer ticking over our heads, the very thing that kept me from being the one to run.

But tomorrow had never felt further away than it did right then.

And I only had Georgie to blame for that.

Nineteen
George

I DIDN'T WAKE UP with a boner, but I *did* wake with a pounding headache and an existential crisis on the horizon. Alex did have one—a boner, not an existential crisis—and he didn't run from me. A fact that he took great joy pointing out as he let the damn thing go down naturally on its own and dressed for the day. We'd both popped pain-killers. He checked my burns before he left, pleased to note that they were looking better, before rebandaging them with the same care he'd previously taken.

That was the last I saw of him.

Because he'd had to do more…competent-wedding-planner-brother things.

Still stuck in my thoughts, I'd wandered to the only place at the camping grounds that felt safe when he wasn't beside me. The kitchen—and my mother. And her distracting, but soothing orders.

But even being commanded to cook did nothing to distract me.

I was stuck in the past.

Trapped.

Like a fly on a sticky tape trap.

When Brendon and I started dating he'd been a lot more focused on aftercare. He'd had a soft hand to follow the hard blows, and it'd been easy to melt when I was held so firmly beneath his thumb. He was never particularly affectionate, but I didn't complain. As that care had dwindled from a full meal into table scraps over the years, I'd found myself grasping at what little morsels of affection he'd decided I deserved. I noticed the change, yes. But it was more lucrative at the time to beg for more than to argue over what I was missing.

Brendon had said my love was "smothering."

He'd said that my standards were too high.

That I asked too much.

That I needed too much.

Brendon didn't like when I argued—unlike Alex, who thrived under my attention, even when it was negative. There were so many differences between the two of them that it was hard to keep track of all of them. What did it say about me that my "practice boyfriend" was better at taking care of me than the man I'd thought would be my life partner?

How had I never noticed?

Scratch that—of course I had. I just…I suppose I hadn't thought I deserved better. It was an awful sort of feeling, to come to terms with the fact that Brendon had been a horrible boyfriend when I'd put him on a pedestal for so long.

What was the opposite of rose-colored glasses? Green…spectacles? I had no idea. But it felt like I had a pair of *those* on. In the light of the morning, after spending time with a man that treated me well, it was suddenly easy to see all of Brendon's faults.

I didn't understand how Brendon could treat me the way he had, and yet—Alex didn't? It was an equation that didn't make sense. Two plus two equalling six, or something equally as unlikely.

Had the fault been mine? That I simply wasn't worth the effort?

Especially after I'd found out what I was to him. A convenient hole to fuck when he got bored with his "real" relationship—the one I hadn't known about. I was the idiot who spent years in the dark. While Brendon paraded around his fiancé, taking her to dinners, and picnics, and family events like he was proud of her. He'd never been proud of me. Never wanted to be seen with me. No, I was delegated to dark corners to pick at crumbs, and yet he'd expected me to be grateful for that.

So many things felt...confusing at present.

My job, for one. Because thinking about Brendon, obviously, made me think about work. And when I did, dread filled me. The icy fear of *seeing* him again, of returning to the pattern I'd lived in ignorance, now that my eyes were open, and I saw it for what it was.

A hamster in a wheel, running round and round.

Was I remaining there because it was what I'd always done? What was expected of me? Out of...stubbornness? Because I didn't want to let my mother down? Or...was I staying because it was what *I* wanted.

Alex certainly cared about what I wanted.

Maybe I should start caring about that too.

It was odd.

Not once...had I thought about Brendon's feelings.

Nor did the dread feel nearly as...debilitating as it had. It was still there, of course. Like a shadow clinging to my shoulders. But I could breathe through it. And that, in itself, was improvement.

As I stared listlessly into the giant pan of scrambled eggs I was helping my mom prepare, I couldn't help but come to the conclusion that I...was beginning to maybe...care more about what Alex might do in the future than what Brendon had done in the past.

Steps forward.

Practice.

Practice at being…valued.

By a man that was Brendon's antithesis.

Where Brendon had been calculating, Alex was spontaneous.

Where Brendon had been cold, Alex was warm.

Where Brendon rationed out his attention, Alex dumped his in overwhelming armfuls. So much so that I had no idea what to do with it. I'd been starved before, shriveled and needy, and I had no doubt that under Alex's care that would not be the case. He'd glut me with affection if he could. Spoil me in ways I'd never been spoiled, simply because he wanted to.

I had an empty well and Alex wanted to fill it.

Which was…intimidating—but not…not bad, maybe?

Because I felt lighter than I had in days, maybe years? And I could only blame last night. The kisses, the compliments, the praise, the laughter. The way Alex had taken me apart then held me together. The way we'd gone to bed with laughter in the air. And woken up to gripe and swipe at each other all over again.

The lack of Alex at my side was frankly jarring.

We'd only just met.

And yet here I was—falling for his charm when I'd promised myself I was done with this. That I would never let another man control my emotions. That I'd never give someone power over me again. I didn't know how to stop. I didn't *want* to stop. Content to ride this train till the end, because for the first time in my life I was discovering what it felt like to be treated well.

Which was…infuriating.

And why I hadn't protested when Alex had told me there was stuff he had to do this morning. He'd said he'd catch up with me later with those big blue puppy eyes—and I…believed him. Like a total schmuck. I one-hundred percent believed that he wasn't playing with me. That last night had not been a fluke—a way to get in my pants.

That he'd been genuine.

Honest.

It was so...odd to think the best of someone. To trust them. To assume they had good intentions, rather than bad.

In a way, Alex's absence was a blessing. I wouldn't have been good company right now, anyway. It was better I hide in the kitchen, stewing in my thoughts, so he wouldn't catch my bad mood as I sorted through them.

"You don't look happy," Mom said from my left. "I'm surprised, after last night." She was wearing massive yellow gloves as she prepped bacon strips. This was round one-thousand. All loads of meat had been cooked to a crisp on the ginormous griddle she'd borrowed from Roderick's mom. The one from our house was already full, sitting right beside it. It was literally a factory's worth—and we planned to use every last strip.

My burns felt better today, and yet despite my protests, she hadn't allowed me to handle anything other than the giant spoon I was currently stirring in the eggs. Even then, it'd been a battle.

The attention...was kind of nice.

Even if it wasn't her fawning over me, and my job, and my "big city life".

"I'm fine," I said, even though she was right. The last thing I needed was for her to worry more about me. I really was fine. Having an existential crisis, yes, but fine.

"I'm your mother, I can tell something is wrong," she replied. Like a hound with a bone, that one.

I sighed.

Stirring the eggs more vigorously than was healthy for them, I attempted to calm myself. It wasn't her fault I was agitated. It wasn't Alex's either. He'd done nothing wrong, not last night, not this morning—and yet here I was, "fussy" again.

As enlightening as yesterday had been, I couldn't help but feel overwhelmed. Without Alex breathing down my neck and distracting me, there was nothing to get me out of my head. A good orgasm—oh fuck, had it been good—would help.

But again.

Only eggs.

No Alex.

And ha! Wasn't that a mind fuck in itself?! That I was now associating him with sex. That I was *expecting* sex. That I *wanted* sex.

Who the hell was I anymore?

Maybe I really had been replaced by a pod person.

"Do you want to talk about it?" Mom asked, not dropping the subject like I'd hoped she would. Her tone was loving, which of course filled me with guilt.

"There's nothing to talk about, because nothing is wrong." I'd come to Ohio to bond with her and here I was…shutting her out. Why? Because I didn't want her to think I was broken.

Even though I clearly was.

It was nice having one person think the world of me. Fine, two. Because Joe. Maybe…even three? Dad, though he'd never outright said it, had always seemed proud.

Ahuuughh! I jerked a hand through my bangs, pulling on them in frustration.

"Alright." Mom's hand waved in front of my face, blocking my view of the eggs. "That's enough of that."

Apparently I couldn't even *pretend* to be normal.

"I know you were out with Alex last night." Of course she knew. Alex had literally charmed the cookies right out of her hands. It wasn't as though we were hiding it. "Is that why you're so out of sorts?"

My cheeks immediately flamed bright red and I had to twist away so she wouldn't see. She didn't know we'd been…*physically intimate*, of course. Despite how out in the open we'd been, no one had come close enough to see us.

At least…I hadn't thought so?

Oh, dear god.

What did she know?

"No. Yes. Maybe?" I said carefully, trying not to give anything away. Mom was aware that I was a sexually active adult. It was a fair assumption to make. But—to openly acknowledge it? Absolutely not. Nope. We were *not* doing that. Not today, Satan.

"Two peas in a pod," Mom tacked on, a knowing smile on her lips.

"What?" What did peas have to do with anything?

"You and Alex," she replied, looking pleased. "You certainly looked cute together last night. I don't know if I've ever seen you smile that much." *Had I been smiling?*

"That can't possibly be true." My cheeks were only growing redder by the second.

"Considering...I'm surprised you're in such a foul mood today." Mom was concerned. Rightfully so. I'd done my damndest not to drop my guard around her for years. "Did he do something?" Mom paused, sobering. "You know you can tell me, right? That I'll help you."

Dregs left over from Brendon.

Like tea leaves in the bottom of an empty cup.

She felt guilty for not telling me to leave him.

But we both knew I wouldn't have listened.

"Alex didn't do anything wrong," I was quick to reassure. "He was a perfect gentleman."

"Maybe not a *perfect* gentleman," she tacked on, tension gone, her eyes dancing.

If that was an innuendo I was going to pull my hair out.

"He's...I mean..." Christ, what the fuck was I supposed to reply? "Alex is...nice." That's what she'd told me before. And fuck, she'd been right.

"I like him much more than Brendon," Mom said without an ounce of shame. My heart squeezed, as I nodded jerkily. "He's kinder to you."

"Brendon wasn't *mean*."

I wasn't sure why I was still lying about that.

Pride, maybe.

The last thing I had left.

"*Honey,*" Mom silenced me with a single look. I wilted, shrinking over my eggs with a groan. Clearly she saw through that too.

"Okay, so Brendon wasn't *particularly* affectionate," I admitted reluctantly. I had literally just been thinking about this so this line of questioning felt far too raw. "But I'm not—I mean… Alex and I aren't dating. Officially."

"You *could* be."

"We *could*, except the fact that he literally told me he's not looking for a relationship. And I'm not either. So—actually?" Okay, I was starting to sound a bit hysterical, voice rising in pitch. "We can't. Because we don't want to. Because we can't. I told him I don't want it. I literally—laid down the law. I told him I—"

"Oh, sweetie," Mom pulled her gloves off, bacon officially abandoned. She held her arms out, her bright blue dress beckoning me toward it like a beacon of motherhood. "Come here."

"The eggs are going to burn." I was fragile enough that if she squeezed I was sure to crack.

"Fuck the eggs."

My jaw fell open. *Since when did she swear?* But then again, I'd caught her high as a kite last night, so maybe I shouldn't be all that surprised to see evidence that she was an adult before she was my mother.

I fell into her embrace rigidly. It wasn't like the way I'd melted into Alex last night when he'd had me tucked tight against his sweat-damp muscles, compliments murmured alongside the kisses he'd left on my skin. But this was my mom. So it was still pretty damn good.

This was one thing phone calls didn't replace.

Hugs.

Mom rubbed my back and I had to force myself not to worry that she'd gotten stray drops of bacon on me. Bacon essence. She'd been wearing gloves—it had to be fine, right? At least, that's what I told myself as I finally gave in, curling around her tiny form with a weighty sigh.

There wasn't a problem in the world that one of my mom's hugs couldn't fix.

"It's okay to change your mind, George," she said softly. "You know that, right? That you can—"

Joe came into the kitchen, interrupting our embarrassingly emotional moment with the emotional intelligence of a block of wood. The door slammed against the wall and he grunted, hefting a giant-ass cooler in his arms.

"Where do you want this?" he inquired.

He blinked, eyes narrowing as he finally noticed our embrace. I jerked away from Mom immediately. I'd been vulnerable in front of her and that was already far too much emotional honesty for one day. I didn't need Joe to look at me like I was fucked up too.

At least one Milton needed to think I was perfect.

I retreated to my task—and my only somewhat burnt eggs—with my head held high. Unfortunately my cheeks remained flushed, no matter how hard I willed the heat away.

"Horrible timing as always," Mom chided him, then gestured at the back wall. "There. Back corner."

"I didn't know you guys were gonna be hugging," Joe gruffed, big chest heaving as he hauled the cooler where she'd directed. He set it down with a *scrape, thud* that echoed through the whole room. His back was sticky with sweat, and I grimaced. It was not at all attractive on him like it was on Alex.

"You need to shower," I told him, stirring my eggs.

Joe made a sound, lifted his arm, and sniffed his armpit. He dropped it back down with a shrug. Then he settled against the counter, watching me with hawk-like intensity. "What's in the cooler?" He asked Mom, as stoic as always.

"Beer," she replied. "The ice is melting. I need to refill it so it's ready to go back into the bridesmaids' cabin."

Joe frowned. "How much beer do they need?"

Mom rolled her eyes, hands on her hips. "However much they want, Joe. If they want to drink a gallon of beer every hour on the hour they are allowed to." Joe was the youngest, and their relationship was way different than the one I had with Mom. Less respect, maybe? Just as much love, of course. But he certainly got chewed out more than I did. I wasn't sure if that was because of his status as youngest—or the fact he didn't seem to mind.

He had thicker skin than anyone.

And then—because he was Judas, and wanted the heat off of him—Joe threw me under the goddamn bus.

"Georgie got laid," Joe said.

Mom stopped mid-rant, turning her wide eyes on me. "George...you—" she gaped.

"I am going to *kill* you." I jabbed my egg-speckled spoon at Joe. "Feed you to the fucking bears—or wolves—or whatever horrible creature will take you."

"Enough," Mom sighed, shaking her head at the two of us. "If you're going to fight, do it outside. You're stressing out my bacon."

"How can bacon stress out if it's dead?" Joe frowned, confused.

"It's a figure of speech," Mom replied, miffed at him again.

"Is it?" I teased, surprised by myself. Obviously she and Joe were surprised too because they both swiveled to look at me, twin sets of blue eyes wide. I lowered my spoon to the pan.

"I didn't know you could joke," Joe grunted.

"Of course I can joke."

"Huh." Joe looked at me like I was a stranger.

Had I really never joked with him?

"Just. Ugh. Forget it." I turned back to the eggs, cheeks burning for a new reason now. A reason that had nothing to do with Joe outing my sexual escapades to our mother.

"Did *you* know he could do that?" Joe asked Mom, not dropping the subject.

"It's been a while since the last time he lowered his guard enough, but yes," Mom laughed back, delighted, and not afraid to poke fun—even though that was mortifying. She saw right through me. "Does your good humor have to do with your *adventures* with Alex last night?"

"Can we *please* stop talking about my sex life now?" I was justifiably horrified. And pissed at Joe. Because this was all his fucking fault. And he'd done it on purpose! Giant little shit.

"I don't know," Joe said. "I'm having fun."

"*Joe.*"

The more flushed I became, the more eager Joe and Mom were to taunt me. When Lacey entered the room a second later, a third griddle in her arms, I knew I was fucked. Lacey knew how to use her mouth like a goddamn weapon.

"Why are you all smiling?" she asked. "Except George."

"George got *laid* last night," Joe informed her at the same time Mom said, "George made a joke." They stared at each other for a beat, then laughed.

"*George* would really like it if you all stopped talking about him," I said.

"George should not use third person if he wants the teasing to stop," Lacey said. She set the griddle she was carrying in the only empty spot left on the counter and turned to look at me.

"George is—I mean, *I* am leaving," I said—though…that would mean abandoning my eggs, and they were almost done.

"You're acting like getting laid is a big deal," Lacey said. "Is it a *big* deal, George? Was it *that* good?"

That question made me pause—which in turn made the room explode with excitement.

"I knew setting them up was a good idea!" Mom sounded far too innocent for a demon. Because she was one. Just like Joe and Lacey. Because I was in Hell. *This* was Hell. It had to be. Otherwise my *own* mother wouldn't be gossiping about my sex life with my two younger siblings.

She turned her attention to Joe and Lacey, ignoring me entirely. "I thought they'd be compatible. You know…*that* way."

"Why the hell are you making hypotheses about my sexual preferences?" I squawked.

"We talk about it all the time," Lacey replied, dead-toned.

"What the *fuck?*" I gasped.

"When we have our meetings," Joe added, like I hadn't spoken at all.

"Your…*meetings?*" I was being baited, but I couldn't seem to get myself to ignore them, or leave, despite my protests. Vaguely, I recalled Roderick mentioning something similar at the barbecue. He'd said he was a "member". At the time, I'd thought nothing of it. But now…I was realizing maybe his comment hadn't been random.

Despite how horrible, awful, horrible this was—it was also…nice to be here with my family, even if they were hellions.

I'd missed this.

And before I'd let them see beneath my "perfect" exterior, we hadn't had a single moment like it. Maybe…vulnerability was the price I had to pay to be close to them.

"What meetings?" I poked again when no one answered.

"For our club," Joe grunted.

I was missing something critical.

"What club?" I narrowed my eyes at Joe. Of the three of them, he was the most likely to spill. He didn't have a mean bone in his body, even if he was a giant tease sometimes—exhibit A, right now.

"The We Hate Brendon Club," Joe said the words without any guilt whatsoever.

"The…" *what?*

"We Hate Brendon Club," Lacey filled in the blank. "Alternatively known as the Get George A Better Boyfriend Initiative. That name was too long and too complicated so we scrapped it."

"Dad's still mad about that," Mom muttered.

"The new name makes more sense. It's practical."

"You're *kidding.*" They did *not* have a club. That was—that was ridiculous.

"Do I *look* like I'm kidding?" Lacey gestured to her face, which was as stern as always. Her pale hair was gelled back, not a single strand out of place. And she was wearing a pencil skirt and blouse, despite the fact we were camping.

Intimidating and impractical, just like her.

"You…" I faltered. Lacey didn't *look* like she was kidding. In fact, Lacey rarely, if ever, joked. We were similar in that way, apparently. "You really…have a club? To hate on my ex-boyfriend? All of you?" The more I acknowledged it out loud the more unbelievable it seemed.

"With meetings and everything," Joe confirmed—as though what they were both admitting to wasn't completely unhinged.

"And you were *aware* of this?" I swiveled to look at Mom, hoping to find some semblance of sanity inside the current madness.

"Of course I was," Mom shrugged, totally unrepentant. "I'm Vice President."

I didn't know how to feel about any of this. Maybe I should've been more offended. But the longer I mulled over my feelings the more apparent it became that the strongest of them was simply relief. As odd as this was, it was validating to learn that my family had seen what I had. And that no one blamed me for calling it quits on a relationship that had taken up so much of my adult life.

I wasn't sure why I'd expected to be judged for it.

But it was nice to know I hadn't been.

Apparently I was the only person that viewed leaving Brendon as failure.

"Is this the same club that's been trying to set me up with Alex?" I inquired, though I already knew the answer. All three blond heads bobbed in sync. Flushed, mildly pleased, and mostly horrified, I wilted. "I'm guessing you're not the only three members." Three head shakes in reply. Varying degrees of enthusiasm. "Jesus Christ."

"You can join if you'd like," Mom offered.

"How magnanimous of you," I replied dryly. "To invite me to join a club *about* me."

"There's usually cookies," Lacey gave my back a single, awkward pat, before turning back toward the door. "I've gotta go. I promised Mavis I'd get her ready for the lake early so we could be the first ones down there."

Right, the lake.

Because today was "lake day".

Unbidden, memories from the night before flooded my senses.

Alex between my legs. Alex's hot, wet, tight mouth around my dick. Alex's hands, so big and scratchy, pinning me immobile like it was easy to do so. Alex's words—

"If you keep that up you're going to have bruises on your hips and leg tomorrow. And it's lake day. So everyone is going to see."

"George?" Joe waved a hand in front of my face the same way Mom had a few minutes prior. I startled, jerking away from the eggs. The stove was off, Mom's doing—when? I had no idea—and the spoon I'd been holding was missing.

"Sorry," I shook my head, cheeks bright red. "What?"

"I asked if you were coming."

"To the...to the lake?" Did I really have bruises on my hips? I hadn't checked. It was a testament to how distracted I was that my first thought hadn't been how very little I desired to get wet—fuck, maybe Alex had been onto something when he'd said I was a cat. "Why would I—I mean..."

Oh Jesus.

I probably did have bruises.

Bruises I'd need to hide.

My cock twitched at the thought.

"Lakes are lakes—" I stuttered. *Lakes are lakes? What the fuck was that supposed to mean? C'mon, George.*

"Mavis wants to build a sand castle," Joe told me. He was uncharacteristically chatty now, even going so far as to tell me about the lake and the beach it had. Also wave runners? And boats—*kayaks?* Canoes. Something or other. But my brain was in the past, focus stolen by last night and how very lovely it had been. Only this time, I didn't think about ex-boyfriends, or guilt, or worries—I simply let myself recall the...good.

"Okay," I found myself agreeing.

Joe offered me a fist bump, that I returned, still dazed. "Bye."

"Bye," I had no idea what I had just agreed to but could only hope it wasn't something totally terrible-awful. Mom was less mischievous as I helped her pack up drinks for the beach. She didn't bring up our earlier conversation either, the one about *feelings*. When we'd finally finished, I felt lighter than I had in a long time—more than ready to see the other pea in my pod.

Other half of my peapod?

Pea number two.

Either way.

Alex.

I was on the hunt for Alex.

As ridiculous, and confusing, and earth-shattering as that was. I *wanted* to see him. And maybe…tell him about the We Hate Brendon Club. And maybe, if I was really, *really* lucky, he'd leave some more bruises for me to worry about hiding.

I couldn't wait to get more practice in, my bleeding heart be damned.

Twenty

Alex

IT'D BEEN A WEIRD morning to say the least. After completing the tasks I needed for the wedding—confirming vendors, double-checking that everything was in order, and checking in on Mom, to make sure she remembered her daughter was getting married—I finally had a chance to do the research I so desperately needed to do. Or so I'd thought—until June joined me, interrupting my tiny bubble of peace with her loud perfume and constant questions.

"Shut up, I'm trying to read," I grunted as June invaded my personal space.

I'd retreated to the beach before everyone else in the hopes of some alone time. June had come bearing breakfast—and annoyance, in equal measure. My evil twin was hyped up on Red Bull after pulling an all-nighter and going on her masochistic hike up the mountain that morning with Roderick.

And she was being insufferable.

"How was your date with *George*?" she wheeled after we'd finished eating.

Normally, I'd bite. We shared most things, especially dating stories, but I only had a certain amount of time to figure out what I needed to and I seriously needed her to shut up.

It was a blessing that Hocking Hills wasn't so far off the grid that cell service wasn't available.

"Can I fill you in later?" I asked, tapping into a new window on my phone. A black and red website dedicated entirely to bondage. The images were as stimulating as they were distracting. I couldn't help but look at them and picture George. George dangling from the ceiling, trussed up like a ham. George on the bed with a spreader bar between his legs, and his hands tied to the headboard. George coated in red shibari rope, laced around his puffy pink nipples and up his thighs to frame his cock.

George—

"That bad?" June frowned, interrupting my daydream. "Damn."

"Jesus Christ, June." I put my phone down, twisting to glare at her. She was laying in the recliner next to mine. Sunglasses on her head. Face and upper body in the shade of the attached umbrella. Her swimsuit was an ungodly shade of red that was offending to the eyes, especially given how much of her breasts it showed off. She wore sandals that made no sense. Sandals that wound all the way up her legs like the rope I'd just been looking at.

I nearly gagged.

I really needed to stop thinking about bondage when my sister was right next to me.

It was just…my phone—and all the articles I'd been reading.

They were getting to me.

"I'm sorry. I really thought you guys were getting along." June looked genuinely upset on my behalf. "Fuck. And it's my wedding! And now I've set you up to have a super awkward week—"

This was never going to end if I didn't put a stop to it.

"He's great. Sexy. Cute. Perfect. We're *very* compatible. Last night was like, epic levels of epic. He agreed to my stupid scheme—and now I'm trying to spoil the fuck outta him—And I only have a few more days to do it." I cut her off before she could keep spiraling. "So I need to *research*."

"Research?" June looked less guilty now, and far more intrigued.

She did not get the hint.

Sitting up, June wiggled her sunglasses down her nose by scrunching it repeatedly. "Research *what?*"

"Research for George." I was not getting into it more than that. "To… please him."

"…what?" June blinked.

"During sex."

"During sex…?" she repeated, trying to wrap her head around what I was talking about. "I'm confused. Why the fuck do you have to do *research?* You know more about dicking-down than half the state of Ohio."

"That's not really a compliment," I replied, even though it totally was. I grinned cockily, popping my back to get comfortable and sighing, before I turned my attention back to June. "He's…" How did I explain this without saying something that would offend or betray George's trust? "Fuck." There wasn't a way to do that. "Never mind."

"I won't tell him that you told me," June promised. "I'm good at secrets."

"Feels like betraying his trust if I say anything," I shrugged. "Can't do it. Sorry."

"What if I figure it out on my own?" June batted her lashes. "Then I could help you without you having to outright tell me."

I frowned…but figured that was one way to get around it.

"I don't know. Feels fishy."

June didn't laugh, even though my joke was perfectly timed considering we were lounging at the edge of a lake. Lame.

"Since when do you hesitate to tell me anything *ever?*" June cocked her head to the side. "Be so for real, Alex. I basically know how many butt hairs you have."

"Disgusting."

"Disgusting, but true." June's pale eyes were knowing. And I knew…this more than anything was betraying how strongly I felt about George. Yes, I'd just told her. But I guess…*seeing* it in action was something else entirely. "I'm gonna put my big sister hat on when I say this…" She was barely older than me, by like five minutes.

"Jesus."

"But, Alex. Baby. You *do* realize that if it's something you need to research, maybe having someone to talk to about it would be, dare I say, healthy?"

I groaned, because she was right.

"Fine. I guess…if you're not going to *say* anything—and *I* don't give you details—" June nodded up and down, "and *you* guess it on your own, I can't be expected not to…seek counsel."

God, this whole conversation felt like pulling teeth.

June's expression was thoughtful. "Okay so…you and George did something—something you *haven't* done, despite being Columbus's favorite slut—and you need to research it."

I didn't respond, instead feigning disinterest. In the distance, I could see Lacey and Mavis splashing around in the shallows. They were too far away to hear us, thank god. And thus far, they were the only members of the Milton clan present.

Where one Milton wandered, the rest were sure to follow.

Like ducklings.

I didn't have much time.

And it was *stressing* me out.

I needed to get this right. I wasn't afraid of putting in the work. Wasn't afraid to hunt for answers. But I was on a goddamn time crunch. Tighter than anything I'd ever faced—and I really needed to stop fucking around and figure this shit out before I saw George next.

June kept talking, "You…and George…did something you don't know a lot about." She had literally *just* said that. This time was different though, because her mouth clicked shut immediately after the statement like she'd finally figured it out.

She blinked, then her grin went wolfish. "Oh. My. God. He's *kinky*."

She was right, so I simply shrugged. "*Hypothetically*."

"Oh-my-god he's *super* kinky," June cackled, way too excited about the prospect of said kinkiness. "Holy *shit*, Alex. And you're…what? Figuring out how to…" She mimed throwing a whip.

"Kinda." He was definitely into being restrained. Whips? I wasn't sure yet. I got what she meant though.

"Ah! This is so fascinating. I love this journey for you. Hate it too—obviously—because thinking about you boinking anyone is…ew. But *love* it." June beamed at me. You'd think I told her he rescued puppies or something, not that he may or may not enjoy BDSM. "Are you cool with this?" she asked, because even though she was actually evil, she did still love me. "You're into that too?"

As much as it pained me to talk about kink with my sister, I figured she was right, given how new this was, it wasn't a bad idea to seek counsel—especially when she was bound and determined to be my confidant.

"I think so," I agreed.

"You…*think* so?" June looked dubious.

"Okay fine, yes, I am. I just—I mean, I never knew I was until last night. It's new and I'm a little worried I'm going to fuck it up, but that doesn't mean I'm not interested," I admitted. This felt…very personal. Way more personal than I wanted to get. "I shouldn't be talking so much about me. This is your wedding. We should be talking about your *pending nuptials*."

June snickered, clearly recalling George calling them that, just like I'd wanted her to. But then she sobered. "That's the stupidest shit I've ever heard."

June exited her lounge chair, picked it up like the tiny tank she was, and plopped it directly next to mine. When she crawled back onto it, the first thing she did once settled was smack my arm hard enough it stung. "Rod and I are *old* news. We've been together for ages. The wedding is important, yes, and I'm excited—but you and I both know I've been trying to set you up for years."

"True."

"And now it's worked! Even if it's 'temporary,' it's still more permanent than anything you've had in ages. I still think I deserve flowers, by the way."

"Noted."

"And your undying loyalty."

"You already have that."

June smacked my arm again and I growled at her, intercepting the next slap with a huff. "Right, but... Okay. The point is—" she took a big breath, arm still raised like she wanted to whack me, "I am very, very invested in your kinky—"

"Oh god."

"*Emotional* journey to monogamy." June flopped back onto her back, adjusted her sunglasses, and spread her arms in an arc in front of her like she was painting a rainbow. "I can see it now—you can get married in a kink club. With one of those…cross things at the altar. Everyone can wear harnesses and you can toss a bouquet of dildos."

"I hate you so much." I couldn't stop grinning, even if I wanted to. Especially because thinking about dildos only reminded me of George now—and everything that reminded me of George made me stupidly, embarrassingly happy.

"Look at that smiiiile," June teased when she stopped playing charades. "Christ, you're so whipped. Ha! I didn't even mean to do that. Whipped. LMAO, I crack myself up sometimes."

"You are being totally unhelpful," I groaned again, turning back to my phone with a sigh. "I don't have that much time. I have to figure out how to be what he needs before he comes back from helping his mom."

"Good luck with that. I'm pretty sure there's not a crash course to kink on Google."

"I thought you were going to be *helpful?*" I whined, picking my phone back up and trying to read.

"I am," June said. "Maybe not with the research, but I can definitely distract George if he comes."

"That would be great, thank you." As much as it bothered me to miss out on precious time with George, I needed a minute to figure out what to do next—and how to do it properly. He'd told me he had experience with Brendon.

I had zero experience.

And I didn't want to fuck this up.

Realistically, I knew June was right, that there wasn't a "crash course on kink" that I could simply follow. But I *had* found a website for a local kink club in Columbus after I'd clicked through the bondage website—and *that* website had a number for one of the Doms that worked there full-time.

I figured it wouldn't hurt to reach out.

Learn directly from a trusted source, rather than Reddit threads.

"Anything for you, lover boy." June wiggled her eyebrows playfully before flopping on her back to tan. "I'll make him help me pick my veil."

"I want you to distract him, not torture him," I sighed.

"I'm still deciding what length it should be for the ceremony itself. I want to go dramatic—but short is good too, more—"

"I'm going to go back to my phone now," I informed her, tipping the device up to block the sun so I could see it better. I'd been through the veil thing with her fifty fucking times. I literally could not afford to go over it again. "Don't make George help with your veil."

"No promises," June chirped.

"Phone, June? Remember? Research?"

"With my blessing," she replied magnanimously before putting her headphones in and trying to catch up on our buddy read again.

True to her word, when George eventually showed up, June was quick to intercept his advance toward me. I barely got a glimpse of his cute blond head before she was yanking him toward the bridesmaids' cabin to torture him even though I'd told her not to.

I felt a pang of loss as they walked off, especially when I caught George glancing at me over his shoulder, an adorably baffled expression on his face. I waved, so he'd know I wasn't ignoring him, but settled back in to make use of the time June had bought me when he was out of sight.

It really *was* a shame there wasn't a quick guide to becoming a Dom, but I knew with tenacity, maybe some outside help, and a whole lot of stubbornness, I was bound for success.

Ha.

Bound.

Fuck, I was no better than June.

No better at all.

I wandered off to speak to the Dom from Columbus. A phone call that I'd expected to last a couple minutes at most, had gone on for well over two hours.

By the time I returned, the sun was high in the sky. The lake water glistened as I approached George's blond, fluffy head from behind. He had neglected to style his hair today. Which meant the waves were downy, drifting up in lazy spikes with the brush of a pleasant breeze. He didn't look traumatized by his time with June. In fact, he appeared flushed and somewhat rejuvenated.

The scent of the lake itself was thick in the air. Along with mystery pollen, and whatever algae was lurking below the surface.

Off in the distance, Roderick was zooming around on a wave runner with his pack of groomsmen, June riding behind him. I could hear her laughter, loud and riotous, from all the way across the lake.

Trees lined its edges, dipping reflections in the water, as the great blue sky above filled in the rest of the gaps in the waves.

Beside George sat Mavis. Across from them, Mrs. Milton, Mr. Milton, Joe, and Lacey sat in the sand, holding various types of popsicles and other sweet treats.

Man, what I wouldn't give to see George eat a popsicle.

Especially wearing those goddamn shorts.

Joe was halfway through burying one of Lacey's legs, a wrapper at his side. Lacey was on her phone, not paying attention to him, aside from delivering a scathing comment or two that I saw more than heard.

George didn't see me at first, as engrossed as he was in his current project. Specifically, a giant sand castle that Mavis was "helping" construct. And by helping, I mean knocking it down every time he built a new tower. I could practically hear the maniacal giggle she emitted before the sound escaped. Her wicked glee was written all over her chubby, unicorn-themed-swimsuit-wearing form.

"Bigger!" she said, like a tiny tyrant as George gamely began to shovel sand into a castle-shaped cup. He'd flip it over when it was packed, pull the cup off, then smooth the edges just like he had with all the other peaks she'd demolished, based on the wreckage of sand lumps surrounding them.

"This is the only size I have," George responded, patient as ever. He was only ever patient with children. Like he found nothing at all irritating about them. Not their questions, or their chaos, or their sticky, sticky hands. It was charming, to say the least. Personally, I'd always been fond of kids. I liked their honesty and I had an excess of energy of my own that I enjoyed burning off with my nephews and nieces.

They were kind by nature.

Hate was taught.

And it was humbling to spend time with creatures that were so quick to emote, as though emotions were not the tricky, uncomfortable things they were.

They didn't have walls like I did—at least not yet. And I hoped they never would, even though that was maybe a bit naive.

Seeing George with Mavis only served to remind me that we had that in common. Which was…maybe even more overwhelming than my revelations about my own sexual preferences. Or the conversation I'd just had with "Dominic the Dom" who had agreed to, for all intents and purposes, "tutor" me if I needed it.

Slowly, I stalked through the sand, careful not to alert George to my presence until I was literally right behind him.

"Hi Georgie," I said, leaning into George's space from behind with a grin. He jerked in surprise and dropped his shovel. When he swiveled to look up, he was glowering. "Didn't you see me coming?" I teased, amused to discover that he most definitely had not.

"I am too busy building a masterpiece to care about where you are," George groused, turning back to his half-filled bucket. His red ears betrayed him, as did the way he peeked at me through his lashes, like he was frightened his ire would scare me off.

Quite the opposite, really.

I'd just spent all morning dedicating every ounce of brain juice I possessed to learning how to please him. He didn't know that, sure, but still. There was no way a little snarking was going to frighten me away. I was made of far sturdier stuff than that.

Besides. We only had a few more days left. And I refused to waste any of them.

Until the end of the wedding, George was stuck with me.

I was the peanut to his butter, after all.

"You're pink, Georgie," I said, crouching into the sand at his back. "Did you put on sunscreen?" I kept a watchful eye on his bandage-covered fingers, but he dutifully kept them out of the sand as much as he was able.

"Of course I did," George huffed, stuffing his bucket full as his shoulders climbed higher and higher. "I'm not an idiot."

"Idiot," Mavis repeated, her small ears sharp as always.

"Are you sure you did?" I teased, still crouching. The sand was cool, which was unsurprising, given the fact that the beach had been mostly shaded all morning. Soon it'd heat up just like the water, molten to the touch. "It doesn't look like you did." Reaching up, I skimmed my fingers along the edge of his oversized t-shirt, just to taunt him.

He wasn't shirtless, which came as no surprise.

What was a surprise, however, was the sheer size of the shirt he sported. It was *huge* on him, drooping over his slim frame and gaping at the shoulder where it slipped low. The skin there was especially pink—and not because he was embarrassed.

Which meant my teasing turned to real concern.

"How long has it been?" I'd been gone for a while. And I genuinely had no idea how long June had kept George occupied. Judging by the piles of sand surrounding him, he had to have been out here in the high heat for quite some time.

"A while," George admitted, shivering as I continued to stroke the pink skin.

"Baby I don't know if you realize this—"

"Stop calling me that."

"You like it," I shut him down immediately, keeping my voice quiet enough his family couldn't hear.

"Ugh."

And then, as if he hadn't interrupted at all, I continued, "But sunscreen doesn't last forever. And you are paler than milk."

"Okay, so maybe I didn't put it on my shoulders." George flinched, like he expected me to get mad at him. Why? I frowned, squinting. Reading his mind was my new favorite hobby. George betrayed himself before I could figure it out on my own. "I wasn't *trying* to lie," he shrank, peeking at me through his lashes again, head tilted away. "I know you don't like liars."

"Don't like…" It took me a second to remember why he knew that. Right. The car ride. My ex. I'd told George I didn't like liars. Outright. "Oh. *Hey.*" His cheek was warm beneath my hand as I tipped his face back toward mine over his shoulder. "I didn't mean stuff like *this*, Georgie. Everyone lies a *little*."

"Right," he sniffed, obviously confused.

Sweet thing didn't want to do something to upset me.

"It's just the big stuff that bothers me," I promised. He still did not look convinced. Mavis made an angry sound, diverting both our attention. I'd honestly gotten so absorbed in him I'd nearly forgotten we weren't alone.

Across the mess of sand, George's family was observing us with blatant curiosity. Mrs. M looked like she was going to begin applauding any second. A frankly diabolical smile graced her lips—almost as evil as June's, but not quite. Lacey and Joe were more subtle, but the hand gesture Lacey made to simulate sex made it clear that she was just as open to teasing despite her stoicism.

"Sorry," George hadn't noticed, absorbed by Mavis once again. "Alex distracted me. I didn't mean to ignore you."

Mavis gave me the stink eye. God-level stink eye. And I couldn't even be mad, because honestly, she'd had George first, and here I was, swooping in and stealing him. I deserved that. But...I was also too stubborn to leave.

I'd been aching for him all fucking day.

Bending over backward, putting myself out on the line for him, taxing my brain when I was supposed to be on *vacation*. The least I deserved was a bit of banter, right? Some solid attention from my grouchy blond beau? It was only fair.

"You got room for a second architect?" I asked Mavis, "after I get some sunscreen on your uncle, of course."

She squinted like it was very, very difficult to imagine a world where I was allowed to join them. And then she nodded, a jerky up and down that made her off-center pigtail bob. "You can make the moat."

"Sweet," I offered her a fist bump that she did not return. Apparently I was on her shit list. No matter, I'd win her over again eventually. She'd always liked me before. Before I'd stolen her uncle, that was. Turning my attention to the gaggle of voyeuristic Miltons, I addressed them directly over George's shoulder, "Any of you have the sunscreen?"

Lacey chucked a bottle at me with no ceremony whatsoever. She looked disappointed when I caught it easily. Her stank face was the exact same as Mavis's.

"I'm gonna scoot your shirt over, baby, so I can get your back and shoulders," I warned George, aware that his family was watching and not wanting to cross a line.

"Why?" George asked, unsure.

"Because I want to take care of you."

He held very still for a moment, before he nodded. "Do what you have to," George grunted, shoveling sand into his bucket again.

His shoulders were tight by his ears, the pink skin growing pinker. A few freckles—maybe moles?—speckled the flushed skin. I caressed them, ghosting my hand across the imperfections before I squirted some sunscreen onto my hands and got to work.

He shivered when the first swipe stroked along his nape, but otherwise didn't react, simply melted into the care like he was starved of it.

I had never despised a stranger more than I hated Brendon.

Which I thought was pretty justified, all things considered.

I could still remember what George had said last night, stars in his teary red eyes, *"Eight years and he never...I thought it was my fault. That I wasn't worth the effort? Or maybe it was just normal to feel lonely, even when you were with someone."*

"Alex!" George's voice snapped me out of my reverie. I jolted, hands stilling. "Are you okay?"

"What?" I blinked, confused. "Of course I'm—" and then I realized that I'd been squeezing his shoulders, *hard.*

I released him quickly.

There were marks where my fingers had pressed. Marks that could've turned to bruises if he hadn't stopped me. *Good,* a small dark voice in the back of my mind murmured, *maybe if you mark him enough, Brendon's touch will fade.*

It was a nice thought.

Fuck.

But not without consent. Never without consent. I'd had that beaten into my head over my phone call with Dominic. Since I was new to this… experiencing what I'd privately dubbed as my "Dom awakening" it was even more important that I made sure to ask before I did things.

"Sorry," I apologized, maybe belatedly, since I'd begun spiraling again.

"It's fine." George didn't seem nearly as grumpy, almost like that little bit of pain had leeched the grouch right out of him. He offered me a smile. "What made you so angry?"

"Unca George," Mavis interrupted again, even more miffed this time.

"Sorry, sorry," George laughed, turning his attention back to her. "I keep doing that."

"Yes." She glared at me again, round face bright red.

To pay for my transgressions I was banished to moat duty.

Which wasn't all that much of a punishment even though Mavis clearly meant it as one. The sand was heating up already as I made room for myself half behind George, eager to feel him but not enough of an asshole to outright climb on top of him in front of his family. Sitting to his left a little, with one pec brushing his side, my legs folded, I finally felt at peace.

Every time he moved, his leg brushed against mine, which was tantalizing to say the least. Despite her serious approach to castle demolition, Mavis lost focus pretty early in the process. Rather than smoosh the towers George built, she turned her attention to his legs—surprisingly hairless—and began burying him the same way Joe was burying Lacey.

"Anyone want a drink?" Mrs. Milton offered, looking pleased as punch beneath her umbrella. "We've got…" She twisted, rifling around inside the cooler to her left. "Beer, a bottle of vodka, water, and…lemonade."

"That's mine." Mr. Milton took the bottle of vodka out of her hand with a grunt. Mrs. Milton just rolled her eyes, passing out a variety of drinks to the rest of us with a motherly smile.

"Here you go, honey." She handed me a water bottle. "You must be parched."

"Very," I winked.

George choked. "Must you flirt with my mother?"

I gave her a wink, and she tittered. "I must."

When I pressed my chilly water bottle against the back of George's neck, he flinched.

"Asshole," he muttered, reaching back to pinch my nipple, *hard*. I laughed in disbelief, batting him off and rubbing my chest with a pained groan.

"Jesus, you've got like—super aim. That was a direct hit."

"It's like his superpower," Joe frowned, rubbing his chest in commiseration, like he didn't even notice he was doing it. Huh.

"I didn't know you were a bully," I took a long sip of water. I really had been parched. George scowled at me.

"I'm not a bully."

"Just like you're not a hypocrite."

Wow. That was a new level of scowl. Scowl 2.0. I was proud of bringing that one out of him, actually.

"You and June never messed with each other like that?" George questioned.

"She bleached all my underwear once?" I frowned, then snorted, because the memory was honestly hilarious.

"How the hell does that happen?"

"She was super annoyed that our boxers kept getting mixed up. I wore hers to football practice one too many times and she figured if she 'marked' all of mine, I'd never get confused again."

"And did it work?"

"Of course it worked! All my underwear was mutilated. I never made the same mistake." I shuddered. "Figured if I did, my ass was next—so…" I shrugged.

"I am *actually* horrified."

George did not look horrified.

He looked entertained.

"Bleach your *ass*?" He shook his head in disbelief. "You're telling me you think June would be vindictive enough to physically go in and…oh god. *No*. I don't want to picture it. And why your ass of all things? Isn't that extreme?"

Now it was my turn to be freaked out.

He was right. Picturing June creeping into my room in the middle of the night like the evil gremlin she was with a tube of ass bleach was just—no. *No*. "Fuck. No! I meant more like, she'd replace my soap—didn't you ever read that article about the Nair in a shampoo bottle? Like…like *that*. Not… Oh god. I didn't mean she'd be all up in my—oh god. Ew. Ew. Ew." The more I thought about it, the more awful the thought became. "Why did you put that thought in my head?! I was innocent. Now I need brain bleach. That's seriously diabolical. You've got an evil mind, Georgie Porgie. *Evil*."

George laughed.

It was my *favorite* laugh.

Bright and happy.

Squawking and awkward, like he was choking on the sound—too embarrassed to be loud but unable to help himself. "That's what you get for calling me a bully."

"You're saying this was *premeditated*?!" I gasped in mock offense. "God, you really are a bully."

He laughed harder.

Suddenly, my justified disgust was no longer important. The more over the top I acted, the harder George cackled. Like a mad scientist or some shit.

Cute-cute-cute.

I was so fucking tempted to bite him I had to clench my jaw to stop myself.

After pushing my theatrics as long as I could, I finally broke. I grinned and wiggled even closer so that George's quaking back was brushing against the side of my chest. I wanted to *feel* that laugh. Wanted to be shaken apart by it. When George's guffaws softened to chuckles, my heart threatened to beat right out of my chest. He wiped a tear away, struggling to get a solid breath in.

I glanced up, unsurprised to find that the Milton clan was watching us with obvious glee. Even *Lacey* looked excited. God, they were as bad as June was. Or worse! Nosy bastards.

Instigators, all of them.

Though…I couldn't be mad about it. Not when they'd all been right. George's laughter was a testament to our compatibility. They saw it, just like I did. They *knew*. And sharing George's joy with his family was a new kind of intimacy, maybe even more precious than having him down my throat, or being trusted to carry his weight.

Family was *everything* to George.

It would take an idiot not to see that.

"Shut *up*," George grunted defensively toward said family, tossing another handful of sand fruitlessly in their direction. "Stop looking at me like that. I *laugh*."

"Apparently." Mrs. Milton looked pleased as punch, her giant blond hairdo bobbing. "A joke and a laugh—all in one day. Aren't we lucky?"

There was a story there—but I didn't get a chance to investigate. Unfortunately, while George had been snorting his head off, he'd twitched his leg—which meant that he'd accidentally broken through Mavis's hard work burying it, his pale knee poking free of its sand prison.

"Stop. Making. Unca. George. *Happy*." Unlike the rest of George's family, Mavis was *not* pleased by the hand I'd had in George's joy.

In fact, her body was *shaking* with fury as she glared fearlessly at me. I'd never incited the wrath of a toddler before, and frankly did not know what to do. Kids usually liked me. Actually, scratch that, kids *always* liked me.

"Ah—I'm sorry—" I said.

"Mavis, honey," Lacey's voice was a welcome distraction. "Why don't you come help Uncle Joe bury the rest of Mommy?" Jesus that sounded dark out of context.

Mavis didn't even give the decision a second thought. Apparently she was tired of my shit. Not George's though, because she gave his cheek an adorable sandy peck before storming off, her sunhat bobbing.

"Sorry," I murmured, leaning my cheek against the bare, sun-kissed skin of George's shoulder. It was slightly sticky and definitely a higher temperature than usual. Baby had for sure gotten sunburned. Good thing I was here to rub aloe on it later. "I didn't mean to scare her off."

When George twisted to look at me, his eyes were dancing.

So not angry then.

"It's fine. We played for a long time," he said. It was like he'd reached inside my chest and squeezed right around my heart. "Don't worry about it."

I took a sip of water to give myself something to do—otherwise I was pretty sure I'd have pulled George right into my lap and had my merry way with him, audience be damned. It was getting increasingly difficult not to grab him. To grope him. To kiss that sweet, grumpy, joyous mouth.

I knew him intimately in a way I hadn't the night before. And now that I'd seen that tasty little cock, I couldn't wait to touch it again.

Glancing around, I noted the boathouse that was tucked between the edge of the lake and the woods, out of the way of the beach. There were dumpsters behind it. And it was off the beaten path. It looked like a good hookup spot. Secluded. And since the boats were out on the water it'd be entirely empty. Unbidden, visions of what exactly we could get up to in there assaulted my senses.

Namely, George trussed up with the rope June had handed me with a cackle before she'd left to join Roderick on the wave runners.

Calm yourself.

You don't need to get a hard-on in front of George's family.

But then George leaned into me. Of his own free will. He wiggled that sweet ass to the side and back, settling against my chest—stiff—but solid. I didn't know what to do for a second, my dick waking right the fuck up despite my earlier protests.

When I glanced down I had to bite back a groan.

Yellow short-shorts.

He was wearing yellow short-shorts.

Even shorter than the ones he'd worn on the hike—the tiny shorts that'd made my brain want to melt right out of my ears. They left nothing to the imagination. Nothing. Barely covered his ass, Jesus Christ.

Those had to be the sluttiest slut-shorts I'd ever seen. They reminded me of some of those scenes in movies from the eighties. Totally straight dudes parading around, playing sports in shorts that barely came down their thighs. My hands twitched, aching to reach down and slip under the hems.

My nose skimmed along his shoulder, and George shivered.

"Behave," he told me, prim as ever.

"I'm trying," I whined. My cock was not trying. Not at all. Already at half mast I knew there was no way he couldn't feel it snug against his ass. "Sorry. You're just…"

"Think about something else." George was being awfully bossy for a guy who had climbed into my lap. I bit my lip, burying my face against his back and trying not to outright hump him. It would be so easy. No one would see. When I glanced up again, scoping out our would-be audience, the Miltons were all occupied with something else.

Mr. and Mrs. Milton were chatting animatedly. Which mostly meant Mrs. Milton was talking, and Mr. Milton was nodding occasionally. Lacey and Joe were playing with Mavis. And…none of my cousins who populated the sand or the water were paying us attention at all.

My hips flexed—slow and deliberate—and George's responding gasp was shallow.

"*Alex*," his voice was a warning.

"You're the one that sat on my cock, Duchess," I murmured against his ear, keeping my expression neutral so we wouldn't get caught. I stretched, motion casual just so I could push my hard dick between his cheeks a second time.

He clenched down, and *god*, wasn't that just…fffucck.

One of my hands slid to his belly, lying there possessively. My watch glimmered, catching the light and drawing his attention down to where I held him.

"I didn't," George protested. His body betrayed him. Still rigid, but relaxing by the second, his hips doing this very distracting, minute shake that caused just enough friction against my dick to make me lose my mind.

"You did," I teased. "Did you forget that I was there?"

George's voice was breathy. "Stop doing that with your hips."

I stopped.

He hadn't safe-worded, but even I knew one good grind was the best I was going to get right now. I didn't want to embarrass him. Even if this whole… exhibition thing we had going on was making me so fucking hard I could barely breathe.

It was fine.

This was fine.

I could behave.

I could totally—

Okay fine, I could not behave.

"I've gotta get outta here," I said, looping both my arms around his waist and giving him a squeeze. George wilted. I could literally *feel* his disappointment.

"Okay," he agreed. "I get it."

I frowned, confused. "What do you…"

"I can give you a break." George shrank even further.

"A break?" What the hell was he talking about?

"From me."

"A break from—"

"That's why you asked June to distract me, right?" Christ, he was far more observant than I'd given him credit. "That's why you need to get out of here. You need space to—"

"Fuck no." Alright. So I wasn't leaving him. I curled my arms around him tightly, squeezing with all my might. Till his bones popped and the tension in his frame eased. "I don't need space from you. And I only asked June to distract you because I needed to figure some stuff out, not because I didn't want to be with you."

"Oh." George relaxed. "Not because you feel smothered?"

Smothered?

What the fuck?

Why would he—

Brendon.

The answer to most every question was *Brendon*.

"No. I was learning sex stuff." My cheeks burned, embarrassed to admit that I didn't know something. I dropped my head against his shoulder, nosing at the sun-warm skin, hiding a little, still careful so we wouldn't be overheard. "Sex stuff I would love to *show* you—if you…want me to?"

George made a sound in affirmation.

Once more, I couldn't help but find his hypocrisy cute. Here he was, upset that I had "run from him" when he was the one that'd done all the running between the two of us.

"Are you coming?" My voice was low with intent, a clear invitation. "You don't have to." Consent, consent, consent. "But if you do…" I squeezed him even tighter, placing a light kiss right below his flushed, pink ear. "I'm going to touch you." George shuddered. "I am going to touch what you've got hidden in those slutty little short-shorts." George made a squawking sound like he wanted to protest what I'd just called his outfit. "And maybe…if you're my very good boy again…" Another shudder, and a gasp. "I'll stuff that pretty pink pussy nice and full, just the way you like."

It was a gamble whether or not he'd like that.

Judging by the breath that escaped him, he did.

"You like that?" I spoke even quieter, directly against his ear. "You like me calling your slutty little hole a pussy?" He'd said he was into breeding. And while the kinks didn't go hand in hand, I had a feeling he'd like this too.

"Y-yes."

"Me and my silly nicknames," I clucked my tongue, pressing the hand I had on his stomach tighter. "Embarrassing, huh, Duchess?"

"Alex."

"*George*," I countered. "C'mon."

George didn't need to be told twice.

Obedient as ever.

And so fucking ready for whatever I had in store, he was gagging for it. Like I wasn't too much for him at all, even like this, loud and unrepentant.

Twenty-One
Alex

THE BOATHOUSE FELT MUGGY, the cool breeze from the lake's surface noticeably missing now that we were hidden inside the large wooden shack. The stilts it rested atop creaked, the steady lap of lake water like a metronome to mark the passing seconds. George's skin was pink, glistening, and slick with sweat. He tasted like salt and summer, as I pushed him against the back wall, my tongue in his mouth.

He grunted when the wood pressed against his shoulder blades, but returned the kiss just as eagerly.

I loved how obedient he got when we had sex. All his contrary nature thrown out the window. He was a different person entirely—needy, soft, desperate for affection. Touch-starved and eager, George was a waking wet-dream.

"That's it," I murmured into his mouth, my hands sliding greedily beneath the hem of his t-shirt. I'd kissed his shoulders, grateful that we'd taken a detour to the showers to clean off the sunscreen and sand before heading back out. His backpack, hiding the lube and his freshly sanitized dildo sat at our feet, momentarily forgotten.

"Mmnff," George gasped, melting into me. Already his back was tacky, the kinda spongy feeling that only came from heat and perspiration—remnants caused by our trek to the boathouse on the hot summer day. I couldn't wait to taste it. Couldn't wait to lick across the salt and see him naked. Couldn't wait to see his hole. To touch it. To see how much it could stretch.

I'd shot a text to June—because she'd offered to help—unbeknownst to George. She was our lookout, far enough away that she couldn't hear, but close enough to make sure that no one stumbled upon us.

She'd been almost creepily pleased to be given such an important task, as she sipped the Bloody Mary Roderick had just delivered to her along with her book. He had been on his way out onto the water, probably on one of the wave runners again—or a canoe this time—the same canoes that were usually stored in the empty boathouse we currently occupied.

With everything prepped and ready, and our safety secured, there was nothing left to do but enjoy the fruits of my labor.

"Relax, Georgie." My hands dragged higher, bringing the hem of his damp t-shirt with them as I tugged it up and over his head. "Let me take care of you."

Bare now, his chest heaved with a shuddered breath.

He was gorgeous like this, a sunburn line glowing along his shoulder where his collar had slipped. More freckles and moles dotted his chest and abs. And the trail of hair that led from his belly button to his covered cock looked like spun gold. Thicker than you'd expect from a guy who had practically no body hair anywhere else.

George didn't balk at the nickname. In fact, already, his eyes had taken on that sexy fog they'd had yesterday. Like he was sinking into his head, trusting me to take the reins and keep him safe. So much faster than last time.

Like I had house money now—since I'd taken such good care of him the day before.

It was heady.

"What do you…what do you want from me?" George asked, his voice shakier than normal. He was quaking with anticipation. Or maybe the fear of getting caught? He liked that. Liked that a lot. If his reactions the night before hadn't made that clear, the way his dick was threatening to poke through his slut-shorts would have.

"I just want you to stand there and look pretty," I said. George cracked a smile, making it obvious he knew I'd said that on purpose to set him at ease. It was our thing now. Not intentionally—but…hell.

Who could blame me?

He was the definition of pretty.

Long, leggy, golden in every way. Like a twinky Adonis, all compact, corded muscle. There was a softness to him too, around his center, belly a flat scoop rather than hard-trained abs. He was fucking gorgeous. A work of art. Something to be proudly displayed and coveted.

If I wanted him to never lift a finger again for the rest of this trip, that was my prerogative.

"You always say that," George laughed, interrupting my ogling. He shivered, and my gaze snapped to his nipples, perking up despite the lack of chill. No…that was all arousal. Fuck. *Yes.*

"I always mean it," I countered. "Okay…" My hands found his hips, sinking into the skin hard enough to bite. No bruises from last time, unfortunately. But I could leave some if he wanted. Gentle waves continued to lap away at the wooden stilts in the water. The wood at George's back was a honeyed color, perfectly complimenting his natural color palette

"Before we go any further I need to make sure you understand how important it is that you are honest with me when we're in the middle of a scene. I'll be honest too, I promise. But communication is *really* important, as uncomfortable as it might be to…voice some of the things you might want. Especially because I am…new to this." I hated admitting that. Hated showing weakness when I was asking him to rely on me.

But if I couldn't be honest with George, how could I expect him to be honest with me?

George tensed, and to combat it, one of my hands slid up the center of his chest, cupping his throat in my hand. His Adam's apple bobbed when he gulped. I squeezed, just enough to get his focus on me and not the thoughts in his head.

If I start it'll be easier for him to open up.

"I want to restrain you," I told him. "With rope."

"O-okay."

"I want to fuck you when you're bound."

"R-right." Christ, his stuttering was adorable.

"I want to call your hole a pussy. Want to talk about impregnating you. Want to cum in your ass." Jesus, just laying it out like that should not have been as sexy as it was. It should've made it feel clinical, but it didn't.

Maybe communication was half the fun?

George groaned, the sound vibrating beneath my palm—like simply hearing the list of kinks I wanted to try was getting him off.

"I'm going to try a few things. And I want this to be organic, natural, just you and me. We may progress places I don't plan sometimes, and that's okay. But I need to know that if that happens you're going to tell me if you're uncomfortable, need to slow down, or want to stop."

"I can do that." George's voice was throaty. Maybe not as hoarse as mine, but certainly affected by what we were doing. I gave his neck another gentle squeeze. His heart was beating like crazy. Skittering all over the goddamn place.

"I never want you to lie to me George," I said firmly. "Do you understand that?"

"Yes."

"Even if you *think* I want something, I don't want that to alter your judgment. You choose based on your own desires, not mine." There was no room for argument in that statement, and I hoped he understood that, though I doubted I'd manage to get away with such a decisive command without some push back.

"But…" George protested.

I grinned, proud that I'd seen right through him. "*George*," I made a point to use his name again, not his nickname, "No buts. I'm serious. If you lie to me about your boundaries we will not be having sex again. Do you understand? That is *my* hard limit. You will break me if you lie. Don't."

"Okay."

Apparently phrasing it like that did the trick. Suddenly George was eager to be honest. Which I definitely preferred over having sex with a yes-man. He was a pleaser. It was obvious that George would bend over backward to make his lover happy—to his own detriment.

Which…was adorable.

And sad.

And not what I wanted from him.

I wanted to make him feel good the way *he* preferred.

I wanted his focus to be completely, entirely on me like it'd been last night. Only better. Because this time I was prepared.

I wanted to eclipse every other relationship he'd ever had.

I wanted to become the only thing that existed in his world and his mind.

I wanted to be the standard he set for himself.

I wanted to matter to him. To matter more than anyone or anything he'd experienced. There would be no skeletons in our closets. There would be no exes to taint what burned molten bright between us. There would be no "not enoughs" or "too muches."

Just George and me, and the trust and camaraderie we'd built, brick by brick.

"What about you?" I asked, voice soft enough I hardly recognized it. "What are *your* hard limits?"

It took George a second to respond. He was distracted, which was fair—*hell*, the heat that was simmering between us was difficult for me to ignore too. If I'd been more of a brute—or we'd been further along in our "practice relationship" I would've already been balls-deep inside him, grunting away. But I wasn't, and we weren't. And I was genuinely excited to learn more about him, as odd as that sounded.

"I…I need…"

"Yes?" I waited patiently.

"I need to know you won't hurt me—at least…not too badly." George trembled, like getting the words out was physically painful. "Bruises are welcome. Um…rope burns? That's fine too. Spanking is…is definitely…*yes*. But nothing too hard or lasting. And if I say red, you s-stop."

Anger, blinding and bright licked at my fingertips. I had no doubt this particular limit was because of Brendon.

"I can do that. Anything else?" I made sure to keep my voice kind, even though a solid ninety percent of me wanted to hunt Brendon down and show him what real hurt meant.

"After we're done…can you hold me?" The request was barely a whisper at all, vulnerable and quaking. "I don't need a lot," George was quick to tack on, probably out of fear that he was coming across as high-maintenance. "But a little would be nice."

Again, I wanted to beat Brendon into the ground.

"Of course." My heart squeezed—and just like that, my fury fled, replaced instead with affection for this sweet, needy man, and how brave he was to plead for comfort. "I'll take such good care of you after, sweet pea, I swear. Like last night. You liked last night?"

George nodded. "*Yes.*"

"What are your safe words?" I asked, pulse thrumming as fast as George's was. This was it. The final question before my first *real* scene as George's temporary Dom. God, even just *thinking* that felt surreal. Like I'd stepped into the pages of one of the books I'd read. I had never, ever anticipated that I would be into something like this.

But I definitely fucking was.

So fucking into it.

And hard enough to pound nails.

Harder than I'd ever been before.

It felt as though a part of me that had been dormant had woken up.

The idea that George would trust me with his body, his mind, his *pleasure*, was exhilarating.

The world was prettier this way, yet narrowed, because nothing mattered but Georgie. Not the beams of wood above us, or below. Not the lap of water at the scaffolding. Only the way his breath made his chest rise and fall. Only the way his Adam's apple bobbed beneath my palm when he swallowed. Only the skip of his heart beat, dancing away, as eager as he was.

There were a lot of things in my life I had never had control over.

My family's rise to wealth.

My mother's eccentricity.

The way I was perceived.

How previous potential lovers reacted to my actual personality.

The accusations of nepotism at my job, no matter how good I was or how hard I worked.

My dad—his car accident—and the deep, very real fear that seeing him so battered had instilled inside me.

Life could be unexpected, terrifying, and impossible to predict.

Having control over George didn't change all of that. But it grounded me. Like I had a purpose—and that purpose was pleasing George.

That purpose gave me peace.

The parts of me that were usually drifting loose had fallen into place exactly where they were meant to be.

None of my pieces were abstract anymore.

My watch caught the light, a reminder of mortality. A reminder of what I could lose if I didn't hold tight enough to the things I cared about. Nothing was forever.

And yet…this felt like it surpassed that. Like these moments with George would survive the passage of time in ways even my watch had not. The memories would remain long after we'd gone back to our separate lives.

Our tiny bubble was in sharp focus.

A slice of heaven hidden in the woods, the lap of water kissing the beams beneath our feet.

"Safe words, baby?" I urged, forcing my thoughts back to the present.

"Red, yellow, green," George replied. He'd taken a second to gather himself like I had. I figured if he was feeling even half of the high I currently was, he needed it.

"And your color right now?" I whispered, sliding in closer. My leg bumped between his, my ankle skimming his and skirting up his inner calf.

"Green."

"That's my sweet boy, so obedient." I dropped my leg before it could make contact with his needy-as-fuck cock, and George *twitched*. Christ, teasing him was fun. "No." I crowded against him, my breath ghosting his lips. His dark blue eyes were already glazed with lust, peering at me through pale lashes like I was God himself—like he *needed* me more than air. Like his heart was beating for me and me alone. It was the kind of attention I'd always craved.

"No complaining," I chided, our lips brushing.

George sucked in a breath.

"You will take what I give you, nothing less, nothing more." George's pulse skipped faster, thrumming like a hummingbird's wings. I applied a bit of pressure to his throat, at the fingers, so as not to cut off his breath—only the blood flow—and only enough to make his knees weak. "You don't need to fear that," I said, our lips still barely brushing.

George didn't press up to connect them.

I didn't think he would, even if I wasn't restraining him.

He was simply obedient like that.

"I'm very generous, Duchess. I'll take *very* good care of you," my voice dropped gravelly soft.

That was a vow I refused to break. And I think George knew that. Because the swirling storm in his eyes calmed, and he slipped under, under, *under*. The fog came forth, threatening to overpower his sense of self, and he…he *let* it.

Simple as that.

Like he really *did* trust me.

Which was as humbling as it was thrilling.

I'd never had another person entirely at my mercy before him.

And this was twice. *Twice*, that he'd offered me such a gift.

Fifteen minutes later, I had his wrists trussed up with the rope June had given me. It was red, which was gorgeous when paired with the milky, sun-marred alabaster of George's skin. It wasn't shoddy work. I'd been a Boy Scout after all. I'd made sure I hadn't tied it tight enough that I wouldn't be able to get him out. I'd also been conscious of his burned fingers, and the bandages I'd reapplied that morning.

The burns were a lot better today but that didn't mean I wanted to cause him pain. A little bruising? Yes. Just like he'd approved. But not anything serious. I refused to get even close to the line he'd drawn, clear as day.

My back pulled, the sting of the scratches he'd left behind tugging with every movement. A reminder that this was mutual. That he could inflict as much pain on me as I could on him.

"You hold the power here, George," I murmured as I finished checking the knots. "I need you to know that." He met my gaze, half gone already, and nodded. "Done."

I stepped back, releasing him to admire my work.

He dropped his hands, embarrassed.

George was a vision with his wrists tied together, hands covering his cock.

Covering the wet spot on his yellow shorts—I'd spotted it when he'd had his arms out for me to tie. The fabric had never gone fully see-through, even though I wished it would. It had, however, darkened. Sticky and slick enough it almost looked like George had already cum.

If I gave him shit for being wet later, he wouldn't even be able to deny it. It wasn't a lie.

He was fucking *soaking* for me.

"Christ, you're beautiful, sweetheart," I promised, taking another step back to get an even better view. The veins on George's hands caught the light when my gaze dragged down his quaking chest to where they cupped his cock for a second time. "You don't need to hide from me."

George didn't move his hands, and I didn't make him. There was something submissive and downright breedable about how *shy* he was currently acting. Like even though he knew this was going to end up with his pants around his ankles and my cock in his ass, he couldn't help but cower.

It made me feel powerful to know that I could hurt him—but never would.

Aside from a few bruises and maybe some well-timed slaps to his ass—to make it as red as his sunburn, of course. But *never* anything lasting, marks on his soul, invisible but scarred all the same. I suspected he'd had that before, based on his request for kindness. He was the kind of person who was weak when it came to the people he loved. Would carve away pieces of himself to make them happy.

He wouldn't have to worry about that with me.

That was the point of this, wasn't it?

For us both to experience the kind of love we'd always craved without fear of heartache.

"Turn around," I commanded, swirling my finger in a circle to demonstrate what I wanted. "Nice and slow. Wanna see your slutty ass in those goddamn shorts." George did what he was told immediately—and god, what a power trip that was. He moved away from the wall enough he could spin. "Very nice," I groaned when his perky butt was right in front of me. Sweat glistened at his back, a beam of sunlight creeping in through the windows above. "Bend over a little."

George bent, and his tight ass flexed beneath the fabric of his shorts. Highlighter yellow, totally an eyesore, and yet somehow the sexiest fucking thing I'd ever seen, especially when paired with the sneakers and knee high socks he'd put on after we'd bathed off the sand. He was a jock's wet dream— nerdy, trembling, and eager.

George wasn't particularly voluptuous. His body was lean, rather than curvy. But that didn't mean his ass wasn't fucking delicious. If anything, it was his masculine angles that made him so goddamn desirable.

"Color?" I echoed, part of me still nervous that I was doing this wrong.

"Green," George repeated, his voice this quaking, needy thing.

I reached down to squeeze my cock to ease the ache. "Alright, straighten back up." I stepped into his space again, this time from behind, my dick brushing the top of his ass as I did so. "That's my sweet boy."

I caught George's throat with a hand, pulling his head back with my grip on it, while simultaneously kicking his feet wider so I could settle between them.

"Do you feel that?" I asked, flexing my hips deliberately against him so he could feel how hard he'd made my cock. It twitched the second we made contact and I had to bite back a groan of my own. George nodded, a sharp jerky motion that was barely any movement at all.

"I'm so hard, baby," I murmured. "Because of *you*," I said against his ear, enjoying the full-body shiver that wracked his frame in response. "But you knew that, didn't you? That you're the reason I'm all hot and bothered. That I've been walking around for the last hour with my cock pointing right at you." George nodded again, and I clucked my tongue. "Words, Georgie."

"Y-yes. I knew."

"So obedient. Thank you, Duchess." George swallowed beneath my palm.

I rutted forward again, slow and easy, basking in the way my own shorts caught on the head of my cock, and my length attempted to bury itself between his cheeks despite the layers of clothing separating us.

"How do you feel about roleplay?" I asked, genuinely curious.

"R-roleplay?" George echoed, distracted by my cock.

"Like we're at summer camp." Christ. He really did fit that particular fantasy, with the way he was dressed. "We've snuck off while everyone is at lunch—"

"Guess it's not much of a fantasy, considering that's exactly what we did," George laughed. The sound was breathy and horny. "We could get caught. We're not supposed to be here."

"Fuck yes." Now that my mouth was moving things felt easier. This wasn't *that* difficult. I could let my mouth run and run, the way that I always wished I could, and George was forced to listen.

He liked it, if the way his ass kept twitching like he was doing his best not to hump the air—and failing—was any indication. At the end of the day, I could call his ass a pussy all I wanted, and threaten to get him pregnant, but he was still a man. Which meant his cock wanted to fuck.

It was a shame that I didn't have a fleshlight to stick his dick inside. The idea of having George stuffed and doing the stuffing at the same time was fucking awesome. Making him cream himself in it then lick out his own pleasure while he was still sitting on my dick.

Maybe later—if I could get him in a bed some day.

No, no.

Best not to think about a future we didn't have.

Present.

I needed to stay present.

To keep the fantasy going. To follow the thread I'd sewn. For a second, I let the scene I'd painted build in the back of my mind. "You've been naughty, George," I told him, my cock pulsing.

"I…I have?"

"You have. Taunting me all day in those fucking shorts. Knowing as your counselor," George gasped, body snapping to attention, "that I couldn't touch you—not in front of the others. Not at all, if I was a good person."

I paused for a beat, vulnerable as I waited to see if George would take the bait. If we'd be compatible this way.

"I knew you were looking," he replied, far from contrite. "That's why I packed them for the summer." I appreciated the backstory he was giving his character. "I knew you'd be here again—so half my bag is full of shorts like this."

"Christ, you're a slut," I groaned, rutting against him happily.

"For you," George said, voice trembling. "Only for you. After last year, I...I kept thinking about you. I couldn't wait to see you again. I hoped...I hoped you'd pay attention to me this year. Hoped the shorts would make you notice me."

"I thought about you too," I murmured. "Told myself I wouldn't touch. I was so good last summer. But this year you're so fucking...*ugh*."

"I just wanted your attention."

"And I don't have self control, obviously." This was fun. So fucking fun. Definitely the most fun I'd ever had during sex, if I was being honest. "And who can blame me? You've been...*taunting* me with the cunt you've got hidden in there. Every time you bend over, teasing me, making me dick-drunk on the idea of sinking into your tight, tight heat."

George made a pitiful sound.

Jesus, he really did like that.

Good.

I liked it too.

"Do you know why I tied you up?" I asked him, enjoying the way he shuddered.

"No?"

"Think about it." This was bullshit. Total bullshit. There'd been no reason behind my desire to immobilize him other than my need to see that pretty pale skin trussed up because of me. But if the idea I was this diabolical, conniving Dom made George hard then I would let him believe it.

It was part of the show.

That's what Dominic had told me. That sometimes it was the mind games that made it better, not necessarily always the physical.

"You…wanted me to…be…" George's voice was so faint I could barely hear it despite the fact his mouth was close to my ear. "You wanted me to be still."

"That's right," I agreed, a shiver running down my spine. "Why, George? Why would I want that from you?"

This time his answer came faster. "Because it helps me relax. It helps me… pay attention."

Huh.

Yeah.

That was great. I liked that. "I like when you pay attention to me," I husked. "Love it, actually."

George whimpered. His legs were shaking, not because this position was particularly challenging, but—probably the adrenaline of being tied up in a semi-public location.

"I want you over there," I told him, releasing his neck and hip and stepping back. He whined, a sad forlorn sound.

"Over t-there?" George peeked over his shoulder at me. It was the same look he'd given me on the beach, demure and through his lashes.

"That's right. Leaning on that—" Fuck, what were they called? "The hoist. Over there." I would've had him hold his arms high up and dangle a bit to get his blood tingling, but I worried that position would exacerbate the burn on his hand. "I want you to be still when you get into position. Doesn't matter how I touch you. Doesn't matter what I do. You hold position until I tell you to let go. Do you understand?"

"I understand." George stumbled toward the wooden beam I'd indicated, his hands already held out in front of him. With his forearms against the wood for balance, the ropes that twisted around his wrists were even more obvious. So fucking pretty. Jesus. He was a work of art.

"Are the ropes too tight?" I double-checked as I stepped behind him once more. "How do they feel?" I had no idea if the new position would tug them uncomfortably, and hoped to god it wouldn't. George shook his head, and I relaxed.

"They're fine," he promised, in that same throaty tone that made me want to pound him into the floorboards. "They feel good."

"*Perfect*. If that changes, you tell me."

"Yes."

His response felt empty. Like it was missing something. It was easy enough to figure out what that was.

"Yes, what?" I asked, kicking his legs apart for a second time that day. He wiggled, sneakers skidding on the wood as he settled into place.

"Yes, Counselor."

Christ, that was a thrill of its own. He was so fucking perfect it made me feel like I was losing my mind. "How's your burn, baby?" I slipped my hands up his forearms, fingering the bandages still wrapped around one of his hands. "Is it hurting at all?"

"No."

"Okay." I pecked his flushed ear in appreciation. "That's it." It was impossible to retreat now, not with his back pressed flush against my chest. I angled my hips, slotting my cock against his ass as I leaned back to admire him. "You have no idea how long I've wanted to feel your ass like this," I told him, eyes slipping shut as I focused on the feeling.

The fabric barriers between us were slippery with sweat and precum, damp as the head of my cock twitched and caught between his cheeks. When I lowered my hips it dragged my foreskin up, and god—was that…Jesus.

"Mmm," I sighed, flexing forward, then back again, enjoying the way his ass cheeks clenched. "You…"

"I…?" George replied, breathless. He was still like I'd requested, frozen. But the way he trembled, and the flush to his cheeks and ears made it obvious he was as into this as I was.

"Are you hard too?" I asked, falling into character easily. "Do you…I mean—when you look at me…do you…"

"Yes," George whined. "When you sit down, you…you spread your legs. I don't know if you noticed you do that? But I can't help but…*imagine* how big your dick must be if you have to sit that way."

"Christ, you really are a slut." Back to mean, my voice dropped even lower. "Bet you like to picture what my dick tastes like too."

"Y-yes," George agreed, his ass pushing back into me to encourage more grinding.

"Bet you can't stop thinking about what it'd feel like splitting you open."

"Y-yes," this admission was even breathier than the last.

This was fun. So fucking fun, but I was—Christ. More than eager to move on. I released his arms, hands finding his hips instead. The skin there was a lovely sort of sticky, the muggy air of the boathouse leaving its touch behind. Swiping along the sweat slick skin, I slid toward his center, one hand curling around his hard dick through his shorts.

George fucked into my grip with a gasp, his trembling only growing worse.

"So fucking wet," I breathed, thumb rubbing into the damp patch overtop his slit. "Just like a girl."

"F-fuck." George's hips snapped forward again, and I nibbled on his ear, debating if we needed more foreplay or not. I didn't have a ton of time even with June guarding us, so that cemented my choice.

"Stay right there," I commanded unnecessarily as I released him all at once and stepped back. George sobbed, head falling against the wooden beam as he waited for my return. The ziiiip of his backpack opening was impossibly loud in the quiet. Not as loud as his panting, but close.

Dildo in hand, and lube ready, I returned to my place behind him with a wolfish grin. "I'm going to pull your shorts down," I told him, yanking them over the curve of his ass one-handed. He jerked, gasping as his cock bobbed free and the highlighter yellow fabric slipped down skinny legs all the way to the floor. It pooled around his white socks, and I groaned.

"Slutty fucking socks too," I whispered against the trembling skin of his speckled back as I popped the cap open and slicked up my fingers. His legs were wide enough already, but I still kicked a leg out to force them even wider. Wide enough that with his body half bent over like it was, his sweet pink hole was on display.

It was so fucking sexy, all shy and twitchy, like him. Pink. Furled. With no hair—hinting at the fact he probably waxed it. God, that was hot. Picturing Georgie with his legs spread, getting his little cunt ready to be fucked. Prim and proper-like.

"You have such a pretty pussy, George," I told him, warming the lube between my fingers then slipping my hand between his cheeks to thumb over the trembling pucker. His hips punched back, proving what a fucking bottom he was with that one deliberate push. Most people would flinch away, but not my Georgie.

No.

My Georgie was a size queen.

The kind of pretty boy who was meant to lie in bed with his legs spread and his ass stuffed and dripping.

"It's…it's not—I mean—" George spluttered. The way his hole twitched as I pushed a single, solitary finger inside it made it clear how much he liked his ass being referred to in such a way. It was taboo. Not something a lot of people were comfortable with, and that was what made it hotter.

"Color?"

"Green."

"God, look at the way you suck me in," I husked. Squirting more lube onto my fingers made the next push inside emit a filthy, slick sound. George heard it too, because he squirmed, ass clenching tight, then releasing, like he was beckoning me deeper.

"Look what I found in your bag, Georgie Porgie," I purred. "You brought a dildo to summer camp?" I tapped the slightly chilly silicone against his ass cheek at the same time I thrust my fingers out and in. He gasped. "Did you do that because you were hoping I would find it? I bet you like to shove it inside your pussy and think about me, don't you?"

"Yes," George's voice broke.

"I bet you pound that sweet little hole till it's red and puffy. Bet you clench your thighs and bounce and bounce and bounce—"

"Y-yes."

"What a naughty, *naughty* boy." I let the silicone slip closer to his crease, my fingers finding a rhythm that had his ass canting back with every thrust forward. He welcomed me inside him like it was natural to do so. Tight at first—trembling, but relaxing a little with every glide of my fingers. "We should teach you a lesson, shouldn't we? Naughty boys get punished. That's only right, don't you think?"

George gasped, head dipping lower. His ears were practically fluorescent they were so red. The way his back heaved with each breath was gratifying to say the least. All that gorgeous, sweaty skin—unblemished, and entirely at my mercy. He didn't respond, which presented the perfect opportunity for the punishment I'd hinted at.

Bringing the dildo back, I smacked it against his ass. George jumped. His head twisted, dazed blue eyes meeting my own. He looked surprised, and for a moment I waited, gauging his expression. Soon enough he sank back into the fuzzy place in his mind, maybe even deeper? Because he simply hung his head forward, leaning even more of his weight onto his bound arms.

His hands kept clenching and releasing, over and over, which again—was sexy as fuck.

He was driving me completely fucking nuts.

"Answer the question," I urged, dildo slipping along his ass cheek invitingly. "Tell me what I want, and I'll stuff you so full you'll forget what it was like to be empty."

"I..." George started, roughly. "I...yes. I—naughty boys. They..." he struggled, whimpering as his hole clenched tight around my fingers, betraying his arousal. God, it looked so fucking inviting. Silky. Tempting. I wanted to feel it constrict around my dick. "They get...punished."

"Slutty boys," I added, my cock pulsing between my legs. "Slutty boys who tempt their counselors into quiet corners because they want their pussies played with."

"Y-yes."

Christ, he was just as unhinged as I was.

Fucking amazing.

When he was loose enough, I slipped my fingers free. Immediately, they felt cold, no longer enveloped in his heat. After liberally lubing up the blue dildo, I shuddered, grabbed his ass cheek with still-sticky fingers, pulled him open, and notched the blunt tip against his hole.

"Ready?"

"Y-yes."

George jerked, but otherwise didn't react. Not when I gave his hole a rub, or when the round crown of the dildo popped right in. It was somewhat see-through, not enough to give me a really clear view, but certainly enough that as it slipped inside I could see the stretch of his inner walls.

"God, you were made for this," I groaned. "Bear down." He did as he was told. "There we go." Another inch slipped in. I'd never been jealous of silicone before but I was now as I stared at the way George's hole stretched around his toy, welcoming it deeper and deeper. With every inch that sank inside, his body became more lax, as though the tension was being fucked right out of him.

"A-Alex," George gasped when it finally slid home, the flared base snug against his cheeks. I gave the base a little snap to enjoy the way he jerked.

"You're doing so good, sweetheart," I promised, nudging his neck with my nose and fluttering a half dozen kisses onto the sunburned skin. "You feel that?" He whimpered.

"F-full."

"Yeah you are. You're so full. Nine fucking inches, and that tiny little hole took it all." I pulled the toy out an inch, teeth sinking into his shoulder, finally getting to bite him like I'd so desperately wanted. George responded to the bite beautifully, his chest shuddering shallowly as he struggled to pull in a breath. "I wonder what else you can take."

"Nnngh," he whimpered as I slapped the base back against him, fucking him full again.

"Could you take me too?" I wondered out loud after releasing him, a pink bite standing stark against his already flushed skin. Glancing down, I was absorbed in my own fantasy. When I wiggled the toy his hole simply gave, well-fucked already. I wanted inside. So fucking bad. Wanted to shove my hard cock in beside the dildo and feel him give for me. Could I…? No. That was ridiculous… There was no way he…

Could he?

Could he fit both?

"How do you feel about double penetration?" I asked him, listening to the squelch of the toy moving in and out. His hips wiggled to meet every slap of my hand, knees quaking. "Color, Georgie?"

"G-Green. So green." I'd never heard his voice do that. There was nothing but open obedience and eagerness inside it. Like he wasn't self-conscious anymore. "Green, green, green—"

"Okay." Fucking him harder, my dick pressed insistently against the seam of my shorts. "Fuck yes." I shoved my shorts down below my balls, cock springing free and immediately skimming George's ass. "Fuck yes."

I'd need to finger him again. Push in beside the toy—make sure there was room, that I wouldn't hurt him. But while I did that there was no harm in rutting against him, was there? Smearing my cum around and marking my territory.

"You're not going to let anyone else see you like this," I warned, uncapping the lube and pouring more directly on his twitching hole. He flinched, and I grinned. "You're my slut now. All fucking summer, you hear me? No one else is going to know what your hole looks like stuffed full and puffy."

"Just yours," George agreed.

"And you're not going to tell the other counselors," I added, fingers slipping in beside the blue toy eagerly. George whimpered, nodding his head up and down in agreement. "It's our little secret."

"Ye-es." His hole gave easily. Far more easily than I'd expected. Barely any resistance at all as I wiggled another finger beside the first. Jesus Christ, he was stretched so fucking wide. How was that physically possible? He was... fuck. He was a wonder.

My cock ached, slick and hard as nails, rubbing against George's body and leaving streaks of pre-cum in its wake. It glistened on his skin, decorating him like he was mine. Because he was. Right now—George was mine. Body, mind, and soul.

"Doing so good, baby," I growled, fucking the dildo in hard so I could feel him clench around my fingers. "So fucking responsive. Jesus. You have no idea how pretty you look right now. Like a goddamn porno."

"Nmmn," George's reply was incoherent at best.

He was so hot inside. Fucking slippery and amazing and soft, in perfect contrast to the harder edges of the toy stretching him open. The silicone had begun to warm, matching his body temperature, and I could not wait to get my dick in there.

"Ready?" I confirmed, waiting for his go-ahead before I slipped my fingers free.

"R-Ready," George agreed, head hanging. It was barely a word at all. Like the bastard between a whisper and sigh.

"Okay." I squeezed my dick to stave off my orgasm before reaching for the lube and slicking myself up. My hands shook a little. Anticipation? Excitement? Fear of fucking this up? All three. I used more than was probably necessary, but I really didn't want to hurt him. And the more lube the better, in my opinion. "Bear down," I commanded as I notched the head of my cock against his hole and began to push.

At first, he didn't want to let me in. He was shaking, these needy gasps escaping him as my crown teased the seam of his twitchy hole. Shiny with lube and slightly puffy, he looked wrecked.

No porno was as good as this.

Nothing could ever compare to this.

My dick ached, balls jerking as I bit my lip hard. The pain helped keep me in check as I waited for him to do as he was told. He bore down, finally, and I slipped in with a grunt. It became too easy all of a sudden, the tight-snug-wet-hot-wet of his hole sucking around my tip.

"Oh, Jesus god fucking fuck," I groaned, dropping my head against George's shoulder. "You are fucking sin, baby. So good. I can't—oh fuck." My hips flexed, barely a twitch, but it was enough to make George sob.

"C-ca-can't," he whimpered, thrashing, though he remained obediently in the position I'd put him.

"You can," I encouraged. "Just…just hold still, sweetheart. Let me in. Let me—I need—" I pressed a little deeper, and George howled. "Fuckfuckfuck." I was not going to last like this. There was no fucking way. Not with him wet and tight, and the silicone a hard ridge against me. "I can't—I can't last—C'mon, take it, take it, take it—"

"M-more," George whined, encouraging me. "Green, green, green." Another inch, another whine from us both. On and on we went, slow and steady. And by the time my cock was sucked up entirely inside all that delicious heat, I was barely holding on to my last thread of sanity. "More, more, more," George begged, spread so wide he couldn't fucking move.

I pulled back a little, sinking in only an inch, but it was enough. Didn't even have to move the dildo at all. We spilled in tandem, George's dick spurting all over the wood beam he was leaning against. "Fuck, fuck," he gasped at the same time I sank my teeth in the back of his neck.

I snapped into him, chasing my own release.

I had enough semblance of self control to reach around for his dick, milking him through the last spurts of come as I rutted into his ass over and over and over, steady, barely there thrusts that we both felt all the way to our toes.

Gasping, and still reeling from how intense that had been, it took me a second to get my head screwed on right. When my thoughts came back online, the first thing I did was release his neck. Another bite mark remained, this one darker than the last. Glancing down nearly made me orgasm a second time. Hole stuffed, my cum began to leak around my cock and the dildo.

"So good," I murmured, kissing over the bite I'd left as my hips flexed one last time, pushing my cum deeper. "You're my good, good boy. Taking what I give you." Another flex. The sound that he made was filthy as hell—and so loud. "I'm gonna take your dildo out, baby, okay? Gonna do it nice and slow."

I was reluctant to leave his heat. At least, right now. Was it too much to ask for a few more minutes? I couldn't wait to feel his hole sans dildo when it was sloppy from the mess I'd made. George nodded, signaling his consent as I carefully began to pull the toy out of him. It was slow going. And when it finally popped free we both audibly sighed.

"Better?" I confirmed, dropping it to the floor unceremoniously. I figured I'd clean it up later, but for now, I needed both hands to make sure George was doing okay.

"Mhm," George's voice was fucked out and submissive.

"You like my cock in you?" I murmured, flitting my lips across his shoulder, the bite I'd left, and up his neck. "Does it feel good?" My hand went to his belly, rubbing over it like I was holding the womb he didn't have.

"Mhm," George agreed, attempting to clench around me and failing. Like his hole simply couldn't close up, it'd been stretched so wide. Fuck. I flexed forward again, the wet slap noise echoing.

"I like your cunt too, baby. I'd fill it up always if I could. Stuff you full and keep you happy." He'd said he liked to be bred, hadn't he? "I'd give you my babies," I husked against the shell of his ear, fluttering it with a few tiny kisses. The skin was hot—maybe the sunburn, maybe the flush? Either way, I supposed it didn't matter. My hand squeezed his non-existent womb again, holding his belly snug so he couldn't move. "You like my cum inside you? Like knowing I'm trying to knock you up? Even if it doesn't work."

I shuddered, my own words getting to me.

"Yes," George didn't even bother denying it. At this point I was pretty sure he'd do anything for me. Say anything. He was innocent and soft and *perfect* like this. All his walls were down—and god…I'd put him there. I'd sunk him in honey, and now it was my job to bring him out of it. To shower him in the sort of praise and adoration that he deserved.

That he'd *always* deserved.

"You did so well, Duchess," I promised. "Such a good, good boy for me. My pretty, lovely, precious sweetheart. I'm so *pleased* with you," George shuddered, a sound escaping him as his hole attempted to squeeze again— once more failing. "You made me so very happy," I continued, knowing he needed this—especially now.

I'd been told that sometimes subs could experience something called a "drop" after a scene if they were not carefully taken care of—and even sometimes then too. And I didn't want that for George. I wanted him to feel dazed, and fuzzy, and important. Wanted his sweet, worried brain to rest like he so desperately needed.

"I'm so proud of you." My voice was gentle as I reached around him, tenderly beginning to pick at the knots of rope around his wrists. "I couldn't be more proud. So obedient for me, weren't you? Playing my games with me."

"Mhmm," George's voice was hoarse. It was difficult to get the ropes undone while reaching around his body like this, but I managed. It took longer than

I wanted, but soon enough, the red rope had fallen to the floor, and I was rubbing feeling back into his arms.

"You want me to pull my dick out?" I asked. There wasn't really a sexy way to ask that. "While I—"

"*No.*" George's answer was quick—*super* fucking quick. I grinned, rutting into him with another greedy slap of our hips. My dick was softening, which sucked, but…I figured I'd let his hole keep me warm for as long as it was able.

"Anything you want, precious," I promised, "but…I need to see you. Need to see that pretty face. You okay if I pull out for one quick second? I promise I'll push right back in and stuff you nice and full again."

George made an unhappy sound, but ultimately nodded. I was quick about it, slipping out of his well-fucked hole and flipping him around carefully. I did accidentally knock Neil with my foot in my haste, unfortunately. Though the plop of the dildo hitting the water where the boats were normally stored was easy to forget when George was docile in my arms.

RIP Neil, you delightful silicone bastard.

Ignoring the wood and possible ass splinters I might get from it, I sat down on the floor with my back to the wall and pulled George into my lap. It was easy to angle his hips just right, and even easier to slip inside his cum-slick entrance. Jesus Christ, it was so good. Hot and sticky and inviting. Twitching around me, George welcomed me back into his body with a grateful sigh. Like I was doing him a favor.

My dick attempted to harden, and I didn't stop it. I had no intention of fucking him again at present—he wasn't ready for that. But if I was somewhat hard it would mean I could stay inside him for longer like he wanted.

My focus was on George.

On his tear-streaked face.

On the way he was shaking, his eyes glassy and lost.

"Oh, fuck, you're so pretty," I said, giving his hips one last squeeze before I slid my hands up his body to cup his face. "So pretty when you suffer. The *prettiest.*"

George cracked a sweet smile—made sweeter by the presence of tears still in his red-rimmed eyes.

"Why don't you lean on me," I offered, "you wanted me to hold you." George nodded. "And I live to please." His head bobbed again before he rested it on my shoulder. I stroked my hands up and down the long line of his back, enjoying the way his chest expanded with each breath he took.

George's shorts were caught around one ankle, tickling my bare leg, but I ignored the odd sensation in favor of giving him what he needed. I moved my hands in languid sweeping motions, then short rubs over his wrists and forearms, keeping him cared for as I beckoned him back to reality, little by little.

Putting George back together after taking him apart filled me with a sense of rightness I had rarely, if ever, experienced.

"How're your knees?" I murmured against his hair, nuzzling into him as I took his full weight. "Is the wood hurting them?"

"S'fine," George slurred, lips skimming my throat. "I...happy."

I happy.

What a *compliment*.

Jesus, he was cute.

"You're such a cutie pie, Georgie Porgie," I groaned, rubbing the back of his neck, amused when he sighed. I swear to god if he really was a cat he'd be purring right now. "The cutest cutie patootie I've ever met."

"Shut up," his response was weak—but very Georgie.

"Christ, I just wanna eat you up." I mimed biting him and he snorted out a laugh. A laugh that made his hole flutter around my dick again—and god, wasn't that nice? I'd never been with someone who wanted to be stuffed after sex was over. It was fucking nirvana. My dick was oversensitive and every weak clench of his hole sent sparks down my spine.

"No more biting." George curled his long arms around me. He gave me a fragile squeeze and I thunked my head against the wall, peering up at the high wooden beams that criss-crossed the ceiling with a happy grin.

"No more biting," I agreed. "For *now*."

"You're like a naughty puppy," he accused. "Always gnawing on things."

"Ooo, now there's an idea for another time," I enthused, still rubbing the tension out of his neck. I moved on to his shoulders, then his back again, enjoying the way he flopped into me like a dead fish. Which may not have sounded sexy, but totally was. "Puppy play," I added, in case that wasn't obvious. "Maybe after I get you a pair of cat ears and a butt plug with a tail. I can try to hump you and you can hiss and bite me like the pretty kitty you are."

"You have a wild imagination." George's face told me he was considering it. "What about as owner and pet?"

"You or me?"

"You, dog. Me, owner."

"Mmm, that *could* be fun," I agreed, imagination already running wild. Me on my knees, sniffing between George's legs, whining at him because I wanted to lick his dick but it was covered. George gasping and getting mad at me, trying to shove me off only for him to stumble—oh fuck yes. George on his *knees* on the floor, with me behind him, humping his ass through his clothes, puppy ears bouncing. "Okay, *yes*. That would be awesome."

"Yeah?"

"*Fuck yes*. I could have a leash. Oh my god—*you* holding my *leash*?! I am so into this. That is so fucking hot. You could tug on it and get mad at me. If you stomped your cute little foot and called me a bad dog I'd cum on the spot."

"Why am I not surprised part of your fantasy involves me being angry with you?"

"I *love* when you're mad." My smile was a testament to that fact. "Actually—scratch that. I love when you pay attention to me in general. Whatever attention I can get is good enough for me, positive or negative."

"You really *are* a puppy." George did not sound surprised, like he'd suspected as much already.

This was trust in its truest form.

George—arguably the most guarded person I'd ever met—was allowing me to see a side of him that he'd never shown anyone else.

And that was…humbling.

The control he'd given me today had been such an immense gift.

My own kink awakening paled in comparison to the wash of uncontrollable feelings I had discovered today. Selfishness was on the back burner. How could I think about myself when George was here in my arms, needing me?

No one had ever needed me before.

Not like this.

Emotions, effervescent and happy bubbled up inside me.

"You were so beautiful, by the way," I said. "I swear to god, I've never seen anything like what you just gave me. What a gift. And this whole conversation? Jesus. So fucking awesome. Everything about you is awesome—and sexy. If awesome and sexy had a baby that would be you. S-awesome."

"Mmm," George's response was lackluster, but he sounded more like himself. We sat there for several long minutes, my hands wandering his limp form, rubbing and scratching, and soothing him back into the world of the living.

When he pulled away to look at me, hands on my shoulders for balance I knew I'd done well. His smile was serene. His eyes were no longer glassy. "Thank you," George's voice was soft as he leaned in and kissed me, long and lingering. "I needed that."

I hummed into it, enjoying the flicker of his frisky little tongue. "Thank *you*," I said when we parted, cupping his face again, thumbs smearing away the remains of tears. "I can honestly say that I *loved* every second of what we just did."

I'd needed it too.

"Me too," George admitted. "It's never…been like that for me."

"Me neither." I agreed, combing his pale hair out of his face the way he often did to himself. "That was *special*."

"Sure was, Counselor." George's smile was playful, and I chuckled, unable to help myself.

"You liked the roleplay?"

"Yeah, I did." George laughed, and his hole clenched around me again. Still loose, but tightening a bit. I groaned. And even though I'd literally just said I didn't plan to fuck him again—I was still upset that my dick hadn't managed to get hard. It was in limbo. Just like we were.

"You want a nap?" I offered. "Or maybe a back rub in our tent? On the mattress?"

George debated with himself. "I want…a sex sandwich."

"You want a—" I paused, then snorted, unable to help the burst of happiness that exploded in my chest. "*Ohmygod*. Are you *teasing* me? Is this what orgasms do to you? You become a teasing little shit?"

"No. That's *you*. I just know your stomach is going to start growling any minute. You get hungry after sex." George was right, so I didn't argue. As much as I'd just taken care of him, he apparently wanted to take care of me, too. Mother-henning me like a motherfucking boss.

"How about I set you up in the tent nice and cozy, check your cute little ass to make sure you're good, and come back with some sex sandwiches for the both of us?" I offered, scratching his scalp and enjoying the way his eyes drifted shut. Goddamn cat, seriously. "That sound good, Duchess? That way you can keep your thoughts fuzzy soft and not have to 'people' until you're ready."

George made a face at the nickname, but otherwise was too distracted being petted to argue. "Sounds good," he agreed.

Full of joy, full of cum, and eager for our next adventure, George and I rose from our spot on the ground. Luckily, sans butt splinters. I could only hope George wouldn't be too devastated when he found out Neil was now swimming with the fishes—literally.

Twenty-Two
George

SEX SANDWICHES. WHO knew?

Apparently carbs hit different after being fucked because when Alex returned to our tent after gathering lunch for the both of us, I was ravenous. I finished my sandwich quicker than he finished his, and his shock was made evident as he watched me dabbing my mouth with a napkin, blue eyes dancing.

"Worked up an appetite, did you?"

"Shut up." I was losing track of how many times I'd said that to him over the last three days. His lips curled into a pleased smile.

"You normally eat like a bitty little bird. It's good to know that that was all an act."

"It wasn't an act." I threw my balled up napkin at him, and he caught it with a leer. Demon. He was a demon. Apparently fucking me made him even cockier than usual. Which was as infuriating as it was adorable.

Christ, I...I was having a hard time unpacking just how good sex with Alex was. Sometimes it really felt like he could read my mind. He knew *exactly* what to do and *how* to do it for maximum effect. The double penetration? Holy fuck, I had not expected that. But I was certain to think about it for… the next millennia, let's be honest.

Normally my skin was too tight for my body, my head like a brittle rubber band ready to snap. But right now…after such an intense scene and the frankly perfect aftercare, I actually felt…good?

Like breathing came easy.

Like my thoughts weren't treacherous.

Loosey fucking goosey.

I'd never realized how much goddamn fun sex could be. That communication itself could make it better. That there were so many options—and ideas, and possibilities. Alex made me feel unafraid to try the things I'd never known I wanted. He was the perfect partner to explore with, all endless enthusiasm and sharp wit.

The fact it'd taken him less than a day to figure out how to take me apart?

He was amazing.

Truly fucking amazing.

I couldn't remember the last time I'd had this much fun. With *anything*, honestly.

"Sure, sure," Alex teased. He finished his sandwich with two massive, disgusting bites, then used my somewhat dirty napkin to clean his mouth. I made a face and he snickered. "You touched it," he shrugged. "It's better than mine."

"You're so gross," I replied, glancing at his clean napkin pointedly. "Do you want me to touch that one too so you'll actually clean your face?" There was a smudge of mustard on Alex's bottom lip that he'd missed.

"Sure." He eyed me curiously, like he couldn't wait to see what I was about to do. Which was so fucking weird and *nerdy* and cute—all at once. After some internal debate, I reached over to grab Alex's unused napkin. *This is so weird, why are you entertaining it?* That thought didn't stop me from pressing a quick kiss to the corner. My cheeks flamed, but Alex looked so pleased I managed to fight through my embarrassment to shove the napkin against his chest.

"There's mustard on your—" I mimed the corner of my mouth.

"Here?" He grinned as he dabbed his face where I'd indicated on mine.

"Lower."

"Here?" He tried again.

"Got it."

"Thanks." Alex folded the napkin up, then stared at it—like now that I'd kissed it he was debating the merit of keeping it versus throwing it away.

Now who was the raccoon?

"Don't even think about it." I laughed, kicking a leg out to connect with his thigh. "It's trash, Alex, not a memento." The motion made my ass twinge pleasantly, and I sighed, leaning into the movement so I could feel it longer. Normally, the sensation dulled by now—and I had no doubt its lingering had everything to do with how fucking full I'd been stuffed.

"I'll let it go if you offer to kiss something else for me," Alex waggled his dark brows playfully, dimples showing he was smiling so wide. My guard still hadn't gone up, even though the fuzz from my orgasm had faded. Another miracle.

"Fine. What?"

"I haven't decided yet, but I promise you'll know as soon as I figure it out."

"I'm not kissing your hockey skates," I grunted. I attempted to extricate my foot from Alex's leg but he latched onto it, fingers digging into the sole like it was second nature. He didn't even seem to notice he was doing it, his hands moving on their own.

"You remembered I play hockey?"

"You told me three days ago." My flush burned even brighter, and I looked up at the sloping tent ceiling so I wouldn't have to see the look in his eyes. The truth was…I remembered everything Alex had told me about himself.

He didn't share much—so I clung to each tidbit almost desperately.

We were on a timer.

I knew that.

But I couldn't help but feel greedy.

We were toeing a line between friendship and something more, and I didn't know how to cross it, or even if I actually wanted to. My mom thought I did. Her reaction when we'd talked had made that clear. But my own feelings were far more complicated. Too difficult to easily understand—not without some deep, thorough thinking.

And I wasn't sure I was ready for that.

If I crossed that line, what would happen? After the wedding? When I went back to New York? Alex had made it clear he had no interest in something outside the terms of our "contract," for lack of a better word.

If he wanted something more he'd say something.

He'd promised to be honest.

Which meant…I was stuck in limbo, waiting.

If I opened my mouth I could ruin what little time left I had with him, and even though "miscommunication trope" was one of my least favorites, I couldn't help but feel like my behavior was justified.

What-ifs were too…unpredictable.

What if these feelings keep growing?

What if he wants more?

What if *I* want more?

Even though I know relationships rarely, if ever, were equal.

It was better to stick to what we'd agreed, and deal with the consequences.

It felt so raw and real and confusing to know that I had walls and fortresses and lines galore—and Alex was somehow allowed behind all of them. I'd been burned before. Badly. And I wasn't talking about my hand—ha! Or my shoulders.

Was I…strong enough to *survive* that again?

Another uncertainty.

I needed to make sure not to take this too seriously, or I'd risk falling even farther for him.

"George?" Alex's voice pulled me out of my head. I blinked, shaking my head to clear it. "Hey…" He was in my space a second later, the scent of his cologne tickling my nose as his fingers danced up the inside of my wrist. "You okay?"

He was worried.

Funny, I'd been concerned about him earlier too—when his focus had drifted at the beach. The parallels between us were as hilarious as they were unfunny. Complementary, just like us. Black and white. Yin and yang.

"I'm fine, I was just…thinking."

"Is that a good thing?"

I wanted to quip at him, say something biting to make him laugh. But…I didn't. I was still fuzzy around the edges, and despite my tumultuous thoughts, I was full of certainty that Alex was here to comfort—no—Alex was *ready* to comfort me.

He saw it as an extension of what he'd done in the boathouse.

And who was I to deny him?

"I'm feeling a little overwhelmed," I admitted, giving him the honesty he'd requested even though we were no longer in a scene.

"What do you need?" Alex asked, instead of dismissing my feelings. "A hug?" God, he was so quick to offer those. "Snuggles? Another sex sandwich? A bottle of water? Some back scratches? What—"

"A hug would be nice," I confirmed—and it ached.

It ached so badly to ask for what I needed. Because I hadn't before. And I was realizing…the more time I spent with Alex, how often I'd ignored my own needs to please everyone else. He paid such close attention it was impossible to be dismissive of myself when he was by my side. As though he wouldn't allow it.

Alex's arms wrapped around me, squeezing me tightly into his thick chest. His breath tickled my ear. One big, solid hand stroked down my back just like it had when we'd been naked and he'd been inside me.

"Do you want to talk about what's overwhelming you?" Alex asked, chest rumbling beneath my cheek. Christ, he was the best hugger in the world. Better than Mom, even. I blamed his pecs.

"It's just…a lot," I admitted—once again surprised by the honesty. "Being with you makes me realize what I've been missing."

"That's a good thing, isn't it?" Alex's hand swiped up and down, and I melted. "That was the point. Why I offered this—why you accepted. So that you could know what it feels like to be treated right."

"I suppose so," I agreed.

His lap looked so inviting.

Inviting enough that I crawled into it—even though it was mortifying to do so—the mattress making a squeaking sound as we moved. It didn't pop or give, which was good. The last thing I needed was to feel more embarrassed. Alex rearranged my legs so that I was sitting sideways, face tucked into the space beneath his ear, hidden away.

Cradled there, I really did feel safe, especially when his hand continued to rub my lower back, and his other hand gripped my hip tight so I wouldn't fall.

"I suppose…" My lips brushed his throat. "It's good to know…that there are better options out there." I paused, gathering my thoughts. "I've never been with someone who…matches my…" What was the word? "Energy? It's always felt so…one-sided."

"Believe me, I totally get that."

"Yeah?" My heart stuttered.

"Sometimes…" Alex trailed off, like he wasn't sure he wanted to keep speaking. He sucked in a breath, uncharacteristically defenseless. "I think… there's not a single person out there who can handle my intensity."

It was a very vulnerable thing to say, made more vulnerable by his tone of voice. All of Alex's masks were gone. I got the feeling this was the most authentic he'd ever been.

"I like your intensity," I whispered, just as soft.

Alex made a noise, crushing me tight as he breathed me in. "You say that," he laughed, "but you've only been with me on good days."

I didn't know what to say to that.

"Anyway." Alex quickly changed the subject before I could get my thoughts together. Which was unfair. But...I'd run from him so frequently, I didn't fault him for his own version of avoidance. "I think it's good. Feeling overwhelmed right now. Shows you the inverse of what you've had, right? So you know what to look for. That's why it's a good thing this is temporary. A trial run. For your next relationship."

"Right."

"Options are always good. Remember what I said about revenge?" Alex was really trying to distract me now. Talking fast. Almost manic. Like he regretted opening up the way he had—like he couldn't get his mouth to stop, even if he wanted to.

Hesitantly, I stroked a hand down his back.

He settled.

"Breathe."

He breathed.

"Are you getting what you wanted out of this, too?" I asked, keeping my tone soft.

"*Yes.*" Alex's voice cracked. "You're the best *temporary* boyfriend ever."

"The feeling is mutual." Understatement of the century. I wanted to push—but this time, Alex was the one at risk of running, so I didn't.

Alex had said the best revenge was being blissfully, happily in love with someone other than Brendon. But what if I...didn't want revenge?

What if I just wanted Alex?

Wanted the days we spent together to never end? This camaraderie. The playfulness. The warmth?

I needed to stop focusing on the future and simply enjoy this. There were still four days left until I left for home. Four days of kissing in the summer sun, of laughter, of feeling Alex's hands just like this.

I really needed to stop thinking that this was anything but temporary. As special as I currently felt, tucked in Alex's arms and pampered by his affection, I knew I wasn't *actually* special. Practice boyfriends weren't real boyfriends, after all.

Twenty-Three
George

THE SUN HAD SUNK beneath the tree line, casting sloping shadows over the lake below. I was exhausted, I could admit that. Day four of Roderick and Juniper's Wedding Extravaganza had been fun but trying in a lot of new ways. The previous night, after Alex and I had taken a much needed post-sex nap and enjoyed our sandwiches, we'd stayed up late helping Mom prep for today. "Bachelor and Bachelorette Party Day."

This morning had been spent setting up the obstacle course for the "Wedding-Lympics" that Roderick had insisted on. And as soon as the adults had begun to populate that, Alex and I had been assigned on kiddo babysitting duty in the main lodge hosting arts and crafts on two of the long wooden tables.

He'd periodically had to go out and take calls. A few from his mom, who he called "Nadine", as well as a couple vendors who were anxious about their roles in the parties tonight. Aside from that, we'd stuck together all day.

There were a lot of craft options.

Shrinky Dinks galore, keychain making, and my personal favorite—friendship bracelets.

I hadn't *really* meant to make a pair of them for me and Alex.

It'd happened without me consciously recognizing what I'd done. When I realized I was nearly finished, however, it felt silly not to commit. So I tied them off and resolved myself to hide them in my backpack later—a keepsake of my first "real" boyfriend, even if he was fake.

There was no way, just by looking at them, he'd realize what they were.

At least, that's what I told myself when Alex came to check on me and my group of preteens and caught me red-handed. The pair of bracelets were matching. One blue, one yellow, with silver charms with a respective G and A on them. In retrospect, it was pretty obvious.

"How's it going over here?" Alex asked, one of his younger cousins, probably six or seven years old, hanging around his neck. There was another attached to one of his legs, smaller, chunkier. But both had the James family dark hair and uncannily pale eyes.

"Good," I reassured, hiding the bracelets beneath my palm as sneakily as I could. "We're nearly done."

"So are we." Alex glanced back toward his side of the table and the marker-laden mess that'd been used to make the Shrinky Dinks. "Mrs. M's gonna cook our masterpieces."

"Right."

Creating Shrinky Dinks was one of the only parts of camping I'd actually liked as a child. Back then, we had to wait until we got home to bake them. That was one of the nice things about cabins—they came with ovens.

I'd been giddy as a kid, sitting in the kitchen with eager anticipation as the colorful charms we'd drawn and cut out of thin plastic would harden and "shrink" in the oven's heat. Over the years, we'd made a variety of fun keychains and decorations for the room Joe and I had shared growing up—

hanging from the windows, our bed frames, and our backpack straps when school came around again.

The kids that populated the Shrinky Dink station looked just as enthusiastic as I had been at their age. Alex did well with them, kind and playful. He had no problem helping—and I'd caught glances of him several times leaning over some of the younger kids shoulders to aid them as they drew.

His work was gorgeous, I could admit that. All straight lines. He definitely had artistic talent.

But what I found most enlightening, was how very patient he could be.

He really would make a good dad.

And Christ, did that thought make my chest constrict.

"What are you hiding?" Alex asked curiously. I was so distracted thinking about him in dad-mode that my reflexes were too slow to stop him. Apparently, I hadn't been sneaky enough because Alex wrestled my hand open, and the friendship bracelets I'd made were revealed.

It was innocent.

Or.

It would've been.

If not for the charms—one to each—with our initials.

Alex gaped at the blue one with the little A like he had short-circuited. He stared at them, spreading them out on the table, long tan fingers tracing the lengths. "Are these...for us?" he asked, voice hoarse.

I didn't know what to do. I hadn't really meant to make them? Except, that I totally had. And his reaction was just—wow.

He looked floored.

Like he didn't know what to do with himself.

As wrong-footed as I often was.

"Yes." My pulse was skipping all over the place.

"*I love them.*" Alex blinked, still staring like the bracelets were something monumental and not a silly mess of string looped together. "Do you...wanna put mine on?" I made a sound in affirmation, too choked up to find words as I reached for the blue one. "No. Um. The other one."

Right.

Of course he'd want the yellow one with the G. I should've expected that.

My hands trembled as I tied it around his wrist, making sure to double knot it so that it wouldn't pop free. The charm made a clinking noise when it knocked against his watch, and Alex grinned. "Your turn." He made an impatient waving gesture, and I offered him my wrist so he could tie the blue one on.

It carried a weight to it that neither of us was ready to acknowledge.

A weight that we lifted together as we finished up with the kiddos, cleaned up the mess, and watched as their parents took them to dinner.

We hadn't had to discuss our schedules—or the fact that neither of us was willing to part with the other. "My plans" and "his plans" became "our plans." Alex was right there when I helped my mom and siblings. And I was there when he needed help setting up the tandem bachelor and bachelorette parties.

He was simultaneously the "Man of Honor", his words, and "Best Man" so he'd been given a lot of responsibility. I'd already known he planned the whole wedding too. I would've had to be an idiot not to notice how much effort he'd put into everything.

Dealing with vendors with kindness—though still delightfully firm.

I had a competency kink, and Alex hit every mark.

Joe helped us set up, because he was great that way. He and Alex hauled the loungers from the trucks down to the lake. They'd be set up for floating beer pong, with cups full of water taped to the plastic, and ping-pong balls made out of fish food.

I set up the picnic tables with the actual drinkable beers, sectioning off a portion so that the balls in cups on the water could coincide with cups on the table.

The James twins were nothing if not environmentally conscious.

Alex worried about my burned hand, but I assured him I was fine. The blisters barely hurt anymore, and besides—as long as I didn't have to get wet, I was happy. It wasn't like I was going to keel over and die while lining up red Solo cups. Christ.

Roderick's party was easy to prepare. The loungers and the picnic tables were the worst parts, aside from filling cups of beer. We had a few mishaps with the loungers spilling into the lake—but since the cups atop them were full of water—and simply needed to be taped again, it didn't matter all that much.

Joe assured me everything would be fine.

And considering how much he loved animals, I believed him.

"You have got to be kidding," I laughed, after we'd finished getting the lake area ready and Alex informed me that a pizza delivery man was coming by to bring food. He shook his head, obviously proud of himself.

"I'm really not. You'd be surprised what someone will do for the right price."

"Jesus Christ."

Alex shrugged. "Roddy wanted pizza from his favorite pizza place in Columbus—and I live to please."

"The delivery guy isn't a stripper, is he?" I teased.

Alex shook his head, expression one of mock offense. The friendship bracelet on his wrist caught the light as he crossed his arms over his chest. It looked good next to his watch. His broken watch—that I was dying to ask about but never had. Not after he closed up anytime things got remotely real.

"Absolutely not." He arched a brow like I was the naughty one for suggesting it.

Joe tripped in the sand down by the edge of the water, and we both held our breath, then sighed in tandem when he righted himself without face-planting. Dude was big enough if he hit the dirt he'd cause an earthquake.

"You okay, buddy?" I called. Joe just nodded, then went about his business.

"Lucky save," Alex whistled, then turned his attention back to me. "Before you ask, there will be no strippers at June's party either."

"Yeah?" I cocked my head at him, figuring there was a story there.

"We don't like it," Alex shrugged. "June and I. It's an opinion we both share.

Not to judge, of course, everyone likes different things."

"So, when you get married, you won't be going to strip clubs in Vegas?" I don't know why I was pushing. Well…actually I did. Because I definitely wanted to know. Especially considering the fact that I had been burned by infidelity before. Every couple has their own rules when it comes to things like that. And I could admit that I was curious if Alex and I would be compatible in this way.

Testing the waters, even though I knew it was fruitless.

"Definitely not," Alex agreed. "I think the whole concept of 'seeing what you're missing out on the day before your wedding' is gross. Why would you be 'missing out' on anything if you're marrying the person you want to spend your life with? It doesn't make sense."

I was oddly relieved.

"What about you?" Alex was testing me and it was even more blatant than my test had been.

"Ah. No. I don't like that either," I said. "Something small and personal like this is nice, though. However, I wouldn't pick beer pong or pizza delivery."

"Yeah?" Alex grinned. He slung an arm over my shoulders, pulling me into him as he steered us away from the empty party skeleton and up the hill toward the cabins. Next, we were setting up Juniper's "spa" night. Alex had informed me that he'd be doing all the heavy lifting—despite my protests—but that I was welcome to do anything else that might not involve bumping my injured hand on things.

No matter how much I told him I was fine, he didn't listen. Which I supposed was fair, considering the fact that he was the one dressing my wound every morning. He hadn't protested me making friendship bracelets—but then again, it would be very difficult for an accident to happen when one was tying string.

"I always thought a joint party would be nice," I admitted. "Because if you're getting married, you'll be joining family and friends. So…it only makes sense that it would not be a separate endeavor."

Brendon had liked to keep his friends separate.

"If you think about Brendon one more time, I can't promise I'll behave."

I jerked, startled. Alex was watching me like he always was, and though his words were extreme, there was a spark in his eyes. A *dangerous* spark. One I did not want to test—unless, maybe, I did?

The thought alone was enough to make my heart skip a beat. Did I...want to be punished by Alex? Yes, yes I did. But I was also nervous. The last time I'd been spanked had not gone well. Brendon had—

"*George.*" My name was little more than a growl. I had hardly any time to react before my back was against the cabin we'd been walking by and Alex's tongue was in my mouth. I moaned around him, fingers catching in his shirt as he licked behind my teeth, curling tongues with mine.

Alex kissed me so goddamn hungrily all thoughts fled my mind entirely. Until I was simply drifting, nothing but a mouth meeting his with sticky sweet glides of our tongues and lips. By the time we parted, I couldn't even remember my name, let alone what we'd been talking about.

"There we go, that's my pretty kitty," Alex said silkily when he pulled back far enough to see my face. His hand was on my throat again. I couldn't even recall when it'd moved there, but I didn't mind. In a way, it felt like a collar, and that was...soothing.

"Kitty?" I echoed, too dazed and kiss-swollen to properly snark.

"That's right," Alex pecked me again, giving my neck a squeeze. "You just need to focus on me, okay? No one else."

"Okay."

"Good boy."

Alex stole at least a dozen more kisses over the course of the next hour. We set up the bridesmaids' cabin the way Juniper had specified, massage chairs across the main floor, and a table full of cupcakes for dessert. There was a pedicure station that genuinely looked delightful.

I made a mental note to visit later, if it was allowed.

I'd been in the bridesmaids cabin only once before, when June had interrogated me about her veil, and I could honestly say—standing back to observe our work—the place was nearly unrecognizable. With pink and green streamers hanging on the walls, and a giant balloon arch that Alex had paid an obscene amount of money to have delivered—there was no denying that it was gorgeous.

"She's got a flair for the dramatic," Alex explained, noticing the way I was staring. "Roderick doesn't care about the frills, June does."

"Right," I agreed, though my attention was now on him. "You…are amazing." The room was truly magnificent—like something straight out of a magazine. Alex shrugged, embarrassed.

"It's not a big deal."

How could he act so nonchalant about something so impressive?

"It *is* a big deal," I argued, keeping my tone tender but honest. "All of this had to take so much work."

"I hired out a lot of it."

"But *you* managed it. That's like ninety percent of the battle. I'm sure it means a lot to Juniper."

Alex's cheeks were red. He didn't often blush, and I couldn't stop butterflies from filling my stomach at the sight. He scratched the back of his neck, thick arms and chest flexing as he cast his gaze to the side, almost shyly.

This room alone had to have cost thousands of dollars. Way more than I was comfortable contemplating. I mean…I figured Alex's family had money—given the obvious signs, but this was on another level.

"The masseuses are supposed to be here in…" Alex deflected, checking his phone to distract me. He smiled when he saw the bracelet I'd made him sitting next to his watch. "Shit. Five minutes. Just in time."

Everyone was still around the bonfire, enjoying a second round of s'mores while they waited for us to finish setting up. Personally, I thought it was a bit strange that no one else had offered to help aside from Joe, but Alex had assured me that he had it handled, and that it would just stress him out to have to command a bunch of people.

Funny, seeing as that was all he did.

Privately, I wondered if he'd simply preferred to put more work in just to spend time alone with me. Or maybe, it was because as dismissive as he'd been of his own efforts, he'd wanted to have a hand in physically preparing for June's big party.

"Alex…" I caught his arm when he was walking past me—presumably to rearrange something. I tried again, hoping this time he'd listen. "This *really* is impressive."

For a moment I worried he was going to brush me off a second time. Which bothered me. He *deserved* to know how goddamn good he was.

Instead, he paused, twisting to look at me.

There was an unreadable expression on his face, like he didn't know what to do with the sincere compliment when forced to acknowledge it. Then, like a pad of butter on a hot pan, he melted. The look he gave me was so gooey-hot it made me feel like I was melting too.

"*Thank you,* Georgie." Alex stepped closer. He pecked my cheek, a soft brush of his warm, warm lips. My grip on his arm softened. "I worked really fucking hard on this. So that was—yeah. Thanks. I appreciate that."

Alex was a hard worker.

And so talented.

But most of all, he had a huge fucking heart.

"June's been having a rough time," Alex admitted. "Our dad was in an accident recently. He's fine—" he was quick to add. "But…I just—I wanted to cheer her up."

I got the feeling June hadn't been the only one having a hard time.

"I'm sorry about your dad, Alex," I said softly, aching for him. My fingers slid lower, toying with his watchband absentmindedly as I spoke. "I'm glad he's okay."

"Fuck. Me too." Alex's eyes took on a faraway sheen. "It's been a tough few months… So I just…I just really needed this to be perfect. For her."

"It is," I gave his wrist a squeeze and his smile returned. His forehead leaned against mine, his pale eyes drifting shut. For a second, we just stood there, absorbed in each other. My heart fluttered, my fingers tugging on the friendship bracelet around his wrist, tracing the knots.

He cared so much and so deeply.

Maybe Alex wasn't the only twin who'd gone out of their way to cheer the other up?

Suddenly, I understood June's matchmaking efforts a lot more.

Though I pushed those thoughts aside quickly, so I could focus on Alex.

"Mmm, you're so great." Alex sighed, nuzzling my temple. No longer running around—a man on a mission—he wrapped his arms around my back, forcing me to release his wrist, and hauled my body against his. Pressed flush together, head to toe, my heart began to riot again. "I needed this, thanks, sweetheart."

"No problem."

It felt like something new had shifted between us. But I didn't get to dissect it—because someone knocked on the door, and Alex was gone. Our moment of peace was over and chaos descended. Noise filled the gaps in my head as the bridal party entered the room with a squeal, closely followed by the masseuses that Alex had hired.

The rest of the night was a blur of activity.

Alex and I had our toes painted, feet in the pedicure tubs I'd eyed earlier. Yellow and blue, to match our respective friendship bracelets. He'd made a point to tie mine on me, and every time I felt the brush of string a flurry of butterflies filled my belly.

I'd made the damn things—and yet…it felt like Alex was the one that'd staked his claim. Like seeing that dangling silver A on my wrist filled him with immense satisfaction.

We both skipped massages in favor of plying Juniper with cupcakes and mimosas like the queen she was. She bickered with Alex. Poked fun at his last hockey game—and the fact that he'd been "stingy." Stingy with what? I had no idea. The puck?

She also kissed him a lot. Smooched his cheeks until he pushed her off with an annoyed huff and a pleased curl to his lips. She made it obvious how much she appreciated all he'd done. Half drunk on Mimosas, June didn't hold back.

"You're such a good brother," she said. "Which pains me to say, because it's like, against sibling rules to acknowledge. And your boyfriend is here."

I flushed, holding on to her glass so she wouldn't spill—because she'd shoved it into my hands.

"You're drunk," Alex said. He arched a brow at me. Following his cue, I set June's drink as far away from her as I could. She looked adorable and ridiculous, cucumbers on only one of her eyes—because she'd wanted to "see", and toe spreaders keeping her…well…toes spread? So that the polish dried properly.

"I just want you to be happy," June sobbed, laying her head on Alex's shoulder, her solitary cucumber slipping down her cheek. "You look so happy." Her hand smacked his cheek. Alex caught it, thwarting the next hit, his eyes crinkling at the corners.

"I am happy," he said.

"But for how long?" June questioned, quieter. "But for—" When Alex released her hand, she patted his cheek again, squishing his face with enthusiasm. His lips puffed out, the devastating fondness in his eyes turning sad for a moment. "How long, Alex?"

I excused myself, because the conversation felt private.

Alex kept glancing at me, like he was uncomfortable with me overhearing. And the last thing I wanted was to betray his trust. Not when he'd been so goddamn thoughtful when it came to mine.

Lacey—because she'd been invited as one of the bridesmaids—kept giving me looks that I ignored, at least until now, seeking her out to distract myself from the twins and their drama.

She was across the room, feet in a pedicure bath, an attractive man kneading her shoulders.

I flopped down beside her, amused to find that she'd painted her toes the same color that I'd painted mine. The masseuse moved on to the next client to offer us some privacy.

"Having fun?" I asked. She paused, fingers on the keyboard of her phone, gaze barely flicking up. Like she hadn't been watching me the entire time I was here. Judging me.

"Not as much fun as you." Lacey's lips curled into a smirk. God, everyone was smirking at me this weekend. I was tempted to abandon her, but of my family, she was the one I'd spent the least amount of quality time with.

"Ha, fucking ha," I huffed instead of leaving.

She was my little sister. I suppose it was…okay she was giving me shit.

"Mom's been telling everyone she found you your soulmate," Lacey informed me.

Of course she was.

She was a gossip connoisseur.

"Can we talk about something—*anything* else?" I begged, leaning back in my seat, bare feet crossing at the ankles.

"Why are your feet pretty?" Lacey scoffed. Mercy, or annoyance? I wasn't sure. "That's just…not fair."

I laughed, wiggling my toes at her just to see her scowl.

For a while we chatted about work. About her new job—and how quickly she was climbing the ranks. We talked about Mavis. About how much she loved being a mom, but how difficult she found juggling her career and being present for her daughter. She admitted that she didn't think she'd ever leave Ohio. That our family's help was the only reason she felt like she was succeeding at raising her daughter.

Which was...food for thought.

If I had children—hell, *when* I had children, because it was something I'd always wanted and couldn't imagine not doing—I couldn't imagine doing it entirely alone.

Missy would help. But judging by the dildo debacle I wasn't sure I could trust her with my kids. Mr. Pickles was a different story. As fussy as he was, he needed far less active care than a small child would. Would it mean I'd need to move? My current apartment was small. Perfect for two adults—but a child? No.

Which meant even if she was willing to help, she wouldn't be conveniently across the hallway.

I knew there were a lot of single parents out there. Like Lacey, for one. And that they managed every single day, somehow—like magic. But I couldn't... fathom doing that. Being a dad—without my mom nearby.

Catching up with Lacey was nice. She was more calm than my mother, and more expressive than Joe and my dad. She was more curious about my work life than anyone else. Even going so far as to ask me questions about things I'd mentioned in passing at dinner that first night.

Alex came and found me a bit later. June had sobered up, which was good.

"She's no longer allowed mimosas," Alex said as he pulled me out of my seat next to Lacey. Like touching me was a natural thing to do, even in front of an audience. He wrapped his arms around me, pulling me snug into him, his face buried in my neck, right where his bite marks still stung. Inhaling greedily, Alex's big frame relaxed fraction by fraction.

"Everything okay?" I asked, hands suspended midair, not because I didn't want to hug him back, but because we were being watched, and I'd never...

with anyone else had to worry about PDA. I didn't know what to do with it.

"Fine," Alex sighed. "Just recharging."

Just recharging.

Christ, that was cute.

As the night wore on and I remained Alex's loyal assistant, running errands beside him, and hovering as much as he'd let me, I couldn't help but face reality. I'd misjudged him. From that very first day, I'd thought him unserious and nonchalant. I'd assumed that nothing bothered him. That he was cocky and manipulative.

But that…couldn't be farther from the truth.

Alex had to be the most genuine person I'd ever met. He was a hard worker. He *cared*. He noticed details about everyone, and everything. He used those details to set people at ease. To make them feel seen.

When he entered a room it brightened.

He took things seriously. Maybe too seriously. His blasé attitude was only there to hide the man beneath. A person who was so desperate to do right by everyone else, I wasn't sure he ever stopped to take time to do right by himself.

His response to my compliment had been awkward at best. Like he didn't know what to do with praise. Like it was foreign—even though it had no right to be.

We were similar in that way.

Mirrors of one another.

And yet, opposites in almost every other regard.

I was beginning to suspect that Alex's flirty persona was nothing but a mask. Something he'd crafted to hide behind so that he wouldn't get hurt. A way to disguise his "intensity" as a flirtatious joke, and not an integral part of who he was.

The idea that a man like Alex could be insecure was frankly absurd.

And yet…the more I complimented him, talking him up whenever I could, making sure the rest of the partygoers understood how brilliant he was—and the more he shied away from it, the more certain I became that I was right.

I'd thought he'd offered to be my "practice boyfriend" because he felt sorry for me? At least, at first. Or because he wanted to get in my pants—which he had, and still stuck around. His motivations had been murky at best. I hadn't understood why a man like *him* would need such a silly, ridiculous ploy just to be able to "spoil someone."

But…as the night wore on, I couldn't help but come to the conclusion that perhaps…the reason Alex had made the offer wasn't because he felt pity for me, but because he was terrified of being vulnerable. Of letting someone see behind his walls.

Maybe this whole ploy had been just as beneficial for him as it had for me.

At present, we were down at the lake, playing a round of beer pong with Roderick. "We" as in Alex, because there was no way in hell I was playing a game that arbitrary. Alex was enjoying himself, gorging on pizza and teasing Roderick between bites about his "shitty aim."

"Hope you're not like that in bed," Alex said around his mouthful.

Roderick chortled, tossed another "fish ball" across the water, and missed.

Alex flitted between both parties like a social butterfly.

Back and forth, back and forth, all night long.

Checking on things, checking on his sister, checking on Roderick, checking on the guests—the vendors—the food, the decorations. Arranging, managing, joking, flirting, dancing between worlds with his silver tongue at play.

If the sun were a person, it would be Alex. So full of light. Friendly. Exuberant. Enthusiastic.

I would've been envious of his social skills if I wasn't so busy being in awe of him.

There wasn't a single conversation he didn't leave without making the person he was talking to smile at least once. When I was beside him, people smiled at me too—like I was an extension of his light, not a shadow following him around. He was charismatic and funny and genuinely so damn good at every single thing he did.

And yet, for some reason…every free moment we found, instead of basking in the attention he'd received, Alex's eyes found mine.

He sought me out like he was drowning.

Like I was a life preserver.

The only thing keeping him afloat.

His smiles would soften, his walls collapsing.

The walks between parties were full of comfortable, wonderful silence. With me tucked against him, his face at my neck, and his deep, needy lungfuls of my scent.

Recharging.

I orbited him and he orbited right back.

More than once, on our trips between the lake and the bridesmaids' cabin, we stole away into the woods. At first, I'd worried about animals, but Alex had assured me we'd be fine. Why I believed him? I had no idea.

But I did.

I trusted him to keep us safe.

Even in the dark—where anything could happen and you wouldn't see it coming.

Even in the woods I'd always hated—but couldn't anymore.

Not when thinking about trees reminded me of possessive kisses, all tongue, and teeth, and *need*. As the night wore on, Alex's hands became greedier, handsier. His groping rougher, more pointed. Sometimes slipping inside my clothing to squeeze and grope my "tits"—and once, memorably, down the back of my pants where he could scrape his fingers over my hole, gentle and insistent, while he asked me how long it would take to get my pussy wet for him.

It was a game we both loved.

And every time he referred to my body like that—as pussy, or cunt, or other equally entertaining nicknames—it sent a thrill up my spine.

More exploration.

Feeling each other out.

Discovering, mutually, how delightful intimacy could be when truly authentic.

It was three in the morning by the time everything had wound down and we'd cleaned the bachelor party at the lake up. Drunk as they were, the party-goers had still managed to help clear the area of any trash. Now, they were gone, stolen off to take a turn at Juniper's spa before the cleanup crew Alex had hired arrived in the morning to take it all away.

Which meant...Alex and I were alone. The stars danced above—reminding me of our picnic and the things that had transpired during it—as Alex and I transported the last bags of trash to the dumpster at the back of the boathouse. It was difficult to look at it without feeling the phantom slither of ropes around my wrists.

Everywhere I looked, I was reminded of Alex.

The path where we'd kissed, the tree we'd made out against. The boulder he'd groped my ass next to. The boathouse—for obvious, obvious reasons. Fizzles of heat buzzed through me at the reminder of what exactly had transpired in there.

It was heady—and overwhelming—and frankly fucking *amazing*.

"You tired, Duchess?" Alex asked. His beefy arms flexed as he yanked the lid for the dumpster open like it was easy. I knew for a fact that thing was heavy as hell. I tried not to swoon as his biceps bulged and the friendship bracelet dangled on his otherwise bare wrist, and wasn't certain I managed. Clearing my throat, I tossed my bag in first. Alex arched a brow at me, amused. He was still wet from his dip in the lake—as he'd been the one who'd dragged all the loungers to shore.

"George?" Alex said, easily keeping the lid open as he threw his own bag in. "I know I'm pretty, but I asked you a question."

My cheeks burned.

So he'd noticed the staring then.

"Are you tired, sweetheart?" Alex inquired again, softer this time.

"A bit," I admitted, because I was. Even though I hadn't done much talking myself, it'd still been a long, long night. Long enough that I didn't even grimace when Alex used that godawful nickname. I was…maybe starting to like it.

I *was* tired.

I hated socializing and I'd just voluntarily done it for *hours*.

The night had been endless.

And yet—I didn't want it to end.

"How do you feel about a shower?" I blurted, before I could stop myself.

"A shower?" There was a hint of teasing in Alex's tone, and the spark in his eyes made it clear he knew what I was up to.

My mouth went dry.

My dick gave a feeble, needy twitch.

I swear to god, I'd been half hard all night—grateful for my cock's size as it was far less obvious on me than it was on Alex.

"Correct. A shower. You know, for *showering*," I over-explained. "You're…wet."

"Not as wet as you, I'd bet," Alex grinned.

I made a high-pitched sound, and he snickered.

The summer heat had a way of making all my clothing feel sticky.

I'd had to borrow yet *another* shirt from Joe—seeing as I'd run out of clothes from my backup backpack. Which was not…inspiring a lot of confidence. Me being…sticky. Alex being…covered in lake water?

Luckily for the both of us, he'd mostly dried off by the time we made the journey back up the hill.

We made a detour to the tent to grab clothing to change into. Alex, because he was nosy, noticed immediately that I had not grabbed a new shirt to wear. He frowned, his own suitcase wide open, a pile of designer t-shirts and pants arranged in neat squares.

God, even the way he packed his suitcase was sexy.

You are losing your mind, George.

Before he could open his mouth to ask, I saved him the trouble. "This is Joe's," I plucked at the hem of my too-large t-shirt with a frown. "I ran out of clean clothes. I wanted to do laundry but I've been busy—and my mom is always using the machines and so I've—"

"Been borrowing clothes from Joe?" Alex frowned at me, offended. And then he chucked a shirt at me from his suitcase. I scrambled to catch it, nearly dropping it on the floor before I grabbed it just in time. "Hell no."

"What?" I blinked, squinting down at the black t-shirt—so fucking soft to the touch—held in my grip.

"You're not going to be walking around wearing some other guy's clothes," Alex grumbled, rising from his crouch.

"He's not 'some other guy'. He's my *brother*," I deadpanned.

Alex shrugged, unrepentant. "Yeah, well, *I'm* your boyfriend."

It did not escape my notice that Alex had omitted the "temporary" part. Which was…a first. And should not have filled me with the thrill it did. He'd only left it off to be dramatic. Not because he wanted something more from me. If he did, he would say something.

Alex's shirt smelled like him. Like cologne, and laundry detergent. Unfortunately lacking the delicious musk of his sweat—but beggars couldn't be choosers, and all that.

What in the hell was wrong with me?

Being disappointed I hadn't been offered a sweaty shirt?

Who the hell was I?

"If you need to borrow clothes, you'll be borrowing mine." His tone left no room for argument. Alex gathered a pair of ill-fitting—for me, not him—boxer briefs and joggers from his suitcase. He didn't chuck these at me. These he handed gently, making sure to invade my space as much as possible, as per usual.

When he pecked my cheek, the action nearly took my breath away.

So innocent, but intimate.

"Now, grab your toothbrush," Alex commanded, retreating to his own corner for just that.

I grabbed my toothbrush. And…*more* than my toothbrush. Sliding the bottle of lube Alex had left in my backpack surreptitiously into the pile of clothing. I didn't know where he'd gotten the bottle of lube in the first place, and truthfully, it didn't matter. I was eager. And like him, I preferred to be prepared.

I'd initiated this.

The shower—that we both knew would lead to sex.

Which was something I'd never done.

As we made our way to the communal bathroom—because he was nosy—Alex couldn't help but push. "Why did you only bring a tiny little backpack?"

Crickets were chirping, but otherwise, the world was eerily quiet.

"You don't strike me as the kinda guy who comes unprepared," Alex added, still talking. "That doesn't seem like you at all."

"My suitcase was, regrettably, lost," I sighed, pinching the bridge of my nose. "I asked them to contact me, but as you know, my phone is still in your glove box."

Alex took a second to reply. "So the backpack was…what? A backup bag in case your suitcase got lost—which it did?"

"Correct."

"That is either genius-level of preparation, or paralyzing paranoia."

"Things have a way of biting me in the ass," I replied. "I've learned to… circumvent that." Like the dildo—RIP Neil. Like the snake in the creek. Like my family's matchmaking efforts—though admittedly, the ass-biting from that was far more pleasant.

"Oh." Alex processed this. "What about a suit for the wedding? Are you going to wear what you had on at the airport?"

Fuck.

I'd nearly forgotten.

How was that possible?

"Absolutely not. That is casual linen. Not wedding appropriate." I kicked at a rock, and Alex caught my elbow, twisting me to look at him. "I figured I'd ask Joe to take me to Columbus at some point to find something. I'd rather not look like a schmuck at your sister's wedding. I would've gone earlier but I got…distracted." By Alex.

Alex's eyes held no guile. "I'd be happy to take you suit shopping."

"You're busy. I don't want to inconvenience you."

"Baby, you're not an inconvenience." Alex laughed, like I was being delightful and not an anxious ball of stress. "I need to head to Columbus anyway. I'm picking up my dad. You could come with me? We could leave tomorrow…or should I say, today? Considering the hour. What do you say? Shall we make it a date?" Alex kept talking, but I was stuck on the fact that he'd just invited me on a date.

A *formal* date.

"Dinner could be something fancy—" Alex tacked on, getting excited. "There's this Italian place I fucking love. Best lasagna I've ever had. Oh shit! And the ice rink. I wanna take you there—and no, I won't ask you to kiss my hockey skates." Thank God he'd listened when I said I wouldn't. Kissing his napkin had been weird enough.

"I'll fall on my face."

"Not if I have anything to say about it." Alex winked. "Some of the guys will probably be around—my team," he added unnecessarily. "I could introduce you. Bet they'd like you—and get a kick out of me bringing a date." Alex launched into a rant, informing me that the "rest of the guys" were "nice." That he'd actually met Roderick because he was on the team too. He was convinced that everyone was bound to love me.

I highly doubted that.

But the sentiment was nice.

"Shit, Georgie, this would be so fun! We could get a hotel—something fancy. Yeah, *fuck*. I wanna knock your proverbial socks off. Okay. *Okay*. Yes.

I am very into this plan. Leave tomorrow, take you on a date, spend the night—then pick my dad up the following morning and bring him here." Alex looked genuinely rejuvenated at the prospect of taking me to the city and *impressing* me.

No one had ever—

No one had—

I didn't know what to say.

"I'll buy your suit, obviously," he added at last, finally realizing he'd gone off on somewhat of a tangent. "As well as whatever else you want. That diamond collar? Fuck yeah."

"I can buy my own suit," I interrupted, sharper than intended. Alex paused, watching me warily like he wasn't sure what to say. Immediately, I felt bad. It'd been a long time since I'd genuinely snapped at him.

I hadn't meant to.

I was just…overwhelmed.

And a little lost.

Because the more time we spent together the closer our end date became.

I sucked in a breath, "Sorry, I just…you…"

"Too much?" Alex's smile was sad, and I *hated* that I'd caused him to make that face. "My bad—"

I reached out for him, tangling my fingers with his and squeezing. Squeezing with all my fucking might, hoping the pressure would break through the walls I could see steadily rising since I'd made that stupid-ass comment.

"No, you're perfect." Alex squeezed back, walls crumbling again. His blue eyes were open once more, something tremulous and wary inside them, like he was desperate for me to explain—uneasy, in a way he rarely was. "I didn't mean to get snappy. I just…you realize you're offering me a lot right now, right? And I already told you that no one's ever—I…"

Fuck, pull yourself together, George.

"Suffice to say…It's *not* too much." I swallowed the lump in my throat, well aware that I wasn't just talking about the goddamn suit. "It's perfect. *Really.*"

So perfect it doesn't feel real.

"Yeah?" Alex perked right back up, chest puffing out as he nodded. "I'll double-check with June, but I doubt she'll care if I leave earlier than planned. She'll probably throw a condom at me and tell me to have fun if I explain I'm leaving so I can take you out."

I laughed, unable to help myself.

Alex's answering grin was so fucking sunny it nearly blinded me. He always responded like that when I laughed. Like he loved it. Even though I sounded like a goddamn pterodactyl and I knew it.

"As long as you're certain it won't mess anything up for either of you," I said. "I'm in."

"It won't."

I felt bad leaving my family behind when the reason I'd come to Roderick's wedding was to spend time with them. But…then again, I knew they were all ridiculously invested in me bonding with Alex, so I figured there was no need to stress. My family was just as likely to throw a condom at us.

I didn't need to ask to know they'd much rather I go suit shopping with Alex than with one of them.

I'd been so mad at them for instigating this—but now I only felt gratitude. Without that…I wouldn't be where I was now.

"I'm certain." Alex nodded. "One-hundred percent sure a little detour won't affect June and Roderick's *pending nuptials.*"

I smacked his shoulder.

He cackled.

We'd reached the bathroom, and he paused just outside the doors, listening to make sure we were alone. No one was around. Only crickets. Only the stars. Only the soft grass underfoot, compressing with our every step.

"You don't need to worry about anything," Alex tacked on as he pushed the door open. "I'll take care of it all." I trailed after him, the rest of the world cut off as the door swung shut, enclosing us in the dark space.

Alex flipped the light switch on.

He pressed into my space, forcing me against the door with his body. Around me, he reached out to lock it, the *click* it made sending sparks up and down my spine. The wood was solid supporting my back, cool, and yet I still felt feverish.

I bit my lip.

The thick, sticky heat of him made me feel *small*—but in a pleasant way. Protected. Like he'd use his bulk to keep the danger away, not harm me.

The communal bathroom was completely empty. Which was unsurprising. I was pretty sure by this point even the drunkest of the bachelor party were passed the fuck out. We were the only people awake aside from the bugs and critters—

And fuck, I needed to not think about them if I was going to have a good time.

And I wanted to…have a good time, that is.

With Alex.

Here.

Alex's grin was wicked as he yanked me away from the door. He flipped me so my back was to the showers, and with a hand on my chest, began to walk me backward toward them. My heart beat double-time. On his way past the sink he deposited our clothing. The lube slipped out of its hiding place in my pile, falling to the floor with a clatter.

Alex cocked his head to the side. His hand was still on my chest, holding me in place with a silent command. He removed it as he bent over, retrieving the bottle with a shake of his dark hair and a chuckle that made the hair on my arms stand on end.

When he held up the bottle of lube his eyes were dancing.

"Now, Georgie…" Alex clucked his tongue, "if I didn't *know* any better I'd think you invited me in here so you could have your wicked way with me."

I flushed, but didn't deny it.

I wasn't innocent.

It didn't feel right to go a whole day without touching him. Like something was fundamentally wrong. I felt safe enough with him to initiate sex—which was something I'd never done with Brendon.

He'd called the shots.

He'd decided when, where, how, and how long.

Christ—maybe Alex was right. I really needed to stop thinking about Brendon.

Alex blinked, watching my face with mild surprise. Maybe he'd expected me to contest the truth of his words, and when I hadn't, he...*fuck*. An evil smirk curled his lips. "Really?" he said, moving again. He reached out, using his free hand to gently, but firmly, steer me backward into a shower stall. "How *naughty* of you."

Alex pressed me into the chilly tile of the back wall in the shower. His hand slid up my chest to my throat, gently holding me still.

"*Alex*," I whined, annoyed that this was not at all going the way I'd expected it to.

"What?" Alex moved his hand from my neck to flick my ear. "Am I teasing you too much?" The sting made me jump, but made my dick twitch too. "You thought we'd come in here...you'd be all suave, pull out the lube, and seduce me?"

That was exactly what I'd thought would happen.

"It was a good plan," I complained—though my ire was lessened by Alex's delight. "And you ruined it."

"You're right," Alex purred, lips skimming my jaw as his body moved to bracket mine. The tile was chilly against my damp t-shirt, forcing it to stick to my skin. He was the one who had been in the lake—and yet, he felt drier than I did. "That was mean of me. Should I let you try again?"

"Try...again?"

Leisurely, *deliberately*, Alex stepped back, out of my space. He handed me the bottle of lube. It felt foreign in my grasp. I stared at it, heart racing.

"I'm a top," Alex husked. "But if you want to dominate me, baby, be my guest."

And then he slid to his knees at my feet, cold tile be damned.

And now it was my turn to short-circuit.

Twenty-Four
George

HAVING ALEX ON HIS knees for me felt like a religious experience. Earth-shattering. Not because of the action itself, but because of the control he was handing to me. Control that, I suspected, was another of his masks.

His pale blue eyes were somehow even more impossibly gorgeous while peering up at me from below—and for a second, all I could do was *breathe*.

I was so overwhelmed by the weight of his surrender.

I'd never been offered something like this before. My inexperience was intimidating—but it was also *exhilarating*. This was a chance to be someone I'd never been allowed to be. A pivotal moment. And the offer of a new… kind of intimacy.

I wasn't afraid of it.

Not with him.

Alex wouldn't become angry with me if I fumbled. He wouldn't yell or ignore me. He wouldn't ice me out.

If I made a mistake, we'd figure out how to fix it together.

There was no "failing" when I was in bed with him. I couldn't imagine myself ever feeling this comfortable with anyone else—as preposterous as that sounded.

I shouldn't trust him so much, he was practically a stranger, and I knew that.

And yet…when Alex was around, all logic flew right out the window.

Bad decisions became good, simply because they meant I'd get to have more of him.

Grounding myself, I closed my eyes.

I let the scene wash over me.

The faucet dripped. Outside, the world was silent—the sound-proofing in here was frankly impressive, all things considered. All I could hear was the *woosh* of both our breath, and the way my own heartbeat tripped in my chest, as eager to get this right as I was. I nearly strangled the bottle of lube in my hand.

"I'm not sure what to say," I said, honestly, eyes still shut.

Normally, it was difficult to admit weakness.

But not here.

Not with him.

"I want this, but I…don't know how to do it."

"Just do and say what feels right," Alex reassured. "I promise I'll like it."

"What if I sound silly?"

"You won't."

Comforted, my free hand found its way blindly into Alex's hair.

It was as thick and soft as it looked—slightly damp from the summer heat, a reminder that as perfect as he seemed, he was human. He'd never gotten it wet down by the lake so it was untangled. Almost buttery smooth to the touch.

Alex didn't pull away, so I gripped his hair tighter, curious to see what he'd do. Testing the waters, so to speak. Alex made a sound and tipped into my touch—just a little—enough to send all the blood in my body rushing south.

When I spoke again, my voice was more steady.

"Do you want to fuck me, Alex?"

"*Yes.*" Alex's answer was a growl—gravelly and soft.

I opened my eyes—and *Christ*, he was a vision. Dark hair clutched between my pale fingers, colors in stark contrast. Peering up at me obediently, awaiting orders like the eager puppy I'd said he was.

I liked this *way* too much.

I almost said okay—like a total idiot—but caught myself before I could hand over the reins prematurely.

"I want you to get my cock out." Voice both breathy and firm—I attempted to sound in control. Though my face and voice were behaving, my dick was not. It twitched, steadily filling and betraying my interest.

Without doing as he was told, Alex pressed his face into my crotch.

His nose skimmed up and down the length of my dick. Barely-there pressure, that made my skin buzz. Diving lower, he nuzzled my balls, inhaling hungrily. I was sweaty, half-tempted to shove him away—as contrary as that was, considering what I'd just told him to do.

But I didn't.

Somehow I knew Alex wouldn't mind a little sweat.

He didn't speak.

But he didn't have to.

The way he was sucking in breathfuls of my scent made it clear how pleased he was by our current position. His breath was hot, lips rubbing my sac through the fabric.

Misbehaving…misbehaving meant…I should…punish him, right?

Yes.

That made sense—

The punishment I delivered was a sharp tug to his hair. Which wasn't much of a punishment, because Alex looked completely unrepentant as he groaned. I yanked his head away from my dick, just a few inches. His big chest was heaving, this fucked-out hungry look in his eyes that was far less present than usual when we were together like this.

"Do as I say," I chided.

The sound he made was even more pitiful than the last one. "Anything you want," he promised, and I believed him. "Seriously. *Anything.*"

Immediately, he went for the hem of my shorts. The elastic gave beneath his fingers, sliding low on my hips as he yanked it down along with my underwear. My dick popped free, flushed and leaking at the tip, bobbing toward him.

My dick looked so small next to his hands. Barely the length of his thumb. Maybe not even that?

His hands framed my hips, tan skin scratchy soft as he fanned his fingers out to hold as much of me at once as possible. It was a lot of me—considering how much thicker, and broader he was. He kept his grip gentle, allowing me to continue to be in charge.

I bit my lip hard as Alex stared up at me.

He was waiting for his next command—only I was still so new to this that I wasn't sure what to say next. Obviously, I should ask him to suck me. But…

Oh fuck.

There was a glint in his eyes that promised untold mischief if I wasn't quick enough. And it was *that* chaotic energy—and its familiarity—that got me out of my own head.

"Open your…" I hesitated, mouth flooding with saliva. "Open your mouth." My heartbeat was drumming in my throat, my fingertips, and my cock as Alex parted his lips. "Tongue out, *please.*"

It was polite to say please, wasn't it?

Even in this situation?

"Yes, sir." Alex taunted, before he stuck his tongue out as instructed. He wasn't exactly…*submissive* so much as he was obedient—but I found I didn't care. Semantics, and all that.

I watched his pink tongue wait, muscle trembling the longer we stood in silence.

He'd made me do this too. In a different setting, for a different reason. But the parallels were impossible to ignore.

This was the time to praise him, right?

That's what I would've liked in his place.

"Um…" I stalled, cheeks burning as I debated how exactly to go about that. "Good boy, Alex." His lips threatened to pull into a smile despite the way his tongue was out in the air. Like a switch had flipped, the mischief in his gaze settled. "That's…very…*good*. You're so…" With every word it became easier. "You're so good for me."

And he was.

So good.

"So good to me," I added, because it was true. "So strong, and lovely, and caring. The best, most wonderful, most amazing man I've ever met." It was true. It was all true. "You're being so very good." He was. "I am so…I am so grateful to you. This…"

Alex's lashes fluttered, affection dancing in the depths of his gaze.

"This is such a gift. If your tongue starts to hurt you can put it back in," I murmured softly, mind swimming. "I don't want to hurt you."

I had no doubt he'd ignore his own comfort for my sake at this point. I sucked in a breath, suddenly overcome with emotion as it truly hit me why exactly he'd pushed for this. That he might need it, the way I did. And that he…

He might have wished to teach me a lesson I desperately needed to understand, the best way he knew how.

Because it wasn't until I was the one doling out orders and praise that I realized how easy it was to do so. How natural. How right. To take care of the person who relied on you. To…be kind to them. To watch them.

Experiencing Alex in his obedience made me want to cradle and protect him.

Not hurt him.

Not like Brendon had hurt me.

What was it about me that had ensured Brendon did not feel this... protectiveness? This desire to care, and covet, and please? Was it truly my fault? Was I lacking some important, essential component?

No.

Something clicked inside me. A cog. Tiny, mechanical. Fixing itself. Part of a door that'd been wedged shut for long enough I'd forgotten it could open. My systems fired, running smoother than they had in years—thoughts swirling, heart warming—memories...so many memories, climbing to the surface.

No.

Maybe Brendon was the one who was broken, not me.

I really had deserved better.

Was that...what Alex had been trying to teach me through this?

Staring down at his quivering tongue, at his pale, needy eyes—at the way he gave himself to me, trusting me to care for him—all I felt was an immense desire to keep him safe.

"George," Alex's tongue went back inside his mouth. "You okay, baby?" His voice was soft, breaking through the fog in my brain. I had no idea how long I'd been observing him—a long time probably. Simply holding his hair and ogling his tongue as my world came crashing down.

Even while on his knees, Alex was watching out for me.

"I'm good," I promised—and suddenly I was. The shadows of my past fled as quickly as they'd come. I sucked in a breath, a weight on my chest I'd hardly noticed was there, gone with them. "Color?"

"Green," Alex's lips twisted into a smirk.

I put the bottle of lube in the shower caddy behind me before refocusing my attention on him.

"Tongue out again, Alex," I whispered, steadier this time. "Round two." Apparently, he sensed the difference in my speech too, because he straightened and his blue eyes went foggy soft.

Out his tongue went, pink and inviting.

I was forced to spread my legs so that I could sink low enough he could reach. The shuffle slide of my feet on the tile was as awkward as it was tantalizing. Alex's breath ghosted over the tip of my cock as I lined us up. Aiming at his open mouth, I guided the crown onto his extended tongue. The first rub of wet heat made my head drop down, hips threatening to snap forward of their own accord.

I was supposed to be in control.

This was my *chance* to be in control.

But I'd been teased, and prodded, and taunted all night long. I'd had my dick groped, my nipples sucked, my hole rubbed. I'd had Alex's tongue so far down my throat that I felt empty without it. I'd breathed his air for hours, tasted where his cologne clung to his throat, I'd grown intimately familiar with how slick his fingers could become if he massaged my slit long enough. Therefore—I figured it was only fair that I cut myself *some* slack.

It was natural to be overwhelmed when the entire night had been foreplay.

"Fuck yes," I gasped out, shoving an inch inside without preamble. As soon as I'd given myself the grace to take what I wanted, the pressure lifted. "God, you're so *good*. Hold still. I'm going to..." I pushed a little further, enjoying the way Alex's tongue twitched beneath my length when I did so.

He was observing me, a look of longing in his gaze that was so powerful it made me feel like I could climb mountains. Who cared if I wasn't the best at taking control? Who cared if this was a learning curve? Alex certainly didn't and he was the person *willingly* submitting to me.

It was a choice he'd made.

I hadn't had to intimidate him, or manipulate him, or force him. I had a big, confident, *delicious* man on his knees for me—simply because he desired to be there.

I'd never had a large dick. It was something that used to make me feel insecure, but...I'd learned to love it. Especially at times like this, when all it took was a steady thrust and my length was entirely enveloped in tight-hot-wet—and Alex didn't have to struggle whatsoever to take me in.

He blinked, swallowing around me, and I whined.

Out, in. My hands tightened in his hair as I fucked the slippery glide of his tongue.

"Harder," I commanded, curled over his head with another snap. Alex slurped, the sound lewd in the quiet. "Again," I said. *"Again."*

Alex groaned, the vibration sending tingles down my spine as I humped his face. His nose pushed into my pubic bone, and I shuddered, forcing myself as deep as I could. He inhaled sharply and I felt it. Felt the *whoosh* of his breath out of his nose.

Close.

I was so fucking close.

Only made more so when I pulled out all of the way, dick slipping free only to skim against Alex's cheek. He made a sound, this broken, needy thing. His eyes were dazed, like he'd fallen as deeply as I had into this.

"So good," I murmured again, the praise spilling freely as I released his hair so I could rub my fingers across his glossy lips. "You feel so good, Alex." Lips turning up sweetly, Alex's eyes met mine.

He was hunting for approval—approval I gave freely. "So perfect."

When I glanced down between Alex's legs I shuddered. His dick was fighting against his pants, attempting to poke through the fabric. Rock hard and swollen. I couldn't help myself. I stepped out of my sneakers, kicking them out of the shower stall. Alex continued to stare, obediently waiting for his next command. There was no reaction whatsoever. At least…not until I lifted one socked foot and pressed it between his legs directly over his hard cock.

"Fuck." His voice was throaty-soft, lashes fluttering. Eagerly, his hips jumped up, grinding into my foot.

"You're so hard, *Alex*," I purred, surprised by my own forwardness. "I bet it hurts, doesn't it?"

"*Yes*," Alex agreed. His hands flexed at his sides, the tendons dancing.

"I bet this big," I dug my toes into his crown, then jerked my foot down, "*thick*, cock—" Alex folded over my foot with a gasp. "Wants a nice wet hole to fuck." I'd almost called my own ass a pussy. Jesus Christ. He was rubbing off on me.

Ha!

Literally.

"*George*." Alex had never said my name like that. A grunt—a plea, all at once. "I need—"

"I know what you need," I said, skimming my toes down low to his balls. Reaching one hand out, I sought the wall for balance so I could trace the shape of him without fear of falling. "Spread wider."

Alex did as he was told, shuffling his knees outward. The fabric of his joggers pulled tighter, making the shape of his hard dick even more prominent. He was delicious. Chest expanding with each choppy pant, t-shirt translucent as the muggy air in the shower made it cling to his sweat-damp skin. Even his nipples were hard, pressed against the white fabric.

"Good boy," I murmured, flicking his balls lightly with my toes. He sobbed, dark brow pinching. "You like this?" I cooed, flattening my foot against his length again and giving it a liberal rub. "Needy as a fucking puppy."

He'd mentioned wanting to try puppy play. I didn't know much about that kink, but figured he hadn't been entirely off the mark when he'd thought I'd like it too. Degrading him was just as fun as praising him—especially when his hips fucked up, and the pitiful look on his face made it clear he liked it.

"And you call *me* slutty," I clucked my tongue. "When I know if I keep doing this." Another rub, root to tip. "You'd come in less than five minutes. Humping my foot like a dog."

"G-George," Alex shuddered, hips rutting upward fruitlessly because I pulled my foot back with the motion, taking the pressure away. "Jesus *fuck*, you're sexy when you're mean."

His cock throbbed.

"Dogs can't talk," I told him, pressing down hard again just to soak in his responding growl.

"*Woof,*" Alex replied. I wasn't sure if he was teasing me, or giving in. Either way, I rewarded him with another full rub. I even squeezed his crown between my toes at the end, just because I was magnanimous like that.

My own dick was throbbing, pointing right at him, fluid building at the tip. It was still shiny from his mouth—oh.

Yes.

His mouth!

"Open up, puppy," I commanded, pressing into his dick with my foot, careful to keep my hips open enough that I could lean my pelvis toward him. "There you go—" Alex's head sank forward, taking me inside his wet-hot-hot heat again. He made a slurping, sucking sound, and I rewarded him with a few sharp rubs to his massive, needy dick.

I could come like this.

I knew I could.

But...

Alex's big blue eyes were black with need. The twitches of his hips were taunting me. And his cock—Jesus Christ, so fucking big—would feel even bigger when it was inside me. Thick, long, so satisfying. Twitching and throbbing, desperate to spill.

"*Okay.*" I pulled my foot away. Alex sobbed around me, nearly nicking me with his teeth. I didn't admonish him though, pressing my foot to his chest instead, right between his pecs. I forced him back with a push, his back arching to accommodate the motion. "You have a minute to get us naked and rinsed off or I'm leaving you here to jerk off alone."

It was an empty threat, but Alex didn't seem to realize that.

He jumped to his feet fast enough he stumbled.

Reaching out to steady him, my cock pulsed as he yanked his t-shirt and pants down in quick succession. He kicked them away just like I'd kicked my shoes. With all that gorgeous tan muscle on display it was difficult to decide where to look. His chest? Still expanding with each ragged breath. His flat belly, sucking in and out in jagged bursts. The V-cut that led to the dark riot of curls between his legs. Or his cock, long, veiny, and soaked with his own pre-cum. It leaned against his thigh as it throbbed and throbbed, begging for attention, foreskin pulled back to show the slightly lighter pink tip.

He truly was gorgeous.

And so far gone.

"Color?" I checked in, breathless.

"So fucking green, baby." Alex's hips jerked forward, rutting into the empty air like he was trying to fuck me before he'd even gotten inside my body.

We made quick work of my clothes too. And the shower. Rinsing off the lake water, the sweat from the day, and some of the fluids we'd already shared.

"Grab the lube," I commanded when the shower turned off.

In a blink Alex was back, lube in hand, cap already open. "Slick up your fingers," I directed. A thrill swooped through me as he did what he was told immediately. Apparently, Alex was an unrepentant tease—unless he thought it would delay his opportunity to fuck my ass. Then he was obedient as a lamb. "Good," I said, watching his fingers become glossy with the slippery substance. "Now wrap them around your dick."

"No—" Alex keened. "No, no." His hand shook. "I want to—to *you*—"

Obviously he thought I was going to make him jerk off because he hadn't cleaned us quick enough. I wasn't that cruel.

"If you're going to fuck me, you'll need to get that big cock nice and wet," I said. Alex immediately relaxed. "Don't you want to put it in my—"

"I want your pussy so bad," Alex whined, circling his length and giving it a languorous rub. "Please, George." He looked pathetic in the sexiest possible way, head tipped down, eyes beseeching. Like he really was my naughty puppy. "Let me breed you. I need it—I need—" His hand tightened to the point it nearly looked painful. "Need to fuck your cunt."

Jesus Christ.

This man was going to kill me.

He really looked like he needed it too. Like he'd die if I didn't let him stick his dick inside me and go to town.

"Here," I held a hand out, and Alex immediately squirted lube on my fingers. "I'll get myself ready for you."

Alex whined again, squeezing his dick hard enough the tip looked nearly purple for a moment. His foreskin slid back as he yanked himself almost violently, like he couldn't help it. If that was an indication of how hard he was going to fuck me, I really needed to be thorough with prep.

We both gasped in tandem when my now-slick fingers slid home inside my ass. It felt odd, the angle uncomfortable, but I didn't mind. I was quick about it, bearing down and adding more fingers faster than was smart. But I just...

God.

Every time I saw his big hand slide up and down his cock, the heat inside me burned brighter.

When I was ready, it felt like a century had passed. Alex was fucking his fist now, and judging by the way his gaze hadn't left the spot where my hand had disappeared behind my back, he was genuinely unaware. He looked drunk on this, a dark curl falling forward and sticking to his forehead, lips parted, eyes glassy.

"Such a good boy," I sucked in a breath, three fingers sliding free. Glistening, I smeared them down his abs, tickling low till I could rub the mess around the dark curls at his base. Alex whimpered, the slippery slap of his hand rubbing up and down impossibly loud. "You ready for—"

"Yes, yes, yes." Alex squirted more lube onto his fingers and liberally spread it across his dick. "Please, please, please, please."

I paused—just to tease.

And that pause apparently terrified Alex, because he began to beg. "Please,

Georgie. I'll be so good. I'll be so, *so* good for you. I'll be your best, *best* boy. Anything you want. Anything in the world—please just let me—I need to fuck you. I need it. I need you—I need, need, need—"

Before he'd finished talking, I'd turned to face the wall, ass angled out.

"Have at it, big gu—"

Alex's cock was shoving into my ass before I could finish speaking.

It was my turn to sob.

Apparently, I'd pushed him past his limit. Alex wasn't gentle or careful the way he normally was. An inch popped inside, then a second. All the while, his gasps of gratitude were hot on the back of my neck.

"Thank you," he whimpered, rutting in another inch. "Thank you, Georgie." Another. I bore down on him to ease the push-slide, and Alex howled. His hands found my hips, squeezing tight enough to leave real bruises this time as he shoved into me bit by bit. It hurt a smidge. I probably should've made him prep me with his giant ass fingers—to ease the stretch, but I hadn't.

"So good," I whimpered, spreading my legs wider to accommodate his width. It didn't help. He was simply too big. "Jesus."

Luckily, I enjoyed a bit of sting, and soon enough, even that faded.

Till all I could focus on was how very full I was, split wide on his cock.

"Such a good puppy," I gasped. "Breeding your master."

"Mnnn," Alex gasped when he finally rutted the last of himself inside me. His pelvis ground against my ass, these greedy rubs that made it clear that as deep as he could go was apparently not deep enough. He wanted to fuck his way into my stomach, my heart, my throat. "Gonna knock you up, Georgie," Alex threatened against my shoulder, faint enough I wasn't sure he even meant for me to hear. "Gonna—knock you the fuck up."

My hole squeezed and his teeth sank into the meat at my shoulder. It stung even more than his thick dick had. And I loved it. Loved it so much. Loved that I'd somehow pushed him into a head space where he was this uninhibited.

He'd never been this way when he was in charge.

Without his walls in place…Alex was far needier than he let on.

"So good," Alex's voice was muffled, his tongue rubbing my skin as his teeth sank deeper.

"Fuck me, baby," I promised, lashes fluttering. "You can go hard—it's okay. I know you need it. You've been so patient for me, haven't you?"

Alex responded with another of those impossibly distracting hip grinds. Like he couldn't fathom the idea of pulling out—even if it meant he'd get to fuck back in.

"It's okay," I said, reaching back to assist him. I needed to keep one arm on the wall to brace myself, otherwise I'd face-plant—but my free hand, luckily the un-bandaged one, found Alex's hip. He made a desperate sound when I gripped the bone, forcing him out of me by a few inches with a sharp tug. "I'll help you."

"No, no, no," Alex whimpered, too respectful to fight me even though I knew it would be easy for him to overpower me. "You said I could—"

"It's okay," I said. "Just…shift back a bit, let me help." When I'd gotten him to move till he was halfway free, I finally let go. "Now in," I commanded. Alex didn't need to be told twice. He snapped his hips forward with a brutality that forced a groan out of the both of us.

I didn't have to demonstrate for him again.

Alex growled, starting up a pace that was unrelenting. Brutal thrusts that made my eyes roll back and my feet skid across the damp tile. I gripped the wall for balance, chest shoved into it as Alex went to fucking town on my ass.

He'd never been this uncontrolled before—and I loved it.

Loved that I'd brought him to this point, all animal instinct.

Even more, I loved how full I felt.

How *needed* I felt.

Split open, the clutch of my ass parting and spreading for the rough jerks of his hips. I was so stuffed it was all I could think about. The way Alex's crown was slightly fatter than his base. The way it pounded directly into my prostate with every slap. So fucking delicious. Alex's mouth dragged over my neck, my shoulders, leaving more bites, hickeys, and spit in his wake.

He didn't speak again, too far gone to do anything but breed me the way I'd told him I wanted him to. He did make noises though. These hurt little sounds—grunts, and gasps, as he rutted into my hole like he was about to make good on his promise and knock me up.

"So good," I gasped, my dick bouncing with every thrust.

At this rate, I was going to come untouched.

Stars swam behind my eyelids. My toes curled. My dick was leaking a trail of need against the wall. Chilly, but welcome pressed to my feverish skin. "That's it, baby. Give it to me. I know you need to."

Alex's hand slid from my hip down my leg, and before I could process what was happening he'd folded my knee up, forcing me open wider. The new angle was even better than the last one had been, my entire weight wobbling on one leg as Alex's hips jack-hammered against my ass.

So close.

I was so close—I just needed—

And then he bit me. Hard. Hard enough I was almost certain it'd draw blood, his teeth sinking into the meat of my shoulder with a sharp sting. I came all over the wall, gasping and clenching down on him.

"Fuck, fuck, fuck—fuck this delicious fucking cunt," Alex gasped out, breaking his silence as I spasmed around him. His hips continued to rut. Over and over and over, faster now—and then…he *groaned*, low and luxurious.

Wet heat spilled inside me, flooding my ass as Alex's thrusts slowed.

He let my leg down, and I sank against the wall, chest to belly. The chill was a balm on my feverish skin. Alex kissed over the bite he'd left, lapping at it with apologetic swipes of his tongue. His hands massaged circles over the bruises on my hips, half apologetic, half appreciative. Afterward, they ducked inward, chasing the shower-damp crease at my groin, fingers tucked between my balls and upper thighs.

He didn't seem to care that we'd both finished, or that his cum was going to start leaking out of me—he simply luxuriated in our shared pleasure. The steady swipes of Alex's thumbs were explorative, running along my pubic hair and down my softening length as he wiggled his fingers lower, lower, possessively around my balls.

"Mine," Alex's voice was soft as one of his hands cupped my dick and the other snugged around my sac. To hear talkative, charismatic, "everything man" Alex, reduced to a caveman was erotic as hell.

"Mmm," I murmured in agreement, so sucked up in his touches my mouth refused to work.

"*My* tiny cock," Alex gave it a squeeze, and I whined. "My balls." He gave them a liberal rub. "My pussy." The last word was punctuated by a needy flex of his hips, driving his softening dick deep again.

"Mmm," I repeated, lips against the tile—germs be damned.

"My…" The hand that had been on my balls slid up my belly, my chest, and settled around my throat. He squeezed. "My *Georgie*."

Those words were a promise as much as they were a declaration.

"Yours," I agreed, without thinking too much about the words.

This was only sex, after all. It wasn't like he really meant it.

I was supposed to give Alex aftercare. I'd made such a point to ask for that when he'd been the one in charge. And yet—here I was, basking in his touch and offering no praise or comfort of my own.

"You did so good," I managed, though it was difficult. Far more difficult than it should have been. "Such a good—"

"I wanna lick your hole," Alex's voice was right next to my ear. I shivered, my good-Dom-etiquette fleeing. Were we…were we not done? "Please," Alex's tongue flickered out to trace the shell of my ear. "Let me lick my cum out of your cunt."

"Oh, Jesus Christ." I shuddered like a total asshole. "But you…I mean—

aftercare—I need—"

"I'll cuddle you when I'm done," Alex promised.

"I meant that I need—to give *you*—" Oh god, why was this so difficult?

My words were wasted, Alex wasn't listening.

That was made apparent when his cock slid out of my ass with a hiss from the both of us, and the protective weight he'd been at my back slid low to the ground. His breath was hot against the globes of my ass.

With little to no preamble, Alex's tongue tickled the top of my crease. He rubbed it there imploringly, only a few inches above where I was twitchy and empty, as his hands gripped my ass cheeks and spread them wide. "Say I can," Alex begged. "Give me permission—George. I need you to give me—"

"Lick my pussy," *Oh god.* The words were out before I could stop them. I hadn't meant to say the word myself. Hearing him say it was one thing, but uttering it myself? Totally another. It was filthy. Taboo. Something I had barely even read in books, let alone thought I'd experience in real life.

"Thank you," Alex's tongue slid down. "*Thank you.*" And then he was sucking around my hole. My fists thumped the tile, lips skimming the surface. Alex ate ass like he kissed. Possessive, with no shyness whatsoever. He rubbed his tongue against the rim of my hole, chasing his own flavor inside it, coaxing it out with each, curled flick.

I convulsed, fingers slipping along the wall.

Now it was *my* turn to beg, because that was what I did—pleas falling from my lips as I arched my back and pushed into him.

Brendon hadn't liked eating my ass.

He'd thought it was "dirty".

Alex apparently did not share such qualms.

He was voracious about it. Long fat swipes, then needy little flicks. Like he was trying to coax my hole to open even more for him—even though it was already loose from his big, hot dick. "Thank you," Alex breathed against my ass, his teeth lightly worrying the edge of my rim. Then he slid his tongue deep. It wriggled, and I sobbed—in particular when he did this scooping motion with it right after, pulling his own cum right out of my gaping ass.

If my dick hadn't literally just spilled, I would've come again.

Alex ate my ass until there was nothing left inside it. And even then, he didn't stop. Not until I had to reach back to push his head away weakly. My legs were so wobbly I was fairly certain if he didn't stop trying to impregnate me with his tongue I was going to fall on my face.

"E-Enough," I whimpered. "Sore."

"Sore?" Alex's voice was a pleased purr. "That's good." And then he did this frankly unhinged thing, and brought his hand up to lightly spank my hole. It stung, and I jolted.

"Jesus Christ." I whined, unable to stop him because he was still holding my ass open with the other hand.

"God, you're so pink back here," Alex growled. "So fucking pretty. Wanna stick my dick right back in and go again." He fingered my hole, and it attempted to close—to no avail. Finger slipping in easily, Alex located my prostate right away, and gave it a pointed rub.

"C-Can't." My hole squeezed around him and he made a pleased sound.

"*Fuck.*" Alex pulled his finger free. I thought we were done, until his fingers came back—two this time—and he pushed them in.

"A-Alex."

"Don't pretend like you don't like it." Apparently, he was no longer foggy-brained and dick-drunk. Well... Actually, maybe he was still dick-drunk. "I'm just checking to make sure my pussy isn't hurt." And then a second later, "It isn't."

Thank god.

He took pity on me though, only teasing my prostate one more time to hear me gasp, before he slid free and rose to his feet.

My head was spinning, our roles reversed so effortlessly back to the way they normally were that I hardly noticed the change. Not until Alex had turned me around and my face was tucked against his shoulder. His big hands swiped up and down my back, fingers taking a minor detour to slip inside my ass on a couple glides south.

"You're so pretty when you're in charge," Alex promised against my ear. "Such a pretty, pretty kitty."

"Nng." My response was lackluster at best but Alex didn't seem to mind. It took every ounce of brain power I had, but I managed to sling my arms around him, squeezing tight. "You were so good," I gasped, the words aching as they slipped free. "So perfect for me."

Alex made a soft sound, melting around me like a giant, muscly blanket.

Apparently, even men as self-assured as Alex needed praise after intense scenes. It felt odd to voice the words I'd often ached to hear, but it was therapeutic too. Like it healed part of me that had been shriveled and full of cracks.

"You did so well," I continued, stroking his muscular, solid back. "Thank you for giving me that."

This felt…dare I say…equal?

Which was something I hadn't known a relationship could be.

Alex kissed the top of my head, his hands mirroring mine as we embraced in the quiet, dark room. It was a perfect moment. Special. Full of eye-opening epiphanies, fun, and orgasms.

I was glad it was Alex here with me.

Glad to be learning what love meant from someone as precious as Alex James.

Fifteen minutes later, we were under the spray of the shower again. Neither of us spoke, but we didn't need to. We took turns sudsing each other up and stepping beneath the spray, unhurried this time. Alex was maybe a little too thorough when it came to my ass—but I wasn't complaining.

When we were finally dressed and clean—with the shower spotless and as innocent as it'd been when we'd entered—I knew with certainty that I was going to sleep well that night. Bugs be damned, woods be damned, impending trip back home to New York be damned.

Because Alex was by my side.

And when he was there, it was easy to forget that the world could be an ugly, scary place.

Twenty-Five
George

I SHOULD HAVE KNOWN our happy bubble could only last so long. The universe was out to fuck me over any way it could, like usual. Life wasn't fair. I knew that. And apparently…my bad luck was rubbing off on Alex. Because this was…horrible. Worse than dropping Neil at the airport. Worse than Brendon's texts.

Way fucking worse.

Monumental levels worse.

Not because it was embarrassing, or mortifying, or humiliating. But because after spending three days attached at the hip to Alex, I was privy to most of his facial expressions. I knew his smirk, his grin, the gooey-proud face he made when he saw June and Roderick together, hidden behind a playful grimace. I knew what he looked like when he was cocky, or horny, or kind. I knew when he was shy, or bashful, or embarrassed by my praise.

But this expression?

This was new.

One second we were squabbling playfully on our way to the tent from the bathrooms, and the next, everything went to shit.

"Wait," Alex's voice was hoarse as he pulled me to a stop. His lips twisted down, brow furrowed, distress evident as he stared at his bare wrist like he couldn't seem to fathom what he was seeing. The friendship bracelet dangled there. On its own.

And with sickening clarity I realized what was gone.

His watch.

Oh shit.

Fuck.

He'd told me the watch was *important*.

But like him, I hadn't noticed its absence—too drunk on our love affair to be anything but blind.

"Your watch?"

Alex nodded, yanking me around—not that I needed encouragement—as we headed back toward the bathroom.

"It's fine." He was self-soothing, though the words were directed at me. "It's probably on the counter. I took it off, right?" I'd never heard his voice that hollow. "Before we…and I just…forgot to put it on. It's on the counter." His voice quaked. "I took it off."

We both knew he hadn't taken it off.

But it wasn't until we'd scoured the bathroom that Alex accepted the truth.

He smiled the whole time, but I could tell it was brittle. The smile was a coping mechanism and nothing more. Fake. Flat. Lacking the life and light that usually clung to him in droves.

"What about the cabins?" I offered. "You had it earlier when we were setting up Juniper's party. We could go check there?"

"It's too late. Everyone is sleeping."

"We can be quiet," I said. "Trust me."

"I…" Alex's lips pinched together. He looked pale, which was not something I'd ever thought I'd say. "*Okay.*" His voice was weak to match the pallor of his skin.

"It's going to be there," I promised, even though it wasn't a promise I should make. But I hated seeing him like this. Alex wasn't supposed to look upset, or distressed, or withdrawn. He was life embodied. Sunshine incarnate.

This felt wrong.

"I hope you're right," Alex said, empty smile in place as he allowed me to lead the way.

Me too, I thought, but didn't say.

Me too.

The watch wasn't in Juniper's cabin.

We searched high and low, ducking around the slumbering bodies strewn across the floor. I managed to be quiet enough not to wake anyone. The shadows in the corners of the room taunted me, and my anxiety mounted with every minute the watch remained unfound.

Alex's sadness was palpable.

It made the air thicker somehow.

He tried to give up again, and I wouldn't let him. Certain he was only doing so for my benefit, and the second I closed my eyes he'd be outside in the dark alone.

"You don't need to—" Alex tried.

"*Alex.*"

"It's dark, George." He was trying to save me. Maybe embarrassed by how much this meant to him? I had no idea. Either way, I stayed stubborn.

"It's been dark for hours. If we stick together I'll be fine." Alex was just coming up with excuses at this point. It was plain as day. He'd had no such worries earlier that night when he'd been sneaking his hand down my pants off these same damn trails.

"We can go to bed."

I glared at him, and he shut up.

We shined flashlights on the path, hunting between the two parties—down by the lake—and inside the edge of the woods behind the boathouse. Both of us were desperate for a glint of silver.

But we found nothing.

Nothing.

Zilch.

Nada.

With every minute that the watch was missing Alex became smaller and smaller. His massive frame shrank. His normally larger than life presence whittled down. Till he was a wisp of what he'd been. A silhouette blending into the darkness, empty and devoid of hope.

"I'm done," he finally said.

That was it.

Two simple words were the only warning I received before the frantic search was over. Alex latched on to my wrist, grip cooler than usual as he tugged me away from the dumpsters at the boathouse where we'd been hunting.

He was eerily silent as we climbed the hill toward our tent.

He wasn't himself.

I wanted to help—to…to *fix* this.

But there was only one place we hadn't checked.

The lake where Alex had been helping clean up.

Hunting through the water would be fruitless in the dark—not to mention *dangerous.* The thought of entering the water at all made my skin crawl. The creek had been bad enough, and entering that had been accidental. The concept of…*willingly* stepping into the lake sounded like a waking nightmare to me.

But…for Alex?

I'd do it.

Hell, if it'd been light enough out to make a difference, I'd be knee-deep in water right now.

"Alex—" I tried, only I didn't know what to say.

"*Don't,*" Alex's plea was hoarse. He squeezed my hand tight, betraying his need for closeness as we approached the tent. I didn't know what to do with this more reserved version of him, but found myself gravitating toward him like I always did. Unafraid, despite his obvious change in demeanor.

It wasn't like before, when he'd shut down because I'd made fun of his watch at the diner.

I wasn't scared of him.

Alex was silent as he checked the sleeping bag for bugs. Silent as he turned on the space heater and the nightlight, always catering to my needs. Silent as he crawled into bed before me, then held the flap open in invitation.

Neither of us were pretending to sleep separately anymore.

"Come to bed, Georgie," Alex said.

Without protest, I did as I was told.

My chest felt tight as I folded my body onto the mattress beside him. I wiggled beneath the slippery fabric cocoon that'd become my home over the last few days. Alex zipped us up without another word. Tense, and unsure how to comfort him—or even if he wanted me to—I lay there unmoving.

A noisy owl hooted somewhere outside the tent—the only sound in the quiet. The tents beside ours were slumbering, and off in the distance, I could make out what I assumed was someone snoring. Maybe more than one person. Like an orchestra of sleep apnea. Far enough away they couldn't hear us.

Which was good.

Because Alex's silence was loud.

Alex's breaths came shallow and short, his usual calm missing. He didn't reach out to touch me and I didn't touch him either. I figured he'd want the space. He was always the one to instigate contact—this had to be a sign, didn't it? That he wasn't open to it?

He'd said *"don't"* and I wasn't sure what that meant.

Don't ask him about the watch?

Don't try to comfort him?

Don't speak?

Don't touch him?

The options were endless. It wasn't that I was frightened he'd be angry if I disobeyed. I just…didn't want to hurt him. Especially not when he was already hurting.

He wasn't a man anymore—but an open wound.

Maybe…Juniper wasn't the only person who had been having a difficult time lately. Maybe…the watch had only been a catalyst. Weddings were high-stress in general. But I got the feeling that Alex's current mood had very little to do with Juniper's upcoming nuptials or the camping trip in general. Something else was going on. Only I didn't have enough puzzle pieces to see the whole picture.

Was it because of the car accident his dad had been in?

Was that it? Why would that have anything to do with his missing watch?

"Distract me?" Alex was so hoarse I barely recognized his voice. *"Please."*

Distract him.

Yes.

I could do that.

Relief flooded my body as I turned to face where he was lying on his back beside me. I wriggled in close, and my hand settled on his lower abs. It inched down toward his crotch and Alex's fingers wrapped around my wrist, stilling the movement.

"Not like that." He chuckled. "But thank you." He didn't release my wrist, simply held it, like the touch was anchoring him. His expression was unreadable, gaze trained on the sloped tent ceiling, blue eyes lost as he peered up at the sky through the see-through fabric panel at the top. The silhouette of his nose and the shape of his lips looked particularly kissable from this angle.

"Distract you how?" I asked.

"Tell me…" Alex trailed off, his brow furrowing. His full lips pressed into a thin line as he mulled over what he was about to say next. "Tell me…what it's like to be George-Arthur Milton."

Well, that was random.

"What?" I must've sounded confused because Alex finally looked at me. It was only a glance, but the moment those pale blue eyes found mine I was no longer drifting. I became tangible. And my world started spinning once again.

"Imagine it's next Monday," Alex said, lips twisting up at the corners. "You're back home in New York. Tell me about your day, start to finish."

"This is going to bore you."

"Nothing about you is boring," Alex replied immediately.

I couldn't help but recall the fact that I'd thought he'd called me boring at the barbecue. Somehow…I believed this over that. Maybe he hadn't meant that before? Maybe I'd misinterpreted that too?

I wouldn't be surprised.

Alex was more withdrawn than usual, but the fact he was talking was good, wasn't it? Better, at least than he'd been. It wasn't as though his request was inappropriate. Certainly not as inappropriate as the fact I'd gone for his dick the second he said he wanted to be distracted. It was innocent, even if it was odd.

"I'm really not all that interesting," I deflected. "But if you—"

"*George*," Alex's voice was nearly as warm as it usually was. "Believe me when I tell you that you are the most interesting person I've ever met. You couldn't bore me. Not even if you tried."

I bit my lip to hide my smile but failed. "Okay. Fine. But I warned you."

"Noted." Alex turned to face me, leaning on his elbow. It felt too intimate, so I wiggled onto my back and stared at the ceiling.

"It's…Monday." I licked my lips, letting my eyes drift shut as I tried to figure out how to make my life seem anything other than ordinary. There wasn't a way to do that though. So I…settled on the truth. "My alarm is set to go off in…fifteen minutes? But Mr. Pickles has decided he's starving to death and I need to be woken up with his ass on my face so I can get him breakfast."

Alex's laugh felt like a reward. "What next?"

"I feed him."

"Right."

"He doesn't like hard kibble. Only the soft stuff. And he prefers turkey flavor over chicken, so that's what he usually eats. It smells fucking awful. I gag every time I open a can, but he loves it so I buy it anyway. Missy—my roommate—doesn't mind the smell. She has horrible taste. In most things."

"And then?"

God help me, this was actually kinda fun. Emboldened by how interested Alex sounded, I continued, "I've got a coffee machine that automatically starts brewing. So after I feed Mr. Pickles I'll chug a cup and hop in the shower. By that point, I'm running early, which always ends up being helpful because I like to um…" I trailed off, realizing I was about to admit that I shaved my legs every morning.

It wasn't a thing most men did. I knew that. And I worried Alex would think it was weird, especially considering the fact I was blond enough the hair barely showed when it was there anyway.

"You sit on your big fat dildo," Alex filled in. I squawked, slapping his chest in indignation. He laughed, this melodic, delightful chuckle that made the hair on the back of my neck stand up—along with my dick.

"I shave my legs, asshole," I countered, crossing my arms over my chest so I wouldn't be tempted to smack him again.

"Why?" There was no judgment in his tone, only curiosity.

"I like how it feels when I wear suits," I admitted. "The fabric slides instead of clinging. Plus…it makes me feel powerful in a way? Which is the same reason I wear panties." Oh Jesus, I had not meant to admit that. Alex made

414

a sound like he was choking.

"Excuse me, *what*?" His voice was all gravel. "How is it I've been fucking you for three days now—"

"Barely."

"And you didn't tell me you wear *panties*?" Alex's incredulity was softened by how turned on he sounded. "Did you bring some? In your slutty little backpack with your Costco-sized dildo—"

"Ugh." I covered my face, cheeks burning.

"Have you worn them around me?" Alex growled. "Are you wearing them right now?"

I almost wanted to say that I *was* wearing a pair, even though I wasn't—to see what he'd do. No doubt he'd pull my pants down to check. Even though we both knew if I said I was, I'd be lying. He'd helped me get dressed, and it was his shirt, his boxers, his pants I was currently wearing.

"I wore them the first two days," I admitted, still hiding behind my hands. "But they're dirty now."

"Fuck." Alex groaned, his hips shifting enough the mattress rocked, like he was trying to relieve the pressure on his cock. "You're telling me…that if I were to hunt through the pockets in your backpack I'd find…" he sucked in a breath, "*Two* pairs of dirty panties?"

"You say that like it's not gross that they're dirty."

"Baby, they're dirty because they've been cupping your sexy little dick all day. You have no idea how bad I want to suck on the fabric while I—"

"Pair one is dirty because I wore it to the airport. Which is not cute. Airport germs, Alex."

"Fine—"

"And pair two is dirty because I fell into a fucking creek." I dropped my hands and leveled him with a glare. "Please control yourself."

"So you're saying…if you'd simply been wearing them around your house, and not here, you wouldn't mind if I…" Alex trailed off with a sharp inhale and then subsequently a low whistle when I nodded, a brief jerk of my head in ascent. "I'm gonna buy you *so many* panties, George," he blurted. "A fucking mountain of them. Strappy ones. Frilly ones. Whatever the fuck you want, baby, it's yours. Jesus Christ."

Apparently my distraction was working.

Alex sounded like himself again.

I hadn't really meant to admit any of that—but in hindsight I was glad that I had. When I peeked at Alex, the color had returned to his cheeks and his pale eyes were dark with lust. Like always, he was already watching me. Which by this point was no surprise.

He wasn't going to do any of that. There wasn't time, but I appreciated his enthusiasm.

"Does it turn you on to know I wanna suck on your dirty panties? Wanna lick where that sweet cock got them wet, hard all day, aching for me," Alex continued playing into his fantasy.

"Christ."

"You look embarrassed," Alex observed throatily. "But pleased."

He was the one that looked pleased, lips curling up into a sexy smirk.

"Of course I'm embarrassed," I croaked. "I just admitted that wearing women's undergarments makes me feel powerful. Most guys would be."

Alex debated with himself before shrugging. "Maybe," he admitted. "But...I don't think you should be."

"Yeah?"

"It's hot," Alex purred. "And if it makes you feel 'powerful,' who the fuck cares if it's not something 'most guys' would do? It's what *you* do, and that's attractive as hell. Just like your stompy little walk when you're pissed off. Just like the way you're always pushing your hair back when you're nervous. Just like the way you won't look at me when you feel vulnerable. It's sexy because it's part of you."

I'd never thought of it that way, but it certainly did make me feel better. No one had ever seen me so clearly before and it was…startling. I nodded, and Alex's smirk turned smoky soft. "Okay. So…" he said. "You feed your cat. You shower. You shave your legs. You put on some slutty panties—"

"They're not always slutty."

"Let me live my dream, George."

"Fine." I huffed, turning back to the ceiling so I wouldn't feel so goddamn close to shaking apart. *You're supposed to be cheering him up,* I reminded myself. *Keep going. It's working.* "Then I put my suit on, brush my teeth, eat breakfast—and brush my teeth again."

"What do you eat?"

"Oatmeal."

"Every day?"

"Yes."

"Huh." Alex's smile was soft. "I thought you said you like to cook."

"I do—on the weekends. I'm too busy on a typical weekday to find time for anything elaborate."

"Continue." He wiggled to get comfortable like I was telling him a bedtime story. The effect was ruined when I heard rustling, glanced down, and caught him with his hand between his legs. He gave his cock a squeeze, and I licked my lips, tempted to reach over and try to help again.

"I ride the subway to work." Alex's hand was definitely distracting me.

"Is it normally crowded?"

"Always."

"What next?" Alex didn't squeeze again, simply held his dick like it was comforting to do so. I turned back to the ceiling as I tried to get my thoughts out of the gutter.

Which was difficult, all things considered.

"You're distracting me with your…" I jerked a shoulder, and Alex laughed.

"What? Is my hard dick making your job difficult, baby?" Alex cooed, playful and unrepentant. "Well, tough. Ignore it. I am."

"Your hand is literally on it."

"For moral support."

"I've never heard of masturbating for moral support before."

"Wanna try? Mutual jerk-off session. We can call it therapy."

"I think my therapist would be offended that you just said that."

"I think that you need to spend less time worrying about how hard my dick is and more time telling me my bedtime story. You're supposed to be *distracting* me, Georgie. Not taking advantage of me." It was obvious Alex was joking. I could literally hear his smirk.

But he wasn't totally wrong.

Even if he hadn't meant to throw a bucket of icy cold water over me, that's what he'd done. If we were going to have sex again tonight—something I was not opposed to doing—I wanted it to be after I'd completed his request, not before.

It only made sense.

"When I get to the office I usually grab another cup of coffee. It's never as good as the espresso machine I have at home. But I need extra caffeine to deal with Brendon."

"Fucking asshole," Alex muttered. "I've never wanted to punch a dude more."

Imagining that was gratifying to say the least—Alex's fist connecting with Brendon's face, sending him to the ground. Brendon wouldn't stand a chance against him. Not with Alex's bulk and athleticism.

There was definitely something sexy about him going all caveman and defending my honor, that was for sure.

"By nine I'm in my office with the door shut—and I will, without fail, always have at least six emails from him. Sometimes texts. He nitpicks everything I do to the point of insanity."

"He's just looking for an excuse to talk to you because he's a bottom feeder who can't let go."

"That's exactly it." I sighed up at the ceiling morosely. "I swear to god, he's such an ass. Calls me into his office to chew me out on a near daily basis—

even though I'm better at my job than he is at his. Always makes a point to turn the picture on his desk of him and his fiancée toward me when he does. He'll make a seedy comment or two about my body—or how "tired" I look. He'll pretend like he cares—even when I am doing my damndest to forget we ever fucking dated and keep things strictly professional. I'll go back to my office for a much-needed break. And then…by eleven-thirty Brendon will come to find me in my office and invite me to lunch with him."

"Gross."

"At the same restaurant we ate at every day when we were together, too."

"It's a mind game," Alex said.

I believed him. It made sense. Brendon couldn't fathom the fact that I'd ended things with him.

Alex's words vindicated me. Because he was *right*. And I knew he was right. And for some…strange reason—even after being single for a fucking year—it wasn't until now, until this conversation that I realized I wasn't sad about the break up anymore.

Wasn't sad I wasn't with Brendon.

Wasn't even sad about catching him cheating, or losing out on eight years of my life.

I was simply…glad.

Glad he was gone.

Glad I was here.

Glad I could laugh about it with Alex—like it didn't matter.

Like it was the past, because it *was*.

"Side note," I interrupted Alex's griping about Brendon.

"Jesus, you're cute. Who says 'side note' like that when they want to—"

"Did I ever tell you that I found out I was his side piece from his secretary?"

"What?" Alex blinked, surprised.

Catching a second wind, I nodded up and down—an oddly manic smile on my face as I relayed what had happened. "She told me not to forget to congratulate him on his *engagement*."

"Jesus fuck."

"We'd been together eight years."

"George—"

"He was everything to me." It didn't even hurt to admit it. The words didn't hurt. Thinking about him didn't hurt. In fact—I kind of wanted to…wanted to laugh?

Oh my god.

How lovely was that?

"I'm so sorry," Alex's hand connected with my elbow, giving it a squeeze. But I didn't need his comfort. I was sick and tired of being hung up on a man who had never valued me the way I deserved. And even more so, I was fucking exhausted of being stuck within the box he'd built for me.

Of feeling like not enough—when I very much fucking was.

I was enough for Alex, at least.

Tonight had been a night full of firsts.

Of discovery.

And I didn't feel like the same George I'd been when I'd fought my way through a rainstorm into the airport a few short days ago. I felt…bolder. Stronger. More confident. Alex had demonstrated through every gentle action the way I should've been treated all along—and I'd always been a fast learner.

Being a sub didn't make me powerless.

I didn't have to make myself smaller.

I could be more unapologetically George than ever before. I could let go. I could trust in the bedroom—and trust outside of it, if I let myself. Sex could be fun and explorative. Kinks weren't hard lines etched on asphalt but wiggles through sand. Relationships were push and pull.

And love—like Alex had said—could be revenge.

But that wasn't what *this* was.

My growing feelings for Alex were not born of a need to get back at Brendon for what he'd done. They were pure and sweet and new—and frightening, yes. But exciting, too. And even though this had an end date, I didn't think I'd ever regret them.

I couldn't.

"I'm not sorry it happened," the words slipped out before I could stop them. "I'm not. I'm grateful, honestly. Because if Brendon hadn't cheated, I wouldn't be here with you. And I am just…"

"Just…?" Alex's voice was oddly hopeful.

"I am so very glad I met you, Alex James."

"Me fucking too," Alex crushed me into a hug that felt like it lasted a century. He smelled delicious. Sweaty again, despite the fact we'd showered. He was, as always, annoyingly hot—given the summer heat and how muggy the inside of the sleeping bag could get when I wasn't icy with anxiety. I didn't mind.

Alex pressed my face into his chest, holding me snug and safe there—exactly like he had when we'd had sex. Only, it felt more intimate now, somehow, without lust to cloud the motion. His fingers carded through my hair, the friendship bracelet I'd made him tickling the nape of my neck where his watch usually was.

Right.

His watch.

I was supposed to be telling him a story to distract him! Fuck.

"My ex was a cheating prick, too," Alex said before I could open my mouth and continue. "Worse than that though, he was a *liar*. Always wanted me to feel inferior because he was born into money when I wasn't." Huh. Alex had never spoken this much about himself, so I consciously tried not to spook him. "He'd take me to the country clubs. Whipped his name around like it was a dick. Undermined me when we hung out with his friends—made it seem like my family's wealth was lesser somehow, just because it wasn't old money. He acted like he wanted me to fit in inside the world I'd been thrust into, like he was helping."

I'd been careful not to form assumptions around Alex and his wealth. Thought it'd been there, right in my face, since the day we'd met and he'd been wearing Armani.

"We were middle class for most of my childhood," Alex admitted. "And I thought he was a godsend. Trying to fucking Yoda me or some shit, you know? Help me fit in. So I could help my dad. Make more connections, further the business, all that. Everything I've ever done reflects on him. I just…I wanted to make him proud. My ex used that to manipulate me."

I nodded and Alex's fingers stroked behind my ears. Which was terribly distracting. His heart didn't skip a beat, didn't quicken, nothing. Despite the rawness of his words, he wasn't angry. I could only hope this meant he was past his ex's transgressions the same way I'd realized I was past Brendon's.

"He was older than me," Alex admitted. "I trusted him to know better and took some seriously horrible advice. A lot of it, actually."

"Like what?"

"Plastic surgery. Eating disorders because he thought I needed to look different to fit in. Bad investments. You name it." Alex sighed. "I used to see a therapist because of all of that. The plastic surgery was luckily minor stuff. Nose job? Yep." He gestured at the bump on his nose. "Not that that lasted. Fucking puck to the face got me one time, erased all that work." Alex frowned. "I got chin lipo at one point because he told me it was starting to look like I had a double chin. Nothing major."

Sounded major to me if his boyfriend was encouraging him to get *surgery* to alter his appearance. That had to have done a number on his self-esteem.

"Didn't help that my mom wasn't around," Alex admitted. "Or that my dad was so busy trying to keep the wealth he'd accumulated to realize I was drowning."

He must've felt…so alone.

"For a while, I was a hot mess," Alex whispered, quiet and tremulous—like he'd never said this out loud to anyone else before. Like we were sharing secrets, like kids at a sleepover. "June thought he was a total dick, but even she didn't know half the shit I did because he encouraged me to. I played it off like losing weight was what caused the changes when it wasn't true. Avoided her when I was recovering so she wouldn't see the bruises." Alex's shrug jostled me, and he murmured an apology. "Anyway—all of this to say that the whole time we were together he made me feel like his wealth was the reason I should listen to him."

"Right."

"But then...a year into our relationship he began asking for favors. Told me his dad cut him off—and like an idiot, I listened."

"Oh no."

"I found out six months later, when he used my credit card to buy himself a new car, that his family was fucking broke." Alex released a breath, nuzzling into my hair. "He was using me. The whole time. It was a giant game. And I wasn't the only guy he had on the hook, either. Me and...I dunno, three others were funding the lavish lifestyle he could no longer afford."

"That's fucked up." I could hardly wrap my mind around any of that. I'd never had the kind of money that meant plastic surgery, or sports cars, or country clubs. But that didn't mean that I couldn't empathize. Or that my heart didn't hurt for how young and lost and betrayed Alex must have felt. "I...am...Christ. I don't even know what to say."

"You don't have to say anything," Alex promised, stroking his fingers behind my ears again. "I'm over it now. At least—for the most part."

He gathered his thoughts. "I dated after that. Mostly women. A few men. I stopped dating socialites. But that was no better. I was a wallet to them, too. And every time I..." Alex trailed off, eyes unseeing. "Every time I thought I was getting somewhere—they'd get this...this look on their face."

"A look?"

"I'd do something. Say something, be too loud. Contact them too soon. Ask for too much. And they'd look at me like I was...freaking them out."

Alex laughed, but the sound was brittle. "I felt like such a creep." I opened my mouth to tell him he wasn't, but he kept speaking. "I wanted to get married. Have kids. Early. That was what I wanted. But after a while, when I realized that the only way to keep my partners happy was to wall myself off, or give them my wallet, it all felt so...pointless."

The owl outside hooted again. I jumped, and Alex made a quiet, soothing sound.

"I stopped dating midway through my twenties. I figured...sleeping with people was easier than worrying they were going to manipulate me. Or that I'd scare them off by being myself." His smile was sad, eyes far, far away. "I'm kinda a jaded asshole—assuming everyone in the world will hurt me, but I do."

"I don't think you're an asshole."

"That's because you're different," Alex admitted. "I can be myself with you. You don't...you don't look at me...that way." He used his grip on my hair to tug my head back so he could meet my gaze. "You wear your heart on your sleeve, Georgie. You're so colorful, and expressive, and...and *genuine*. And for some, completely un-fucking-fathomable reason you're not freaked out by me."

My cheeks flushed, gaze darting away—his words too much for my already frayed nerves to handle. "You've been nothing but wonderful," I said softly. "I hate that those people...those people made you feel like—"

"Too much?" Alex sighed. "And not enough, at the same time."

"I...can relate to that." I had to look at him then, so he could see I meant that. "Maybe too well."

"I hate that," Alex replied. "I hate that anyone could make you feel that way."

"The feeling is mutual," I said. "Mom says we're...two peas in a pod."

"That's accurate," Alex's voice quaked with joy. "In some ways." His eyes danced, lips impossibly soft as he smiled at me, his earlier unease forgotten. "I'm sneakier than you, though. I don't think you have a manipulative bone in your body," Alex added, his lips pressing quick and soft to mine. "You know what's amazing? I don't need my guard up around you—in fact, I don't think I even have a guard at all when you're around."

My eyes burned.

That was…

Fuck.

That was the sweetest thing anyone had ever said to me.

"I can relax and be myself. You push me—I poke you. We laugh. We fuck. We start it all over again. There isn't a moment when you're near that I don't enjoy."

"A-Alex." If he didn't stop, I was going to cry.

"Even now," he continued, despite my protests. "We both just admitted some seriously fucked up shit and I'm *smiling*." I glanced at his mouth—unsurprised to find that he was, in fact, smiling. "I lost my watch, the most—the most important thing I own—and I'm *smiling*. And it's not because I feel like I need to smile to placate you, or because it's easier to pretend like it doesn't hurt. I'm smiling because even *talking* about sad, awful, horrible things with you is nice. Do you…do you realize how fucking weird that is?"

"It is weird," I agreed, because it was. A giggle escaped—which was better than crying, so hey, I wasn't complaining.

"It's so weird." Alex pecked me on the lips again, and my mouth tingled. My everything tingled. "The weirdest thing ever. I'm in my thirties, man. I thought I was done with this juvenile crush bullshit."

"You have a crush on me?" I teased, butterflies swarming in my belly. The look Alex gave me was flat as hell. "How embarrassing for you."

"Shut the fuck up," Alex laughed, smooching me longer this time. Longer, wetter, needier. He yanked my head in, his other hand finding my waist. He pressed our torsos together, his heart beating against mine as he licked behind my teeth with a groan. "Fuck—" Alex murmured between kisses. "You're so fucking cute sometimes, I can't stand it."

"I have a—" I whimpered as his hand sank lower, grabbing my ass. "On you." My freshly fucked hole twinged. "Too."

Alex's voice was sugary sweet. "That's no surprise—"

"Asshole," I countered, lapping at his bottom lip, begging entrance. He let me in, allowing me to play dominant for a minute or two before he chased me back into my mouth. His tongue was hot and demanding, curling and swiping over mine as he released my waist. He fumbled for the zipper, yanking the sleeping bag open to give us more room. When we were free of it, he hauled me up and over onto his lap.

"We're going to wake people up—" I protested, straddling his lap, his hard dick poking insistently at my ass.

"Not if you're quiet."

It was a sound enough argument I didn't protest, not when he stuck his tongue back in my mouth. Not when he wrestled my pants off, and then his. And not when the slap of his cock met my ass cheek.

"Lube—" I mumbled.

With a growl, Alex rolled me over onto my back, barely pausing his kisses as he fumbled to the side for the abandoned bottle of lube. When he found it he made a triumphant noise against my mouth. The faint click of the lid slipping open felt almost as lewd as the wet sounds our mouths kept making.

The push and pull was fucking amazing. It felt like I was melting every time his tongue wriggled next to mine.

"Need you," Alex gasped out between kisses. "C'mon." It was a plea as much as it was a command. I was back in his lap only a few seconds later, the sleeping bag pooling around his legs. Alex made quick work of slicking up his cock, and when he reached for my ass, eager to finger me open, I batted his hand away.

I was still loose.

And besides, I wanted to feel a bit of the burn.

"George," he warned. "I don't wanna hurt you."

"You won't—"

"*George.*" There was no arguing with that tone. Or the look he gave me. I conceded defeat with a whimper, my cock dripping onto his t-shirts—the one he was wearing, and the one I'd borrowed. It was so hard it hurt, jerking between my thighs as Alex slicked up his fingers and shoved them home.

He was impatient too—but apparently less than I was.

What a trip.

I'd never been the more impatient person during sex before.

"So precious," Alex cooed, slipping deep inside, his index finger tapping at my prostate. Stars burst behind my lids and I whimpered, head falling back. "I know it feels good, sweetheart," Alex purred, sliding his middle finger in along with it. The stretch burned, despite my earlier proclamation that I was ready for something bigger. "But you need to be quiet. Remember? Cover your mouth, okay? You can—"

I jerked my borrowed shirt up, cotton catching between my teeth as I shoved it into my mouth as a makeshift gag.

"Holy fuck," Alex said, rubbing my prostate liberally.

"How's that?" I asked, voice barely intelligible.

"Fuck yeah. That's…yeah." His hips jerked up like he couldn't help himself. His chest was heaving, testing the fabric of his t-shirt with every great breath as sweat beaded at his temple. Dark hair spilled along his pillow, that same curl—the infuriating one—stuck to his forehead.

Apparently, being quiet only extended to me. Because though Alex's voice was low and sweet, he was still running his mouth.

"Look at those pretty titties," Alex groaned, his free hand sliding up to cup one of my pretty much nonexistent pecs. They were tiny. I didn't exactly spend time trying to enhance them. And my natural build was slender. Alex didn't seem to mind. He squeezed my chest inward, pinching my nipples between his fingers like he was trying to create cleavage.

"Alex," my whimper was muffled enough to hardly be a word at all, but he seemed to get the picture. His fingers stopped spreading me open, dropping down to slick his cock up again, before notching the head against my hole and sliding home.

427

We groaned in tandem.

Felt like I was transported to another dimension entirely as my eyes rolled back and his thick, long dick filled me up. He was so fucking big. Big hairy thighs prickling against my inner thighs as I sank down. Big cock testing the limits of my hole. Big chest, bouncing with every greedy breath.

If anyone had tits it was Alex, not me.

All muscular and built with pecs that looked particularly squishable. I reached down, intrusive thoughts winning as my hands framed his chest and gave it a tight grope. He flexed into my grip, which only made the muscle harden. Not like breasts at all—but definitely attractive.

"Naughty, Georgie," Alex groaned, snapping his hips up into me and making me whine. "Touching my tits without permission." I gave his chest another squeeze, and he grinned, wide and unrepentant. "Again?" Alex clucked disparagingly. "Bad, bad boy."

He didn't sound like he thought I was being bad.

Not at all.

So I didn't stop.

Not even when Alex's hand lightly slapped my ass cheek. "Naughty boys get punished," Alex promised. The sting made me jolt. Alex waited, hand hovering as he watched my expression. "Color?"

I couldn't exactly answer him with my mouth full of soggy t-shirt. I glared at him and mumbled a muffled "green".

"Squeeze your ass three times if you want me to smack you again." Alex looked incredibly proud of himself for that one. I whined. Because that wasn't fair either—and I just…ugh. I wanted it. I wanted it so fucking bad, even if it was embarrassing to admit.

I did as requested and after every tight clench, Alex's lashes fluttered.

After the third deliberate clutch, his hips pulled back and snapped in, dark brow furrowed. "Shot myself in the foot with that one," Alex admitted hoarsely. "Jesus Christ. One day I'm gonna make you do that till I come.

Gonna make you sit on my dick and clench your little ass over and over and over. Watch you get frustrated—fuck."

I made a muffled sound in protest, and Alex's grin came back. "Right. Where was I—? Oh. Yes. I was punishing you." I glared at him, not impressed. My hips wiggled, trying to force more friction and Alex's smirk grew wicked. "Slut," he cooed, slapping my ass cheek again, harder this time. "Can't sit still, can you? You wanna be fucked so bad. Wanna touch, and be touched—want that sweet cunt stuffed full." Another smack. More stars danced behind my lids.

God, that was good.

And even though this was technically a *punishment*, it certainly didn't feel like it. It was fun. All of this was fun. Everything with Alex was.

My dick jerked, precum slipping from the tip and decorating Alex's stomach.

"Making such a mess," Alex murmured disapprovingly. "What am I going to do with you?"

I ground my hips down, and Alex pulled his back, making me chase friction. "What?" he said when I growled at him around the t-shirt. "Did you want something?" He snapped his pelvis up, and I sobbed. "That, maybe?"

Christ, he was driving me out of my mind.

I was at the end of my rope.

So far gone by that point that I barely noticed he'd yanked the spit-soaked t-shirt free. And that I was babbling. Crying, more accurately, tears streaming down my cheeks. "Please, please, please, please, please—"

"Shhh, shhh." When I could force my eyes open Alex's gaze was adoring. His tone was as warm as his expression. Fingers swiped through my tears, comforting me—and then embarrassing me when he brought his tear-soaked fingers to his lips and lapped at them. "It's okay," he promised. "I've got you. Quiet, baby. Just—"

Alex pushed the t-shirt back into my mouth.

And then he was forcing my legs open wider, directing my hands to his chest for balance, and his hips were rutting into me with a brutal pace that had me half blind with lust. Squeezing, squeezing, in and out, the wet slapping sounds filled the small space.

We were so lucky it was late, and that everyone was asleep.

Otherwise—

Fuck.

George the slut, getting his hole pounded at ass o'clock during Roderick's wedding trip. Mom would throw a party. Hell. My whole family would. I'd never survive the embarrassment. It was bad enough they all knew about the night on the hill.

"I know you can take it," Alex grunted, fingers biting bruises into my hips as he shuffled so his feet were planted wider and he could really fuck into me. I felt every thrust from head to toe, lashes fluttering and wet from tears, my belly tensing, my toes curling as the thick crown of Alex's dick punched in and out of my well-fucked hole.

"Take it—" Alex growled. He was getting close if the way his teeth were gritted was any indication. Or the way he was shaking, his thrusts getting faster and less purposeful. Like he was using every last ounce of energy he had to keep himself going until I finished.

When his hand found my cock, he got his wish.

Scratchy palm, hot and large—I lost the battle with my will, spilling all over him as I drooled into his t-shirt.

"Fuck yes," Alex groaned, jerking into me faster, faster, one-two-three times. "Squirt for me—"

And then he was coming too, filling me up with liquid heat, and several more, slightly less violent jerks of his hips.

"You're so good," he'd murmured as he'd plucked the fabric out of my mouth and pressed a dozen soothing kisses against my raw lips. He'd lapped at them in appreciation. "Such a pretty, red mouth," he cooed, before moving on to the rest of my body.

By the time we'd both wound down I was exhausted—and yet somewhat wired up. Alex rearranged us so that we were laying back-to-chest on our sides atop the mattress, and his cock could soften inside my hole. He clutched me from behind, his hands rubbing anywhere and everywhere.

He worshipped me in a way that made me feel both powerful and small.

Small, because he was bigger.

Protected.

Like I didn't need to worry about anything at all.

Not when Alex was around.

Powerful because I had this big, capable, wonderful man to dote on me—at least…for a few more days.

"We need to get you cleaned up," Alex sighed after a while. He sounded drugged, almost. Out of his mind with exhaustion. "Your ass is—"

"That's the first time you've ever called it that." I was bullshitting. I genuinely couldn't remember if he had before.

Alex snorted. "Fine. Sorry. My bad, King George. Your *cunt*—" I shivered, the grin in his voice not helping with my arousal at the use of the word. "Is full of my cum. We should probably take care of that."

Dried cum in my asshole was not my favorite thing.

Not even in my top ten.

"I could lick it out of you." I didn't have to see Alex's face to know his eyebrows were wiggling.

"Do what you must," I agreed, fucked out and exhausted.

"Drama queen," Alex said affectionately as he carefully pulled out and pushed me onto my belly. I lifted my leg obediently, showing off my leaking hole. Alex groaned, descending down my body immediately, heading right for my entrance. He wasted no time, eating his own cum out of my hole like it was an Olympic sport and he was aiming for gold.

When he came back up, I felt thoroughly debauched. Sore. Sticky. Aching. Empty.

Alex crowded against my back, one thick arm bracing most of his weight while the other worked me open again.

"I swear, I should take Viagra or some shit just so I can stay hard in your cunt all day." Alex murmured against my ear. "It's like my favorite place. I'd take a vacation there if I could."

"You're ridiculous."

"You love it."

"I do." The words escaped and I didn't stop them. Not when it was true. I did love it. Just like I loved—

George.

Not right now.

Not. Right. Now.

You will break.

You will break.

Don't—

Alex kissed along the shell of my ear, allowing me a minute with my ass full before he slipped his fingers free and began caressing and kissing and praising me all over again. He liked this part as much as I did if his thoroughness with it was any indication.

He stayed at my side, fingers skimming my body, staring at me like he always loved to do.

"I eat...lunch in the stairwell," I murmured sleepily against my pillow as Alex's fingers danced up my forearm and began to play with my friendship bracelet. I had failed my mission—to finish his bedtime story before we fucked. And it wasn't till I was half asleep that I even realized.

"You...oh!" He seemed to realize what I was doing pretty quickly, which was good. Because I was far too tired to explain.

"And then I head back to my office. After lunch I do most of my design work."

"Designs?"

"Marketing," I said. "Graphics." Too tired to find the words, I hoped he understood. "Ad campaigns."

"And after work?"

"I ride the subway home and pick up take-out. Mondays are Indian food."

"Tikka Masala?"

"Butter chicken." I yawned. "With Naan bread. Garlic. Missy likes... spicy—so I get her that. She likes me to pick her entrée at random. I'm more...predictable."

"My favorite flavor," Alex said. I wasn't sure if he was calling my predictability his favorite flavor, or the food, but either way I supposed it didn't matter.

"Then I spend..." another yawn, "the rest of the night eating with her and watching *Planet Earth* so I know what to look out for...And I wind down by reading books from my...collection."

"Collection?"

"My BL manga collection."

"What's a Bee-Ehl? Or a mon-guh?"

"Boys Love. Gay manga. Gay comics from Japan? I have...a lot. It's an addiction. I started with one bookshelf and now I have...three? I'd get more if it wouldn't totally overtake my apartment. They practically fill my entire closet."

"They must be good, huh? I mostly listen to audiobooks. I've never thought of reading comics," Alex hummed thoughtfully.

"Really good." My eyes were too heavy to keep open. Judging by how slow Alex's replies were becoming, he was in the same boat. He was leaning heavier against me now, his arm slung low over my waist, anchoring us both. "One day, I want a library with all of them."

"I'd build you one," Alex was quick to offer, pecking the back of my neck.

"With a ladder," I added, even slower. "Like Belle from *Beauty and the Beast*."

"I got you. A ladder. So you can reach the top."

"Mhm. Then I go to bed...and I'll start it all over again on Tuesday." There. I'd done it. I'd done what I'd promised. Alex had received his bedtime story.

And I…well.

I wasn't sure how to describe what I'd gotten.

But watch, or not, as we fell asleep together, sated and happy, I could only come to the conclusion that what I'd received was pretty damn good.

Twenty-Six
Alex

GEORGE WASN'T IN OUR tent when I woke up. Which was…unsurprising. Not for angsty, dramatic reasons, but simply because when I groggily checked the time on my nearly dead phone, it was almost four in the afternoon.

I'd slept in.

A lot.

Apparently George had not.

Even after staying up as late as we had last night, George didn't strike me as the kind of guy who spent lazy days in bed. Knowing him, he'd probably been up for hours—in the kitchen helping his mom—or, if he was *truly* unlucky, getting dragged into more of June's wedding veil drama.

Which reminded me that I needed to talk to her.

I was still hoping she wouldn't mind me leaving early so that I could take George out, even though…that plan had been forced to change based on how late I'd slept in.

The end of June's wedding extravaganza was creeping up on us—as was the actual ceremony itself. I had a lot of mixed feelings about that. I was stoked—because my sister was about to marry the love of her life, obviously! But...I was unsettled too.

The end of George and my arrangement was swiftly approaching.

And as enlightening as it'd been to learn about his "real life" last night, it was also a glaringly obvious reminder that he would be leaving in a few short days. He'd return to his take-out-filled Mondays and creepy ex-boyfriend-supervisor.

And I...didn't like that.

Didn't like it at all.

I didn't want him to go.

I didn't want to be apart from him.

Was it selfish that I wanted him to stay here with me?

It *was*...it had to be.

He'd only seen me on my "good days". Our current compatibility didn't guarantee to extend over a longer period of time. I'd given myself a safety blanket for a reason.

I'd wanted—fuck.

I'd wanted to...just for once...experience the kind of relationship I'd always dreamed of.

And the only way to have that, was to be certain George wouldn't see past what I allowed. Only...I'd already told him more than I'd told anyone else. Last night. I'd opened up in a way I never had—not even with June.

I wasn't the best at maintaining my own boundaries, obviously.

The point remained, though.

I could be a perfect boyfriend for a week. But any longer than that? Yeah fucking right. George would get sick of me. Everyone always got sick of me. I would so much rather remember this...in a prettier light. Let myself believe he was the love of my life—the one that got away—then have every wonderful interaction tainted by seeing the…*look* on his face.

The same look everyone eventually got around me if they stayed long enough.

Still though…I couldn't help but fantasize.

Fantasize about keeping him.

I'd make it my goddamn mission to take care of him. I'd spoil him rotten. We'd try anything and everything he ever wanted. I'd maybe even learn to cook, so I could feed him. I'd build him that library I'd promised. Buy him a fucking cat-tree-paradise for Mr. Pickles. Take him to stores to purchase books for his collection of gay mongooses. Hell, I'd buy him the whole fucking store if that was what he wanted.

We'd spend Sundays split between his parents' and my dad's. Barbecues in the summer. We'd make my place a home—he'd populate it with George-oriented things. Little items. Like his razor in the shower, or his shampoo, that I really fucking loved.

I'd see echoes of him everywhere. Every time I got home.

His dishes in the sink—actually, fuck, more accurately the dish washer.

His shoes by the door.

His clothes beside mine in the closet. Our suits mingling like they were as entangled as we were.

I'd piss him off by leaving my dirty socks places they shouldn't be. And he'd drive me crazy with how anal he'd be about cleaning. We'd argue over crumbs on the counter—and kiss to solve our problems.

We'd adopt as many kids as we both wanted.

The pitter-patter of little feet pounding up and down the stairs. Pencil marks on the door marking every passing year. George would use my empty kitchen the way it was meant to be used. Crafts with the kids. Culinary escapades we'd all benefit from.

If George were mine, he'd lack for nothing.

I'd bend over backward for him.

We'd fight and fuck and make each other blissfully, wonderfully happy.

In my fantasy world.

The world where I wasn't…me. Where I didn't know how unpalatable I was. The world where I hadn't been burned, and burned, and burned. The world where I could still believe that happy endings were possible, and people loved you—no matter how intense, or "much" you were.

Absorbed in my own thoughts, I began my hunt of the campgrounds for George—and food.

But primarily George.

I figured I'd find him in the kitchen, where he often was, spending time with his mom and siblings. *Hopefully they haven't hosted a club meeting without me.* That would suck. I just joined! Mr. Milton had invited me—and wasn't that a trip?

That he'd sought me out yesterday—and offered a personal invitation.

With words.

When I arrived at the main cabin, it was empty. Which was…strange, considering the hour. At this time, Mrs. Milton should have been prepping dinner like she'd done every other day that week—but she wasn't. Which meant there were no signs of Georgie or any of his siblings.

Huh.

Maybe George was showering?

I checked the bathroom next, sandwich in hand. Maybe he was rinsing off the summer sweat? But nope. No Georgie in the bathroom. No Georgie in June's cabin either. No Georgie at our tent—you know, in case he came back. And no Georgie at Joe's tent, either.

I was, once again, perplexed.

Where the fuck was everyone?

And more importantly, where was George?

A small, insecure part of me worried I'd scared him off. That he'd somehow hailed a Ryde all the way out here in the middle of fucking nowhere and headed to the airport to escape.

What if I'd shared too much last night?

What if I'd freaked him out—talking about twenty-year-old Alex's trauma?

What if I'd *already* been too much for him?

By the time I stepped onto the path down to the lake—the last possible place I expected George to be, and the only place left—the sandwich I'd eaten sat like a ball of lead in my stomach. I didn't make a habit of getting overly emotional. Especially not about people I'd just met, so the strength of my current feelings was unfamiliar.

But even I knew George-Arthur Milton was different.

He was... *Georgie.*

My Georgie.

And the idea that I'd been too much for him was terrifying. Scarier than anything else I'd faced in all my life.

Jesus Christ.

My phone buzzed in my pocket. My hands shook as I pulled it out, disappointed to find it wasn't a text or call from George—even though I already knew that was impossible. Dad. Dad was calling. Right. I swiped to answer and held my phone up to show my face.

"Hey, kiddo." Dad's voice was a balm on my nerves.

"Hey, old man." I smiled, but even I could tell it was wooden. After losing the watch he'd given me—and losing my Georgie—I was feeling like shit.

"You look worried." Of course, because he was a fucking mind reader, he immediately clocked my bad mood. Didn't matter that I was smiling, or how good I'd gotten at masking my true emotions. Dad always knew.

"I...I'm fine. *Just.* You know. The wedding is so soon. I'm...stressing." I shrugged, and Dad made an unimpressed sound. "Last minute stuff. You know how it is."

Dad didn't buy my bullshit.

Because of course he didn't.

"What's really bothering you?"

"I…" I bit my lip. June and I had called him pretty much every day since we'd left him behind in Columbus. It was the only time I took away from George. He hadn't ever minded—because of course not. He was a family guy. He got it.

Which meant…Dad knew a lot about George.

I blamed June and her big mouth. My soppy grin, I'm sure, didn't help.

"I…" I almost broke. Almost admitted the thoughts that had been plaguing me. But then I saw the dark circles beneath my dad's eyes. And I just…couldn't. "Let's talk about it later, yeah? My phone's only got like five percent."

"You know you can talk to me, right?" Dad frowned. His phone shifted, and I was staring at a very concerned eyebrow. "I know my accident freaked you out…but I'm still here. I've still got two perfectly functional ears."

"I know." I'd never been good at relying on him. Independent since I was young. His accident had only made that worse. The last thing I wanted to do was burden him with my bullshit.

"I don't know if you *do* know," Dad said, tone soft.

I laughed, but the sound wasn't happy. "Let's just…let's get through the wedding, okay? That's what's important."

"Alex."

"Four percent left—"

"You're deflecting."

"Learned that from you," I replied with a smirk. Dad chuckled, but I could tell he was still worried. "Enough. Please. Can we focus on June? I'll be there tomorrow to pick you up like I promised. We can worry about me and my drama later."

"You carry too much, Alex. Let someone else help. Jesus. You know we all want to." Dad's voice was a quiet rumble. And it did help. A bit. I could admit that. "Open up—"

"Three percent." I scowled up at the fluffy white clouds drifting above, my heart in my throat. "You better not be working."

"I'm not." I could hear Dad's eye-roll in his voice. "And even if I was—"

"You better not be."

"Alright, alright," he conceded with a snort. "I'll see you tomorrow."

"Yep." When I glanced back at my phone he'd figured out the camera again. My heart ached, my internal frustration uncomfortable beneath my too-tight skin. "Tomorrow." The next smile I gave him was softer, more genuine.

It wasn't his fault I was a fuck up. Not that he knew that. I wouldn't let him.

"Charge your phone and call me if you want to talk," Dad said, because he was a nosy, lovable bastard.

"Bye, Dad."

"Bye, Alex. Love you, buddy."

"Love you, too."

All I'd ever wanted was to make him proud. To be…what he needed me to be. And I'd lost the watch—I'd lost the symbol of his love. His most prized possession before he'd given it to me. He may not know now but he would soon. Just like he'd see beneath my cracks if he kept pushing hard enough.

Shoving my phone back in my pocket, I had to stand in the path for a few minutes to get my breathing under control. I couldn't…I couldn't fucking do this. I just—I just wanted *George*. Was that too much to ask? I just needed my Georgie.

This was too much.

It was…I couldn't—if he was gone I just—I *couldn't*.

I picked up the pace, cresting the hill that would lead down to the lake with my heart in my throat. My palms were sweaty. If I was being honest, my *everything* was sweaty. The heat beat down on me, peeking through the branches of trees, each beam like a blow.

I hadn't drank alcohol at all last night, too drunk on George to need liquor—and yet I still felt hungover. Like my brain was a dry sponge, and my mouth was full of sandpaper.

Through a dip in the trees, I could see the sparkle of the lake.

Finally.

When I reached the edge of the forest, I frowned.

A rather large group of people were by the edge of the water.

What the fuck.

Today wasn't lake day.

Why was everyone down here?

Curious, I continued closer—hopeful that I'd finally discovered where my wayward blond kitty had disappeared.

With every step I took, I only became more confused. Because…what I was seeing didn't make sense. George's entire family, as well as my cousins, Roderick, and June were crowded inside the shallows. All of them were shuffling about, hardly moving, faces tipped toward their feet. That in itself was strange.

But strangest of all, was the fact that George was among them.

Even if I hadn't been totally obsessed with him, George would've been easy to spot. His height, his slight build, and his wavy sun-soaked hair were pretty distinct. It looked messy even from afar, and his usually stiff posture was even more pronounced when pitted side by side with Joe's gargoyle-like bulk and stature.

It was tricky to jog in the sand, due to how much I was slipping and sliding, but I pushed through the discomfort as I headed straight for him. My calves were burning by the time I got close enough to see what he was wearing.

Holy shit.

Ten feet away, then five, I paused at the edge of the water, out of breath.

My pulse skipped about, jack-hammering in my chest. George had yet to notice my presence, as he had his back turned toward me. *George.* Germaphobic, water-repelled George. Who was…standing in the shallows while wearing a frankly horrendous pair of…wait, was that—I squinted, shocked—*chest waders?* These absolutely massive plastic overalls sat overtop a t-shirt he'd borrowed from my bag. It was a band t-shirt, and my personal favorite, which only made it even better that he was wearing it—like without me having to tell him, he'd somehow known that was the one I loved the most. The t-shirt drowned him in worn black cotton, but still magically managed to fit his body better than the waders did.

It wasn't my birthday, but it sure felt like it.

This was the stuff of fantasies.

On top of the waders, George was wearing a set of fluorescent orange water-resistant gloves. They covered all the way up to his armpit, protecting him from the water he abhorred. Not that he was digging around in it much—because judging by the state of Joe, that was his job.

No.

George was the lookout. The bossy, adorable, rubber-covered lookout.

"Okay. We're going to need to move to the quadrant at the south end. June's already covered this area," George directed Joe. Joe who was soaked from head to toe, as was his duty as George's obedient minion and the person digging around in the water for him.

Joe spotted me before George did. He rose from his crouch, accidentally splashing George. Annoyed, George began to tell him off—only for him to stop mid-rant when he turned to see what Joe was looking at.

Me.

It was a testament to how tired I was that I hadn't recognized why they were in the water sooner. I was simply…overwhelmed, by my call with my dad, my own guilt and worries, and the fact that George looked like a very fuckable parachute.

George's eyes went wide, dark from a distance, gaze meeting mine.

For a second, the world came to a stop.

The steady lap of the water near my feet ceased to exist. The twitter of birds in the trees was non-existent. The echo of voices and splashes as the wedding party dug through the shallows was nothing but background noise.

There was only George.

George.

Who looked…exhausted. *Fuck.* Dark circles beneath his eyes, his hair sticking up in messy tufts, lips chapped and dry. He was sunburnt. The collar of my shirt swooped low enough over his shoulder the hickey-bite-riddled skin was unprotected.

There was this feeling in my chest.

Like a balloon expanding.

Larger, larger, larger.

"Baby, what the fuck are you doing?" I called out, even though the part of me that wasn't frozen had already figured it out.

"I'm taking a swim because I like it," George snarked with a grumpy eyebrow flicker. "Surrounded by…" he shuddered. "Invisible *snakes.*" His eyes narrowed toward the water like he expected it to be teeming with them.

His grimple was back.

Wet hands went to his hips, his posture nothing short of pure annoyance, he turned his ire back on me. I swear to god, if he stomped I was going to marry him right then and there—whether or not it meant showing up my sister during her wedding.

George didn't stomp.

Which was good—you know, because I didn't want June to snip my balls off—but it was also a *total* shame.

"Are you looking for my watch?" I inquired, heart skipping a beat.

It was the only logical conclusion.

There was no other reason *George* would be in the water like this. His cheeks were flushed, and I wasn't sure if it was the sun, or because he was embarrassed to be so quickly caught out. Either way, he was adorable.

"Nosy bastard," George muttered under his breath. "You weren't supposed to come down yet."

Jesus Christ.

He *really* was out here—doing something he fucking hated—just to…to…

"I decided last night that it was gone for good. There's really no need to put this much work in. Or to make yourself uncomfor—" I started, only for him to cut me off.

"Fuck that. And fuck *you* for telling me that when I'm already standing waist-deep in fish poop." Okay. *Now* there was a stomp. "You said the watch is *important* to you. So I'm going to find it. Stop trying to talk me out of it. I already made up my mind. You'll lose, and you'll just piss me off."

That balloon expanded even more.

Wider, wider.

Till I could barely breathe around it.

"*Marry me,*" I moaned—far too loud, considering we were only ten feet from both of our nosy matchmaking families. Joe's eyes widened comically. George splashed me instead of saying yes. Which again, proved the lengths he'd go to for…for…

For what?

For…*me*?

He was…

Fuck.

And here I'd been an asshole, thinking that he'd run out on me because I told him about my wild, sad youth. And he was down at the lake—the place he'd told me he would never voluntarily go—voluntarily…*going*?

Because he wanted to *help* me.

Because he *cared* about me more than he cared about his own discomfort.

No one had ever—*fuck*. No one had ever gone to these lengths for me. I didn't know what to do with it. I guess now I understood why George had reacted the way he had when I'd made him a midnight picnic. Though…*his* gesture was way better than mine had been.

This wasn't a sad block of cheese, an old blanket, and stolen wine.

This was…everything.

The balloon popped.

And the realization that I was desperately, irrevocably in love with George hit me like a puck to the face. I couldn't laugh. Couldn't smile. Couldn't do anything.

I was frozen.

Broken.

Unable to get my brain to work.

Eyes wet, I covered my face with one hand, squinting up into the sun in the hopes that it would conceal how close I was to losing it.

I didn't want to feel this way.

To be so undone, especially with such a large audience.

Getting caught having sex was one thing, embarrassing yes, but—this was…fuck. This was a new kind of humiliation. Like my chest had been sawed in two and my heart was out in the open for everyone to see.

"One sec." I thought George was talking to me, so I nodded, unable to look at him, my hand still over my face. I quickly discovered that he'd actually been talking to Joe—not me. Because a short time later, after some clumsy sloshing through the water, sun-warm, damp gloves wrapped around my free wrist.

George dragged me away from the edge of the water and back across the sand.

Dazed and blind, I let him maneuver me into one of the sun loungers June and I had adopted as our own. He fussed over the umbrella, making sure I was in the shade—even though he was the one that was slowly turning into a tomato.

I heard him.

Still unable to look.

My face turned away, body curled in on itself. Making myself as small as I could. Wanting to disappear.

A cool water bottle was forced into my free hand as George yanked my shoes off and pulled my feet up onto the lounger. Only then, did I remove my hand, peeking at him warily, my chest this awful combination of full and empty all at once.

He stood back to survey his work, nodding to himself when he'd met his own approval.

"Relax," he commanded with a bossy point of his elegant finger. "And take a nap."

My heart wheezed.

Which was—a confusing, horrible, wonderful feeling.

No one had ever cared about me like this.

Especially when I was…so…

So…

Much.

Right now, I was at my limit of "muchness" and George wasn't…batting an eye.

"But I should be— If you're all out there looking for my watch, shouldn't I be helping?" My voice was barely a croak.

"The only thing you should be doing is following orders." George arched a blond brow.

"As you wish, your majesty," I joked, though it felt hollow. Because *I* felt hollow. And full. Hollow-full. Both. At the same time. Full of butterflies, of hope, and despair. Because even though George was here right now, doing the sweetest fucking thing anyone had ever done for me in my life—it was temporary.

It was temporary.

And that hadn't changed.

Even though I loved him.

Even though I—

Stop it, Alex. Stop it. You know how this will go. You know. Recognizing how deeply you care for him doesn't change that.

"I'll be back when my mission proves successful. Until then, I expect you to focus on feeling better. Rest. Relax. Take a nap. Take some time away from… all of this." George's attention was split between me and his legion of watch-hunters in the lake. "June, you need to go five feet to the left—" he yelled, before turning back to me. "Drink your water. Did you even eat lunch?"

"I ate." I twisted the cap off obediently and took a swig.

God, I loved his mother-henning.

So fucking much.

"Good." George nodded short and quick. "Finish the bottle."

"Yes, sir." I saluted but George didn't laugh. He did…however…lean over me, blocking me partially from view of the others.

"Are you…okay?" he asked, his severe tone dropping.

"I'm fine," I promised.

He hovered for a second, his sweat-soaked, sunburnt cheeks close enough to smooch.

And then he kissed me. Just a peck. But still—a kiss out in the open—audience be damned. A cheer erupted behind us, which only further proved that our families were full of nosy motherfuckers.

"Such assholes," George muttered against my mouth, but he didn't look too miffed. Instead of storming off, or yelling at them all—he…stole another kiss, flashed me a little smile, and stalked off to go terrorize his younger brother again. The stalking part was made less intimidating by the way he waddled in the sand, like a rubber-coated penguin, squeaking all the way back to the spot where he'd abandoned Joe.

I…didn't even know what to do with this.

With any of it.

But I was grateful. So fucking grateful.

June joined me an hour later with a new bottle of water. I woke with a groan, having actually followed George's command like the "good boy" he wanted me to be. Guilt nearly overwhelmed me as she flopped onto the matching lounger at my side with a sigh.

"I'm sorry—" I said.

"Shut the fuck up," she rolled her eyes. "It's not a big deal. I chose to be here. This was a *choice*."

"But it's *your* wedding and I feel like all I've done is make it about me—between getting your advice about George and this, and—"

"*Alex*," June reached out, her hand lying on my shoulder. "For once in your life, stop fucking worrying about me, okay?" She waved a hand at her face, scrunching her nose till her sunglasses slipped down the bridge. "I'm happy. Super happy."

"Yeah?" My lips wobbled.

"Fuck yeah. I mean—look. This is…exactly what I wanted." She gestured out at the crowd still hunting through the water. "I told you I didn't want my wedding to be boring. That's why we came out here for so long. And this is probably my favorite thing that's happened all weekend. No offense. I know you spent a long time planning the other activities—"

"None taken," I shook my head, eyes chasing where George and Joe had disappeared farther down the shore. "I…"

"Plus. You're not alone. And I am so…so glad you're not alone." June's smile was serene, like this was exactly what she'd pictured when she'd decided to start throwing dates at me for her wedding.

"I'm—"

"Shhhh," June understood me better than anyone else. Understood that I didn't have words for what was happening. Couldn't explain how much this meant to me, even if I tried. "Shut up and enjoy your man going all *Devil Wears Prada* on an entire camp of himbos for you."

"But—"

"What about shhhh do you not understand? That's 'nice person' for shut the fuck up."

"My bad." I twisted so I could ogle George even more, and June's hand didn't leave my shoulder. It's like she could sense how badly I needed her comfort, even without me having to say.

I didn't know how to ask, so I was glad I didn't have to.

A half hour later, June had given up on our game of silence and spoiled the ending of the book we were supposed to be buddy reading together. Which was—fucking messed up, if you asked me. She'd caught up to me. Surpassed me. Then made it my problem.

I felt better. Way better. And even her fucked up choices couldn't kill my mood.

It never occurred to me that George would actually find the watch.

I figured it was a lost cause.

As much of a lost cause as my feelings for him.

So, imagine my surprise when I heard what sounded almost suspiciously like a battle cry and George's arms shot straight up into the air. A cheer erupted, echoing along the shore as all the others began to clap, then quickly abandoned their posts.

"What just…" I trailed off, gaze caught on George and his waddling as he struggled out of the water with Joe behind him like a giant duckling. His mom was ahead of him, and she paused by my seat with a knowing smirk.

"Dinner will be ready in an hour," she told me. "Don't be late."

"Thanks, Mrs. M."

"I mean it," she added. "No…*dalliances* on the way."

"Oh my god," June clapped, enjoying my pain.

I did my best not to grimace.

"You too." Mrs. M winked her way, causing June's face to scrunch up in confusion. Then Mrs. M linked arms with her silent husband and headed up the trail. The sun was on the move, still peeking above the treetops, but soon, it'd slip behind them.

June had been disgustingly enthusiastic about the idea of me taking George out tonight. But…given the late hour I wasn't sure he'd still want to go— even considering how badly he needed a suit. The dark circles he'd been sporting made me doubt that taking him ice skating—even if the rink was open by the time we got to Columbus—was a good idea.

I didn't want him to fall or get hurt.

Sweet baby needed his own long, lovely nap.

George was sluggish in his rubber suit.

My heart would not slow the fuck down.

It wasn't until he got close enough for me to see the silver glinting between his orange-gloved fingers that I let myself breathe. He'd...he'd really—had he really done it?

"Have fun, love birds!" June teased, abandoning me the second George was within the general vicinity. "See you at the rehearsal tomorrow?"

"Of course." I agreed. She gave me a dual pair of finger guns before wandering off and leaving me alone with George.

He looked like an angel, sun behind him, sweat glistening at his temples.

"You..." I didn't know what to say.

Without the chatter of the crowd it was eerily quiet. Just the steady lap of the water meeting the shore, over and over.

"Here." George shoved the watch toward me.

It wasn't rusty.

But it was certainly wet.

I grabbed it, my throat tight when my fingers met the chilly metal. I didn't know what to say. That early overwhelm flooding through me again as I clutched the watch close to my chest, eyes pinched shut.

"*Thank you.*" My voice was barely a croak.

"You're welcome." George didn't ask for anything else. He struggled into the lounger at my side with a tired sigh, head dropping back against the seat.

"I'm—"

"If you say you're sorry I am going to strangle you."

I laughed. How could I not?

He'd made that threat so many times by this point, I didn't believe him anymore.

"I was going to tell you that you look cute." I totally *had* been about to apologize, but he didn't need to know that.

The look George gave me could've leveled a mountain. "I look *ridiculous*."

"Ridiculously *hot*. Where'd you get your sexy lil outfit?" I inquired, genuinely curious.

"Apparently the boathouse is useful for more than just..." George's cheeks flushed, and I grinned. "Suffice to say—" he added quickly. "There happened to be a bunch of these detestable ensembles in a closet at the back."

"Handy."

"Very." George didn't speak, though the atmosphere remained friendly. "Roderick told me about it—and then helped me find the one closest to my size. He was...very..."

"*Roderick-y.*"

"Right."

"Thank you, again." My thumb skimmed over the face of the watch, the slick surface drying by the second. "You have no idea how much it means to me that you did this."

"It was nothing."

"It *wasn't* nothing," I argued.

"Fine then. It *wasn't* nothing. But your thank yous are still unnecessary."

I could tell that George had had enough praise for now—and I restrained myself, even though I wanted to kiss the hell out of him in his sexy-silly outfit and declare my undying fealty.

Instead of saying anything else that George would deem "unnecessary", I reached out, fingers tangling with his gloved hand and squeezing tight. He made a pleased sound, but otherwise didn't respond. When he squeezed back, the remaining tension in my body eased.

I loved him even more fiercely then.

Loved him for how fussily he cared. Loved how anxious he was to please. Loved his attentiveness. Loved the fact that his brand of loyalty might seem "smothering" to outsiders, but to me, it was...perfect.

For the first time in my life, I had found someone who could match my intensity.

Someone who was as dramatic and romantic as I was.

Someone who had seen me at my worst, and still wanted to hold my hand afterward.

The other half of my half-empty cup.

It was easier to breathe then, with George at my side, and the sun slowly descending.

And for the first time since I'd lost my watch last night, I realized how much easier it was to carry the weight of the world when I wasn't carrying it alone.

Twenty-Seven
George

"I'M STARTING TO THINK you really do have brain damage," I huffed as Alex headbanged to a song I didn't recognize. He'd had way too much caffeine. It was late. He shouldn't have had *any* at all, but here he was, an energy drink in his cup holder, with the streets of Columbus, Ohio blurring by.

"Rude," Alex snorted, shaking his hair back and forth, a breeze caressing the curl on his forehead, sending it drifting. "You're just jealous because this is your first time listening to modern girly-pop."

"I don't think 'jealous' is an accurate description of what I'm currently feeling," I replied. "ABBA is far superior."

"ABBA?" Alex echoed, eyebrows shooting up. "I feel like I'm seeing you for the first time."

"Oh, shut up." A giggle burst free, and I had to slap my hand over my mouth to get it to stop. I blamed the show tunes we'd been listening to all the way from Hocking Hills and into the city. Discovering that Alex and I had both been theater kids in high school was surprising—especially because I knew he'd also been a jock. In my school, those things had not mixed.

I'd skirted by—as a cheerleader, but only barely.

I supposed private school might be different? But that wasn't something I'd ever know firsthand. Alex was an eclectic combination of perplexing contradictions. And I adored it. Just like I adored the pickles I'd been munching on for half the drive—having retrieved them from the fridge at the main lodge for our journey to the suit shop.

So, yes.

Show tunes had made me giddy.

I'd never driven with the windows down through fields of corn while belting to *Annie Get Your Gun* before. We'd sang a rather horrible rendition of "Anything You Can Do, I Can Do Better", both of us so out of tune it was horrendous.

I'd said we were both in theater.

Not that we were gifted.

It was also possible that my current lingering joy could've been caused by the brand new Armani suit hanging from the suit hook in the back of the car so it wouldn't wrinkle. Armani, to match the one Alex was going to wear.

Alex—because he was a unicorn—had a friend who owned a suit store, apparently. A friend who just-so-happened to owe him a favor, and had been willing to keep the shop open past closing so that we could go suit shopping despite the late hour.

Which subsequently meant that at one in the morning, we'd only just finished purchasing what had to be the prettiest, and most expensive suit I'd ever owned.

I'd let Alex buy it.

I hadn't even attempted to push his credit card away. Maybe it was my way of showing him that things had changed between us. That I accepted him. Or maybe it was his puppy dog eyes? Either way, Brendon no longer felt like a shadow that hung over me. Nor was he a wall between us. And refusing Alex's genuine offer felt like something "old George" would've done. Not new Georgie.

No. *New* Georgie listened to show tunes with his not-boyfriend. *New* Georgie snarked and giggled, and rolled down the windows to feel the summer breeze. *New* Georgie was free in a way old George never had been.

As illogical as it was—after only a few short days—

There was only Alex in my heart now.

There was only Alex's smile haunting me.

Only the whisper of his laughter.

Only the nonsensical way he somehow managed to fill every space he entered with light—even now, when it was dark out, and the only thing keeping us company were the blurred city lights on either side of the vehicle, and the half-eaten jar of pickles that was abandoned at my feet. We pulled to a stop at a train crossing, and the lights outside stilled.

I couldn't even feel embarrassed that his friend had teased him about the hickeys and bite marks on my neck. Couldn't be miffed that Alex was currently bouncing off the walls—being loud enough to shake my tired brain apart—because it was far preferable than the sad, endearing ball of misery that he'd been earlier today.

I'd wanted to hold him, but even I could tell that would be too much.

He was too raw at the time.

Unlike now…now when his guard was down again, and his eyes were manic.

"Where are we going?" I asked, interrupting more of Alex's headbanging. He looked so *stupid*. Stupidly *adorable*. The way he was dancing was out of sync with the beat of the music—and he was lucky that we'd stopped in front of one of the many train tracks that crossed Columbus or his voracious moves would've been a health hazard. He was probably doing it on purpose because he found bouncing off-beat to be fun like the chaos demon he was.

Train cars covered in graffiti zoomed in front of us, the *creak-rattle* of wheels on the track loud in the nighttime quiet—but not as loud as the beat of my heart, or Alex's presence in my head.

"We're going home," Alex answered my question.

"Home?" I blinked.

"*My* home," Alex reiterated. "In Columbus."

"I know what city we're in, thank you," I sighed, though I was…still confused. "I thought you wanted to go to a hotel? What about my *diamonds*, Alex?" I deadpanned, surprised by how natural it felt—and how easy it was to focus on him and push aside my warring thoughts. "You said that you were going to *spoil* me."

"I literally *just* bought you a suit?! Greedy, much?" Alex teased, wild and unrepentant. He wasn't offended by my joke, which was a relief—and only further proved how close we'd gotten over the last few days.

It felt like we'd known each other years, not less than a week.

And the fact that I could joke about money-related issues, given what he'd admitted last night, spoke volumes about that bond.

Alex's still-broken watch was back in its rightful spot on his wrist.

Sitting next to the friendship bracelet I'd made him, it caught the light from the street lamps to our left and right. His forearms flexed, tan hands cupping the steering wheel like it was an old friend. When I glanced back up at his face, Alex's pale eyes were bright.

"You're right, though. I *did* say that. And I meant it. But—plans have changed," he said. "I realized I was wrong."

"Wrong?" I frowned.

"I miscalculated—I've never actually had a *real* partner to spoil." Alex admitted when the rattle of the train had finally stopped, and the caboose passed by in front of us. The red and white railroad crossing gates slowly began to rise back into position. "You're different. You're not one of my nameless exes. Not a Poundr hookup. You're *George*. And if I'm going to *show* how you deserve to be treated, I'm gonna do that in my own goddamn house—in my own fucking bed."

I understood what he meant.

The hotel had been before we'd…reached *this*. A new level of not-boyfriends. At some point, we'd crossed a line into unknown territory. Things were different. Better, more, and stronger. The tension between us flickered liquid-hot and airy at the same time. Like it was simultaneously a scorching iron and a fluffy summer cloud.

I could honestly say I'd never felt this way about anyone else.

A beat passed, companionable silence filling the car as Alex waited for the gates to rise all the way so we could cross the tracks safely.

"Relax." He reached out, fingers looping around my wrist. There was no one behind us, so I didn't worry about stopping traffic. Okay, maybe I worried a bit—but it was only because it was the law.

The muscle at the corner of Alex's jaw jumped, his expression nothing but honest earnestness as he brought my hand to his mouth and kissed the back of it.

"Quid pro quo, George," he said softly. "You took care of me earlier. Now let me take care of you."

It wasn't a look I saw on him often, walls down, open sincerity written all over his face. I'd been seeing a lot more of it lately. Like now that I'd broken through the last of Alex's fortifications, he didn't know how to get them back up again. I didn't know what to do with it. Especially given the direction our conversation had veered.

It was too much.

It was all too much.

I was going back to New York soon. There wasn't—there wasn't room for declarations like that. And yet…Alex made room anyway. Like he was carving space for us in the universe.

Alex lived in a house that was so picture perfect I was half-tempted to take a snapshot to add it to my vision board. Red brick. White trim. A space large enough for a family to grow into. It looked homey and inviting, set inside a neighborhood of other similar fancy houses. Ivy danced up the walls, the yard was spacious and flawlessly manicured, and the cement walkway that led from the covered front porch to the street was lined with perfectly spaced rose bushes.

This was not the bachelor pad I'd anticipated.

And…it spoke volumes of the life Alex wanted—but had never let himself have.

Alex pulled into the driveway and the garage door rose with nary a creak. Perfectly oiled, probably. The kind of perfection only money could buy. An automatic light illuminated the space as Alex parked the car. We exited in tandem, both of us eager to head inside, though that didn't stop me from taking in the space around me with awe.

I clutched my pickle jar close, for moral support.

To my left, a parked motorcycle—presumably based on the shape—was covered in a drop cloth for protection. The wall at its back housed a set of shelving units painted a glorious firetruck red. Tools hung in perfect precision along a matching pegboard inlaid into the unit. There were a few empty spots made glaringly obvious by its organization.

A honeyed wooden workbench connected the first set of shelves to a second even larger set that spanned the connected wall all the way to the door that led inside the house. These were clearly used for storage of a different sort. Hockey skates, gear, and other miscellaneous sporty knickknacks populated the shelves along with what had to be the remainder of Alex's camping gear. There were quite a few empty spots here as well, though it didn't take a genius to realize that was because half his camping gear was in use at the wedding.

"You done stalking me yet?" Alex teased. I jolted, twisting to look at him across the hood of the car.

"You brought me here, it's not stalking." My tone was certainly defensive, which did not help my argument.

"Gathering intel, then?" He looked far too pleased with himself, eyes dancing. "Spying?" I flushed, and Alex's gaze flickered to my cheeks. A Cheshire-like grin curled across his lips as he cocked his head.

He didn't tease me again. He simply led the way through the garage and up the steps. The kitchen door swung open silently, and Alex waited at the top, eyes watching me hungrily. He usually looked at me like that, so it wasn't particularly alarming.

Things felt different though…stronger.

Alex wasn't hiding.

And his desire was blatant.

Apparently by paying attention to the contents of his garage, I'd pleased him.

"You can ask me questions, you know," Alex said as I climbed the steps. He didn't move out of the way, studying me from the doorway he was blocking. My heart skipped a beat. "Anything you want. I'll answer to the best of my ability."

"Why a motorcycle?" I inquired immediately. Alex laughed, shifting to the side barely enough to let me through. Our chests brushed when I squeezed by. I couldn't help but shudder—a motion Alex caught, as he licked his lips, pale eyes dancing.

"I like the way it feels," he answered. "Makes me hard when I ride it and it buzzes between my legs." I choked, stumbling into the dark open kitchen with a shocked noise. I must've looked annoyed because Alex shut the door with a click and immediately crowded me into the kitchen island. "I'm not lying," he promised. "Or teasing. That's really my main motivation."

"Why am I not surprised you bought a death-trap simply because it makes you hard?" I said, breathier than I meant to.

"Because you pay attention to me," Alex husked, watching me with those all-knowing pale blue eyes. Like he saw right through me. "Because you *see* me." He dropped in close, nuzzling our noses together in a tantalizing back and forth that sent a shiver down my spine. My breath hitched. Alex's eyes were swimming with emotion.

They asked, *am I right?*

They begged, *please tell me I'm not making this up.*

They begged, *don't let me down.*

"I do see you," I whispered, lashes fluttering. "I…"

"You're so precious, Georgie Porgie," Alex murmured before stealing a needy kiss. It felt different here, surrounded by his things. Private and special—and personal. I whined, my free hand twisting in the back of his sweat-damp t-shirt. His skin was molten where I brushed it, muscles in his lower back clenching as he pressed into me with greed. The pickle jar dug into our bellies, trapped between us, but neither of us cared.

Big, scratchy palms skimmed up my forearms, tickling the hair on them. Leisurely, they climbed, tracing my biceps, my shoulders, till Alex was cupping my face in both his hands and holding me steady.

Obedient.

Sipping from my mouth like he was parched and I was the only thing that could quench his thirst.

We kissed and kissed and kissed.

Soft, hard, sweet.

Insatiable, ravenous, delicate.

Alex's tongue was as desperate and domineering as always, taking what he wanted from me. He didn't hesitate to force my mouth open wider with his thumbs when he wanted to lick deeper. He didn't pause or second-guess tilting my head to change the angle, the wet sounds our mouths made impossibly loud in the quiet space.

At one point, he pressed so close I nearly dropped my pickles.

When he pulled back I was panting.

Alex's eyes were pools of black desire, his mouth as kiss-swollen and glossy as my own. He licked his lips, like he was chasing my taste, his fingers sliding deeper into my hair, palms scraping my ears.

"Do you want a tour?" he inquired, like he hadn't just fucked my mouth for ten minutes.

"W-what?" It took me a second to figure out what was going on. I squirmed, half hard already. "Oh. Yes."

Right. A tour. A tour was good. A tour was…yes.

I could learn more about him if we went on a tour.

And as desperate as I was to yank his pants down and take his hard cock into whatever hole was closest—I was equally eager to discover new things about him. Maybe he wasn't the only person that was starved.

"Alright." Alex gave my scalp one last parting scratch, making my lashes flutter. Then his hands were sliding back down my body as slow and deliberate as they'd climbed up. He tangled our fingers together, pulling me through the moonlit kitchen, before flipping a light switch on.

Once illuminated, the space looked even more inviting.

"For a man who claims not to cook, you certainly have a well-equipped kitchen," I said, honestly shocked. This was a chef's wet dream. Everything was massive. Granite counters, a farm-style sink, and appliances that looked so new I wouldn't have been surprised if they still had the stickers from the store.

Alex was delighted. "Well," he said, tugging on my hands to catch my attention. "I'm nothing if not well-equipped."

Only Alex could twist what I'd said into a dick joke.

I snorted, and his eyes lit up.

"That was a pretty good one," I admitted, trying not to smile and failing.

"Damn. Did I win the lottery today, or what? Keep laughing at my dick jokes and I'll start to get cocky." Alex waggled his eyebrows, and I rolled my eyes. He took my bottle of pickles from me and put them in the fridge. Then he flipped the light switch off, plunging us into darkness, before he continued the tour.

The living room was a lot more lived-in than the kitchen and definitely more on par with what I'd expect from Alex. Just as massive, just as sparkling— with an inviting-looking sofa and a TV that was large enough it belonged in a Megaplex. A few rolled balls of socks decorated the foot of the couch, betraying Alex's bad habit of kicking them off and lying down.

He surreptitiously tried to kick them beneath it before I saw, but failed.

I didn't react to the socks.

A laptop sat on the coffee table beside an empty takeout container and a half finished bottle of Diet Coke. I didn't react to those either.

Alex made a sound, embarrassed.

"I—clearly—was not expecting visitors," he said. "Sorry for the mess."

"I like it," I admitted—which, of course—went against everything I'd ever thought I'd say. My own apartment was far smaller than this place. In fact, I could probably fit the entirety of it inside Alex's living room alone. But it was neat always. Every item had a place, and the only clutter that populated it were Mr. Pickle's toys he often left lying around and the occasional manga I was half-finished reading.

I didn't like putting them back until I was done. Having unfinished business made me antsy.

"You do?" Alex looked appropriately shocked. "I figured the dirty socks would be a deal-breaker for you."

"I don't mind," I blurted. My cheeks burned, but I ignored the growing flush. "I like that you're human."

"Of course I'm human. What did you think I was?" He was teasing. I could tell it was because he didn't know what to say. He was as flustered as I was, having me in his space like this, seeing his flaws.

I could relate.

I, too, had an issue with appearing less than perfect.

"I just mean…" Instead of joking, I simply spoke the truth. "Since we've met you've been so put-together. You always know what to say to get what you want. You're prepared in a way even I wasn't—and I make a habit of always prepping for the worst-case scenario." Alex's eyes were swimming with emotions I couldn't name. "You're attentive. So fucking attentive. You're smart. Capable. Hard-working. When you enter a room, it brightens, every single time." My cheeks flushed. "During sex, you always seem to know what you're doing—even when you don't." At that, he laughed. "And while all of those things are true…you also…" I didn't know how to say this the right way—but I tried.

"You have masks—so many of them I've lost count. You use them to protect yourself. A fact I admire, truly, as no matter how hard I try I can't seem to do the same. But to see beneath the masks…to see you…*vulnerable*…and… imperfect…" I trailed off. Alex was watching me, the weight of his gaze like a warm blanket.

"To see Alex James as a *whole*…picture? Not just the put-together-bits you want everyone to see is an honor." I continued, bolstered by his attention. *God, how to phrase this.* "And I find…I like you more this way, without the masks. Dirty socks and all."

Maybe he'd needed reassurance after earlier.

After being laid so bare before me.

Because Alex's eyes were wet when I met his gaze again.

Wet.

Glistening, as he stared at me for a beat, processing my words.

And then he cleared his throat.

It seemed I'd made him speechless.

Whether or not that was a good thing, I had no idea. At least, not until he tugged me into his side. And suddenly, I was smashed into a wall of heat and Alex was pressing a kiss to my temple. He held me there, recharging, all that manic energy from earlier missing.

"I'm glad you don't mind my dirty socks, Georgie," Alex finally said, voice hoarse.

Embarrassed by the emotion I'd exhibited, I was tempted to pull free. But that would mean losing Alex's embrace, and I wasn't willing to do that.

At least…not yet.

The rest of the tour was enlightening. Alex wasn't a slob, by any means, but he wasn't a clean freak either. It was entertaining to see what spaces he kept the most organized. As we went through his study, a few empty bedrooms with a couple sad bookshelves—because he said he preferred audiobooks—and his well-stocked back porch with its high-end grill and patio furniture, I made a mental list of all the objects that had been given a home in spots that were not their designated areas.

Alex's bedroom was the most interesting of all, for obvious reasons.

Sleepy and vulnerable, this was where he retired after every long day.

While his house, as a whole, was his private domain, his bedroom was arguably the most personal space inside it. It smelled of expensive cologne and a hint of clean sweat. The walls were painted navy blue with a rich wooden trim, and beams across the ceiling. A sturdy four poster bed was stationed in between two floor-to-ceiling windows sporting rumpled sheets the same color as the walls.

One half of the room remained pristine, while the other housed a hockey stick, a pile of dirty laundry—and a basket that was full of clean clothes. The whole area was an eclectic mix of homey and refined. Like the two sides of Alex's personality were mashed together in the space.

Alex entered before me, dropping my hand as he side-stepped toward the bed and surreptitiously attempted to kick his discarded socks beneath it before I could see them.

"What did I *just* say?" I laughed, amused.

"Sorry, old habits die hard!" Alex apologized. That was when I spotted the takeout container on his night stand. I frowned, and Alex snorted. "What, you're fine with laundry but you draw the line at take-out?"

"It's unsanitary."

"You're so fucking cute." Alex pinched his face together with a nose scrunch. "It's unsanitary," he echoed, in a lower tone of voice, like he was trying to mimic me.

His easy grin made it obvious he was not upset. In fact, he looked *amused*, if not a little embarrassed.

"I'm not judging," I promised. "I told you most of what I eat is take-out too. Only, I have the common sense to not eat in bed."

Alex snorted.

"Glad to see you're fine with dirty socks but you draw the line at crumbs on the mattress."

"I have to draw the line *somewhere*." I had so few lines with him. So few I wasn't even sure I could count them. Nothing he did truly annoyed me, which was as fascinating as it was overwhelming.

"Is this a dealbreaker?" Alex's eyes were still oddly vulnerable, despite his teasing tone.

"No."

"Good." He melted, flopping onto the bed with a sigh. He leaned back on his arms, legs spread wide to accommodate the girth of his cock, his chest flexing. When he arched a brow my way, my stomach filled with butterflies.

"Where have you been all my life?" Alex said.

It was an accusation as much as it was flirting.

Like he was irritated I'd waited until we were both in our thirties to stumble upon Roderick's wedding. Like we should have met earlier. Which was…a sentiment I shared, despite how fanciful and illogical it was.

I ignored the question, twisting around to catalog the rest of the details of his most personal space. Like the sporty posters on the back wall. As well as the walk-in closet stocked with designer suits in a neat row on one side, and a half-open dresser on the other. Ticket stubs to hockey games littered the window sill, draped curtains framing the moonlit panes. Beside the takeout container on the nightstand, a few wayward coins sat in a clunky-looking ceramic bowl I was almost certain one of Alex's cousins had made for him.

Alex didn't interrupt me. His eyes carried a weight to them as he watched me wander. He snorted in amusement when I bent to pick up the socks he'd tried to kick beneath the bed, before tossing them into the dirty pile where they belonged.

"I *knew* they bothered you, you adorable little liar." Alex's eyes were dancing as he stayed reclined.

"They don't." I glared at him, reaching for the takeout container next. I stacked it along with the empty Diet Coke bottles I'd found littered about. Alex chuckled the whole time as I walked into the en suite bathroom—oh nice, a glass shower!—to deposit them in the trash bin beside the sink.

"If they don't bother you, why are you cleaning them up?" Alex called after me. He sounded way too amused. But still…I liked that. Even if he was laughing at me.

When I returned, I paused a few feet in front of him, scrubbing my hands off on my pants. I huffed and crossed my arms. It was hard to look at him, my cheeks burning, eyes downcast.

Why was I cleaning?

It was rude, wasn't it?

But Alex didn't seem to think so.

"I…don't know," I admitted, because I *didn't*. It was almost as though I felt…the need to care for his space like it was my own. "I…"

"Are you nesting?" Alex teased. "Marking your territory with your neat lil fingers." I scowled and his voice went honey sweet. "I don't mind, baby. Fuss over me all you want."

"You read too much omegaverse."

"What can I say? I like my books knot-ty."

"Ha, ha." I rolled my eyes, but my cheeks still felt hot.

"I'm serious," Alex's cockiness was back. "I like that you care. I like that you're nosy. I like that you can't help but fix things. I like that you feel welcome enough here to touch my stuff. I want you to." He spread his legs invitingly. "Now, come here—unless there's more cleaning you're dying to do before it's finally my turn to take care of you."

I followed his command immediately, pulled by the magnetic force of his warmth. Pausing between his spread legs, my heart pounding, I took a moment to get my bearings.

It was late. Far too late, considering the lack of sleep I'd gotten the night before. I was running on fumes and nothing else—and yet, somehow—I'd never felt more awake.

"Sit on my lap, Duchess." Alex's voice went low and buttery. I shuddered, nipples perking up, as I straddled his hips. The mattress dipped beneath our combined weight, and Alex lifted up, shifting back a few inches so we were more steady as though my weight didn't matter at all. "That's better."

I didn't know what to do with my hands, so they simply hovered, useless at my sides.

Alex was different now. His earlier teasing energy was gone. Instead… replaced by the almost predatory intensity I'd grown to associate with him, maybe even more than his smile. Like he was looking at me—*really* looking at me. Seeing beneath my surface to the gooey center hidden deep inside.

And I let him.

I let him see me as clearly as I saw him.

I was happy…to let him see me.

As vulnerable as that was.

"Arms around my neck," Alex said, voice rumbling. Relieved to be told what to do, I slung my arms around him, eager to hear what he'd say next. "How's your pussy feel?" Gravelly and soft, Alex's voice was full of concern. "Is it still sore?"

I squirmed as the use of *that* word sent a fizzle of pleasure zinging up my spine. I shook my head.

"Should we *make* it sore again?" Alex straightened enough his arms were no longer supporting him. Strong hands cupped my ass, digging in and spreading my cheeks. A frankly ungodly sound escaped me. "That wasn't a *yes*, Georgie," Alex taunted. His fingers slid into my crease, rubbing at my twitchy hole through the fabric. "I'm gonna need a yes."

"Y-yes."

Thirty minutes later, I was face-first in his pillows with Alex's cock in my ass. In and out, the thick, sticky glide made me feel like I was losing the last dregs of sanity I had left. The back of my neck tingled and stung from all the hickeys Alex was leaving. His heavy body blanketed mine, my legs spread so wide I was practically lying on the mattress like a useless, needy starfish.

Every thrust sent stars exploding behind my lids.

Alex knew exactly how to angle his hips to strike my prostate. Which resulted in a brutal bounce-slap that forced sobs from my lips, and air out of my lungs. His movements were syrupy slow. So slow that they'd been maddening at first.

I clawed at his thighs, fingers slipping along the prickly hair atop them as I attempted to urge him faster. No matter how I scratched or pulled, Alex never relented. It was easy for him to deny me. And every denial only further reminded me who exactly was in charge here.

At least—on the surface.

Alex had made it clear that I was the one that called the shots. And it was that reassurance that allowed me to hand over control in its entirety.

One of Alex's hands tangled into my hair, sending another fizzle down my spine. Periodically he'd tug my head to the side so he could see my face—but for the most part, it was simply a reminder. A reminder that I was *his*, and he was *mine*, and I was entirely at his mercy.

A reminder that he wanted to see the mess he made of me.

That he liked it.

That he liked me, drooling, sobbing, and tear-streaked.

"*Squeeze*," Alex commanded silkily against my ear, teeth nipping playfully at the lobe. "C'mon baby, I know you can. Squeeze my cock." I whimpered, hole clenching around him obediently. "Fuck yeah. Again." Again, I pinched. My entire focus was on my hole—on the way he split it open. On the squelch-smack of our hips as Alex ground into me, his sac bumping my ass with every glide.

"A-Alex—" I keened.

"Arch your back."

It was an impossible request. How was I supposed to do that when my legs were spread like this? Still, I tried. Alex purred, pulling all the way out, my empty hole twitching, before he plunged back in with a brutal thrust that had me seeing stars.

"Such a good boy," Alex's voice was barely more than a growl. "Squeeze me again, Duchess. That's it. Such a pretty, pretty pussy." He released my hair, straightening up as his hands fanned over my ass cheeks and he spread me wide open. "You have no idea how slutty you look right now, do you?"

The noise I made was barely human. The puddle of drool beneath my face was steadily growing, and it was a testament to how undone he made me that I hardly cared. When Alex called me slutty it was a compliment, and the shame the word should have inspired was absent.

"God." Alex pulled out until only his crown remained, his thumbs digging into my cheeks to keep them spread. "So fucking slick and pink. You have to stretch so much to fit me, don't you, sweetheart?"

I whined.

"Yeah, you do. But you don't mind." My hole fluttered, and Alex groaned. "Because we both know you like it. Size queen." His hips snapped forward, and I howled, trembling beneath him as his hands slid up my lower back, across my shoulders, down my forearms, to wrap around my wrists.

Every grind of his pelvis forced mine into the mattress, the pleasure of the comforter scraping against my dick an addicting back and forth that made me feel like I was losing my mind. I didn't even notice when I came, the shockwaves caused by every flex of Alex's body unstopping. It went on forever, on and on, the wet spot beneath my dick growing as I spilled and spilled.

"Jesus," Alex gasped out, losing the battle with his own control. His teeth sank into the back of my neck—a new spot this time—his pace stuttering. Faster, harder, quick needy jabs that made my head swim.

The hot spurt of his cum filling me was nirvana.

Sighing, my body lost all tension as Alex pumped his load into my well-fucked hole. "Christ, you pretty fucking princess," Alex groaned, his tongue lapping stripes up and down my neck. "Such a good boy, for me. Such a good, good boy."

He settled down, smashing me into the mattress, his fingers skimming over my wrists as his cock began to soften inside me. It was the oddest sensation, but not unpleasant. In fact, my hole clung tighter, trying to urge him to stay.

"You're so perfect," Alex murmured into my ear, laving its curve with his tongue and a few flickering kisses. "You take my cock so well. My perfect, perfect baby. Fuck." He wiggled to get more comfortable, and I whimpered, his dick jostling deep. "Don't worry. Gonna keep you full, sweetheart," Alex promised. "Gonna take care of you—just like I promised."

His hands were on the move, running over my body, tracing its contours with reverence. He rubbed my shoulders, skimmed my ribs, scraped his nails in the groove between my leg and hip. "So lovely," he praised with a flurry of new kisses. "Thank you. That was—fuck. Thank you."

He cupped my spent dick, simply to hold it. I was so exhausted, the most I could do to respond was gasp. His hand was so fucking delicious, the calluses just the right scratch to feel heavenly on the overstimulated skin. It hurt a bit, in the best possible way.

"Such a good cock," Alex continued, fingers slipping lower to cup my balls. "Sweet little balls too. God, you're a gift, you know that? Not a single inch of you that's not perfect. My pretty, cute lil Georgie. My precious little sweetheart, aren't you? So obedient for me. Such a tight, pink hole you have." His hips flexed, and I sighed, full and happy and content.

No worries or thoughts of the future plaguing me.

Dazed, relaxed, and sated, there was no denying the fact my feelings had grown far more than was natural in such a short period of time. It wasn't until I was half-asleep, my eyes catching on a wayward pair of socks I'd missed, that I realized why Alex's flaws didn't bother me.

Because I loved them.

Just like I loved his strengths.

Just like I loved him.

Dirty socks and all.

Twenty-Eight
Alex

"NO." GEORGE SLAPPED MY hand as I tried to sneak another slice of bread from the pan he was using on the stove to toast it. I'd already snuck two slices from it. The first one had been because I wanted to see what he'd do. The second had been because seeing his "grimple" this early in the morning was an absolute treat.

I reached again, slowly—then dropped my hand when he outright glared.

"*Alex.*" George huffed at me, his cute scowl made the balloon in my chest expand once again. I leaned against the counter at his side, far enough from the flames not to get scolded.

"Can I help?" I offered, even though I was pretty sure I'd ruin anything I touched.

"No." George's brows were furrowed as he glowered into the pan of eggs he was scrambling. "If you help, you're only going to steal more food and spoil your breakfast."

He'd somehow…miraculously found ingredients in my fridge to make a classic American fry up. Hash browns, buttery toast, eggs, and sausage. All sizzling on different burners. Like he was that muppet—with the zillions of arms—he managed to flip and stir and scowl every food item into submission.

"Are you—"

"Stop asking." George grumbled to himself, something about me and my "sneaky, greedy hands" and "nibbling problem".

"What if I promise not to steal food from the pans?"

George paused, his angry stirring halting as he considered. Then he shook his head. "No," he said, softer this time. "I've got it covered."

His back looked lonely, despite being drowned in a borrowed t-shirt from my closet and nothing more. It hung past his cock, and I was half-tempted to yank it up so I could see what was mine beneath it. But I didn't. Instead, I latched on to his back like an overgrown barnacle, hands at his hips.

"This okay?" I confirmed, lips finding his nape—my favorite place to sate my "nibbling problem". "Not too distracting?"

"Is this your version of offering moral support?" George's response was dry.

"Maybe?" I squeezed his hips, unfairly turned on by how good he felt like this. Domestic. Like this was our everyday life—and not just a blip in the monotony of my world. A single bright, delightful moment.

I ran my fingers along his hip bones, tracing them beneath the fabric before enveloping him in a tight hug, my teeth sinking into the meat of his shoulder. "Or maybe…" I murmured after releasing him from my bite, tongue soothing the sting. "Maybe I just want to hold you."

Way too fucking close to the truth, Alex, Jesus.

"Oh." George's ears flushed and I had no doubt his cheeks were an even ruddier pink. I grinned, hiding against his nape again.

"Maybe I…love holding you."

You are playing with fire.

"*Alex.*" George's voice quaked.

I didn't know what *that* tone meant. It was certainly needy. A plea. Maybe it meant that he needed me to sink to my knees, pull his ass cheeks open and—no. *No.* He was cooking. With flames. Flames that could hurt him—and he'd already been burned once this week. Distracting him, even with my tongue in his ass, was dangerous. *Later.* Later I'd eat him out till he cried, one long leg anchored on the counter, my t-shirt shoved up his back.

Except…

Would I?

We only had a few hours before we were due to pick up my dad for Juniper's rehearsal. And then tomorrow was her wedding—and then…George would be flying back home to New York where he belonged.

I had just over a day left with him at best.

The thought was sobering.

And I didn't…I didn't know what to do with it.

Every time I acknowledged it, my chest began to squeeze. So tight I couldn't breathe. So tight I couldn't—

It was better not to think about it.

Definitely better.

I needed to survive this—and at this point, I wasn't sure I would.

"Breakfast is done." George's voice shocked me out of my reverie. I pulled my lips back, amused—and unsurprised—when I realized that in my distraction I'd left a rather dark hickey. My body was apparently as possessive as my thoughts, even subconsciously. George's whole neck was covered in a myriad of bruises that he'd never attempted to conceal. A painting of our love affair written in varying shades of purple on his sunburnt skin.

These would last longer than our relationship.

Stop it, Alex.

Stop it.

George's lack of shame was uncharacteristic.

I think…maybe he was proud of them. Or—maybe…just maybe he was as reluctant to let go of signs of us as I was.

"Hell yes." I pulled away. Silently, I gathered two dinner plates and tried to ignore the elephant in the room—the timer ticking above our heads. George ignored it too. His focus was aimed at piling our plates high with the prettiest damn breakfast I'd ever seen. George had been modest when he'd talked about his culinary skills. This was a fucking masterpiece.

The smell was almost as good as the presentation, if that was any indicator of taste? I was so screwed. I'd probably ask him to marry me again. Like an idiot. Luckily for me, he'd thought I was joking before—when I really… embarrassingly…had not been.

"I like your kitchen," George said, as he plopped a few sausages on my tray. "It's nice. I like…your whole…um—house."

"I'm glad." My heart fluttered. I raised my voice and asked Alexa to turn on my show tunes playlist. Immediately, music filled the room, overtaking the silence.

George flashed me a smile, a private smile. So small I knew it was honest. A smile that was meant for me.

I kissed his shoulder and took the plates, bringing them to the dining room table I'd only ever used for work. When I pulled his chair out for him, he arched a judgy brow my way but otherwise didn't complain. He simply slipped primly into his seat and dug in.

Sweet baby was hungry, apparently.

His bitty little bites had morphed into something more normal-people-sized. Maybe because he was more comfortable here. With me. A lot had changed since the day I'd taken him to the diner. It felt like a lifetime had passed.

I groaned when I took my first bite, fist smacking the table in appreciation. George's nose scrunched like he was annoyed by the theatrics, even though his eyes said otherwise.

They said, *thank you for letting me take care of you.*

They said, *thank you for not thinking I'm too much.*

"You're an idiot," he teased, looking way too pleased with himself. "Do you really like it that much?"

"'Course I do. You made it." I stabbed a bite of buttery egg and wagged it at him. "I love everything you make." The friendship bracelet on my wrist dangled, proving the truth of the statement.

George cleared his throat, his cheeks flushed once again, betraying him. His lips pressed into a flat line that was more smile than scowl as he shrugged. "Okay."

That was it.

Okay.

No snarky comment. No denial.

Only…simple acceptance.

George dried the dishes while I scrubbed. He was meticulous about it, holding each dish up for inspection, hunting for stray water droplets. When he found them he'd squint and scrub each drop to submission before he set them to the side on the drying rack. There was something so *seriously* adorable about how *seriously* he took such a basic task.

When I'd finished washing the last dish—and boy, did I need to put some elbow grease into that bad boy—I pulled the plug and let the dirty-soapy water drain. *Glugging* away, the suds sucked down the pipe while I turned the faucet on.

It was so sickeningly, wonderfully domestic I could hardly breathe.

And the companionable silence was a double-edged sword. Because I could not fucking stop thinking about what he'd done for me yesterday—or what he'd said to me about the masks I wore.

I needed a distraction.

Stat.

After cleaning my hands, I playfully flicked some water George's way. He flinched, set the pan he was drying down, and swiveled to glower at me.

"Did you just *splash* me?" George sounded as indignant as he was surprised. Like he simply could not fathom the fact I'd do something so terribly horrible as flicking water at him. Jesus Christ, he was such a cat.

"So what if I did?" I teased, flicking water at him again. "What are you gonna do about it?" It was a challenge, as much as it was a taunt.

He looked so adorably offended, I simply couldn't help myself. I was, however, not prepared for George's response. Because he grabbed one of the freshly cleaned spatulas from the counter, raised it above his head—and with an evil glint in his lovely, dark blue gaze, began to beat my back mercilessly.

"Ah!" I gasped, batting him away to no avail. It didn't hurt. More of a tickle, than anything. The damn thing was plastic, after all. But still. As the sweet crooning of the music on the speakers morphed into something more upbeat, George's smacking began to match its rhythm.

A metronome of rage.

"Splash me again, motherfucker," George aimed the spatula at my ass. "See what happens." *Smack, smack.* He wanted to see it jiggle, the little slut. I choked on a chuckle that quickly evolved into full-blown guffaws. Skidding away from the never-ending barrage on socked feet, I barely managed to avoid another swing.

George was not deterred.

In fact, my fleeing only seemed to egg him on.

Rather than stop and concede defeat, he gave chase.

What George lacked in athleticism he made up with sheer force of will.

His socked feet skidded on the tile as he stalked me around the center island, spatula raised threateningly. His lean chest heaved with every breath. When he finally caught up to me—I maybe-possibly had intentionally slowed enough to allow him close—he whacked my ass again. A maniacal giggle escaped his mouth, eyes gleaming with mischief as I scurried away and he chased me around the island for a second time.

Five smacks to the ass—that was the price I paid to get my hands under the faucet again. The second my "ammo" had been "loaded", I began flicking my fingers at George with vengeance.

"You sneaky little shit!" I cackled, flick, flick, flicking away. Pretending like I hadn't let him catch me because it was more fun that way. "Take that!"

"Gah!" George's spatula smacked at my chest in retaliation, because of course it did—kinky fucker liked my tits. "Fuck you! You giant titty-ass bitch." *Flick, flick, flick.*

"Giant titty-ass bitch?" I echoed, amused. Was that his idea of an insult? Cute.

I loaded up on more water—

George abandoned the fight and scrambled away, water droplets slipping down his cheeks and chin, and dotting the collar of his borrowed shirt. Apparently, it was my turn to chase now. Laughing all the way, I stalked after him, dripping fingers wriggling.

"Fucker—" George hissed, slip-sliding on the tile. He bonked into the corner of the counter, a pained hiss escaping.

"Are you okay?" My smile faltered.

"I'm fine!" He grabbed a dish towel and launched it at me, instigating the chase once again.

Around and around and *around* we went. We made a detour into the living room for a time, scrambling up and over the couch—before returning to the kitchen to finish our battle where it had started. By that point, the water on my hands had long since dried, and my only goal was capturing my wriggling, giggling blond.

My heart was pounding for more than one reason by the time I found success.

"Got you!" I caught George by the hips. His body was quaking with glee— and these snort-y giggles shook his entire chest. They were as endearing as they were attractive. Imperfect in the most wonderful way. Eager to taste his snorts for myself, I yanked him through the air and up onto the kitchen island with a grunt. My hands slid across his cheeks and into his wavy golden hair, holding him captive while I pulled him into a ravenous, lingering kiss.

George tasted like sunshine, happiness, and peace.

Like someone who cared too much, who loved too hard, who needed to be accepted just as he was. He tasted like the kind of solid, loyal love I'd stop believing in—like short-shorts in the summer, shared pleasure, and domesticity.

Suffice to say, he tasted amazing.

So *amazing* my goddamn toes curled, the heat in between my legs simmering, then climbing high, wrapping tight around my dancing heart.

George's giggles softened, the heavy bursts of his breath growing quiet as he moaned into the kiss. Delightfully strong fingers curled in the back of my matching t-shirt, tugging me closer. His heels dug into the back of my thighs. I growled. *Deeper, deeper,* I licked, unable to get enough of him.

We didn't stop kissing.

Not when I yanked him into my arms. Not when I walked us up the stairs to my bedroom. Not when I laid him down on the sheets, crawling between the sprawl of his long, bare legs—the place that had quickly become my personal slice of heaven.

There was no need for foreplay.

No drive to play the games we both normally enjoyed.

Without anything to hide behind there was nothing but raw need between us. A mutual desperation to get as close as two people could possibly get. To be bare with no walls or obstacles in our way.

The lube was close, which was a relief, because even the brief separation from George's pouty mouth felt too long.

Too long to be away from him.

George was fully naked when I returned from gathering lube in the nightstand. I settled back inside the space between his legs. His t-shirt had been tossed haphazardly at the end of the bed along with the too-large boxer briefs he'd borrowed.

His hands were demanding when I leaned into his space, lube bottle in hand. He wasted no time yanking my shirt over my head, and my underwear down my legs so that we matched, skin against skin.

Once more, with enthusiasm, he parted those lovely legs for me—welcoming my touch. I pressed into him, an undeniable sense of rightness settling over me as our hips slotted together. George's hole was fluttery and inviting as I stretched him with lubed fingers, sipping kisses from his lips with open desire.

"Enough," George murmured a few minutes later, voice vibrating with need. "It's enough. I need—"

"Me too." I scrambled to do as I was told.

When I finally pushed my dick inside, he gasped. That was it. A simple, *glorious* gasp. A gasp I tasted—along with the butter from our breakfast. It wasn't perfect by any means. We were still sleepy and sex-rumpled from the night before. Sweat-damp from our impromptu battle with dark circles beneath our eyes. I wasn't the perfect male specimen I always attempted to project myself to be.

I wasn't a son.

Wasn't a brother.

Wasn't a wallet.

Wasn't wearing a mask.

Wasn't pretending to be someone else—simply because I needed to.

Wasn't scrambling to fit in, or stick out, or please—or perform.

My barricades demolished, all that was left was…me.

Alex.

Sweaty, *imperfect*, needy Alex.

And George still wanted me.

George who was—who was *everything* I'd written off as a fantasy.

Welcoming, warm, and icy when necessary. He invited me behind his walls, not because they weren't important, but because he trusted me not to betray him. He welcomed me into his body like it was a privilege to have me there. Like he wanted me as desperately as I wanted him. Like our need for one another was equal.

And as I filled him, my heart filled as well.

I'd never understood when people called fucking "making love." It seemed like such a silly, cheesy, stupid term. I'd had enough relationships to know that it was a myth, right along with love at first sight. Experience had taught me my lofty dreams of the romantic were naive and ridiculous. I'd written off the term entirely.

And yet...now I was a believer.

Because as George and I shared breath. As our two became one, as I held and *cherished* and caressed him. As his nails raked down my back, heels at my hamstrings, I could acknowledge that *this*...this was not "fucking".

It wasn't.

As ridiculous-awful-fanciful-naive as that sounded.

And in that moment, we weren't two star-crossed lovers, destined to part. We weren't a summer fling. Weren't "practice boyfriends", a fond memory—something that would eventually fade into sepia, with disintegrating, well-loved edges.

Here and now, my world started and ended with Georgie.

My Georgie.

As we made love.

For what might be the only time.

And for the first time in almost a decade, I let myself be naive. I let the romantic in me awaken. I let the young man who'd been crushed by disappointment again and again break free from the walls where I'd shackled him.

For this one perfect morning, I let myself believe that there was nothing wrong with dreaming of happy endings.

The romantic in me could die tomorrow.
But today, I'd let him live.

Twenty-Nine
George

ALEX'S DAD WAS PRETTY much his older, more silver doppelganger. Which was as shocking as it was…ah…*stimulating*. I couldn't stop stealing glances in the rearview mirror. Every time I did, my cheeks became more red.

Alex…because he was *Alex*, found the whole thing incredibly funny.

He'd clocked my attraction the second his dad had exited his front door dressed in a charcoal three-piece suit—a suit that perfectly complemented the gray in his hair. Honestly, it wasn't my fault. I'd have to be dead not to notice his dad was good-looking.

And besides…there was something *extra* attractive about the fact it felt as though I was catching a glimpse of what Alex might look like in a few years, silver at his temples, laugh lines around his eyes and mouth.

I felt robbed that I'd never see that.

"Are you sure you don't want the front?" I confirmed as we pulled into a gas station. I'd already offered what felt like fifty times, but it genuinely felt wrong to be sitting in the passenger seat. I didn't want to relegate Mr. James to the back. It felt disrespectful.

"I'm sure." Alex's dad was entertained. His eyes danced the same way Alex's did, lips curled up. "Though I am a bit parched."

"Oh! Right." I unbuckled. Before I could even touch the door handle, the older gentleman was shaking his head. I paused, confused.

"Alex?"

"Yeah, yeah. Iced tea and lemonade. I know, old man." He rolled his eyes good-naturedly, shoving his own door open. He was dressed in blue jeans today. Jeans that cupped his thighs so obscenely they should be arrested. The outline of his cock was difficult to ignore—easier, knowing his dad was nearby.

Still challenging though.

Especially when my ass was a little sore from sitting on it.

Once out of the car, Alex leaned back into the space. "You want anything, baby?"

I shrank, glancing surreptitiously toward his dad. His very hot, very nosy dad. Who was watching us. Smirking. "Um."

"Water? Juice? A donut? Whatever you want."

"Water is fine."

"Alright." Alex paused. His pale gaze darted to his dad in the back seat before his attention was mine again. After a second of deliberation, he pecked me on the mouth. "Be right back."

My hands drifted up, tracing the memory of his touch as he disappeared. The door slid shut with a thunk.

And then it was just me.

Me and Alex's dad.

His *hot* dad.

Who was hot.

Did I mention that?

Flustered, I didn't know what to do. Was it polite to speak to him? I'd never met the parents of anyone I'd dated before. Not that *we* were dating. I was under no illusions. Roderick's family didn't count. They were practically my aunt and uncle.

"It's—" I started, unsure what I was about to say, at the same time Alex's father spoke.

"It's a pleasure to meet you," he purred. He leaned forward, an imposing figure—or he would've been, if his energy didn't feel so welcoming.

"Likewise." *Likewise? Who the hell even says that? C'mon, George.* I twisted to look at him. "Alex is uh…um. He's—" Oh god. Why had I began the sentence this way? Anything that came out of my mouth was going to sound horrible.

"Alex is smitten with you," Mr. James finished for me. My heart lurched. I shook my head.

"No. He—I mean."

"You don't need to be so nervous around me," he reassured, eyes dancing. "I'm not going to bite."

"It's not that—it's just…"

Apparently more time had passed than I'd accounted for, because Alex's door swung open and Alex was leaning back into the car.

"He thinks you're hot," Alex said. "Don't tease him."

Like an idiot, I belatedly realized that the window had been rolled down and he must've heard the whole thing.

Alex was the one teasing. The shit.

"I do not—" I gasped, offended. "That would be *wildly* inappropriate."

Mr. James chuckled. "Would it? Considering he'll look like this in a few years if another puck doesn't mar his pretty face." He gestured toward himself. "Maybe slightly less handsome though," he added with a wink.

"Ha, *ha*. So *fucking* funny." Alex rolled his eyes, moving to chuck the aluminum tea can he was holding at his dad. Only he paused, rethinking the motion, and carefully handed it to him instead. Suddenly, the air in the car thickened, tension growing.

Until that moment everything had been lighthearted.

"I'm not going to break," Mr. James growled, popping the tab on his drink with a grumpy huff. It was so unlike his earlier amusement I shrank back. "Jesus Christ. You drive me nuts."

"Feeling's mutual, asshole." Alex flipped him off, and I was genuinely shocked speechless. If I'd flipped my mom off I don't know what would've happened. The apocalypse probably. Even thinking about it made me shudder.

Was this…because of the car accident Alex had mentioned?

I wasn't surprised if that was the case. Alex cared a lot, was attentive. I could assume he'd been babying his dad the same way he babied me when I was hurt.

Alex turned his attention back to me, offering me a bottled water after popping the lid open. "I got you some fruit too," he said. "They had these fruit cup things? I dunno. I hoped you'd like it." The "fruit cup" he was talking about looked genuinely delicious. Cherries, peach slices, a few chunks of pineapple. The perfect snack to stress eat while Alex play-not-play-fought with his dad.

"I also got you a donut." He handed me a paper bag. "You don't have to eat it if you don't want to. Just…you know. *Variety*. I figured I'd give you options."

"Thank you," I said.

"Oh, aaaaand I got you more pickles." My favorite brand. Yum! I'd left the other jar in his fridge. A fact that had filled me with immense sadness. "Not apology ones. These are 'good morning' pickles."

"Thank you." My cheeks still felt flushed.

"Where are my pickles?" Mr. James teased from the back. Alex's cheeks darkened, his tan skin adorably pink.

"I'd bet it's in your pants, Dad," he responded without missing a beat.

"Alex!" His dad scoffed, offended. I nearly choked on air. Alex ignored him, smooched my cheek, then disappeared to fill up the tank.

The rehearsal dinner went off without a hitch. Alex invited me as his plus-one—officially, and to June's utmost glee. He'd had this eager grin on his face the whole time. Smile growing even brighter as he stood beside Roderick at the altar as his best man. Juniper, as always, looked incredible in her usual puffy skirt and cowboy boots.

She kept adjusting her dress—not her wedding dress, at least, not yet—as she walked down the dirt path that they'd made the "aisle". "When you get fake boobs, no one ever warns you about the boob sweat," she whispered to me as she passed where I waited in the audience.

I snorted, and she beamed.

Even though it wasn't the real ceremony, Roderick cried. Tears dripped down his face, smearing across his chin. Snotty, and hardly attractive at all— and yet, Juniper looked at him like he was the epitome of beauty itself.

Roderick wasn't the only one with wet eyes. Mr. James sniffled as he clung to her arm, leading her toward the wooden platform that would act as the altar. He kissed her head before parting and taking his seat.

Alex's eyes took in his sister, full of love, his smile blinding.

There was no denying how proud of this he was—as the person who had planned it. Alex was devoted. It was obvious in the way he ducked his head, his heart in his eyes and on his sleeve, for once.

The night came to a close with stars in the sky and the wedding party populating their tents early in preparation for the early morning—and ceremony—the next day.

I should've been with them.

Should've joined Alex in our tent. Should've soaked up his heat and taken advantage of my last night here in Hocking Hills with him. But…I couldn't.

Not yet.

Not without speaking to someone about the feelings that had plagued me since the dirty socks—and my epiphany.

I'd learned that being vulnerable was the price for love.

And even though I'd spent my entire adult life projecting perfection, when I felt truly lost—the first person I went hunting for was my mother.

I found her where I always did, in the kitchen, bustling about in a dress as colorful as her personality. Mom smiled my way, though her smile dimmed when she saw the expression on my face.

"What's wrong?" Her voice was uncharacteristically soft.

I shut the door behind me, debating if I was going to open my mouth or not. Ignoring it would be easy—in its own way. I could pretend that this was what we'd set out for it to be.

Casual.

Temporary.

A lesson for both of us.

But I didn't want to.

I needed to tell someone what Alex meant to me or it was going to eat me from the inside out.

"I'm in love with Alex." The words were barely a whisper. Saying them aloud hurt, but it was freeing too. Like a weight that had been constricting my chest was gone. I could breathe again, an overwhelmed gasp escaping—and evolving—into something more like a sob.

"Oh, *George*," Mom's voice was soft. "I know."

I fell into her arms, tears soaking into the floral of her dress, my truths laid bare. "I love him but I can't have him," I choked, arms stiff at my sides. She enveloped me, squeezing me close, the warmth of her round frame as soothing as only a mother's embrace could be. As always, she smelled like sunscreen, cookies, hairspray, and laundry detergent.

"Why not?" she asked, hand scrubbing over my back. Back and forth. Like I was five years old with a skinned knee. Like I was still the little boy whose problems could be fixed with a Band-Aid and a kiss.

"Because I'm *leaving*."

And I was.

I was leaving.

It felt more and more real with every hour that passed.

Tomorrow night. The ceremony would wrap up and I'd be on my way to the airport—and back to my life. My real life. The tall, shimmering buildings. The job I'd worked so hard for. The ex that wouldn't leave me alone. The horrible, awful texts on my phone. The career I'd stubbornly stuck with, though now I was starting to wonder why.

Back to the same fucking Mondays I'd suffered through for nearly a decade.

At least I'd see Mr. Pickles, right?

And Missy.

And my manga collection.

My bright points.

And yet…I felt…so fucking empty.

So empty.

"What if you didn't?" Mom said, still rubbing back and forth. "What if you stayed? What then?" I had never in a million years expected her to say that. The same woman who bragged about me to every single one of her clients. That made a point to mention my job and my "big city life" every chance she got.

I was…confused to say the least.

Wrong-footed.

"I've spent…I've spent so long building the life I have." My voice broke. "Won't it…mean all of it was for nothing if I leave it behind? That all those years I was away were a waste of time. That moving to New York in the first place is just…another failure? Like—" It was hard to breathe all of a sudden, all my rawest insecurities laid bare. "Like Brendon."

"Sweetheart." Mom's voice was firm, her arms tightening. "Life is about the journey, not the destination."

"W-what?"

"It takes a lot of bravery to change paths so far down the road," she murmured softly. "But turning back when you've realized you're going the wrong direction? That's not failure—it's wisdom. There's no shame in changing your mind. It's how we grow. If you never try new things you might never discover what matters most."

"I could get a job here, yes. But I'd be starting from scratch, abandoning everything I've built. And why? Because I spent a week in the woods with a stranger, and decided I was in love with him? It's illogical," I said.

"So?" She squeezed me tight. "The best things in life are."

My chest hurt, and my worry slipped free. The same worry that'd kept me up at night for years. The worry that made all my other concerns pale in comparison.

When I spoke, my voice was barely more than a croak.

"You won't...you won't be less...proud of me?"

"Oh, honey, no." She shook her head, and her blonde hair tickled my cheek. "*Fuck* no." I laughed, but the sound was brittle.

"You won't get to brag about me to your friends anymore."

Mom pulled back briefly to glare at me. "I will brag about you no matter what you're doing—no matter where you're doing it."

My eyes burned.

"I want you to do what will make you happy—not what you think will make me or anyone else happy. You've always been such a sweet, loyal boy. You put everyone else first. But maybe it's time to do something selfish. Maybe it's time to choose your own happiness." She wasn't the best with words. Wasn't a philosopher. Wasn't a psychologist. Wasn't my therapist.

And yet...her words struck a chord. Like she'd reached inside my chest and enveloped my heart in her embrace directly. I was no longer cold. No longer half as worried—even if I was nervous. So fucking nervous.

Maybe it's time to choose your own happiness.

"Alex...makes me happy," I confessed. "Even when he pisses me off, he makes me happy."

"I know."

There was a lump in my throat that I couldn't seem to swallow. It clogged me up from the inside, made me feel like a stuck drain. "What if he doesn't want me too? What if I implode my entire fucking life—"

"Then we'll pick up the pieces and build something new."

We'll pick up the pieces.

We.

As though she considered my problems hers. Like I was part of a team. A family.

God.

Had I really let myself forget what that was like? Suddenly, the We Hate Brendon Club made a lot more sense. All this time…had they been waiting for me to remember that I wasn't alone? That I could rely on them? That they were in my corner?

I was struck again, the levity of that driving the breath right from my lungs.

"If he wanted me…wouldn't he say something?" I asked, trembling. "He's the most honest person I've ever met. I…trust him. Don't you think he would—"

"Alex is a nice boy," Mom said. "But he's *not* perfect. Maybe…" Mom's voice was loving, her rubbing continuing. "A lot of these worries could be solved if you'd talk to him?"

I quaked as I nodded. "I know. I just—"

"Brendon did a number on you, I know."

"That's not it." For once, Brendon hadn't factored into this at all. "I'm scared I care more about him than he cares about me. That I've misread this. That I'll ruin what could be a good memory by being honest."

"Honesty very rarely, if ever, ruins good things," Mom promised.

Mom's advice was helpful, but difficult to implement. As I retired to our tent after showering off my emotional funk, I couldn't seem to get my mouth to open. Not when Alex was already stressed, and on the phone—despite the late hour—talking to a vendor. *The night before the wedding.* Apparently the company that was supposed to be dropping off the chairs for the guests early that morning was pulling out.

It was wildly inappropriate and unprofessional. Which was what Alex told them, an angry fire in his eyes, his jaw jumping with tension as he sprawled on our mattress, legs spread. Immediately, I took a step back, ready to retreat and give him privacy but he shook his head. Deliberately, while he was politely, but sternly telling off the vendor, he patted his thigh in invitation.

I took a seat, pleased when some of the stress in his frame eased the moment he had me in his lap. His lips found my neck, a single peck that sent a shiver down my spine.

"I understand that you are apologetic," he responded, kissing my neck again. "But being *sorry* doesn't change the fact that my sister's wedding is tomorrow morning and we now have no seating. If it's a matter of money—"

He and the vendor went back and forth for a while until they found a compromise. Benches would be delivered as opposed to the original chairs. Which was frustrating, but workable.

Alex hung up the phone with a groan.

"Jesus Christ." He looked stressed, sweat at his temples, his hair mussed from the way he'd been angrily tugging on it. "That was a nightmare."

"I'm sorry," I apologized, shifting on his lap to alleviate the pressure between my legs. Apparently, listening to him go all "corporate" on the phone while I was straddling his thighs really did it for me. His voice went growly and flat with anger—a tone I'd never heard him take.

He was kindness personified.

"*Are* you sorry?" Alex shifted his hips up, our dicks aligning. "You don't *feel* very sorry." He arched a brow, and I flushed, chastened. "Mmm, that wasn't an admonishment, baby. I'm just…" His phone dropped to the floor unceremoniously as Alex found my hips, fingers digging in. "Really? Seeing me pissed off really revs your engine, does it?"

My nose scrunched, because the question itself was horrendous—even if the answer was yes.

"Now I *really* wish I could take you to one of my hockey games," Alex laughed. "They're just for fun, but I can't help but get pissed." I shivered, ignoring the sad reality of that statement and instead focusing on the part that mattered. "You like that? You like me mad?" One of Alex's hands cupped my throat, giving it a squeeze. "Fuck, I should've guessed. You always fight with me. Is that why? You wanna get me all riled up. Want me to fuck you like I hate you?"

Okay. I hadn't realized that was a thing I desired until he said it.

Breathless, all thoughts of talking about our relationship flew out the window. Alex growled, jerking me onto the mattress with a grunt I felt right between my legs.

And then he made good on his promise, yanking my pants down with no finesse. Insistent, lubed fingers snuck between my cheeks. His cock followed—filling me up till he was all I could think about.

Till he was all I could breathe.

Till I was simply a hole for him to pound his frustrations out on. Eyes rolled back, his hand covered my mouth to keep me from alerting the neighboring tents to what he was doing. With feigned disregard for my wishes—Alex fucked me brutally enough, I swear to god, my ass was bruised.

Sweat dripped down his temple onto the mattress, his blue eyes wild.

Betraying him, as always, because despite how rough he was being, there was no denying the affection in his gaze. The awareness, never to push too hard. Never to hurt me.

When he finished, my hole felt as sore as he'd wanted it to. Well-fucked, stretched, and full of his cum. He tucked his fingers up inside me, scraping it out, then made eye contact as he slurped his own cum right from his filthy fingers. He sank back over my body, reaching for his cock and aiming it at my hole again like he planned on shoving back in despite the fact it was only half hard.

I was a limp sated mess, and therefore didn't protest when Alex's other hand covered my mouth again.

"You want my cock back in your pussy?" he purred against my ear, his crown notched against my loose hole. "Want me to breed you nice and full, Duchess?"

"Guyyyysss," a tired, annoyed voice echoed—way too close for comfort. "Seriously? Some of us are trying to sleep."

I didn't know who had spoken—and was glad for that. A horrified *eep* escaped me.

"Fuck off, Martin," Alex called—before burying his face in the back of my neck with a dry laugh. "Apparently our 'quiet' isn't so quiet," he chuckled, totally unrepentant about the trauma he'd caused his extended family.

"I want to die," I told him when he removed his hand from my mouth. "I want to—" Alex put his hand back.

"None of that." He clucked his tongue, kissing the back of my neck. Still, his cock pushed against my ass. "We're just sleeping," he promised. "Gonna fill you up so you can rest."

He was shameless.

Seriously shameless.

And I loved him for it.

Just like I loved the puff of his breath on the back of my neck, echoing in the silence as Alex settled in for the night. His fingers looped my wrist, playing with the bracelet there absentmindedly.

Awake, despite the fact he'd promised we were only sleeping.

His cock was softening inside me. It slipped out of its own accord—a shame, really.

"Are you asleep?" Alex asked several long, quiet minutes later.

Now's your chance.

"No."

"Good." He pecked my neck. And then he was moving away from me. I frowned, twisting to glare at him only to be floored by what I saw him doing. His watch came off with an easy click, like he'd done it so many times it took no effort at all. He was oddly reserved as he crowded against my back again and wound the watch band around my wrist. It was a tad big. He had to close it all the way on the last hole.

"Looks good on you," Alex said, running his fingers across the band, underneath it, against the sensitive fragile skin where my veins stood stark and blue.

"Alex?" My heart skittered as he linked our fingers together, pulled my hand up, and leaned over me so he could kiss along my wrist.

"This was my grandpa's," Alex explained between tender presses of dry lips. "Dad gave it to me when I turned sixteen. He'd worn it his entire life until that point." Another kiss. "Grandpa was dead and gone by that point—a horrible man, if you listen to my dad's stories. But still…important."

My heart skipped a beat.

"It was the only nice thing grandpa ever did for him," Alex murmured, lips skimming up along my palm. "He told him it was a 'symbol' of what he expected from him."

"And your dad…gave it to you."

"He said it was because I'm important," Alex replied. "That he wanted to give me the most important thing he owned, so even though he couldn't be around as much—busy as he was—I'd always know he loved me."

My eyes were burning. Which was unfair. Because this was Alex's heart-wrenching story, not mine. And yet…

He kissed each of my fingers, still looming over me.

"He could've died," Alex's voice cracked. "And he's okay now—but I can't…" He pressed his face to my skin, body shuddering. Seeking comfort. From me. Like simply holding my hand, simply seeing the watch on my wrist, was helping. "When it was lost, I kept thinking what if…what if this was all I had of him?"

"Alex." I didn't dare hug him. Even though he was quick to offer them, I got the feeling when he felt this…torn apart he didn't appreciate being huddled. Not the way I did. "I think that's perfectly understandable, given the circumstances."

"You do?" Alex clutched my hand to his face, hiding against it, his watch hanging on my wrist.

"It sounds like June isn't the only one that's had a rough few months."

He laughed, but his voice cracked. "Y-yeah."

And then he curled around my back again, his big frame cuddling up like an overgrown octopus. "Thank you for finding it," he said softly.

He'd already thanked me.

"I told you not to do that," I sighed. Alex snickered—lighter this time.

"Whatever guy you date next better treat you so fucking good," Alex growled. "Or I'll fly to New York and—" He cut himself off. "I shouldn't say things like that."

"Shouldn't you?" My heart was skipping.

Now, George.

Just tell him.

Tell him how you feel—

"We should sleep," Alex deflected. "We've got a big day tomorrow. If you want to wake up early with me, we could get ready in June's cabin together?" He unknowingly interrupted me, his brain back in planning mode. "Otherwise, I'll hardly see you. There's too much to do, unfortunately."

It was our last day together.

Of course I was going to wake up early to spend what time with him I could.

"I want to," I admitted, ashamed that I'd missed my opportunity once again.

"Good." Alex squeezed me tight, his earlier sadness forgotten. He cleaned me up with wet wipes he'd stolen from somewhere, making sure I was safe and comfortable before we actually fell asleep.

He left his watch on my wrist.

All night long.

I returned it in the morning, obviously.

But I felt the whisper of its touch.

Like an omen almost, of what I couldn't have—but wanted, more desperately than I'd ever wanted anything.

Illogical as it was.

Thirty
Alex

JUNIPER HAD NEVER BEEN more beautiful than she was at her wedding. Her dress puffed around her calves, exposing the white cowboy boots she'd had custom made. Her veil dragged behind her in the dirt, long enough I was relieved it hadn't managed to trip anyone up all day. She'd ended up picking the ultra long one for dramatic effect.

She didn't mention boob sweat.

Not once.

Dad ugly cried the entire time he led her down the aisle, and Roderick did the same. Both of them were loud as hell, tears slipping down their cheeks. It was impossible not to react, and I found myself shedding a tear or two as well, especially when Roderick began "lasso-walking" Juniper the last ten or so steps, and the benches full of wedding guests erupted into booming, eager applause.

In a blink, it was over.

Just like that.

Years of preparation all leading to the single, perfect moment that was Juniper and Roderick exchanging rings, and kisses, with a canopy of leaves—and all their loved ones, all in one place.

I felt lighter, already.

Lighter still as they ran down the aisle together, arms held high, more cheers echoing through the picturesque morning. Even Mom had showed up—standing on the front row beside Dad wearing her signature sunglasses and a soft smile.

It felt like a *perfect* moment.

A movie moment.

Like from an eighties rom-com where everything turned out in the end.

I was floating when I met George's gaze—somewhere in the middle of the crowd, tucked between his parents and siblings. His eyes were as fathomless as always. Surreptitiously, he glanced around, searching for the missing exhibitionist from last night, probably—before he raised his hand in a shy thumbs up, aimed my way.

I mirrored the motion, heart fluttering like crazy.

I couldn't stop thinking about how my watch had looked on his wrist. And how heavy it felt now. Heavy in a way it never had before. Like it wasn't mine anymore.

Couldn't stop thinking about the way he'd watched me as I'd shaved this morning, all dark, lovely eyes. Or the way he'd offered to help me get the corner of my jaw—then let me return the favor, steady swipes of my blade on his skin.

I didn't see him again until later. Mom left early. We'd done family pictures—Dad, Juniper, Roderick, and I. The whole time I'd felt the empty spot at my side keenly. I'd done my best not to focus on it, however—instead making sure Juniper felt seen and appreciated on her big day, even though my hovering was apparently pissing her off.

Because by the time the photos were over and it was time to join the reception, she confronted me. "If you don't stop looming over me I'm going to scream."

"I'm only—"

"Helping, I know." She laughed then smacked my chest. "And you've been *very* helpful." Her tone softened. "The most helpful. And I appreciate it, so, so, so much." It was an uncharacteristic show of genuine emotion. We'd had way too many of these moments lately. But I supposed that was what happened at weddings. We both shifted on our feet, uncomfortable. "But I will be here tomorrow for you to celebrate with. And I'll be here the day after that—and the day after that—and the day after—"

"Okay, I get it."

"So go…I dunno. Fuck off and have fun with your date."

"Oh my god."

"I feel sufficiently supported and loved." She gave my chest a pat. "Really." I sighed, tension bleeding away as I nodded. "Besides—you got to hog Dad all day yesterday, and I've barely seen him."

"You see me every day," Dad dead-panned, where he was not even pretending he wasn't eavesdropping to our left.

"I'm trying to make Alex not feel guilty for spending time with George instead of me," June groaned, hands flying up. "You're not helping."

"Right." Dad adopted an air of mock seriousness. "Go forth. Be gay."

"He's bisexual," Roderick supplied helpfully, still clinging to Juniper's arm. He was the one that was truly hovering. But when he did it, it was cute, apparently.

"Go forth and be bi," Dad corrected himself.

"Not too bi, though," June teased. "Wouldn't want to traumatize any more of our cousins."

"It was one time, and one cousin." I rolled my eyes. "And I shouldn't have told you."

"But I'm soooo glad you did. You know Mama loves her drama." She blew me a kiss, and I stormed off, eager to find George—especially now that the resulting guilt felt far, far away.

And yet our timer kept tick, tick, ticking.

George was, as always, with his family. This time, Joe. Joe, who was staring morosely down at his white button up—that was now red, seeing as he'd apparently spilled wine on it. George was dabbing at it with a paper napkin and making fussy, grumpy sounds.

"It's not going to come out."

I approached slowly, catching Joe's attention and pressing a finger to my lips so he wouldn't react. His eyes widened, lighter blue than George's. A little smile curled across his lips—a smile that would have betrayed my presence if George had not been mid-mother-henning.

"I swear to god," he griped, "you need a bib—"

Leaning in close, I held my breath so as not to alert him to my presence at his back. He didn't notice. Joe's eyes danced.

Three...two...one—

"*Boo.*" When I pinched George's sides, he squawked, arms flapping. He whipped his head to glare at me, spooked.

"You scared the *fuck* outta me," he gasped, the napkin he'd been holding fluttering to the ground.

"You helping Joe?" I murmured, arms sliding around his waist and pulling him back against my chest where he belonged. Pressing a kiss to that long, mole-speckled neck, I melted—finally feeling as though I could actually settle.

Recharging.

"Helping would be a stretch," George sighed. "I've made him a smidge less wet. Everything else is a lost cause."

Joe frowned. "Won't kill me."

"Wasn't that suit a rental?" George snarked.

"Oh." Joe's brow furrowed. "Might kill me."

"I'll take care of it," I promised, lighter on my feet than I'd been since I'd parted with George this morning.

"Really?" Joe perked up, focusing his puppy eyes on me. "You'd do that?"

"Absolutely."

"Thanks." Joe offered me a fist bump of gratitude—before he wandered off to presumably congratulate Roderick and June.

"Why aren't you with your family?" George didn't turn around to face me, still looking at the dessert table, though his pink ears betrayed him as always.

"I was banished." I gave him another squeeze before pulling back so I could do the turning myself. He was pliant in my grip, allowing me to maneuver him until we were chest to chest with no complaints.

"Banished?" George arched a judgy brow, though he was staring at my collar, and not me. And that simply wouldn't do. I grabbed his chin, squeezing and tipping his head up so he'd be forced to meet my gaze.

"Banished," I confirmed. "Apparently June is sick of me."

George snorted. "Believable."

He didn't mean that.

We both knew he didn't mean that.

I grinned, not taking the bait.

"I feel like I haven't seen you in years," I sighed, thumb skimming over his bottom lip.

"It's been two hours."

Two hours of dealing with my mom, with the ceremony, getting my picture taken—which I hated. Two hours George-less.

"Two hours too long. Dance with me?" It was a formal request, dripping with affection—and ignoring the ammo my pretty kitty always seemed to have loaded. His mouth was as sharp as it was soft. "Please?"

He melted, blue eyes meeting mine, his flush splotchy and endearing where it smeared across his cheeks and throat. "O-okay."

I pulled him toward the dance floor, waiting along the edge for the next song to play. June had wanted to forgo the whole first-dance tradition, and instead, had opted for a more group oriented approach. Therefore, the live orchestra had been playing since the reception had begun, even before she'd arrived.

George was a horrible dancer.

Which was surprising.

How the hell had he been a cheerleader?

Or in theater, for that matter?

It was a mystery.

He stepped on my feet more often than not—punctuated by apologies dripping in mortification. I didn't chastise him though. What were a few missing toes in the face of his affection? After the third time he'd stomped on my foot, he whined, this low, upset sound.

"I'm done. I can't do this anymore. It's too—"

Golden-boy George was too embarrassed.

"Here." I jerked him upward, lifting his body up and against mine, until his feet settled on top of my own. "Now you don't need to worry."

The motion silenced his protests, his eyes full of confusion, and then ultimately relief when we started to spin around in graceful circles, and no more toes were abused.

"Everyone's going to see," he muttered, though he didn't step off my feet. The weight of him was nice. The dress shoes I'd bought him were bound to leave scuffs on mine, but I didn't mind.

In fact, I'd put them on a pedestal. Right next to the family photos we'd taken in the woods.

"No one's watching your feet, baby," I promised, hands wrapped around him to keep him steady. I stole a grope of his ass, wagging my brows until he giggled. He quickly caught himself, adopting a scowl instead. A scowl that was ruined by the light in his eyes, and the way his lips kept twitching like he wanted to smile.

"Monogamy is a good look on you," June's voice startled me out of my staring match with George's mouth. I snorted, and George flushed, glancing toward her sheepishly.

"Fuck off," I laughed.

"That's not a very nice thing to say to your sister on her wedding day." June and Roderick were spinning around in lazy circles off beat. Which…if that wasn't a symbol of why they worked, I didn't know what was.

"Yeah, that's not going to work anymore. Not after you're the one that chased me off."

"Touché." June's eyes were warm as she ran them over the two of us. "Cute," she said simply, before leading Roderick away—and leaving us alone.

The rest of the afternoon was full of little comments.

Mrs. M told us we were "quite the pair." Mr. M grunted. Lacey and Joe both offered me a thumbs up—at different times, and with varying degrees of enthusiasm. Mavis was…as always…not impressed by me stealing her uncle—but hell, who could blame her? In a way, I was jealous of myself too.

That I was the one who got to hold George-Arthur Milton close. That I was the one he fed bites of his wedding cake to—germs be damned. That he accepted my kisses. That he wore my hickeys. That when he smiled, it was for me—and me alone.

It all came to a stop way too soon.

The ceremony ended.

June and Roderick departed to go on their honeymoon.

The vendors started the arduous process of taking things down.

And then it was just…pieces.

The scraps of what had been a monumental day—a perfect week, over a year of meticulous planning—strewn across the campground like they were as temporary as party confetti. The cousins were mostly packed up, and Mrs. M was chatting with Roderick's parents. They were determined to clear up the cabins themselves—to "save me money"—despite the fact I'd hired a company to do that, and it really wouldn't.

I didn't have it in me to fight them on it.

George was silent at my side, leaning into me, his eyes distant.

As distant as they'd been the night I'd made him a picnic and he'd stared at the stars.

Like he was miles away—even though he was right here.

"Do you have a ride?" I asked, heart in my throat.

It wasn't a question I wanted to ask.

"To the airport?" George clarified, blinking out of his reverie. "Yes."

"Oh." I was…disappointed. He could tell, because his tone softened.

"But I already asked Lacey if you could take me." It was presumptuous of him. Which was totally unlike him. A fact we both knew. "She said yes."

"Perfect." I pressed a kiss to his cheek, and he made a soft noise he probably didn't mean for me to hear. Pleased. That was what that sound was. George was pleased. "When do we need to leave?" I asked.

His lips pursed.

That faraway look was back as he sighed.

"Now?" he sighed.

"Now?" I hadn't expected that. So soon? "As in…right now. This second," I clarified.

"Pretty much. Especially if we're dropping your dad home first."

"Dad can wait." That wasn't something I'd ever thought I'd say. Immediately, I felt selfish. But then I pushed that thought aside. "I'm sure he wouldn't mind a detour to the airport." The last thing I wanted was to stress George out and make him worry about missing his flight home.

Home.

To a place that wasn't here.

With me.

Because our time was nearly up.

Sucking in a breath, I tried to calm my racing heart. "Grab your backpack?

I'll go get him."

"What about your tent?" George frowned.

"One of the perks of having money," I shrugged. "It'll get taken care of."

"Okay." George wavered, before he pressed a kiss to my cheek. "I'll go say bye to my mom then?"

"Sounds good," I agreed, missing him, even though he was right next to me. "I'll meet you at the car."

"Okay."

"Okay," I echoed.

"Okay," George said a third time. He stood there for a second, mouth opening and closing—then he sighed, shoulders slumping. "*Okay.*" He sounded defeated, disappointed in himself, and I wasn't sure why. George stalked off before we could get any more awkward, and I watched him go, chest squeezing tight.

Why couldn't I…

Why couldn't I keep him?

You know why, I reminded myself.

There's a reason you only offered a temporary relationship.

You don't want him to get sick of you, do you?

"Fuck." I groaned, fingers biting into my hair and tugging. He was out of sight now, and that loss nearly sent me right to my knees.

Dad was happy as he'd climbed into the back seat. The flower on his lapel had wilted, as had mine, and his usually impeccable hair was disheveled. There was an air of exhaustion about him, but that wasn't unusual. What was, however, was the fact it had been caused by happiness, rather than healing.

He was getting better.

Able to move about now—no bruises in sight.

"This is a refreshing change of pace." He hummed a jaunty tune to himself, buckling up with a prim wiggle. "I never thought I'd see the day you'd put yourself first. And I have *George* to thank for it. New favorite son status: achieved."

I groaned. "Please don't." I leaned my head against the steering wheel. "Don't make jokes like that. I just—fuck."

"Alex…" Dad blinked, nonchalant as ever. "You haven't told him you want to keep dating him, have you? I'm surprised. Considering you're totally inseparable, even when you aren't fucking like rabbits."

"*Jesus* Christ." So he knew about *that* then. I blamed Martin. Or June? Fuck. Maybe both of them. Everyone. I blamed everyone—myself included. It wasn't like I tried to hide how into George I was—or like I'd been particularly sneaky about our nighttime escapades. Last night I'd had less than zero fucks to give.

It was still embarrassing to get called out by my dad though. Especially when he was giving me these *knowing* looks—like he understood that this was different for me, even without me outright admitting it.

My cheeks went hot and I glanced out the window, making sure George wasn't approaching. I was terrified he might overhear. "It…I mean. He's—"

"Only here for the wedding, I know." Dad's voice was sad. "You know, once I—"

"Do not take this opportunity to tell me about your many flings, please. It's not as motivating as you think."

"I wasn't going to—" Dad laughed, wry and soft. He was notoriously a bachelor. His reputation preceded him wherever we went—a fact that was not at all embarrassing. Nope. Totally not. "Okay, maybe I was. But I was only trying to reassure you that long-distance is a totally viable option."

"I don't need advice," I sighed, even though I kind of did. Laying my head back on the cool steering wheel, I took a moment to breathe. "I know what I need to do. I just…need to stop being a fucking bitch and do it."

I needed to drop George off at the airport.

Needed to let this be what we'd agreed it was.

Needed to stop wanting more.

Needed to—

"It's okay to be scared, Alex," Dad's hand was warm against my back. Apparently he'd leaned between the seats, because his voice was louder too. It felt good in a way only a loving parent's reassurance could. "Trusting people can be terrifying."

"*Stooop.*"

I knew that better than anyone. I hadn't trusted anyone outside my family in years. Roderick, yes, but only because I could see how much June loved him. Aside from that, I'd never let myself open up. Not the way I had with George. And that was fucking terrifying.

When I was with George, all the "masks" I wore fell away. If he ended up rejecting me, it meant I wasn't good enough. That I really *was* too much. That the last shred of hope I had left would wither and die.

And if that happened?

I had no idea what I'd become.

I could handle being disliked by my previous partners.

But…George?

I couldn't survive that.

Right now, he liked me. But like I'd told him—he'd only known me on my good days. And a week was…not long enough for him to get tired of me.

Except that you already admitted you've shown him more than you've ever shown anyone else, that same voice whispered. *And he's still here. Maybe that means something.*

"What if he…" my voice came out choked. "What if he decides he doesn't—"

The passenger door opened and my words got stuck.

"What if he decides he doesn't what?" George inquired as he slid into his spot. His backpack was between his legs, his upper body drowning in one of my t-shirts. He'd changed clothes. Apparently. When he'd been saying his goodbyes. And his clothing of choice was an item of mine. That he would… clearly be taking home with him.

I loved that he hadn't asked permission to do that.

Almost as much as I loved his flawless timing.

I didn't want to get into this with my dad. I couldn't believe how close I'd gotten to just that—for years I'd refused to open up to him, careful to maintain my perfect son persona.

It was exhausting to feel like I lived in a constant state of crisis. A fact, in a way, George understood. It was part of why we got along so well. He did the same thing with his family—only better.

Christ, we made such a fucked up pair.

"What if he…" I didn't know what to say. Didn't know how to pretend like I hadn't been about to talk about George.

Dad saved the day, patting George's shoulder in greeting before sliding back into his seat. "Alex was concerned that Roderick might not be able to make it for their next game."

"Oh," George frowned. He glanced at me, a worried look in his eyes. *Are you okay?* he mouthed. I smiled and nodded, even though I wasn't.

Lying.

Like the coward I was.

Lying about the big stuff, like I'd told George I hated.

Who was the hypocrite now?

"You got everything?" I confirmed, reaching over to tweak his nose. He batted me off with a grumpy sound. I felt better immediately. The unease that'd settled cold and heavy around me dissipated.

"Yes." George's grimple winked at me. "Not my suit though. Mom said she'll ship it to me. And my pickles," he sighed. "Those are at your house."

"That's good." And it was. It was totally, completely awesome. Totally. Yep. Totally great that he lived far enough away that my gifts would need to be shipped. Totally awesome that the next time I opened my fridge I was probably going to break down when I saw his goddamn pickles. "I'd be happy to do it."

"You've done enough," George promised, buckling himself up, then turning his attention to my dad. "Don't you dare ship my half-eaten pickles to me."

"Well, now I want to."

"Good afternoon, Mr. James," George said formally—like the nerd he was. I snorted, and my dad looked amused.

"Where's my 'good afternoon'?" I teased. "I wouldn't mind being called Mr. James."

"*Alex*," George growled, embarrassed.

"What? It wouldn't be the kinkiest thing we've done."

"Alex!" George smacked me, and I grinned.

Dad knew anyway. There was no need to hold back. Besides…I was holding back enough, as it was, my true feelings squeezing like serpents around my heart.

The trees blurred by, sunlight dappling through the branches as I pulled out of the parking lot and onto the narrow, winding road that would lead us back to civilization.

It felt weird.

All of this did.

The wedding was over. June was married. Roderick was officially my brother now. Everything I'd worked so hard for had simply…ended. Even weirder, was the fact that my heart hurt.

This giant, uncomfortable cramp in my chest.

I caught myself rubbing it a few times—and George flashed me another concerned look, but didn't comment.

Dad put headphones in, which was genuinely kind of him. He zoned out, gazing through the window and allowing us what little privacy we could have, considering the inside of the cab was a shared space.

George was…unaffected.

His usually expressive face was oddly blank as he watched the trees whipping by. I didn't know what to say to break the silence. I didn't know if I should. If I should pretend like this was normal. Like the idea of sending him away wasn't breaking my heart.

Like I wasn't totally, completely, irrevocably in love with him.

Even though it'd been a week.

A fucking week.

And we'd both sworn we weren't looking for something serious.

We'd agreed this was for practice. That this week was all we'd have. All we wanted.

"Tell me about Monday," George's words were faint—faint enough I barely heard them.

"What?" I blinked, surprised. My hands tightened on the steering wheel, the crunch of the tires filling the silence.

"It's Monday," George tried again, even more stilted. "How do you…how do you start the day?"

Oh god.

My stomach tied itself in knots. Clearing my throat, I realized what he was doing. Distracting himself. Just like I'd asked him to do for me, a few short days ago. My watch had never felt heavier on my wrist—the weight of all that we'd shared in such a short time hanging over me.

"I'm up by six." I hardly recognized my own voice, it was so hoarse. "I go for a run to get some cardio in before I meet my trainer at the gym by seven thirty." Sick, heavy—my heartbeat was sluggish. "Grab a protein shake, then head to work."

"Where do you work?"

"Dublin. This gaudy high-rise with my dad. We manage financial shit. Boring, but pulls in the big bucks." That was simplifying what I did to an almost insulting degree, but I figured George already knew what I was talking about. "He's acting CEO but I'll be taking over for him in the next five years. We're in the home stretch as he prepares for retirement."

George nodded along, processing this. "Okay. You're at work," he urged me. "What next?"

"I handle the big-ticket clients personally. Get updates from my personal assistant." I continued, still feeling off-kilter. "I'll go to lunch with one of my hockey buddies, or more frequently, June and Roddy. Usually some hole-in-the-wall place—where I end up ordering a disgustingly massive amount of chicken and rice—and nothing else."

"Because of your strict diet," George replied, proving he'd been listening when I'd told him about it.

"Yep." June never stopped teasing me about how anal I was when it came to my fitness. But...I simply wasn't comfortable enough with myself to let go. At least, not the way I had this past week. It felt like I'd been living a mirrored life.

Myself, but...different.

More authentic.

Less encumbered by my own insecurities.

"I'll stay at the office late. Usually way later than is probably healthy," I admitted. "My work-life balance is not...the best."

"How late is late?"

"Depends on the day. Mondays are usually the worst though. If it's a good day...I'll hit the ice after. There's a late night drop-in session that a lot of my buddies attend because they know that's the main time I can go."

"And then?"

"Then I head home." I shrugged a shoulder, the pain in my chest only growing. "To my empty-ass house to shower. Order more take-out. Maybe pick away at something work-related to get me ahead for Tuesday. If I'm feeling horny I'll swipe through Poundr for a hookup—meet them at a hotel, and call it good." I maybe shouldn't have added that last part, but I figured George actually wanted to know. "I'm boring."

George snorted. "Nothing about you is boring."

It felt odd to have my own words thrown in my face.

Cathartic.

I sucked in a breath, eyes on the road, my lips curling into a slow smile.

"What about Tuesday?" George asked before we could fall into silence.

"Well…"

It was surprisingly busy at the airport when we arrived. A summer storm had hit about halfway to Columbus from Hocking Hills, and the stubborn gray clouds refused to let up. Miserable, warm drops dripped from above. They'd wet the car, and the road, and the scent of the storm was thick in the air. Despite the stacked nature of the Columbus airport, and the fact I couldn't see the storm as the levels above us blocked it, I could still sense its downfall.

Poetic almost.

It'd rained like this the day I met George in New York. And now the storm was here, like it was guiding him home. Symmetry.

There'd been no trains to delay our arrival.

No red lights.

Nothing to stall the inevitable.

The universe, for once, had decided to present George with good luck. If you could call this good luck. I certainly didn't. Even if I was the one stubbornly clinging to our end date out of a sick sense of self-preservation.

I'd wanted to walk George to his gate, but knew that wasn't a possibility.

So, here we were.

The car was parked behind us, windshield wipers blurring back and forth, back and forth. The thump-glide of them swiping away the last dregs of rain would've been soothing on any other occasion. Today, it, like everything else, only seemed to amplify my emotions.

A metronome of judgment.

My weakness as cold as the chill the rain left behind.

My hands were fists at my side, flexing. The bones creaking. It felt impossible all of a sudden to open my mouth. Cruelly, my silver tongue failed me right when I needed it. George had his phone again, in his pocket. He had his backpack, sans Neil—RIP. He had…everything.

My watch felt heavier than before. It itched and itched.

Beg him to stay, that awful, sneaky voice whispered.

What if it works out?

What if he—

No. No. I knew it wouldn't. I'd had it proven to me time and time again. I couldn't do this. Couldn't expect George to accept me when I couldn't even accept myself. Couldn't ask him to leave his life behind. Couldn't go back on our deal.

Couldn't—

A steady litany of insults and encouragements bounced around inside my head. Back and forth.

Idiot, idiot, idiot.

What a joke.

I was such a fucking joke.

Why would George want this?

*Why would George want **me**?*

"So…" George trailed off, looking up at me—*waiting*. I hated this. Hated that I wasn't strong enough to be brave. Hated that a small part of me thought that this could work out for us—and I wanted to squish it down.

Wanted to bury the romantic I'd unearthed, lock him behind my walls, to protect myself from the heartbreak I knew I couldn't survive.

If George said something…maybe I could push through my own fear. If he gave me a hint that he wanted more. If he crossed that distance first, maybe I could—

"So." I stared back, heart in my throat.

George opened his mouth like he wanted to say something—and I froze.

Was he?

No.

No way.

There was no way, shy, reserved George was about to tell me that he loved me. That he was going to pack up his entire fucking life and move in with me. That he didn't care that we'd barely known each other a week—he knew without a doubt that I was the one for him. That being my "practice boyfriend" would never be enough. That he wanted me—

Unless…

He did—?

And he *was*?!

But then…he sighed.

And his head dropped down.

And he looked at my feet. Silent. It wasn't rejection. But it certainly wasn't the rain-scented confession of undying love that I'd hoped for. I fiddled anxiously with the clasp on my watch.

Back and forth, back and forth.

Right.

"Do you come to New York for business often?" George inquired, without looking up. What he'd just asked was an olive branch—so I was grateful. Even if it hadn't been what I was hoping he'd say.

What I *needed* him to say.

"I'll be there again next month. I could take a few extra days…you know, if *you* were available." This was something, wasn't it? The safe route.

"I'll add it to my calendar," George said. "We're…friends, aren't we?" The question was so devastating it tore my heart in half.

"Yes." I barely recognized my own voice. "We're friends."

"Even if our arrangement is over?" George clarified.

"Of course."

It was a promise that this wasn't the last time we'd meet. Which was *good*—wonderful even. It made the weight on my chest ease some.

But it still…

It still didn't feel *right*.

"And you—when will you…um," I stumbled. "When will you be visiting Ohio next?" I asked, when I'd found my words.

"I have a week off for Christmas," George said.

A couple walking by us nearly whacked him with their suitcase. George side-stepped, leaning into my space with a nervous laugh.

Nothing about this conversation felt even remotely right.

Dad was right.

I was scared.

Scared that if I offered George myself in all my unrefined, unrestrained glory—he would find me lacking.

"Nothing before then?" My hands cupped his biceps, steadying him.

"I mean…I could take a few days for my birthday."

"When?"

"October."

I nodded, up and down. "Tell me the dates. I'll take them off too. I never did get to take you ice skating."

"Okay." George opened his mouth again—then sighed, when nothing came out. It clicked shut with finality. Instead of speaking, he reached for my face, palms cupping my cheeks. "Can I kiss you? Just one more time."

"Of course."

Just one more time.

George didn't hesitate, leaning into my space to steal a long, lingering kiss. He moved away a moment later, and I chased him, unable to let him go so soon. Longer, greedier. My tongue swiped his lower lip, begging entrance. His hands felt cold. Like he was anxious.

"*Alex*," he admonished, "we're in public."

"Don't care."

George didn't fight me. His lips parted submissively. Slipping inside him with a needy growl, felt like coming home. My fingers twisted in his hair, pulling him in tight, sharing his breaths like they were my own.

Someone whistled but I ignored it. Ignored the cars that pulled in and out of the drop-off zone. Ignored the rattle of suitcase wheels on the cement. Ignored the fact my father was watching us from the car. Ignored the elephant in the room—like the coward I was.

One hand slid to George's backpack pocket, fingering the flap as I made the last-second decision to give him something to remember me by. Something important.

This was enough.

Wasn't it?

It was something.

We'd meet again.

That was…that was enough.

Right?

I was nearly home by the time I finally realized what a colossally bad decision letting George enter that airport alone had been. He hadn't looked back. I knew, because I'd watched him until his tall silhouette disappeared inside the building.

Numb, I didn't move for a long time.

My bare wrist hung at my side.

I let the space that George was supposed to occupy echo. He should have been with me. We should have been laughing. We should be sharing rain-soaked *reunions*, not…goodbyes.

I should be hugging him, recharging—after how goddamn long today had been.

But instead…I left.

Thoughts swimming. Chest tight. That horrible ache growing as every George-less minute passed by.

I'd driven out of the terminal, confused.

Upset.

Attempting to rationalize my irrational behavior despite how impossible an endeavor that was. I knew I was trying to protect myself, like I always had. But it didn't feel like it was working.

And the walls that I'd built to keep me safe now felt like a prison.

Trapped by my own fears. Trapped by my own insecurities. The walls closing in on me, showing me in startling, devastating clarity how very alone I was.

And it was my fault.

It was always my fault.

Wasn't it?

I'd built this cage brick by brick. Shut everyone out. And it wasn't until I'd met George that I realized how fucking miserable I'd made myself.

June was right.

Fuck, I'd been saying that a lot lately.

But it was true.

She'd said, "You look happy, Alex." She'd said, "For how long?"

And I'd—fuck.

I'd blown her off. Said she was drunk. Played her words off like they weren't an omen. Like she wasn't looking into the goddamn future.

But she had been.

She'd predicted this.

She'd tried to help.

Just like Dad had tried to help, telling me, "You carry too much, Alex. Let someone else help. Jesus. You know we all want to."

And I'd blown him off too.

Hadn't believed either of them. Hadn't listened. Had thrown up more walls—and more walls—and more—

Only I wasn't brave enough to confront my demons afterward.

It wasn't until the airport was out of sight, the familiar streets blending into one another that I finally gave a name to these feelings.

Loss was palpable in the air.

Filling the car with its thick, cloying ache. Festering like mold. Heavy, and impossible to breathe around.

When Dad had gotten hurt, I'd freaked the fuck out. June too. We'd been a tangle of emotion together, constantly terrified, hovering over him—smothering him. The scare that we might've never seen him again causing us both to walk on eggshells.

And that had been…Christ. So fucking awful.

Something we never could've predicted.

Something I'd never wanted to go through again.

And here I was—choosing to lose George before I had to.

Choosing to bet on my own pessimism, because I thought it would save me from heartache.

But it couldn't.

It wasn't.

Because my heart was a gaping hole in my chest.

The stoplight turned red and I paused, heart ticking along with my blinker. To my left, on the sidewalk, a couple were running, jackets over their heads. I didn't need to hear them to know they were laughing. They looked happy. The light turned green, but I didn't move—stuck, as I watched them kiss beneath the blanket of their makeshift umbrellas.

I'd almost…

I'd almost had that.

And I'd…

Let him go.

My vision began to blur. The next handful of roads blended into one another, my body operating on autopilot as I headed toward home. *Home*, where I could lick my wounds in private. Home. Alone. Without my Georgie. With only the memory of his presence, and the way he'd made my world so much brighter.

Home, with his half-eaten jar of apology pickles.

And the daydream of what could've been.

As I drove over a railroad crossing, my wheels ground over the tracks. *Thud, thud, thud.* There were railroads like this all over Columbus. So common, I hardly noticed I'd passed one—too occupied by my own distress to really pay attention.

What had I expected?

That I wouldn't miss him?

I mean…how stupid could I possibly get?

He wasn't a friend.

He was my *best* friend.

He wasn't meant to be a fond memory.

He was my soul mate, probably.

And he was boarding that plane right now, wondering why he wasn't enough. Again. But this time, I was the reason he was feeling inadequate.

Was this—this awful, horrible loss—really worth it? Wouldn't I have been happier—less…less fucking miserable, if I'd simply told the truth? Why the fuck had I actively chosen to lose him? If that decision was supposed to protect me—it had definitely backfired.

I couldn't recall ever feeling worse.

Sweaty, shaking, my vision flooded with black spots.

My chest squeezed, and squeezed, and squeezed.

I could hardly get a breath in.

And I knew…if I kept driving in this sorry state, I was bound to crash. So I pulled over onto the side of the road, lost in my head, as thunder rumbled above. The tracks were behind me now. I must've been driving at a crawl, if I'd barely gotten this far past them.

It wasn't until I'd put the car in park, and I could actually let my guard down, that I realized my vision was swimming—not because of the rain—but because I was *crying*.

"Alex?" Dad's voice was fraught with concern. He was in the passenger seat now. He'd switched over during my staring session with the door George had disappeared through. I hadn't spoken to him since we'd left. Not a word. And he hadn't said anything either.

Until now.

I groaned, resting my head against the steering wheel as the tears began to spill. Hot and angry. Angry at the situation. Angry at myself most of all.

"*Alex?*" Dad's hand rubbed my back.

My masks fell away, one by, one by, one.

Until nothing was left.

Just me.

Just the aching black hole that was my heart—desperate to be loved. So desperate I'd convinced myself I had to be perfect to deserve it. I kept people at a distance. Pushed them before they could pull away. Before they could see the real me and decide that I wasn't enough.

When had my self-esteem gotten this…bad?

Jesus.

When had I…

When had I begun to think that love was something I had to earn?

I ran, just like George did.

"Alex?" It was the third time Dad had said my name. Three times he'd tried to break me out of my teary-eyed, dazed stupor. My shoulders were shaking. I couldn't get them to stop. Didn't know if I even wanted to, as I folded over the steering wheel and sobbed.

"I hate myself," the words were brittle. "Fuck. I hate myself so much—"

Dad's hand stroked up and down, comforting me. But it wasn't the hand I wanted. Wasn't the comfort I wanted. He wasn't the person I wanted.

"How could he ever love me if I don't love myself?" My tears smeared down the steering wheel as that gaping, cavernous hole in my heart cracked wider. "How could I ask him to stay with me? When I'm like *this*?"

The car was silent as my brain caught up to my mouth.

Only the drum of the rain, and the rattle of a train in the distance echoing through the quiet.

"*I* love you," Dad said, tone as gentle as his hand.

I sobbed again, turning from the steering wheel and crumbling into him. He was smaller than me, but he held my weight, as I maneuvered across the console to cling to him. I couldn't recall ever having a conversation like this with him. Ever opening up. Not even when I was a kid.

"Even like this?" My voice broke, tears wetting his collar.

"*Especially* like this," Dad reassured.

It was…so close to what George had told me. The words that had rattled around inside my head. The words that—as I recalled them—with my walls down and my heart vulnerable, began to crowd into that awful, empty space.

"*I like your intensity.*"

"*You're perfect.*"

"*To see Alex James as a whole…picture? Not just the put-together-bits you want everyone to see is an honor. And I find…I like you more this way, without the masks. Dirty socks and all.*"

Dad's words were there too. As well as June's. Filling in the gaps of that gaping, open wound.

Enough…that I could breathe again.

Enough that I could think.

That my self-loathing faded, and I was able to offer myself the grace that everyone else did. George worried about perfection the same way that I did. George *understood* this feeling better than anyone. He gave himself rules to follow. He was desperate to be seen as perfect. To make his family proud. To not be viewed as a burden. Maybe…if there was anyone in the world who could love me, it'd be someone like that.

Someone who looked at my dirty socks and told me he *liked* them.

Someone who understood my flaws because he shared them.

The storm that had overwhelmed me calmed as the storm outside the windows raged on, the steady beat of the windshield wipers waving back and forth. The sound of a train approaching grew louder, but I hardly noticed.

I breathed in and it hurt.

I breathed again, and it felt a little easier.

"I let him go." The words were knives on the way out.

"It's not over," Dad promised. "There's still time. That's what phones—and planes—and computers are for. Hell, you could even tweet-tweet him."

"You don't *get* it." I clung tighter to him, opening up even further. And it didn't hurt. It didn't hurt like I thought it would. Sharing the burden. "I'm like Brendon. No. I'm *worse* than Brendon. All George ever wanted was for someone to need him like he needs them—and I do. And yet, instead of being a goddamn adult and being honest about my feelings—I didn't fucking tell him. I ran away. I *let* him leave. I let him think that I—"

I let him think that he wasn't special.

That he wasn't enough.

And he *was*.

"I need to call him." My heart was pounding. "I need to ask him to stay—I need to tell him how I feel. I need—" I fumbled my phone out of my pocket. A horrified sound escaped when I saw that it was dead. Dead-dead. Jabbing the power button into submission didn't provide even a flicker of light from the pitch-black screen.

Fuck. Fuck. Car charger.

I needed—Jesus. I scrambled around for it, relieved when I found it where I'd put it. Plugging everything was a struggle when my eyes were bleary with tears and my nose was running, but I managed.

It wasn't until I had my phone turned back on and I'd pulled up my contacts list that I realized I didn't have George's number.

"I don't…" I trailed off, staring woodenly at the screen. Tears slipped down my cheeks as I turned to my dad with despair. "I didn't ask for his number."

"Alright. Get out."

"W-what—"

"Don't fight me on this. You're in no state to drive, and the faster I can get you to the airport the faster you can fix this."

Dad had always been the type of man who took action, and he did so now, already out of the car before I could even process what was happening.

Dazed and confused, I pushed my door open and stepped out. Off in the distance, bells rang, the rattle of the approaching train forcing me to pick up the pace. It'd gotten louder. Loud enough I couldn't ignore it anymore. I scrambled around the car, switching spots with my dad and sliding into the passenger seat.

It was a miracle I didn't throw up.

"Okey dokey." Dad put the car in drive, pulling back onto the street. Only…unfortunately for us, we were too late. The boom barriers were already lowering into place and blocking the way we'd come. "Dammit."

Dad reversed, the back-up camera flickering on.

This was fine.

There were other ways to get to the airport.

We weren't about to get stuck behind a goddamn train.

Everything was fine.

Everything was—

Jesus Christ.

Everything was not fine.

Dad only drove a few feet before we both realized our mistake. Because the clanging of bells were deafening now. And behind us—just like in front—

there was a railroad crossing, its gates swinging closed.

I'd been so out of it, I hadn't noticed we were trapped between two crossroads.

"No." I seriously could not make this shit up. "*No.* No, no, no, no."

"It's fine," Dad reassured, putting the car in park, because there was no reason to ride the break when we had no idea how long we'd be stuck. "We'll fix this."

"You have *got* to be fucking kidding me." My hands sunk into my hair, tugging hard enough to sting. I'd finally found my courage to turn back and go for George and *this* was how the universe repaid me?

"Call his mom," Dad said, trying to soothe me—and failing. "I'm sure she can give you his number."

"Okay." I highly doubted she'd answer, considering the fact she was commanding the rest of the Miltons to pack up as we spoke.

Which meant, the most I could do was message George on Picstogram. I doubted he'd check that. Not after the last time he'd had his phone open we'd posted the picture of us—and Brendon had begun to blow up his phone. Hell, if today's luck was any indicator, my message would go right to spam.

God.

Dammit.

One last tug.

I sagged, defeated.

There was nothing I could do. No way to fix this. By the time these damn trains had passed, George would be long gone.

I couldn't breathe.

I couldn't—

Thirty-One
George

IT WAS SOMEWHAT IRONIC that the reason I was currently sitting in a Ryde, headed to Alex's house—was because of Brendon. For the first time in the near decade that I'd known him, he'd actually done something to *help* me. Funny how it was his same horrible bullshit that'd inspired this rash decision.

I'd been waiting at my gate, fraught with emotion, when I'd turned my phone on for the first time since Alex had made me turn it off. Immediately my inbox was flooded with messages.

Brendon

> Is this another one of your dramatic cries for attention?

> A misguided attempt to make me jealous?

> It's not going to work.

> Did you forget that I know you?

> He's not going to stick around.

And you'll come crying back to me soon enough.

You're pitiful, George. You and I both know that.

And then, a few days later.

Brendon

I need to speak to you when you're back in office, Monday.

Pretending he'd never sent the above nasty text messages at all.

Brendon

I have a question for you about the design you completed before you left. The Donaldson's have asked for a few revisions that I need to go over with you before I meet with them on Tuesday.

Most of the things Brendon had said were commonplace. He often tried to make me feel small. And though this was my first time outright antagonizing him—nothing he'd texted me had been surprising or new.

He'd never been good with boundaries.

He'd never been kind.

He enjoyed seeking me out when I least expected it.

Got a sick kick out of knocking me to my knees with a few, well-planned words.

He knew he had me on the hook—like Alex had said he did.

Only…that apparently wasn't the case anymore.

A week ago, I'd be tied up in knots over this, choking on so much emotion I'd never be able to detangle it. Sick to my stomach. Quaking. Bile climbing up my throat. But that was a week ago. This was now. And for the first time in *years*, seeing Brendon's name pop up on my phone didn't fill me with icy dread.

I felt no longing for a life I didn't have.

I felt no fondness.

I felt no anger, no mourning, no *grief*.

No fear. No apprehension. No anxiety.

There was simply…

Nothing.

Nothing.

Huh.

I set my phone down on my lap, at a loss for words. I wasn't an idiot. I knew why things were different. I'd admitted as much to my mother—twice now—once before the wedding, and once after, when I'd said goodbye and she'd told me to be honest.

But even with that encouragement I hadn't been able to force the words free. Not when Alex had been so impossibly handsome, his dark hair dripping, his pale eyes lost. He'd needed me to chase him. He'd needed me to take the lead like I had that night in the bathroom.

I hadn't.

Hadn't thought I was *allowed*.

Hadn't been brave enough, good enough, strong enough to take a chance on something so irrational. Something that directly defied the lines that Alex had drawn to enclose our relationship. I'd been waiting for him to do it. Waiting for him to tell me what I wanted to hear.

I'd left my future in his hands.

Just like I'd done with Brendon.

Instead of seeking what I needed for myself. Instead of…standing my ground. Instead of becoming the master of my own fate. I'd let someone else dictate my happiness.

In my defense…I'd never been involved with someone who treated me like I mattered. Someone who needed me as much as I needed them. Someone who looked at me like I was as perfect as I'd always wanted to be. Someone who didn't mind my flaws, just like I didn't mind theirs. It wasn't until that hit me—the uncomfortable, shocking truth of that statement—that it registered that my relationship with Alex had the potential to be equal.

Equal.

In a way I'd never been allowed to be.

Equally imperfect. Equally invested. Equally enamored.

And if Alex and I were equals, if what we shared was fifty-fifty and if our intensity matched as well as I knew it did…then that meant I was just as capable of taking that first step toward "something real" as he was.

Mom had said he wasn't perfect.

And while I'd understood the sentiment, in my head I'd disregarded it. In my eyes, there was nothing he could do wrong. In my eyes, he was as close to perfect as a person could get.

But as I sat there thinking about Alex. Thinking about the way he shied from compliments, the way he hid his emotions, the way he seemed genuinely terrified of opening up—a shockingly horrible realization occurred.

Maybe Alex hadn't asked me for more—not because he wasn't interested, but because he didn't think I'd want him the same way.

Maybe flirty, charismatic, good-at-everything Alex was scared too.

Maybe he was just as worried about appearing perfect as I was.

Maybe he would never, ever make the first move—because needing me was something he was too terrified to admit.

And maybe…*maybe* he'd been waiting. Hoping. Worrying. Scared I would be another person to let him down. Beneath the wall of muscle, the smiles, and the outward confidence…Alex was as vulnerable as I was.

My thoughts spun, horror dawning as reality set in.

Confirmation of my lack of feelings toward Brendon was the final nail in the coffin. And as I fiddled with my phone, dazed, and *warm*, I realized the fear that had silenced me earlier was gone. Mom had told me that the best things in life were illogical. She'd encouraged me to take chances. She'd promised she'd be proud of me either way.

She'd given me the cushion I needed to take the fall—if there was one.

She'd offered me comfort—no matter the outcome.

And yet…here I was—in limbo.

But no more.

No fucking more.

If there was anyone in the world I could be vulnerable with it was Alex. He didn't need to be scared of me, just like I didn't need to be scared of him.

We…deserved a fighting chance.

And I was going to fight for it.

If Alex didn't want to be my *real* boyfriend, he could say that to my fucking face. There were more flights home. Who cared if I missed a day of work? In fact, who cared if I missed *all of them.* I'd have to talk to Missy about keeping Mr. Pickles for a little longer, but—

The point was…

While there were endless opportunities to tell Alex how I felt about him, none were as optimal as right here, right now.

I wanted to tell him I loved him for the first time in person.

Wanted to feel his smile.

Wanted to see his expression.

Wanted to twist my hands in that dark, dark hair and prove to him that he wasn't the only person who was capable of giving chase.

It was raining, like a cheap rom-com. The kind Alex had privately admitted he loved.

This would be a ridiculous gesture of disastrous proportions.

By all rights—a horrible, terrible, bad decision.

My worst yet.

It could go so wrong.

But…

It could go so right, too.

It'd be a declaration as silly, as dramatic as we both were.

And that was…*perfect*, wasn't it?

The perfect conclusion to our love affair.

We'd started this thing together—and we were going to end it that way too. At least, if I had anything to say about it.

If someone had told me it'd take less than a week for me to fall in love again, I would have laughed in their face. I would have scoffed and growled, and possibly stormed off. The sentiment was frankly ludicrous. And yet… that's what I'd gone and done.

Mom was right.

It was time to choose my own happiness.

Maybe the best things in life had no logic at all. Because I certainly felt excited at the prospect of seeing Alex again. Of surprising him. Of watching his eyes go wide. Of breaching that distance between us for the final time.

Pulled out of my thoughts, I recognized a familiar glint of silver. Frowning, I moved my bag out of the way, horror dawning when I realized what exactly I was seeing. Alex's watch. His special, precious—most prized possession…. on the floor.

I'd heard a little thunk when I'd retrieved my phone but I hadn't thought anything of it.

Reaching down, my heart skipped a beat as my fingers met the worn metal.

There were a lot of dings in it, betraying its many years. The watch face didn't move, stuck forever on 6:52. Running my thumb over the smooth surface, I struggled to breathe.

Brendon's texts sat open on my phone screen. I'd read them. They'd incited no reaction.

But this?

This was…

I pressed my lips to the watch face, eyes pinched shut. The drum of my heart was louder than the thunder I'd left behind outside. *Thump, thump, thump.*

If there was such a thing as a sign, this was one.

And Alex had left it for me.

What exactly it meant, I wasn't sure. But it certainly meant something.

Emboldened, I opened my eyes and put the watch on. Its weight was welcome. Comfortable. Comforting, more accurately. Like Alex's fingers were looped around my wrist. I sucked in a breath, steadying myself.

I called my mom.

She didn't have Alex's address, but she said Joe did. I figured if I couldn't call Alex—like an idiot I'd forgotten to ask for his number—I'd simply go to him.

That was what Ryde was for, wasn't it?

A man on a mission, I slung my backpack over my shoulder and made my way out of the airport.

I should have known things would not be that easy. It'd been eons since I'd traveled through Columbus alone—and I'd naively thought it'd be a straight shot to Alex's house to confront him and sweep him off his feet, of course.

Only it wasn't.

Because about ten minutes into the drive we were stopped by the tail end of a train. The thing was long enough it'd blocked several roads, and the driver assured me we were better off simply waiting for it to pass.

It was annoying…yes.

But I figured it couldn't possibly delay us for long.

Rain poured down on us, water trickling down the glass and onto the drenched asphalt. Street lights glistened, growing brighter by the minute as the sun sank lower. The sky was a mix of sunset and stormy gray, fat, angry clouds blocking its pastels from view.

Swipe, swipe, went the windshield wipers, a steady beat that would've been soothing if I wasn't so on edge.

On edge because I was so close.

So fucking close.

Nervous energy buzzed beneath my skin, zipping up my arms and down my legs, settling at my fingers. I plucked at my backpack strap, over and over, matching the beat of the wipers on the window. Alex's watch was warm.

My phone vibrated, and when I glanced down, it was Brendon again.

Brendon

?

A single question mark.

What an asshole.

I was tempted to ignore him. But then…it occurred to me that maybe taking a different approach would be more…effective. Fuck it. I swiped up for a call. It rang six times before Brendon answered.

That was another game he'd always liked to play. Even when he'd told me to call him, he'd wait till the end to answer—in an attempt to make me feel like I was inconveniencing him.

It didn't work.

Not anymore.

"Hello?" Brendon sounded pleased with himself. Like this was a battle that he'd won.

I waited to feel something. Anything. Fear—guilt—dread.

But it didn't come.

No flicker of affection, no iciness, *nothing*.

"I'm assuming this means you missed me?" Brendon drawled, in the same tone of voice that had used to break me apart and stitch me back together again. Only now, he was…off-putting. Like he was trying too hard. Throwing up a front to appear more powerful than he was.

A small man standing on stilts.

"I quit."

Silence. Those two words were met with complete and utter silence. For a beat, all I could hear was breathing on the other end of the line. And then Brendon spoke again, "Excuse me?"

"You heard me. I quit."

"You can't quit."

"I just did." And with that, I hung up and blocked his number. I'd call our boss in the morning. Maybe I'd even be *honest* about why I was quitting—now that honesty was going to be my new thing. I could throw Brendon under the bus for the sexual harassment I'd had to endure since we'd broken up.

But...I didn't focus on that.

Didn't feel anything but calm, as the end of the train finally came into sight.

Calm, because I'd be seeing Alex again.

Calm, because he needed me.

Calm, because for the first time in my life I wasn't letting anyone else decide my fate.

The train rattled by, and it wasn't until the boom barriers had risen that I understood Alex and I were more like-minded than I'd thought. Because across the tracks, in front of a second train, was a car.

A very recognizable, very *sexy* car.

And Alex was inside it.

Thirty-Two
Alex

I COULD COUNT ON one hand how many times in my life I'd been shocked speechless. When Dad had told us the company had taken off, for one. When June had told me Roderick had finally proposed, and asked me to be their best-man-of-honor. When I'd found out the surgery had been successful—that Dad's injuries weren't too severe. That after real rest and recuperation, he was going to be fine.

But this…this was a new kind of speechless.

Like all the words in the world—even if they'd been smashed together—couldn't possibly encompass the vastness of my joy.

Emotional whiplash, that was for certain. After I'd been broken down to dust only a few minutes prior. Now I was soaring. Soaring—already transported across the tracks, even though my body remained still, exactly where I'd left it.

Across the tracks, through the torrent of rain, George's blond head was visible. He slid out of the unfamiliar vehicle, all long and leggy. Like a fucking angel. An angel of mercy, maybe?

Time stopped.

Even the rain seemed to slow as I jerked my seatbelt off and shoved my door open.

George raised a hand above his head to block the worst of it, and my watch glinted on his wrist—beside the friendship bracelet I'd tied there. It looked as good on him from a distance as it had up close.

The rain was an odd amalgamation of cold and warm. It soaked me in seconds, drenched my tux through each expensive layer down to the skin beneath. I hardly noticed as I ran in front of my car. The asphalt crunched under the soles of my shoes, still exuding the heat that'd plagued the city before the rain had ever hit.

I didn't feel that either.

All my senses—my sight, my smell, even touch were focused on George.

It was as though he was right there beside me, even though he wasn't yet. I sprinted through the rain, across the barren train tracks, and around the boom barriers to reach him.

George was drenched by the time I'd closed the last of the distance that'd separated us. His thick, wavy blond hair dripped down his forehead and into his eyes. The hand he had in the air did nothing to protect him. Especially not when he dropped it to his side, my watch sliding along that firm, delicate wrist bone.

His eyes met mine.

George had the kind of eyes poetry was written about. There was a sadness in them I recognized far too intimately. Neediness. But strength too. Determination. Determination that showed in his actions, as well as his gaze.

The fact he was here was a testament to that.

They were the same vivid, bottomless blue as they'd been the day I'd met him. But my feelings for them were far stronger now. Because I knew those eyes. Knew exactly how many wrinkles his nose scrunched into. Knew what he looked like when his guard was down. Knew the taste, the feel, the shape of him—so well, if I closed my eyes, I could picture every last, perfect inch.

I knew how to bring him joy. How to make him smile. How to make him drop his precious control. I knew how to make him feel seen, and loved. How to appreciate him, the way he was meant to be appreciated.

As I stood there staring at him, taking him in, there was no denying the honest truth.

And maybe I didn't know how to love myself yet—but I knew with bone-deep certainty how to love George-Arthur Milton.

There wasn't a single man in the world who would love him more fiercely than I would.

He must've recognized that in my gaze, recognized my devotion, my awe, my gratitude. Because the tension in his frame fled, and those dark eyes glistened.

They said, *I'm meeting you halfway.*

They said, *we're not done yet.*

They said, *I need you, I need you, I need—*

"You look like you could use a recharge." George's words broke me.

A laugh escaped before I could help it, and suddenly that terrible, awful ache in my chest was completely gone. As though George's presence had untangled the knots.

"You have no idea." No truer words had ever been said.

When I kissed him, he tasted like honesty.

Nothing existed outside his mouth—soft, pliant, then biting and ravenous.

Teeth, and tongue, and long-long fingers tangled in the back of my hair.

Time blurred along with my vision, rain mixing with tears, with spit and sweat. The thump of my heart was louder than the rumble of thunder above us. The storm didn't let up, but neither of us cared, growing soggier by the minute.

George's skin was chilly beneath my palms, fingers scraping up those sweet cheeks and into his tangle of blond hair. It was knotted now that the rain had made it catch. The gel he'd styled it with that morning made it sticky and hard to card through.

I tugged.

I felt his responding gasp all the way to my toes.

"I was so mad at you—" George's voice broke. "For not admitting you need me."

"But I do—" I licked his whine right out of his mouth. "I *do*."

"*I need you too.*" George's wet lashes were a spiky, dark blond. The whites of his eyes were red, swimming with tears. "I don't want to be friends," his breath hitched. "I don't want to be anyone else's—"

"George."

"I know it was just for practice but can't it be—" George's voice was shaking. "Can't it be forever? Can't we…can't we just never stop?" His hands clung to my shirt, pulling at the fabric. "Does it *have* to end?"

"It doesn't have to end." I kissed him again, overwhelmed—frightened— and elated all at the same time. "Never, George."

"I won't let you down like those other people," George sniffed, his dark eyes swirling with tears. A few rolled down his cheek, mixing with the rain. "I don't care if every day isn't a 'good day.' The way I look at you will never change."

I kissed him again, cutting off his confession.

When I pulled back again this time, he was far more settled. "You don't have to be perfect," George promised softly. "You don't have to be perfect for me to love you."

"I know." My throat clicked when I swallowed. And I did know. I did. Because I realized the feeling was entirely fucking mutual. In fact…it was George's flaws that endeared him to me so very much. His fussiness. His tendency to smother. How loud, how bright he could be. Argumentative and grouchy—and so…so goddamn lovable.

George wrapped his arms around my middle, burying his face in my neck. He shook. Shook so damn hard. I clutched him close, rocking him as I inhaled the scent of his shampoo, my eyes squeezed so tightly when I opened them I saw more black spots.

His fluffy head was right there. So kissable. So I kissed it. Kissed his ear too. Kissed his forehead, and his nose, and his eyebrows—and his cheeks, and his chin and his—

"Ah!" George shoved my face away with a laugh, his earlier upset gone.

It was only when he was smiling at me, this tremulous, eager thing—so goddamn proud of himself for speaking up, for being brave, for taking what he wanted—that my own words rose to the surface.

"I never wanted you to go." My truths spilled free, muttered between kisses that tasted like second-chances. "I don't ever want to be apart from you." George made a hurt sound, but I continued. "I don't want to be without you for a single fucking second."

"You didn't say anything," George said, still smiling, despite the devastating honesty of his words. "You promised to be honest. You promised not to play games."

"I know." I smiled, but it wasn't happy, not like his. His fingers yanked me closer, those gorgeous eyes on mine. He waited, blinking away stray drops of rain, patient as the whirr of the Ryde's engine sounded beside us. "I…"

I didn't know how to explain, but I tried.

"I was scared," I said softly, surprised when the words spilled free.

"Scared?" George blinked.

"I've never loved someone like I love you," I admitted. "I…didn't—don't know what to do. I hate not knowing what to do. I hate not knowing the answers—"

George was quiet for a moment, but only a moment. And then he was reeling me back into a hug, smooshing into me, going so far as to yank my hands around him so I was hugging back exactly the way he wanted.

It was the bossiest, fussiest hug in the history of the world.

And it was perfect.

"It's okay not to have all the answers," George said softly. "Maybe…instead of being stupid—next time we can just…ask each other. Honesty very rarely, if ever, ruins good things," George recited.

I laughed.

Because when he said it like that, it sounded so simple.

"Real boyfriends communicate," George chided. "That's my boyfriend lesson for you."

"Oh, really?" I snorted. "Georgie-the-adorable-hypocrite strikes again. Who exactly was the one that walked into that airport without even looking at me?!"

"If I'd looked at you I wouldn't have left!" George squeezed me tight, far tighter than I thought he was capable.

"I was coming back for you," I promised, sobering. "*I was coming back for you—*" I repeated, days worth of pent-up emotion making my voice quake. It didn't feel like days. Felt more like centuries, honestly. Like I'd spent this life, and the last, and the one before that wanting him, chasing him, craving him. "I was such an idiot, George. I should've told you the truth from the start."

"The truth?"

"That you deserve better than what Brendon ever gave you. You deserve…" Christ…there were so many things it was hard to pick. "You deserve to be with someone that respects you. Someone that adores every messy, dramatic, delightful part of you. Someone that loves you enough to tease you—"

"You do a lot of that," George griped, though the roughness of his voice betrayed how touched he was. And yet—I wasn't done. Wasn't fucking done. Because now that the words were flowing, I couldn't seem to get them to stop. The dam had been broken, the overflowing well of my George-oriented thoughts spilling free.

"You deserve to be with someone you can trust. Someone who wants a future with you. Someone that makes you laugh. Someone that's proud to call you his." Tears blurred my vision and I blinked them away—annoyed at their presence because they were blocking my view of his face. Of the way his lips were trembling. Of the way his breath puffed out, in panicked bursts.

"Alex—" George whined, clearly struggling. But I didn't stop. Didn't stop, because for his entire adult life George had been starved of affection. He'd begged for scraps of attention. Bent over backward for praise he never received. And I could see in his eyes that my declaration was doing something to him.

Breaking him down.

Breaking him so that he could build himself stronger.

So that we could be something better. So that he could stand on his own. So he could understand his worth didn't come from a boyfriend's feelings or perception, but because he deserved better.

We could reconstruct our foundations in tandem.

We could fortify one another.

I wanted to be the standard he set for himself.

Wanted that standard to climb and climb and climb.

Wanted to spend my life striving to surprise him with my devotion.

"You deserve a ring on your finger. Anniversaries. A wedding—exactly the way you've always wanted."

"I-I can't."

"You…" My heart kept jumping. I could feel it in my fingertips where they pressed into George's skin. Feel it in my chest, knocking each breath free. In my throat, tightening with my words. "You…deserve someone who knows he has flaws." Jesus, did I have those. "Who's not perfect—but never stops trying. Someone who struggles sometimes…but…loves you enough to never give up."

A car honked but we ignored it. I had no idea if it was the Ryde driver, or someone behind my dad. But it didn't matter. Nothing mattered. Nothing but George's eyes. Those fathomless, swirling depths.

And the way they warmed with every rain-streaked blink.

"Alex—" George sounded wrecked.

"But most of all, you deserve…to feel like you're enough. Fuck. Like you're more than enough—because you *are*."

"F-fuck." George gasped.

"I would make you so happy, Georgie." Candid was best. I'd nearly lost my opportunity to be that—to do this. I was tired of being an idiot. "I would." It was a vow. "I'd take such good care of you."

"A—"

He tried to stop me again, but I wasn't done. Wasn't done—because I'd almost lost this. This was the most important negotiation I'd ever make. "I need you." My stomach filled with lead, those words far heavier than anything I'd ever thought I could admit. "I need you. I can't fucking breathe when I think about losing you. I can't imagine my life without you in it. Can't imagine a future where we're not together."

I could keep going.

I wanted to keep going.

All my private, most personal thoughts were escaping—but George... lovely, wonderful George, anchored me in the present.

He stroked up and down my back.

Recognizing my rambling for what it was, an anxious ploy to convince him he'd be making the right choice. His hands slid into my hair, petting through it, holding me still as he pulled my face back so he could meet my gaze.

"Okay." George's eyes were red-rimmed. "*Okay.*" It took me a second to process the word through the ringing in my ears.

"Okay?"

Now it was my turn to shake. Trembling like a leaf in the wind, weak in a way I'd never been for anyone but him. Allowing myself to show weakness— because I knew he wouldn't judge me for it. Knew he'd help steady me. Knew he'd understand.

The hands George had in my hair tightened, as I sucked in a breath.

"*Okay,*" George repeated. "Let's do it."

"Which part?"

"All of it." George blinked. "If you're up for it."

"Of course I'm up for it. I can't promise I won't mess up—"

"Good, because I'm sure I will." George said this wryly enough it startled a laugh right out of me. "Long distance?" George's voice was soft. "For now. While I pack up my apartment."

"While you—"

"Pack up my apartment, yes. I'll need to give my roommate time to find someone to take my place. But that shouldn't take long."

Had I hit my head?

This could not possibly be that easy.

"That's it?" I couldn't rationalize what was happening. George nodded, a short jerky thing. His hands slipped out of my hair, tangling around my wrists instead. "You're just...going to...move here?" I blinked. "But what about your job?"

I was clearly out of my mind.

Why the hell was I trying to convince him not to stay?

Shut up, shut up.

"What about your *life?*" My voice cracked again. Again. How fucking embarrassing.

"I quit my job on the drive here," George replied dryly. My mouth dropped open, and my expression must've been ridiculous because it made him smile. "It was a long time coming, Alex," he confessed. "But I can't help but... admit...you had a lot to do with it."

"You love your job."

"I loved parts of my job," George corrected. "I didn't love working with my ex. Didn't love walking on eggshells everyday. Didn't love being away from my family. Didn't love the fact that I was only staying because I was worried I'd disappoint my mom if I left."

"Oh."

"You made me realize that there is...so much more to life than staying stagnant." George sucked in a breath. "You made me realize...I could have fun. I could be myself—and be accepted, fuck. Even celebrated for that. That there are…*better* options. *You* are the better option."

George was quoting something I'd said as a joke, but obviously he'd taken it to heart.

"I wish we would've said all this earlier," George huffed. "We both were idiots."

"But we're not idiots anymore?"

"No," George laughed. "We're still idiots." He shook his head, and his hair flopped onto his forehead. I snorted, because he was right. We were.

"Idiots together," I agreed.

"Too true." George's lips curled into an indulgent smile. It was gorgeous. Private, and soft, and all mine. Then his expression hardened. "We should set some expectations."

Expectations were good.

I liked expectations.

We really were two peas in a pod.

"I'm not moving in immediately," George started.

"What—"

"I need my own space while we date. Four months should be long enough, right? Then we can move in together. Your house, obviously. It's perfect for my needs." He was planning our life. Planning it as intently as I'd planned Juniper's wedding. "We can have date nights on Fridays."

"That's reasonable."

"I'll allow a proposal between month four and six. I like being surprised."

"You'll *allow* it, huh?" I chuckled, chest so warm and light I was surprised I didn't simply explode. "I'll add it to my schedule."

"I prefer silver over gold."

"Gotcha."

"You'll need to buy litter boxes for Mr. Pickles."

"Not a problem."

"And stock up on his cat food. For the nights I stay over."

"Will do."

"I don't want a long engagement," George added. "I hate those. Six months maximum."

"Sounds perfect."

"Be mentally prepared for me to be involved in the wedding planning." George's thumbs skimmed my inner wrists as I sank my fingers into his hair, then down to his nape, scraping across the chilly skin. "I have a lot of opinions. I know you handled June's ceremony—and you did a beautiful job. But I want to be hands-on. I want ours to be a joint effort."

"I wouldn't expect anything else. George, the bridezilla. That tracks." George rolled his eyes, but ultimately looked pleased.

"I want kids," he added like a challenge. "Lots of them."

"Believe me, you'd already be pregnant if I had any choice in the matter."

He glared at me, but his cheeks were pink, so the effect was ruined. George cleared his throat, shuffling his feet as he got his mouth going again. This adorable, bossy little negotiation was lighting me up with each bulleted stipulation.

"I'm serious, Alex," he said.

"So am I." I grinned, and he stared at me. *Stared.* How had I never noticed the way he looked at me? It was suspiciously close to the way I looked at him, stars in my eyes.

"I don't want to be limited," George added. "There are a lot of kids of various ages in the system. Any kid that needs a home is welcome in our family."

"I wouldn't have it any other way." My heart fluttered.

It was so easy to picture the life George was painting. A yellow brick road to a happy ending I'd always craved. *Swipe, swipe* went George's thumbs, anchoring me in the present.

Anchoring me to him.

So I could orbit him the way I always did, sucked into the gravitational pull that was George-Arthur Milton. His fingers wiggled under the edge of the friendship bracelet I still wore.

I felt like I was floating.

"I want my library."

"I'll start building," I said immediately. "Anything else?"

He pursed his lips together, eyes narrowing thoughtfully. "Saturdays at my mom's? I miss her...and I..." His eyes hardened. "I don't want any other relationship to get in the way of spending time with her."

"I love your mom. That's easy."

"We can do Sundays with your dad."

"Perfect."

George softened, head tipping back a bit more. His lips were still swollen from our kisses, and it took every ounce of self-control I had not to lean down and taste him again. "I want..."

"Anything."

"I want you to still be mean to me sometimes," George's voice went hoarse. "Especially in bed."

"Jesus Christ, Duchess."

I couldn't stop myself. I had to kiss him. Kiss his lips, and those words, and the ache behind them. He moaned into the kiss, pressing into me greedily, like he'd been waiting for me to take charge and take this for the both of us.

Like my kiss was a gift.

"This is the easiest negotiation I've ever participated in," I murmured when we parted, both of us breathless.

"I'm glad." George's cheeks were flushed, but his eyes were unguarded. His walls were gone. Left somewhere back at the airport where he'd had to tear through them to chase me down. Because that's what he'd done. Worked through his own fears to meet me halfway—the way I'd always dreamed a partner would.

For the desperation we felt to be a mutual affliction.

We had more in common than we didn't, despite being opposites.

Maybe that was what happened when you fell in love with your best friend.

Because, despite how odd that felt—considering we'd just met—I knew for a fact it was true.

George relaxed, the tension in his frame dissipating as his fingers slid up my arms to tangle in the back of my hair once more. The icy bite of his fingertips against my scalp sent a shiver down my spine.

He needed out of this rain.

Needed to be warmed up and kissed silly.

"So…what does that make us then?" I asked. Another honk sounded, but again, we ignored it. When I kissed the vulnerable shell of his ear, he tasted like summer rain. "Real boyfriends? *Lovers*? Love birds—"

"Equals." George's voice was soft.

"Equals," I echoed, squeezing him tight. "That's the most poetic shit I've ever heard, you giant sap."

"Shut up."

"I won't," I grinned. His frame trembled with laughter, betraying his amusement. "You have to know that."

George snorted in agreement.

And suddenly I had to taste him again. Had to taste that mouth, and its laughter. So I did. It was easy to yank him into my arms—to pull his soaked sneakers from the asphalt and support him with my bulk well above the ground. Reed thin, and lovely, George was the most welcome weight I'd ever carried.

He made this delightfully shocked sound as he stiffened—then relaxed, meeting my kiss bite for bite, lick for lick.

Equal, the way all partners should be.

Equal, the way I'd never felt with anyone else.

Thirty-Three
George

MY FAMILY WAS ECSTATIC to say the least when they found out I was staying for a few more days. Even more so, when I explained that I was moving back indefinitely. Missy, my roommate, was equally unhinged in her reply when I'd told her what happened.

"I honestly never would've expected this," she said over the phone, sounding amused and delighted for me in equal measure. "Good for you, George. Taking a chance on the unpredictable."

The truth was, I'd never expected this either.

Falling in love in less than a week.

Abandoning my life—and all I'd known—to chase a fairy tale that shouldn't have made as much sense as it did.

But…every time I saw Alex's grin, I was reminded why being illogical might be the most logical thing I'd ever done. Because picking this "ending" for my story had meant that I was going to see as many of those smiles as I wanted.

And Christ, that was a gift.

I'd never forget the way he looked at me, standing in the rain. Drenched. Eyes red-rimmed. Defeat written over every inch of his large, drooping body. He'd looked so small. So needy, and so grateful to see me.

All it had taken was one glance at that tear-streaked, heart-broken face to know that I'd been right. Been right about everything. And I'd never been more glad in all my life that I'd taken a chance on something with no discernable outcome.

Alex needed me the same way I needed him.

We filled each other's wells.

I'd never regret my choice.

Alex's house was as messy-clean as we'd left it. The dishes were still sitting on the counter, dry now—a reminder of how quickly we'd left the previous day when we'd realized we were running late. Cum-stained and flushed, we'd abandoned responsibility in a way both of us rarely did.

This…didn't feel like that.

Leaving behind my career.

Leaving New York.

It didn't feel like a rash decision—even though it kind of was. Even though it was ridiculous, really. Even though by all rights it should make *no* sense. And yet…it did.

I was abandoning a miserable, monotonous life for the chance at one that could be everything I'd always dreamed. There was nothing more logical than that.

"Are you going to come back home?" Mom asked when I'd called her next. Alex and I were still warm from the shower we'd shared. We'd warmed up in other ways too. Ways that involved mouths, and fingers, and the bottle of lube that Alex apparently kept in his shower.

Another round of that syrupy slow, delightful sex we'd shared in his bed yesterday morning.

More kisses.

"What do you mean?" I asked, shaking away the inappropriate memories.

"For dinner, before you leave," Mom explained.

"Maybe." Alex's hands were on my feet, kneading the arches, his blue eyes watching me hungrily—like even though he'd just had his dick so far inside me I could still feel his cum leaking out—he was ready for another round. "I need to hunt for an apartment. Alex said he'd—" I bit my lip as he pushed his thumb in deeper.

"Alex is helping you?" Mom's voice quivered with amusement. "Of course he is."

"Anyway. I'll um. I'll be back permanently soon. If we can swing by later, we will. But we'll be pretty swamped apartment hunting in Columbus for the few days I've extended my trip—and afterward, Alex took time off to come with me to New York to get my life packed up."

When I'd told Missy about my plan to live there a few months while she'd found a new roommate she'd immediately shot me down. Apparently, she already had someone in mind, and didn't think it was necessary for me to drag out the inevitable. Plus, and I quote, "That way, Lord-Ass-Face can't beat your door down now that he knows you're leaving."

She'd never liked Brendon.

A fact that brought me glee now that I was well and truly over him.

"Sounds like you've got it all planned out," Mom said, again, delighted. "And you're…"

"Happy?" Alex's smile curled at the corners, his eyes drifting up my body, settling on my mouth as I spoke. "I'm very happy," I confirmed.

It felt odd to admit that.

I couldn't remember the last time I'd said such a thing.

"That's all I've ever wanted for you," Mom said. "I could not be more proud." Mom's voice was full of acceptance, of blatant affection—and relief, almost. And suddenly, any lingering anxiety I might've had over her reaction to the news was gone. Just like that.

"We'll come to dinner." We were busy, yes. But…

"Monday?" Alex offered. "I'll drive us."

I'd make time.

"Monday," I repeated.

"I'll make your favorite," Mom promised. She went quiet, her words muffled as she turned from the phone to yell at someone. Presumably Joe. "That goes in the other truck!" When she came back on the line, her voice was sugary sweet again. "I gotta go, sweetheart. Joe's making a mess."

"That's okay, Mom."

"I'm proud of you."

"Tha—"

"I swear to god." Mom hung up as she started yelling again. I set my phone down with a laugh, amused—and *relieved*, now that I didn't have anyone else to call.

"Feel better?" Alex dug into my arch again. I sighed and nodded, slipping low onto the couch, foot pushing into his grip. "You look like you feel better." He sounded entertained.

"I feel like I can breathe," I confessed, eyes flitting to the high ceilings, my heart skipping a beat. "Is that…weird?"

"No." Alex's hands walked up my legs, rubbing at my thighs as he hummed thoughtfully. "I think that's a good thing."

"I just willingly chose to uproot my life," I said—once again, managing to sound *giddy* about that, rather than upset.

"And you're *smiling*."

"I am?" My hands slid up, phone abandoned so I could brush along the shape of my smile—memorizing the feel of it, because it was simply that foreign. "I am."

"You are."

"I'm happy about it." Even though I'd admitted that to my mom, it still felt odd to acknowledge out loud. "Are you…happy?"

I knew realistically that he was. His rain-soaked declaration had been far prettier than my own. Way longer too. Like the dam had broken and all his thoughts had spilled free. I was still reeling from some of the things he'd said—and some of the promises we'd made.

But still…

June's words haunted me, even now.

And I needed confirmation that Alex was as happy as I was.

Alex stared at me for a second.

It was a new expression.

Like he'd never been asked a more stupid question in his life.

I couldn't help but giggle. Giggle, and then squawk, when his annoyance meant those big warm hands yanking me up—and across—and into his lap. "Of course I'm fucking happy, Georgie Porgie," he sighed. "My cat came home."

And then he kissed me.

His mouth was hot and needy, this kiss lingering long enough to make my toes curl.

With hair damp from the shower, Alex was as delicious as he ever could have been.

Delicious, because he was as mine as I was his.

"Ask me if I'm happy again, and see what happens," he murmured threateningly against my lips, hand cupping my throat to hold me still.

I laughed—and he laughed too, the sounds vibrating between us.

"Alex—" I started.

"Don't you dare." The hand on my throat squeezed a fraction. "George—" If he was trying to intimidate me, he was going to fail. I wasn't scared of him. And that realization, along with the others, only seemed to make the love I had for him expand in my chest.

All my life I'd wanted to be enough for someone.

And as Alex's chest rumbled against mine, as his eyes spoke truths, truths about our future, about his feelings—about the absurdity of all of this, and the rightness of it too—I couldn't help but recognize that I was.

Not because he'd said so.

But because he *showed* me.

With everything he did.

If there was one thing falling in love with Alex in such a short time had taught me, it was this: sometimes the worst, most illogical, most impractical, most unbelievable bad decisions were the best decisions of all.

Epilogue

Alex

GEORGE'S EXPRESSION WAS DUBIOUS as he squinted at the pair of figure skates I was currently holding. He eyed the toe pick—the almost star shaped grooves at the front—distrustfully. His nose scrunched.

"June only wore them once," I promised, wiggling the black boots at him so he could familiarize himself with them. "And I sanitized them."

I planned on buying him his own set, but those would need to be molded to his feet and we simply hadn't had time for that. In the interim, these were better than rentals—far more support for him, and surprisingly a perfect fit, considering his size disparity with June.

"It's not that—" George reached out, fingers closing around the toes so they'd stop swinging. "I just…the fronts look sharp. Are those the brakes?" His breaths were coming a little faster.

"Absolutely not." I didn't figure skate, but June did. And she'd made it clear over and over and over again—even though I already fucking knew—that

555

the toe pick was for jumping, not stopping. "You won't be using the toe pick today," I promised. "I bet you won't even notice it's there."

"Unless I stab myself in the leg with it," George sighed. He took the boots from my hands and sat down on the bench inside the front end of the arena. Behind him, the ice rink was being resurfaced, the whir of the Zamboni filling the air. I could practically taste the ice—which was far preferable than the smell and musk that filled the locker room when I was back there getting ready for a game.

"You're not going to stab yourself in the leg," I promised, even though… now that he'd brought it up, I was kinda worried he would. "And even if you did—which you won't—" I cut him off before he could stress, "I'd make sure you were fine. Trust me."

George relaxed.

And fuck, wasn't that a trip? That my reassurances were enough to make his loud mind quiet.

"Okay." He put the boots on the ground, scrutinizing them like he'd never seen a pair of shoes in his life. "How am I supposed to—"

I knelt on the floor. It wasn't made of tile, but a softer substance. Something that wouldn't damage the blades when you walked—aside from if you stepped on a wayward pebble or some shit. That'd never happened to me, but Roderick wasn't nearly as lucky. He'd started wearing hard guards for that reason, always wary it was going to happen again.

"They're a bit different than shoes," I said, reaching for his foot. He didn't protest as I cupped his ankle, gently sliding his foot free from his "casual loafers." I never wore formal clothing outside of work. George was…his own specimen of man, that was for certain.

"How so?"

"They're supposed to fit tighter, for one thing." I fully intended on buying him his own pair but we hadn't had time. Between apartment hunting, visiting with his family, returning to New York to pack things up—and then flying back here to await the arrival of his possessions, both of us had been swamped.

We'd come so far in such a short amount of time.

Just thinking about our trip to New York brought a smile to my face.

Partially because George's roommate had been a goddamn riot, and twice as hilarious as I'd hoped, for obvious reasons. Also, because his apartment had been simultaneously nothing like I'd anticipated, and exactly like I'd expected.

It was far more cluttered than one would think, though clean. You could see a divide between George's "common areas" and Missy's, as anywhere George often occupied was perfectly organized without a speck of dust in sight. I couldn't say the same for Missy, and was surprised that George not only put up with her messiness, but seemed to enjoy her.

They quipped back and forth the entire time we'd been packing.

She poked fun at him in a way that reminded me of his siblings. Like she was his other, grayer older sister. Her hair was a mess of curls, and the first time I'd seen her I'd been shocked into silence because she was wearing yarn.

An entire *outfit* made of yarn.

Head to toe.

Even her earrings were made of yarn—tangled balls dangling from her ears in colorful blobs.

She'd been friendly, an air of peace about her as she swung the apartment door open with a flourish and welcomed George home.

"Your baby has missed you," she said in greeting. "And Lord-Ass-Face has been here six times since you called me to delay your trip home." Then she'd enveloped George in a hug so snug I heard his back pop. "Welcome home, Bubba."

"Hi, Missy," George greeted, patting her back.

"Bubba?" I echoed, delighted. "*Bubba?*"

"Because of his bubble butt," Missy released George, her voice a dreamy sigh—that I quickly learned was her default setting, not just because George's ass was a thing of legend.

I liked her immediately.

"I'm stealing that." I grinned unrepentantly, and Missy smiled beatifically back.

"No, you're not," George grunted, standing to the side to gesture between us. "Alex—the pain in the ass I told you about—"

"The tall drink of water you're head over heels for," Missy corrected.

"Missy, my gremlin-asshole-roommate." Then, now that introductions were over, he stalked off into his apartment to go find his cat.

"He's so fucking cute," I murmured without meaning to, to which Missy just nodded, her long gray hair swaying.

"Like a cat," she agreed. "A big, grouchy, snarky cat."

"You and I are going to get along swimmingly." I offered Missy my arm, and she took it with grace, her yarn-covered mittens tucked inside my elbow.

"I already like you better than the other one," she cooed, leading me into the apartment and shutting the door behind me.

"I should hope so," I said. "I'm not an ass-face."

"Depends on who you talk to," George quipped from the kitchen.

The apartment was smaller than I'd expected but I kept my opinions to myself, absorbing the energy of the room—the plants dangling from the ceiling, the exposed brick wall, and the framed pictures of George's family that hung perfectly spaced upon it.

George re-entered the room, his eyes bright, a giant grin on his face. Not because of me. No. Because of the cat he was currently wearing like a scarf. A huge, fluffy white monstrosity with bug eyes. The creature was purring, his paws covered in yarn mittens I assumed were handmade by Missy herself.

"You look so handsome," George cooed at his hairy baby. "Look at you, you precious, perfect, beautiful thing. Daddy missed you. Yes he did. He missed you so, so much." He kissed the cat's head, continuing to shower it in praise as he made his way across the living room, dodged around the leather sofa, and stood in front of me.

I was suddenly jealous of Mr. Pickles.

As ridiculous as that was.

"Do you like the mittens?" Missy asked, her grip on my elbow light.

"Do I like the—" George pulled his face out of Mr. Pickles fur. "Of course I like the mittens. They're brilliant." He picked up one of the cat's paws and gave it a wave. "So itty bitty, tiny—"

"So this is Mr. Pickles," I cocked my head, staring into the creature's eyes curiously. I liked cats. I liked all animals. But that didn't mean I'd really... interacted with them. Mom had one—but I hadn't been to her villa in Italy in probably a decade? And I genuinely couldn't recall if she'd had a cat the last time I was there, or if that was a more recent development.

"It sure is," George's smile was blinding. He wiggled his grip around, fingers sinking beneath the armpits of the beast as he held him up to me— our faces inches apart.

He smelled like...fur.

And his eyes...

His eyes, I swear to god, could see inside my soul.

"Mr. Pickles, meet your new dad," George said.

And suddenly—I was no longer jealous of the cat.

Happiness flooded my chest, bubbly and effervescent.

"He's annoying sometimes but he means well," George said, his dark blue eyes blinking at me from behind the plume of fluff. "You better be nice to him—"

I wasn't sure if the threat was aimed at me or Mr. Pickles, but either way, I figured it was fair.

"Here." George blinked, waiting.

What was he—

Oh.

Was I supposed to hold the cat?

I blinked, startled into action as I latched on to the animal, and George let go. Then suddenly, I was holding the purring beast, all his fluffy white fur clutched to my chest as I arranged his limbs so he could comfortably curl against me.

"His pecs make good pillows," George whispered conspiratorially. "Enjoy."

And then he abandoned me, stalking off toward his bedroom to pack. Missy laughed at the shell-shocked look on my face, patted the arm she'd abandoned so I could hold my current arm full of fur, and headed off to grab the boxes she'd gathered to help George.

I felt like I was missing something.

Something crucial.

Like in my haste to make a good impression on George's roommate and pet—and take in his home as greedily as he'd taken in mine, I'd forgotten something I really shouldn't have.

A fact that was only proven to be true when seven hours into our group packing project, the doorbell rang.

We were expecting pizza, so none of us were surprised. George was the first to rise, all his long, skinny limbs straightening as he shuffled past where I was huddled on the floor, packing his manga—not mongooses.

That had been a fight in itself.

The whole collection was hidden in his closet behind rows of clothing—and when I'd offered to help pack them he'd immediately shut me down at first.

"Absolutely not," George had said, yanking me out of the closet like I'd just discovered a bomb about to go off. "Those are for my eyes and my eyes only."

"How am I supposed to build you a library if I'm never allowed to even look at the books inside it?" I asked, amused by his dramatics. He shut me out of the closet without reply. I could hear him rustling around in there. And I waited to see what he'd do next.

Leaning against the wall, I watched the door for a few minutes, unsure if I should give up and move on to another section of the house, or wait him out.

My patience was rewarded because only a few minutes later, the closet door creaked open and one of George's cute eyes peeked out from the gap. "If I let you help—" he hesitated, "*If.*" I nodded. "You are not permitted to open any of the books."

"Why?" I couldn't help but push. "Are they porn?"

George's cheeks went bright red and he slammed the door on me again.

Oops.

Another few seconds passed before it opened again, only a crack once more. "I'm not ashamed," he said quickly. "There's nothing wrong with liking what I do."

"Yes," I agreed, because there wasn't.

And that was why I was being so pushy. I didn't want him to think there was a single thing he had to hide from me. Especially not stuff he loved.

"I just…haven't ever…let anyone else touch them." The door creaked open a smidge wider, revealing his nose and the corner of his mouth. "And some of the things I read are…"

"Creative," I finished for him, throwing him a bone.

"Yes." George waited for a beat.

"Baby, the first time we met I told you my favorite genre to read is erotica," I pointed out, wiggling closer to him. Just a bit. Not enough to spook him. "Besides, you know I like anime. I promise you that I'm more likely to become obsessed with your mongooses than I am to judge you. "

"Mangas," George corrected. "Mahn." He enunciated slowly. "Gahs."

"Mangas," I echoed, pleased when the door pushed open more. Now I could see his whole cute face, in all its anxious glory.

"Okay…" George waited. "You can help."

I was tempted to fist pump, but through sheer strength of will managed not to. "Thank you."

Which was why I was knees-deep in a box full of Japanese comics. Some of these covers were wild. I could see why he'd been a bit nervous for me to see. The most memorable had been one with a man totally covered in bondage gear, tear-streaked face, a tall stranger behind him smirking like he'd put the beefy bottom exactly in his place.

Some of them were on the cuter side. Adorable little anime-men snuggled up together. Some with ears, and tails. Some smooching. Some simply leaning into each other's sides innocently—hiding the filth that populated the last quarter of the book's pages.

Okay, yes, I definitely skimmed a lot of the volumes as I put them in the boxes. But who could blame me?

The art was cute and I was curious.

I was certainly not disappointed, and made a mental note to ask George to recommend me his favorites when we got home.

Anyway—I was distracted by censored penis illustrations, and cute twinks getting railed—which was why George was quicker than I was, and made it to the door first.

"I'm surprised he let you touch those," Missy said from the back corner of the room where she was messily folding George's casual wardrobe. Neither of us were "permitted" to touch his suits. It was a rule.

"Oh, me too," I agreed, flipping to the end of another book and whistling. "Jesus this dude's dick is huge. Like. The size of his forearm."

Missy tittered.

"I'm not complaining," I shut the volume before George could catch me. Looking at it reminded me of how much I liked to stick my very own massive cock inside George's tight little—nope. Nope. Do not get a boner right now, Alex.

It's pizza time.

Not boner time.

Only…I could still hear George talking—and there was no pizza.

I swear to god, if the delivery man was hitting on him, I was not going to be happy. Mangas abandoned, I rose from my seat with a groan, and headed out of his bedroom and into the main room to defend my territory.

I froze, frowning, when I spotted what was most definitely not a pizza delivery man standing in the open doorway. His hand was on George's wrist. His brown hair was immaculately styled, and his dark eyes were dead, steely, as he stared at George like he was his property.

"Get your hands off me," George's voice was clipped. "I'm serious, Brendon."

Brendon.

Brendon.

Bren—

I was across the room in seconds. I even leapt over the fucking couch in my haste to get between them. Through a red haze, I recognized how my own behavior might've been frightening to George—but…when he turned and saw my approach, the only look on his face was relief.

Relief.

Not fear.

Because while I knew George could fight his own battles—and he had, for over a fucking year, Jesus.

He shouldn't have to.

"Please tell me I can punch him," I begged the second I was close enough for him to hear. Brendon's eyes widened but I barely noticed, all my attention on George. "*Please.*"

He laughed, this soft, airy sound.

Then he yanked his wrist out of Brendon's grip and stepped to the side.

I grinned, wide and unrepentant.

"Fuck yes. I have been dying to do this since the day I heard your name, Brandon with an E." I cracked my knuckles, hopping from side to side as I revved myself up. "You've got three seconds."

He was within the doorway still. On George's property.

"You better get a head start," George drawled, eyeing me with hunger. His eyes caught on my biceps, on my chest, and I flexed a little extra just to show off. "He's faster than he looks."

"You can't punch me," Brendon said, arms crossing. "I'll sue."

"Please do," I hummed, getting my stance ready. I wanted to make this count. "I'd like to see you try to win when you are currently trespassing—and you put your hands on my fucking boyfriend. From where I'm standing, anything I do to defend his home is fair game."

And then I pulled my hand back, clenched my fist—and with a sickening, delightful, wonderful crack, pounded it directly against Brendon's goddamn face.

He went flying back out into the hallway—far enough he smashed into the wall on the other side. My fist stung a bit, but I hardly noticed, a sick sort of satisfaction running through me as I smirked down at his crumpled form.

"I gave you a warning," I shrugged, leaning against the doorway. "Not my fault you don't know how to listen." He groaned. "Now kindly see your ugly ass-face out. Please and thank you." I slammed the door, locking it for good measure, before I turned back to George.

"You called him ass-face," Missy's voice was hysterical. "You called him—" She wouldn't stop laughing. Apparently she'd followed me into the living room, because she was crumpled against the wall, wheezing her lungs out. Even Mr. Pickles had come out of wherever he'd been hiding to see what the fuss was about. "Oh, I like you," Missy wiped a tear. "You got an older brother?"

"Sadly, no." I smiled at her, but turned my attention back to George.

George, who was leaning against the wall, face turned away from me, shoulders shaking.

"Oh, baby." Shit. I'd scared him. I'd—

And then I heard it.

The squawking wheeze of his giggles.

"You scared the shit outta me!" I grabbed him by the shoulders, spinning him around so I could see with my own eyes that he wasn't upset. He wasn't. Tears were streaming down his cheeks, and his whole face was red as he choked on his laughter.

"Did you hear the sound he made when he h-hit the w-wall?" George wheezed. "Oh my god. I'm going to Hell."

It was impossible not to join in.

Impossible not to feel George's amusement, the monolith that had been Brendon reduced to the butt end of a joke.

"I can't b-breathe," George snickered, falling against my chest as I wrapped my arms around him, breathing in his joy like it alone could sustain me. Hell, maybe it could.

The next time the doorbell rang it was actually the pizza delivery guy.

Which was good—even if I was a bit disappointed I wouldn't get to acquaint Brendon's face with my fist again.

Oh well.

So yeah.

Part of why just thinking about New York made me smile was because of Missy—and seeing George's home up close and personal. But the biggest reason I'd enjoyed New York? Was because I'd gotten to rearrange Brendon's goddamn teeth.

"Alex?" George's voice broke through my reverie. I was grinning like a fool, probably worrying him—considering the fact I was supposed to be teaching him about ice skates.

"Sorry, sorry," I shook my head.

"You were thinking about punching Brendon again, weren't you?" he asked, amused and annoyed all at once.

"Guilty."

He emitted a soft sound. It was one of my *favorite* noises. He only ever made it when he was trying to look grumpy, but was too pleased to be successful. Half sigh, half snort.

"While I understand—really, I do," George grouched. "Can we focus on the problem at hand? I'd rather get my untimely death over with, please and thank you."

"Okay, okay." I helped him get his foot inside the boot, lacing it up. "Noted." There was no way in hell I was letting him get hurt.

He knew that, I knew that.

It was the only reason he'd agreed to come to the ice rink as our first Friday date night—considering the fact we were about to be walking around on "knife shoes"—his words, not mine. He trusted me. And fuck, that was the greatest gift of all.

Once he was all trussed up, I got to work on my own skates. I'd been worried they'd stink, and had pretty much soaked the insides with a can of Lysol in preparation. Which meant they smelled like fucking daisies as I slid my feet inside and laced up far quicker than I'd worked on George's.

Muscle memory.

"Okay." On my feet, I held a hand out for him. "You remember what I taught you?"

"Fall to your side," George rolled his eyes but recited dutifully. "Bend your knees."

"Right."

"If I feel like I'm going to fall, bend more and put my hands on my knees."

"That's perfect, Duchess."

George smiled, this soft tentative thing. Pleased that I was pleased with him, no doubt.

"Slow and steady, baby. We got this."

"You got this," George huffed. "Me, I'm not so sure about."

He was worried for no reason.

An hour later, he was gliding around all on his own. Okay, maybe calling it "gliding" was a stretch. But he was definitely moving.

"Look at you go, you precious little cutie pie," I purred from in front of him, watching him wiggle forward with a pinched brow, his lips pressed into a determined line.

"Stop flirting with me, I'm trying to concentrate."

He was so full of shit. We both knew he loved when I flirted with him.

"Bend your knees more," I encouraged. He bent, and I cheered. "Better."

"It's so…slippery," George complained, breathing through his nose as he focused on getting his feet to move.

"That would be because it's ice," I teased.

"Shut up."

He was moving faster now. More confident. Way better than I'd done my first day on the ice when I'd been a kid.

"Alright, now glide," I coached. "You got moving, now keep your feet shoulder-width apart and glide—" And he did it. He fucking— "Fuck yes! You're doing it! Yes, yes, yes!"

George was beaming, this wide bright smile—the smile he reserved for me and Mr. Pickles, and no one else. "I'm doing it!" he said, still sliding on the ice. It was a snail's crawl but it was enough.

"Again! Push your sexy lil feet and then gli—there you go."

"I'm a fucking pro," George said, gliding along. "Look at me!"

"I *am* looking!"

"I'm so—" And then he fell.

He hit the ice on his side like I'd told him to do, sliding for a few feet as his eyes went wide and his mouth dropped open. For a moment, I wasn't sure what was about to happen. Worried his fear of appearing less than perfect would rise to the surface—that our night would be ruined right as it had begun. Even more, I worried that he'd be distressed. That falling would crush his already brittle ego to dust.

I skated close, terrified he was about to give up, or cry—or that he'd been hurt for real.

But as always, he surprised me.

Because he *laughed*.

"Too cocky," he said, grumbling to himself as he shakily got back up onto his feet. "Just need to—"

And then he was off again.

By the end of the night, George was a self-proclaimed "professional figure skater". He'd seen a few people out on the ice for public skate, a teen most notably in the center of the rink performing tricks. Spins I didn't know the names for—and a jump or two. George's eyes had gone bright, this almost manic smile on his face as he'd stared and stared and stared.

I got the feeling we would be going ice skating together a lot more often.

Which was definitely surprising.

And fucking awesome.

I knelt at his feet to help him get his skates off. I figured he could do it on his own, but it was more fun this way.

"I want to do one of those things that girl did," George told me, leaning back and letting me take care of him. "The...swirly things."

"Spins?"

His cheeks flushed, embarrassed he hadn't guessed the word. "That, yes."

"We can get you lessons," I promised, unlacing his second boot and pulling that one off too. I rubbed his feet, even though he kicked at me, grunting something about his socks being sweaty. I leveled him with a look, and he didn't complain again.

"Can't you teach me?" George asked.

"You want me to teach you how to spin?" I clarified.

"Yes."

"Baby, I play hockey, that isn't the kinda shit I know how to do." Some of the guys on the team got fancy with it and mimicked the figure skaters sometimes, but it was always far less graceful—and without toe picks on our skates, there wasn't much I could do when it came to jumping.

George sighed, glaring at me like I'd planned this all along. Like I'd brought him here to get him obsessed with figure skating only to pull the rug right out from under him.

"How about I teach you all I can do, and then we go from there?" I offered, pressing my lips into a line so I wouldn't laugh at his adorably disgruntled face.

"I suppose that's acceptable."

"Glad to hear it." Okay, I lost. Because then I laughed—unable to help myself, and George kicked at me with his free socked foot.

I was on cloud nine the rest of the night. I took him to the Italian place we'd never gotten to visit. He ate his spaghetti in the bitty bites I knew and loved—not because he was uncomfortable now, but because he hadn't wanted to spill on his sexy little outfit.

We snarked and joked and kissed at every opportunity.

And life…life was good.

So fucking good.

I'd started seeing my therapist again. We'd only had one session, but already that had helped. George didn't mind my "affirmations"—homework, that I'd been given between now and the next time I'd see my doctor to try and help me boost my self-esteem. George liked to listen. Liked to stand in the doorway to the bathroom as I stared at my own reflection and attempted to find good things to say. Confidence building.

When he was watching, it made it easier to be kind to myself.

Sometimes, when I'd draw a complete blank, he even stepped in.

"You have a nice smile," he'd say. "Maybe start with that."

Or.

"You're clever," he'd say. "Begin there."

It was the baby steps I needed, the small push, to see myself through his eyes that gave me the courage to keep going, even though it was difficult. Somedays, it felt impossible, really. Silly, to look at myself and try to see past all my flaws. Maybe one day, I'd believe the words I told the mirror. But until then, I was grateful to borrow George's perspective.

He saw me as I was in my plainest form.

And he liked me.

Loved me.

Like my dad and June, he didn't ask for anything in return. It was a pure kind of love. The kind of love I'd written off as a fairytale in my bitter youth.

The kind of love I was learning was there—if only you could look past your own self-loathing to see it.

George had bad days too. He'd become withdrawn sometimes. Especially right after we'd returned to Columbus, and his life had irrevocably changed. He didn't do well with change. That was his explanation as he'd curled up in our bed, dressed in only my clothing, and shyly inquired if I might hold him till he felt better.

It was no hardship to love him when he was down.

A fact that certainly helped me be kinder to myself—as it was impossible not to see the parallels.

George was still on the hunt for an apartment, currently living with me until he found the perfect place—and his stuff was set to arrive the next morning. I'd offered to store all his boxes in my garage for the foreseeable future, and he'd accepted. Another thing that showed how far we'd come.

George accepted my help willingly, and all the time.

He looked to me for guidance and support.

For affection.

For strength.

And when I needed him—he was there, folding into my chest where he was meant to be so I could recharge.

We were laughing as we pulled into the driveway at home after our night on the town, distracted by each other—distracted enough neither of us noticed the package sitting in front of the garage until after we'd parked inside it.

"Weren't my things supposed to arrive tomorrow?" George asked when he exited the car. I'd opened his door for him, and his pleased smile had morphed into confusion.

"They were." I frowned, ducking around him and heading for the box to inspect it.

It was clearly addressed to him.

But it was a package—not from the movers.

"It's from Missy," I said, picking it up and bringing it toward him. The thing wasn't all that big. It easily fit in my arms. In fact, it hardly weighed anything at all. "Maybe you forgot something?"

George frowned. "I'd never forget anything. I had a list, remember?"

"Right."

He picked at the tape, pulling the box open with a grunt so he could see inside. On top of tissue paper was a note. George pulled that out first, unfolding it with a confused pinch between his brows. "It says…it's a parting gift?"

"Awe, that was nice of her."

"I told her not to get me anything." George set the note aside, reaching for the tissue paper. He was voracious as he tore through it, overeager for his gift. I'd have to remember that—how much he liked presents—for the future.

While he made confetti out of the tissue paper, I glanced toward the note. It read:

In case you ever get lonely, here's a little parting gift to remember me by.

–Missy

George made a sound.

I tore my eyes away from the note and nearly dropped the package when I saw what was inside it.

"No fucking way," I gawped, unable to help myself as George's exuberance caused his gift to fly from the package and fall to the garage floor. A shiny silicone dildo rolled a few inches, tapping against my foot as it finally came to a stop.

George's horror was soon replaced with good humor as he bent and grabbed the offending item.

"At least she didn't put it in your backpack again," I wheezed, trying to hold myself together even though I was currently dying.

"Small mercies," George agreed, before he dissolved into giggles along with me.

We didn't stop laughing for a long time.

And as reality set in, I couldn't help but be grateful to Missy and her mischief—for June and her matchmaking. For Mrs. Milton, and George's siblings—because they'd seen our potential and known we could bring each other bliss if only we let our guards down.

As George's joy and mine mingled, that gaping black hole in my chest was missing.

I was full in a way I'd never been before.

Accepted in a way I hadn't known was possible.

I knew life could be an uphill battle. That there would be twists and turns—unexpected events I couldn't plan for—just like Missy's package. But somehow, that felt exciting rather than intimidating.

Because I wasn't facing things alone anymore.

I'd found the partner I'd always wanted.

My perfectly imperfect equal.

And I couldn't help but come to the conclusion—good days or bad—that having George-Arthur Milton in my life made every day better than the last. *He* was my happy ending—my fussy, smothering, detail-oriented, high-maintenance, *perfect* happy ending.

Snorty laugh, and all.

And I had Neil-the-dildo to thank for that.

The End

If you loved *Cloudy with a Chance of Bad Decisions*, make sure to keep an eye out for the next trip to Belleville, Vermont! Joe, George's brother, will be getting his own book.

If parts of this story feel familiar, please know you're not alone.

Everyone deserves to feel safe, respected, and heard in their relationships. If you're hurting or unsure, there are people who care and want to help.

In the U.S., you can call the National Domestic Violence Hotline at 1-800-799-7233 or text "START" to 88788.

For sexual assault support, reach out to RAINN at 1-800-656-HOPE (4673) or visit www.rainn.org.

author note

THANK YOU SO MUCH for reading *Cloudy With a Chance of Bad Decisions*. I hope you loved Alex and George's story—I certainly had a blast while writing it. These two mean the world to me. They were my first contemporary couple, created way back in 2022, before I'd even published my debut *Bite Me! (You Know I Like It)*. Some of you may remember them from their early days as a newsletter serial titled *Cloudy With a Chance of Dildos*. For others, this might be your first time meeting them in their full-length glory. Either way, Alex and George have always held a special place in my heart. They were my original loves—the first time I dared to step outside the PNR world.

A lot changed between the early version and the one you just read. At one point, I even thought it might be an office romance! I had so many plans, so many notes on my phone dedicated to them, so many versions of their happy-ever-after. But what I ended up with is so much better than anything the 2022 version of me could've imagined. Their story feels timeless now, and honestly, I'm glad I waited. Back then, I didn't have the tools to do them justice.

I feel so incredibly lucky to have come back to them with fresh eyes. To get to reimagine their journey—and share it with you—has been such a gift.

My hope for this book is simple: that it would make you smile. That it might bring you a little joy in a world that so often feels joyless. That, through Alex and George, you'd find a soft place to land. A space where fairy tales still happen, and even two disastrously adorable men can find their way to love—messy pasts, emotional baggage, and all.

Special thanks to DL, Molly, and all my wonderful alpha readers. You helped so much throughout the process and I could not be more grateful for your support, encouragement, and love.

Thank you again, for taking the time to read this book. My words would mean nothing without you beautiful readers here to enjoy them. You are the reason I do what I do. I am so grateful to be given the opportunity to share my art with all of you.

Love,

FAE

about Fae

FAE IS OBSESSED with anything romance. From a young age she realized she had a passion for falling in love over and over again. She loves to tell stories through both her art and writing. With a passion for classical monsters, meet-cutes, and contemporary romance, you can often find her with her nose stuck in a book and her pet corgi, Champa, on her lap.

She currently resides in Utah with her amazing husband and her collection of squishmallows. When you read one of her books you can expect to find love stories between humans, monsters, and loveable assholes that will make you laugh (and cry) as you get lost in their worlds for just a little. Every story comes with a happy ever after guarantee.

Find her online at:
WWW.FAELOVESART.COM

www.ingramcontent.com/pod-product-compliance
Lightning Source LLC
LaVergne TN
LVHW042032040625
812831LV00003B/78